We Were Stardust

Kathrin King Segal

Published by: Bucket List Books
First printing: September 2011

Cover photo: Mitera's, MacDougal and 3rd
Robert Otter, photographer © 2011 Ned Otter

Cover design: Blue Sky Creative
Author photo: Steve Kaplan
Interior Layout: Lighthouse24

LIBRARY OF CONGRESS CATALOGUING-IN-PUBLICATION DATA:
Segal, Kathrin King
We Were Stardust/Kathrin King Segal—1st edition

ISBN: 978-0983518112
LCCN: 2011933499

Also by
Kathrin King Segal

Wild Again

for Charlie

I *found my grandmother on eBay.*

There's her life in fragments, the life I know so little about. Three dollars for an acetate demo recording from 1965; a dollar for an 8x10 glossy photo of a band called the Folk Brigade. I unearthed the dress she supposedly wore on a TV show no one remembers, and her diary from 1967 (Summer of Love!), one of those little spiral notebooks with the wires that unspool and stab you in the thumb. A lot of her entries are bi-polar ramblings, and there is way too much yearning lovesickness for a lot of different guys. She wrote her name about two dozen times, trying out variations: Julie. Juley. Juliette.

The last one is the name I ended up with. She was a lot prettier than I am but they tell me I got her voice.

I just want to know what happened to her, why she dropped out, tuned in, or whatever they called it back then. When she was seventeen – the age I am now -- my grandmother was right in the middle of the whole Greenwich Village folk music scene. That's what my Dad told me, although he never liked to talk about her. He was bitter because she dumped him as a baby, and he was fostered out, even though he was eventually adopted by nice people. He never knew who the hell his real father was. It could have been the rocker or the manager or just some guy she picked up on the road.

Dad got screwed in the genetic sweepstakes, too. He didn't inherit her music talent but he got her manic depression. By the time Dad came along, it was called bi-polar disorder and there were meds for it, but none of them saved him in the end. He made it to thirty-nine before he crashed, in every way, on the Long Island Expressway last year—leaving me and Mom in a Queens apartment very much like the one my grandma grew up in. Some families are just downwardly mobile, I guess.

That's when I found out that Dad was sort of obsessed with her; his mother, I mean. He had been quietly gathering information about her for years, and was planning a book—memoir or novel, I don't know—but the notes were in his desk and in his hard drive and on disks. He'd been thinking about this for a long time. Since DOS. I found a geek at school who could open the old 5 ¼" floppies. Once he stopped laughing.

I'm coming out of the subway at West 4th, my boots crunching on the snow, heading to a singer-songwriter night at the Bitter End, which is still there after, like, a century. I close my eyes and imagine a time machine that will take me back forty-some years to a night very much like this one. It must have been amazing to be in the Village when Bob Dylan was just coming out of nowhere, and there was so much hope.

COLLECTIBLES

February 1965 issue of *Sing Out!* Article about "promising new duo Luke & Julie", $5.95 on eBay.

A grainy video of the duo, backed by John Sebastian, harmonica, and Felix Pappalardi, bass, from *Music After Hours*, a short-lived local (NYC) variety show, 1965. YouTube.

Flier: "Appearing at The Fat Black Pussycat: Tiny Tim, Richie Havens, impressionist David Frye, folk singer Julie Bradley." No date. $1.59, eBay.

Program: "Elliot J. Levine presents: Hootenanny Night featuring Luke & Julie, the Au Go Go Singers, and more!!" 1966. 99¢, eBay.

Demo tape: Julie Bradley, one song, *"All the Wide World"*, composer unknown. Signed, undated. $19.99, eBay.

Part One

I was standing on the corner of
Bleecker and MacDougal
wondering which way to go

Fred Neil, "Bleecker and MacDougal"

1

MacDougal Street began to vanish into the snow. Really, it was like being inside a snow globe, Luke was thinking when he saw the girl through the restaurant window. She stood under a streetlight, still as an ice sculpture, staring up into the white night sky. Her bare hands clutched the narrow end of an upright guitar case. Long hair, an odd shade of reddish gold that reminded him of the copper pot his mother used to polish when she was angry, flowed over the shoulders of an oversized coat and down to her waist. Snow illuminated her with millions of tiny crystals, and tears trailed down her cheeks.

Luke felt the pulse of the city beating inside him. He'd been in town less than two months and was dazed from lack of sleep. He wanted to turn everything into a song, and was certain that this could be done.

Food was placed in front of him, and when he looked outside again, the ice girl was gone.

2

Julie draped her coat on the lumpy, sprung couch in the Bitter End's crowded backstage greenroom. Had anyone noticed her entrance? Her outfit? It appeared not. Folk singers, comics, musicians, poets milled around, smoked, talked, laughed, tuned their instruments, creating a cacophony of clashing sounds and rising chatter. They threw their heavy wool jackets and scarves on the furniture and in the corners, over chairs, the rest squashed together on bowed wire hangers on a bent clothing rack. Instrument cases leaned against the walls and were stacked on the floor. She found a space in the corner of the sofa and arranged herself in what she hoped was a nonchalantly seductive pose. Her moods rose and fell from moment to moment. Alternately, she pondered her own extraordinary musical genius and totally mediocre insignificance. She could not pass a mirror without looking into it, not because she had any confidence in her beauty, but to reassure herself that she continued to exist.

She gnawed the cuticle of her left thumb—it began to bleed—and recalled her fifth-grade teacher, Mrs. Green stein, who'd told the class a story about a little girl who bit her nails. Mrs. Greenstein said that the tiny, undigested nails accumulated inside the child's stomach, sharp edges slicing away until her guts were all cut to ribbons and bleeding and the little girl died a terrible death. Julie switched from biting her nails to tearing at her cuticles until they bled.

The MC came backstage and read the running order of the people who would be performing—blah blah blah blah blah Julie Bradley—she was way the hell down the list. According to Open Mic Night code, the best spots—between nine and eleven—were saved for regulars who came in to try out new material. Or singers being promoted by their record companies. Or people with Important Managers. Or the club manager's friends. She was none of these.

Meyer Norman pushed through the door, lugging a beat up Guild guitar. Meyer was small and rat-faced, with quick nervous gestures and nicotine-stained fingers. He had the affectations of a young man who'd ridden the rails, driven trucks, lived off the land, when in actuality he was a Jewish boy from Flushing, Queens, not far from where Julie grew up. He played the basket houses from West 3rd to Bleecker, just like she did: a set here, another one there, scrounging through the nights, playing till her fingertips hurt too much to even touch the guitar strings.

The Village music scene was a distinct hierarchy. The lowest tier, other than playing in the street or the subway, was the small store front cafes where performers passed straw baskets or tin cans for tips. Usually, you'd have to do at least a half-dozen sets a night, often in different places, to accumulate enough money to survive. The basket houses, which could squeeze in maybe twenty to thirty patrons, opened and closed quickly, lasting a few weeks to a few months, although some, like the Basement, the Raffio, the Four Winds and the Why Not?, had managed to stay around for several years. For most of them, one week the place would be a coffeehouse, and the next week there'd be a city marshal's sign taped on the window, and the week after that, it would be a pizza parlor or cheap jewelry store.

The clubs on the next level up booked acts on a regular basis and carried a little prestige, but didn't pay much: the Cafe Wha?, the Fat Black Pussycat, the Cafe Bizarre. The bigger- name acts appeared at Gerdes' Folk City and the Village Gate, the Bitter End or the Cafe Au Go Go or the Gaslight for a run of a week or two, but nearly every club held Monday or Tuesday nights for Open Mic.

"I hear there's an A&R guy out front," Meyer said, rolling a cigarette from the pouch of tobacco he always carried. "From BigWheel Records."

There was nearly always a rumor, even in the smallest coffee houses, that someone *important* was coming in later, or just stopped by. What you wanted was for the Artist and Repertoire man (they were all men) to hear you and say, let's do some demos in the studio, or, better yet, we'll sign you for an album. It seemed like *everyone* had a record deal. Even Meyer Norman had done some demos, and he just wasn't all that good of a musician or singer. Well, her turn would come. She was eighteen, and felt both young and old. Young because other people, even those her age, appeared to know how life was supposed to work, while she was perpetually baffled. Old because she had been on her own for almost two years, and imagined that this made her wise and sophisticated.

Her nights were crowded with music. Days, she slept until four, five in the afternoon, got up, watched *I Love Lucy* reruns and wondered how she was going to catch up on three months' back rent on the one-room basement shithole. Later, she'd hit the basket houses again. When she got her record contract and some concerts, she'd have money to get a big apartment. Because she was *brilliant, absolutely brilliant...*

There was this feeling she got sometimes that she was on the edge of a great abyss, and she could fly or fall, but something invisible was shoving her from behind; she could hear the scrabble of pebbles under her feet as the earth gave way.

Julie glanced at Meyer, who was tuning his guitar. If he's no good, she mused, and he and I play the same places, what does that say about me?

"So you're goin' solo, huh?" Meyer rasped.

For a few months, she had been the pretty chick in a big group called the Folk Brigade. They were supposed to be the next New Christy Minstrels, the next Serendipity Singers. Except the group fell apart before that could happen. Maybe if they hadn't been fighting all the time, or had a better manager or an agent to intervene.

"Heard Casey went to L.A. Got some new group starting," Meyer continued.

Some of them blamed her for making lead guitarist Casey Mahoney's life miserable, like she made him fall in love with her, like she was some Delilah who compromised his guitar-playing ability; or, as the musicians called it, his "chops." Casey had packed up and split one morning, leaving her the roachy but rent-controlled pad on Grove Street. "You'd have a better chance of getting a record contract if you're in a group. It's hard for chicks on their own, you know? Record companies got their Joan Baez, their Judy Collins, their Judy Henske, one chick per label, you dig?"

"Hey, my name begins with a 'J', too."

He soberly considered this as he knocked saliva out of his harmonica with the heel of his palm. He blew a few thin notes. She wanted to shove it into his teeth. Instead, she pulled herself out of the couch and went to see if her friends were in the audience yet.

3

Elliot Levine exited the subway at West 4th Street. Despite the snow, the streets of the Village were bustling, as if every-one had tacitly agreed to ignore winter's final fuck you. He paused briefly to search his pockets for the small packet of Sen-Sen breath mints he always carried, realizing he'd left them home in Brooklyn. He adjusted the gray fedora that camouflaged the humiliation of losing so much of his hair so unfairly young, and which, he believed, gave him a bit of a rakish look. Elliot had already piled up an excess of life failures: college dropout, Macy's sales clerk (fired), comedian (unfunny), songwriter (unsung), junior accountant (bored). He endured a week walking dogs for a pet service, his hands snarled in a tangle of leashes, a half-dozen yapping, bounding canines dragging him through Central Park. On his recent twenty-fifth birthday, he re-upped his personal deadline for success to age thirty. Elliot passed the Purple Onion, a club with an identity crisis, alternating between strip shows and folk singers, and the tiny Zig Zag and the Night Owl Cafe, where he'd heard a fat, rich-voiced singer named Cass belt her heart out. He'd felt it then, the prickly excitement of finding prey: raw talent. She was with a group called The Big Three, and she already had a manager. He resolved not to be too late the next time he spotted a potential star.

The Gaslight featured Carolyn Hester. The Cafe Wha? was having its weekly "Hoot Nite." He paused in front of The Fat Black Pussycat: Richie Havens, that young, toothless, black blues singer who tuned his guitar in an odd way and beat it so hard his broken picks littered the stage after each set; a couple of unknown comics, Dave Frye and Richard Pryor. And that very strange, androgynous Tiny Tim.

At Brooklyn's Erasmus High, Elliot's sole moment of glory occurred in a chess tournament in his senior year. He came in second, earning a small medal: Chess Club Reserve Champion, 1957. Chess had lured him to Greenwich Village, to the Washington Square hustlers he checkmated from time to time. He passed many lonely nights in the coffeehouses, watching the talented and the not so. Hungry musicians and singers, their hopes and ambitions nakedly obvious, filling the clubs and the streets, encumbered by their folk instruments, sitting, sleeping on the park benches, waiting for that cliché: the Big Break.

It seemed to him, at first, that *anyone* could play a guitar. Elliott gave it a try, imagining that he would be a singer of protest and union ballads, a leader of men and a magnet to women. He bought a Kay steel-string and a booklet: *Teach Yourself to Play Guitar in Ten Easy Lessons*. The cover showed a serious, thin man bent over the instrument, raptly concentrated, with an aura of genius and mystery. The first time Elliot placed his soft fingertips on the hard strings, pain went shooting up his arms. *What?* Music wasn't supposed to hurt, was it? After several attempts, he managed to ignore the agony long enough to create a chord of sorts. It sounded like this: mmmph, ump, dink, sproing, unh, bzzz. Discouraged, Elliot put the guitar back in its case and stashed it in a closet. He had a new respect for musicians, enough to know that he wasn't one. He also knew what talent looked like, what it sounded like. Hadn't he gotten the shivers hearing Dylan that first time when nobody knew who the hell he was? And Joan Baez? He *knew*.

Left on Bleecker, another block toward Sullivan. At the Cafe Raffio, he cupped his hands around his eyes and peered in the window. A folk singer was on the stage with a harmonica rigged up in front of his face like an orthodontic device. He continued to Thompson Street, increasing his stride to a fast tiptoe-hop over the ice.

The Bitter End Cafe was holding its Tuesday Open Mic Night. The regular weekend bill was also posted outside: their in-house group, the Bitter End Singers, and the Chad Mitchell Trio. Across the street, the Cafe Au Go Go had their competing group, the Au Go Go Singers, and a revue featuring Vaughn Meader, whose career, based upon impressions of the Kennedys, had taken a precipitous decline in the year since the assassination.

Of all the possibilities, Elliot chose the Bitter End that night. Elliot J. Levine (the 'J' didn't actually stand for anything, he just liked the way it looked on a business card), seeker of gold nuggets of talent in the dark espresso-scented caves, in the six-string guitar, five-string banjo, upright bass, twelve-bar blues, hootenanny honky-tonk 1964 Greenwich Village. Elliot J. Levine, star-maker.

4

"Hot chocolate. Lots of whipped cream," Rochelle told one of the annoyingly wraith-thin, black-clad waitresses. She lit up a Parliament, poking her tongue into the recessed filter, the reason she smoked that particular brand.

"We haven't missed her, have we?" Arlene whispered.

"I don't think so." They were squeezed into a small space in the back row. The Bitter End was set up with rows of benches and narrow plank tables facing the stage.

Rochelle enjoyed the Village, but often felt as if she were visiting from another planet. The planet of Queens. A year out of high school already and she was still living with her parents. Her clothes were wrong even though she'd brought a change of outfits to the office: stiff, new jeans and a blue and white checked blouse, and high-heeled pumps to make her taller than her flatfooted five-foot three.

I look like a bad impersonation of a cowgirl, she thought. *Or Howdy Doody.*

Her thick, curly dark hair was tamed into a chin-length flip, a recent change from the teased beehive that had been her high school look, but just a bit too fussy for a room filled with skinny, longhaired girls and even a few men with beards. She recalled her one sexual tryst with a beatnik, a recollection that was embarrassing, but also boosted her secret longing to be a wild girl.

It had happened when she was sixteen, shortly after Arlene dragged her and Julie to a coffeehouse for the first time. A man with a goatee sidled up to her and made an explicit suggestion. His candor took her so much by surprise that, a few nights later, she told her parents she was going over to Julie's and instead took the subway into Manhattan. The beatnik lived in a fifth-floor walkup near Chinatown, hardly what she envisioned as a hip Village pad. He gave her some wine, the first she'd ever had that wasn't sweet and kosher for Passover, and explained that administering oral sex would raise her to a higher level of consciousness, and yet allow her to retain her virginity.

Rochelle still scanned the coffeehouses for the beatnik, dreading the prospect of running into him, and yet hoping she would.

Arlene was annoying but she had her advantages. She was what Rochelle's mother would call "a good person to know." Arlene had no shyness about talking to strangers, and she flouted her plainness—only slightly improved by a sweet-six-teen nose job and extensive acne treatments—by sleeping with any man who asked her. Tonight Arlene was wearing a snug yellow Banlon sweater and a tighter black skirt. Arlene was awkwardly designed, all hips and thighs, with barely a hint of breasts. She didn't wear a bra and her puckered nipples poked against the sweater, a sight that horrified Rochelle.

When the hot chocolate arrived under a puff of Reddi-Wip, Rochelle let its steamy fragrance warm her face and hands. She was always edgy when Julie was going to sing, almost as if it were her own self up on stage and not her best friend. Now, the MC was positively groveling his next introduction, like maybe Jesus had dropped in to do a set. "She's just signed a big contract with Vanguard Records," the MC *kvelled*, "and we have high hopes for this girl, who started right here. So let's have a great big Bitter End welcome for…Liz Gainsborough!"

As Liz's folkie alto caressed the microphone, Rochelle decided that Julie was a better singer, and had much more fabulous hair. She watched the audience watch the singer, and wished she had the nerve to get up in the spotlight. And the talent, of course. Rochelle had mixed feelings about her friend's singing. She loved her and was her biggest fan, but resented being perpetually in her shadow. It wasn't anything Julie did on purpose to make her feel bad, but that was often the result. Julie didn't understand why Rochelle hung out with Arlene, but at least with Arlene, she could be the pretty one.

Tired from a long day's secretarial toil, lonely from being here with Arlene instead of on a date, Rochelle slipped off her shoes, forgetting that the floor was inch-deep in sawdust and god knows what else. The sensation was like stepping in soft dirt, and she drew her feet back up sharply.

"Ouch!" A man was squeezing between tables on his way to the corner, and she had accidentally kicked him in the shin.

"Sorry!" He had a smooth, pale young face and wore a business suit, topped off by a ridiculous hat like in a detective movie. He removed the hat and placed it on his lap.

Liz Gainsborough finished her last song. Eventually the applause died down, and the house lights went up for a break.

"Wow, she was great!" Arlene said.

"She was okay." Rochelle spotted Julie near the back wall. Her friend was wearing black sailor pants that flared below the knees, over white boots, and a snug black turtleneck sweater that highlighted her fair skin and slim frame.

Arlene nodded toward the man in the business suit, and murmured to Rochelle, "I bet he's someone *important*."

"He looks like your basic garden-variety putz to me."

Rochelle hugged Julie, whispering, "That Liz is *so* boring. When are *you* going on?"

"When I'm forty."

"Come on. You'll be great."

"Yeah, singing to a couple of waitresses and the kitchen cat."

The next act was a listless male singer ruining "Kisses Sweeter Than Wine." When the song ended, the MC grabbed the mike, milking applause. "Let's have a nice hand for…" He looked at the list in his hand. "Grant Dilfer!" An over wrought Dilfer claque in the corner shouted and clapped.

There was a genuine, spontaneous burst of applause when the MC announced that Fred Neil and Vince Martin were doing a surprise guest set. The two musicians were well-known in the Village and had just released an album. They carried heavy twelve-string guitars over their heads as they passed through the crowd. On stage, they messed around with the mikes and then set a strong rhythm that had the audience stomping and clapping to Neil's song "Mississippi Train." A backup musician played what looked to Rochelle like a pregnant guitar.

"That's a *guitarron*," Arlene informed everyone.

The music's irresistible energy restored Rochelle's good mood. Anything was possible.

Julie fell in love with all three men for the duration of their set, an attraction mixed with envy. She was transfixed by their sinewy arms, strumming, stroking the guitars, the casual drape of their jeans, the way they stood, arrogant and relaxed, in the spotlight. Maybe you had to be a guy to be so confident; to be so certain you belonged where you were standing.

When they ended their set—with two encores—she slipped back into the greenroom. Cigarette smoke thickened the air. The three musicians burst in. "Great, man!" people exclaimed, hands shaking hands, slapping shoulders, the camaraderie of musicmen. Lissome women waited patiently outside the action. Julie couldn't think of anything to say to the men that didn't sound dumb and fawning, just another simpering "old lady." She took out her small spiral notebook and wrote down the date. A few poetic lines came to her; she jotted them on the page. At least she would look intelligent and possibly mysterious, but it was hard not to be distracted by all the commotion.

Martin and Neil were talking about their new album on Elektra. The entourage of hangers-on helped carry out their instruments. Girlfriends followed, silent and devoted. She wondered if any of those girls were talented, and decided they probably weren't.

With Martin and Neil gone, the room's energy rapidly faded into an anticlimactic funk. People called for checks and got up to leave.

The guy with the hat was watching Rochelle watch Martin and Neil.

"You know them?" he asked.

"We've met," she lied.

"I helped get them their record deal," he lied.

"You work for a record company?"

"Manager." He handed her his card.

Elliot J. Levine

Talent Manager, Songwriter, Promoter

Arlene nudged her. "I *told* you he was Somebody."

"My friend's singing here tonight," Rochelle told him. "You should hear her, she's great."

He pulled up a chair next to Rochelle. "Do you mind if I join you?" he asked. Arlene leaned forward. "I'm Arlene Slotnick."

Ignoring Arlene, Elliott turned his attention to Rochelle. "I'd love to hear about your friend, the singer."

"She's *my* friend, too," Arlene said. "Would you like a drink? My treat. You, too, Rochelle." She waved at a waitress.

The MC was trying to rally what was left of the audience. "Hey, we got some really great acts coming up!"

"She's not famous or anything, *yet*," Rochelle continued, "but she's really good. *I* discovered her," she added.

"You did." A hint of a smile broke through Elliot's businesslike demeanor.

"Where are you from?" Arlene asked him.

He hesitated. "I'm just getting a place in Manhattan."

"But where do you live *now?*"

"I, well, I'm just helping my folks out, in um, Brooklyn. Flatbush."

"Oh, my god, how much of a coincidence is *that*," Arlene said. "I lived in Flatbush till I was eight, before Daddy bought our house in Forest Hills."

Rochelle remembered the other reason she couldn't stand Arlene: money. Arlene had more than most everyone they knew, and made no secret of it. While Rochelle's father was toiling at the IRS, Arlene's dad, a gynecologist, had a spacious office adjoining their big, ivy-covered house in the posh Forest Hills Gardens enclave. The few times she had been at Arlene's, she kept envisioning Dr. Slotnick and his naked women patients on the other side of the wall.

"I feel that fate is so...oh, I don't know...*randomly amazing*, don't you?" Arlene went on, "like in my philosophy class the other day—that's my major at NYU."

"And are you in school, too?" Elliot asked Rochelle.

"No," she said. "I work for this lawyer. Talk about boring, I should never have learned to type or answer a phone, but in high school, my grades were shitty—pardon my French—so I took the Commercial course, you know steno and typing? I mean it pays okay but some days it seems like I'll be spending my whole paycheck on the rush-hour E train."

Arlene moved her chair a few more inches closer to him.

"Have you read this?" She pulled a book out of her enormous purse: *Existentialism from Dostoevski to Sartre.* "Don't you think the French really understand *ennui*?" Arlene had spent a summer as an exchange student in France.

"Well," Elliot faltered, "I saw a really depressing French movie once."

Rochelle stood, pushing her chair back. "You mean there are some that *aren't* depressing?"

"Oh, don't go yet," Elliot said. "I mean, I haven't even met your friend. The singer."

"I'm sure Arlene will entertain you till I get back."

The greenroom was uncharacteristically quiet. In the brief hush, Julie's ears picked up a new sound: the strains of a blues guitar. It twanged and cried and soothed, over a solid thumping rhythm. The guitar player was partially hidden behind a ratty curtain, but Julie could see his hands moving with assurance over the strings of a scratched Martin D-28.

He stood up and bumped into a dangling bare light bulb, causing it to swing back and forth. A young man who seemed taller sitting down, his head and shoulders almost too big for the rest of his body, he had light-blue eyes and uncombed, black curly hair that made the eyes more startling. He'd rolled up the sleeves of his plain white shirt, revealing fine, strong forearms and expressive hands. His back was very straight.

Julie had a visceral urge to run her hand the length of it, like petting a feral animal; to place her hands just above his, as he played, not touching, but absorbing the heat and energy coming off his skin.

He chose that moment to look at her, keeping the gaze for longer than necessary. Unnerved, she turned away and pretended to be absorbed in unpacking her guitar from its case. He probably thinks he's Some Hot Shit, she thought.

"Ice girl," he whispered.

5

Two months ago, Luke was still driving around Columbus, Georgia in a battered '53 Plymouth, a big dumb boat with split upholstery and suspension like jello—the car a symbol of all that was wrong, like living in a half-trailer in the back of his folks' place outside Fort Benning. He wanted a goddamn *fleet* of cars: Jaguar E-type...Pontiac GTO...Shelby GT-350...Ferrari 250-GT.

The MC poked his head into the room and read the name of the next performer.

"Luke Bella...vita?" he said, pronouncing it "vyta."

"It's Bella veeta, man. Like Velveeta."

"You're on next."

"Guess I'll go out there and kick ass," Luke said. What he needed was a sharp shot of bourbon to calm his nerves. Maybe one of these days, he wouldn't be so damned scared. Maybe he shouldn't have changed the strings two nights ago. This playing by himself was a ball-buster, he could get away with it in the subway where he could just play and ignore the onlookers, but here he was supposed to put on some kind of a show.

"Guys and gals, a newcomer here at the Bitter End, so let me make sure I pronounce his name right...Luke Bellavita!"

Scary. Lights hurt his eyes. Goddamn guitar out of tune.

"'Scuse me, folks. I ain't never done this alone before."
They laughed, out there in the darkness.
"I mean, I'm used to a band drownin' me out."
More chuckles, kinder this time.
He began to play.

Luke could just imagine what his daddy would have to
say about Greenwich Village. It was almost funny, picturing
tough Sgt. Vinnie Bellavita in a folkie club. A non-com
friend of his dad's in Germany gave Luke his first guitar, a
cheap, toneless thing. But from that moment, his world cen-
tered on the only object that gave him real pleasure. He hid
in his room and practiced for hours, recreating the riffs he
heard on the Helicrafter radio, which pulled in rock and roll
on the Armed Forces Network. He also had a small record
player in a red case with snap locks like a suitcase that
played 45s and 78s. He mastered Chuck Berry's style and
Elvis' smug, sensual singing, played every blues lick he could
find on the R&B singles he borrowed and "race music"
from the colored soldiers, and was astounded the first time
he heard B.B. King. Lucas thought that King's naming his
guitar "Lucille" was genius and he thereafter named each of
his instruments after different girls he lusted after from afar.

He launched into the Everly Brothers arrangement of
"Lucille" His foot tapped the stage floor, causing a hollow
thump, and the audience picked it up, a throb of rhythm
connection.

Since before Luke was born, he'd traveled. They flew in
an old four-engine C-54 Flying Tiger over to Germany,

France and Japan, then back to Texas and North Carolina, Kansas and Oregon, packing up about every eight months from the time Luke was walking. He learned to tie his shoelaces with the help of a sausage-maker in a small German village; his first words were in French (long since forgotten). The military bases had little contact with the countries they inhabited. They were self-contained all-American universes. The non-com families lived at the edges of dry desert towns where newly planted trees looked like sad leafy sticks in front of each identical house. In Europe, tucked away from the native culture, they ate hot dogs and burgers and made fun of the foreigners.

"Martha, what the hell is that noise?" his father would yell as soon as he got home and heard Lucas practicing in his room. He played the same chord changes, the same melody lines over and over until he got them right, and sometimes that took weeks of repetition. His door banged open and there was Sgt. Vinnie in his soiled fatigues, beer in hand. "Give it a rest, alright?"

Luke's playing took an angry, edgy turn. He played a searing guitar solo. Pretending he was alone, just playing for the hell of it.

In Japan, Lucas' band, The Teen Beats, did weekends for three months at the NCO club. Vinnie came into the club one night with three buddies, drunk from hitting a strip of bars in Tachikawa. The club was already pretty noisy when they crowded around a table down front. Luke led a rousing rendition of "Johnny B. Goode." He took the solo in the middle, making the guitar ring out, and even imitating Chuck Berry's duck walk. The crowd yelled.

"Can't hear yourself drink," said Vinnie, laughing, full of bourbon. "Shut up! I wanna hear my goddamn son play!"

When someone hollered for Vinnie to sit down and shut up, Luke saw the Red Mist—that's how he thought of it—come over his father's face, and knew that it was a matter of seconds.

"Hey motherfucker," Vinnie growled, spinning around and catching the offender neatly on the chin. Even drunk, his coordination was excellent, and the man he hit—a corporal who worked at the PX—lost his balance and tilted toward the stage, falling against Luke's microphone stand. It slammed down on the bass player, a fifteen-year-old kid from Kentucky, knocking his hand away from his instrument. He recoiled with a howl of pain. Every one was on their feet now, the word spreading that there was a fight.

"That's my son!" Vinnie hollered over the din. The MPs charged in and grabbed him. Luke tried to disappear behind the amplifier. His father yelling, "Lucas, Lucas! Tell them it's all right, give me a hand here, hey, you son of a bitch, you pussy!" keeping it up as he was being dragged out.

The family was shipped back to Fort Benning, Georgia, where Vinnie took semi-retirement, worked as a jeep mechanic and spent his free hours either at the bars or sunk into his Barcalounger in front of their brand-new, twenty-inch Emerson color TV.

Luke got on a train in Atlanta and rode it all the way to New York City. The only thing he didn't get to do before he left home was tell his daddy to go fuck himself.

He played his final song. Blues. God*damn*, he'd never felt it like this, an energy reverberating from the blood of his heart out through his hands and in some impossible way, touching the people in the room. He wondered where the girl was, if she might be watching him, and the thought of this excited him more. He stood, rested one foot on the stool, and tilted the guitar neck up. There were yells from the back of the room. He grinned at the unseen crowd and wondered when they would figure out that he didn't really know what the fuck he was doing; he was just making it up as he went along.

6

Elliot's talent radar pinged inside his head. He took a quick look around the room: As far as he could tell, the other agents, managers and record execs had departed after the sets of the "hot" acts, Martin & Neil, and Liz Gainsborough, and had missed the new kid, this Bella-something.

Luke finished his last song to an enthusiastic response. Elliot followed him to the back and found Luke chatting with sycophantic musicians who wanted to know where he had learned this or that riff.

As soon as he could get a word in, Elliot stuck out his hand and introduced himself. "I really enjoyed your playing," he said. "I manage a few acts. And, you know, the only thing I might suggest is—no, never mind, just can't stop being a manager for five minutes!" He gave as engaging a grin as he could: "You don't need *my* two cents. It was great hearing you." He turned to leave.

Luke stepped away from the crowd. "What were you gonna say? Something about the music?"

Elliot had noticed an odd thing about artists: Not one of them, at least none that he'd met, could resist an implied critique. It didn't matter who it came from, if it was helpful or destructive. That was why they needed someone like him to protect and nurture them.

"No, no, no, not about your playing, that's just about perfection. But it occurred to me the set would be stronger if you switched those last two tunes. No big deal."

"You think so?"

"Hey, listen, if you ever want to talk about the business, I can probably, I don't know, help point you in the right direction." He handed Luke his card. "Look, why don't we get together for a cup of coffee? You tell me your ideas for your career, I give you mine. Nothing lost but a little time. Just off the top of my head, this is the way I see it: Luke Belladonna—"

"Bella*vita*—"

Elliot bit the inside of his lip.

"It means beautiful life. My daddy's Italian and his family was named after a town in Sicily. And I'm also half Cherokee," Luke invented. It sounded good.

Elliot lowered his voice to an intense near-whisper. "I can see your first album! A single climbing the charts! The whole shammoo!"

"Shammoo?"

"*The Ed Sullivan Show! Hullabaloo! The Tonight Show!*"

Luke gave a laugh. "You sure make it sound easy."

"Oh, don't get me wrong," Elliot cautioned, "it isn't easy. No way."

Rochelle pressed her hand to her stomach. Had she been alone, she would have brought it lower, to quench—or expand—the sensations provoked by Luke's crystal-blue eyes, the loose curls that flopped onto his forehead, the husky voice that dampened her underwear. She had barely heard what he played—some sad, sexy thing about a lost woman and a deep river. All she could think about was the specific fantasy of her hand slipping into his jeans.

She watched Luke leave the stage and move across the room, and wondered what his skin felt like. Even if she could get to him, what was she supposed to do, bring him home to Queens, with her parents in the other room? Her friends were all moving into the city. Arlene already had a place—her parents paid the rent, of course—and suggested that Rochelle be her roommate. It would be better than schlepping home to Queens every night.

Rochelle resolved at that moment to move to Manhattan. She would invite Luke over; she would have candles and French wine and something elegant, like fondue. At work, she would say things like "my boyfriend—the musician."

The ice girl was looking at him. He began to pack up his guitar, harmonica and slide, pretending he wasn't acutely aware of her.

"I didn't figure you for a guy who wore lipstick," she nodded at the brass metal cylinder he used to play slide guitar. It did resemble a lipstick case and, in fact, some musicians used those in a pinch.

"It's a slide."

"I *know*. That was humor. As in 'sense of'." She shifted her weight to her right side, her left hand on her hip.

He noticed her breasts move slightly under her sweater. "Oh, humor. Right. I think I remember that." Awkward pause. "So. Would you like to go get a cup of coffee? Or a drink, or something? Let me just get all this sh- stuff together."

"I'm going on soon. I sing, *too*." She had an insolence he liked. "And you can say 'shit,' you know. It's allowed."

"What about 'fuck'?"

"Fuck, yes."

He laughed. "When are you singing?"

"Any year now."

"Well, then, I'll just wait around and hear you. If that's okay."

"Suit yourself," she said.

"Julie!" Rochelle poked her head into the back room. "Oh, hello," she said to Luke, as if surprised to find him there. "I really liked your songs a lot."

There was some intangible energy in the room. She looked from Luke to Julie, and back. Oh, I see how it is. "Okay, then. Well, break a leg. Isn't that what they say?"

An exhilarated Elliot returned to the table. Arlene moved her chair around so that she was practically leaning against him.

"What you do is so *fascinating*," Arlene told him. "You should definitely sign that Luke."

"I don't want to take on more clients than I can handle." He actually didn't have any signed clients yet. Just a few ragtag acts he occasionally booked into the Catskills hotels: a comic, a magician, a piano player.

Rochelle rejoined them, looked irritably at her watch. "If Julie doesn't go on soon…"

"I think she's next," Elliot assured her. "I pulled some strings and had her moved up." This, at least, was true. The MC was an aspiring comedian who wanted Elliot to manage him.

"I'd love to work for a record company or something, you know?" Rochelle said. "Anything but being a dumb secretary. But I suppose you have to know somebody."

"I might be able to arrange a few introductions," he said.

As her turn drew closer, Julie's panic increased. This was a Death Row kind of anxiety, a waiting-for-the-terminal-diagnosis terror. What made her think she should get on a stage? She hated everyone who had ever told her she had singing talent. If they *really* cared about her, they would not want her to endure this torment. If she blew it, they wouldn't want her back, or she'd be relegated to the bottom of the Tuesday night lists, one of those pathetic acts everyone talked over.

"Julie Bradley..."

The MC helped her adjust the mike. People were talking, oblivious. What was she starting with? "All My Trials"? That would put them right to sleep. Better change it. Something tougher, louder. Like jumping into cold water, she sang:

> *"I know you rider gonna miss me when I'm gone*
> *I know you rider gonna miss me when I'm gone*
> *Gonna miss your lovin' woman rollin' in your arms"*

Her hands were slippery and cold, and she struck a wrong chord on the guitar, made a quick adjustment, but anyone with a musical ear *had* to have heard it.

Elliot watched Julie. Her voice was pretty, not quite as pure as Judy Collins, a little edgier, and she needed to bring her keys down to a lower range. She looked ill at ease. That was no big deal, he could work with her. A beauty, a real beauty. Her body was amazing. He considered what she would be like in bed, with that hair floating over her bare breasts with their pink nipples—yes, they would have to be pink—and those long, slim legs. He fantasized running a hand up the inside of her pale thigh. Abruptly, he pulled himself back to reality. If she was to be a client, he couldn't be one of those sleazes who think their female clients are fair game. She'd have to fall in love with him all on her own. But he had never had a woman fall in love with him before, and had no idea how to go about it.

Ping!!! Her guitar's high E string broke. The pitch dipped disastrously flat and sharp all at once.

When the guitar string broke, Elliot's heart just about broke, too. She needed someone like him. She needed him.

Julie was starting to succumb to despair when another dimension of sound joined her voice. Someone was backing her up. The guitar player was sitting just offstage accompanying her. He added harmony on the chorus. Together, they finished the song.

The MC shook both their hands. "Come back next Tuesday, I'll give you a prime spot," he promised.

Luke and Julie regarded each other warily.

"We're not a *duo*," she said.

"Maybe you ought to be," said another voice behind them. Elliot took Julie's hand. "I enjoyed your singing. I've already told Luke here that I think he has real potential. To be quite honest, you two might be marketable as a duo. But if that doesn't sound like something you'd consider, I'd be happy to work with you separately, Miss Bradley. Please feel free to call me." He handed her his business card, turned and walked away.

She stared after him, amazed. A real *manager*.

7

Luke drained a third cup of espresso, and inspected the depths of the empty cup and the leisurely drift of smoke rings from his cigarette. He and Julie were the last customers at a funky old cafe two doors down from the Bitter End, so late in the night it was nearly morning, the street sounds soft as a dark mellow chord.

"Where'd you grow up, Julie?" Saying her name for the first time was shockingly intimate, the word on his tongue like tasting her.

"Right here in the city. Well, Queens."

"You Yankees got some damn strange names for places: The Bronx. Flushing."

She laughed, coquettish. "Well, ah jus' luuuv the way ya'll speak," she said in an exaggerated Southern accent. "Is that where you grew up? The South?"

"Army brat, actually. We lived everywhere."

"So where'd you learn to play the guitar?"

"Taught myself, mostly. In high school—we were living outside Fort Benning by then—I used to play every weekend in Columbus. Le Club Fransay, a crummy saloon with a fancy name, till my fingers were bleedin'—rhythm all night long— chunka chunka chunka" (she laughed at the face he made imitating how he played) "behind a hotdoggin' sax player called himself Joey B and couldn't play his way out of a small room with a map and a compass. Customers were so classy you had to duck the Coors bottles that came sailin' toward the bandstand. Owner put up chicken wire to keep us safe. Even the MPs didn't want to go in there. This owner was a lunatic, one night he got so pissed that one of his strippers didn't show up, he started shooting. At the fucking band! We hightailed it outta there like jackrabbits!"

She was wide-eyed, listening.

"The Fransay was next door to the Emerald Isle," he went on, grinning at the memory of the places he'd left behind. "A regular United Nations outside Columbus, Georgia, but over the state line in Alabama, where the liquor laws weren't so tough."

The two clubs were divided by one very busy package store with a steady flow of traffic in dry Muskogee County. They were called "bottle clubs" because you had to bring your own booze. The clubs sold set-ups for a higher price than they would've gotten for the liquor, so they were happy, and the store next door was happy, too. The bandstands of both clubs were situated right near the exit doors, which conveniently led straight into the store. Between sets, the musicians made a bee line for the whiskey and then headed out to the flat gray parking lot behind the buildings. If you walked around to the front, you'd see the flashing lights of Le Club Fransay spelling out the name in giant metal sequins, closely matched by the blinking, rippling green Emerald Isle marquee.

As Joey the bandleader signaled the end of a long version of "Honky Tonk," Luke managed to get in a few closing licks and earned a glare from Joey, who didn't like anyone stealing the spotlight. The other guys—electric organ, drums and bass—all deserted the bandstand in record time and headed out the door.

He leaned against the wall of the package store, pouring half the contents of a bottle of 7-Up onto the gravel and filling it with bourbon. He shook the bottle gently, then tipped his head back and drank half of it in three swallows, the tepid stinging sweet liquid burning a path down his throat to his belly. It took his mind off the stifling heat inside the club and the sweat that wriggled along his face and back and left dark wet patches on his shirt, and stung his eyes blind while he was playing. He took off his jacket and loosened his tie.

The bass player sidled up. Luke passed the bottle to him and took a Lucky the guy offered. They both lit up.

"Been playin' 'round much?" the bass player asked, wiping his lips on his sleeve. He couldn't be much older than Luke, maybe twenty, twenty-one at most, but he already looked worn out.

"Here an' there."

"You're good, man." Handed the bottle back.

"Thanks, man." Luke stared out at the parking lot. Three stocky women were getting into their car, a '63 Fairlane.

"I know a place over t' Phenix City lookin' for a guitar player. Strip club called Chuck's Little Flower Emporium. Ain't that a mouthful? Only thing, though, band's colored, so if that's a problem for you…"

"Black, white, don't matter to me, long's they can play."

"They play, all right, helluva lot better'n ole Joey."

"Ain't sayin' much," Luke laughed.

The bass player continued, "Their guitar player went to jail for coupla months."

"No shit?"

"Yeah. They got him on a morals charge? Seems he slipped it to his thirteen-year-old cousin jus' like ole Jerry Lee."

"No shit."

"Yeah. Makes you wonder, don' it? Wouldn't mind a little sample of fresh young snatch m'self."

"Yeah," Luke echoed, thinking: What the *fuck* am I talking about? Some times he had the feeling that the ladies who hung around the band stands were interested in him, but he didn't know how to get to the next step and by the time he'd started to figure it out, they'd gone off with the drummer. It was that primitive beat turned women on or something. One time Luke had screwed up his courage, so to speak, and approached a woman he'd seen in the club a couple of times. She was a bottle blonde who looked like she'd been around the world and back again. He knew she liked his playing because she smiled at him a lot. He asked if he could buy her a beer.

"Sure, honey," she said. They sat there awhile, at the bar, and she told him about her job at the Piggly Wiggly and how much she hated all the customers. He put his arm around her.

She looked at him with a kind of bemused sadness in her eyes and said, "You like girls?"

He nodded, unable to speak.

"Well, honey, so do I."

For a moment, he didn't know what the hell she meant and then it came to him, what she was saying. It was the kind of thing he'd heard about but never actually believed in. Like UFOs. She hopped down from the barstool and blew him a kiss as she left.

Luke stopped. He had made that last part a little cleaner as he related it to Julie. He replaced "fresh young snatch" with "pretty young lady," which kind of changed the meaning, but hell.

"It sounds wild."

"Am I shocking you?" he wanted to know.

"Of course not," she replied haughtily. "I read *Lady Chatterley's Lover*. And *City of Night*, too."

"Well, then," he said. "Guess you're a woman of the world." Although he hadn't read either book himself, at least he'd heard of one of them.

Julie tapped him playfully on the arm.

Luke resumed his story. "I got the job. At Chuck's Little Flower Emporium—sounds real exotic, don't it? Well it wasn't!"

The band consisted of maybe four pieces, maybe ten if the horn players showed up, which was an iffy thing. More often, there were five or six guys laying down a consistent, hot rhythm, heavy on the drum beat. The musicians wore white shirts that glowed in the black-light, which served to emphasize the strippers' pale bodies. Luke wore a battered straw hat pulled down over his eyebrows, not that it made him appear any less white if anyone cared to look close. And a couple of times, cops came in and there was just time for the manager to hustle him out the back before they saw the white face in the black band. He could just see, from beneath the brim of the hat and through the gauzy scrim that kept the white strippers and the equally white spectators separated from the Negro musicians, the opaque shadow of the strippers' backs writhing and wriggling out of their clothes, in an endless parade of tacky "acts" that went on until two in the morning. The concept of the scrim, "protecting" the lady "dancers" from the view of potentially predatory Neeeegroes, was a joke to the band, of course, because when the gals exited the stage, bare as babies, they passed in full view of the musicians, most of whom had seen it all too many times to take much notice anyway.

The strippers were not exactly Gypsy Rose Lee caliber but even so, after a couple of months of playing weekends, Luke had a favorite. She was a big woman who called herself Lydia Lickit—tall and wide in the shoulders, big-breasted and hipped with thick dark hair that fell to her waist when she let it down at the end of her "act." Luke didn't know why, but that was the most exciting part, better even than when she slipped off her bejeweled bra and peeled off her pasties, revealing long succulent brown nipples, or the bikini bottom she pulled slowly between her legs, then whipped around and around and tossed back over the divider, occasionally landing on the neck of Luke's snazzy new white Fender Jazzmaster. The strippers peeled down to G-strings and then fled behind a curtain while the clientele whooped and got sloshed.

Lydia's gimmick was that she wore black-rimmed glasses and kept her hair up in a schoolteacher's bun until the climax of the act. It was when she removed those glasses and let down her hair that Luke—and a lot of the audience—got hard. Luke was inspired to play a fierce quick solo, firing out notes like lightning up and down the neck of the guitar, prompting Big Dog, the seasoned keyboard man, to look up, sweat running rivulets down his dark skin, and murmur appreciatively, "White boy plays the blues!"

Maybe it was the music that fired his senses, or the presence, the smell of the women—between shows he could hear them giggling and squealing in their crowded one-room dressing area. The owner, Chuck, always paid a visit then, passing among them like a rooster checking out his henhouse.

"Where you get all that soul, boy?" asked Big Dog after a particularly feverish set. Luke shrugged, embarrassed. What could he say? That it came straight up from his dick? Although he had a feeling Dog would understand. They were out in the parking lot, a stretch of gravel that looked just like the parking lot behind the Club Fransay and the Emerald Isle. Luke wondered if this was to be his life, if he'd never see any place that looked different or smelled of something other than old smoke and sweat, cheap perfume and stale booze. He knew guys who spent their whole lives this way; they ended up playing weddings or gave it up altogether to work in a garage.

The other men joined them, lighting up reefer. They passed it over to Luke like he was a regular part of them. He was ashamed to let them see he didn't know what the fuck to do with it.

"Hold it down, man," Big Dog rasped, showing him.

This time Luke did it right, sucking in his breath until he thought he might pass out and, in a few seconds, he felt a slow spreading of time from gesture to thought and back. He sighed aloud and the other musicians laughed.

"Watch how he play now!" the small, wiry drummer remarked.

The next set was a sensual blur, although it did seem they were up on that stage for a long, long, long time. Lifetimes passed, he got older and then younger again. He was brilliant and his fingers had a life of their own.

Lydia Lickit was watching him pack up his guitar and for once, he had the courage to go right up to her.

"You're here late," he said. She was almost his height, five-eleven, and he looked right into her black eyes. Her hair was still down and he impulsively reached over and touched the trailing ends of it, near her waist.

"You like my Cherokee hair?" she asked.

"That where you got it?"

"My Gramma, she was full-blood Indian."

"Me, too." His black hair came from his Italian daddy but he preferred the idea of Indian ancestors; it suggested something wild and free.

"Maybe we're related then," she said.

"Not too close, I hope."

They had moved together, almost touching. He was hard, as usual. She edged toward the back door, the red Exit sign just barely illuminating her profile. He followed, mesmerized by the idea of being in bed with her, feeling her bare skin all over him. When they got to the parking lot, she paused.

"I like you, Luke," she said, touching his face gently with her forefinger. "In fact, I more than like. I want you so bad I'm meltin'...but I got two kids an' a babysitter waitin' for me."

"I want..." he said. "You're so..." The ache in his groin made him nearly double over. He leaned against the wall.

She pulled him into the shadows. He could see the highway, cars whooshing by one after the other. She knelt down and unzipped his pants, slipped him out; the night air touching him in a new way. He felt her fingers and her hands and then her tongue, which sent his brain soaring up into space, fast, like a rocket. It was all happening much too quickly and then it was over, she'd put him back in his clothes and wiped her mouth with a handkerchief she took from her purse. His legs felt wobbly and he sank down to the doorsill to catch his breath. She sat next to him and she seemed to be waiting for something.

He turned to her, his heart so full of gratitude he couldn't contain it. "I love you," he told her.

She smiled. "Well, that's nice, honey, but it ain't gonna pay my rent."

His brain registered this new idea. She wanted *money*.

He thrust his hand into his pants pockets and pulled out the small wad he'd just earned, peeled off bills until she looked happy and put the rest away.

Lydia Lickit got up and stretched. "Oh, boy, I ain't as young as I once was, these long nights are gettin' to me. See ya later, kid."

He sat there in the dark for a long time and when he finally got up the energy to go home, his father was sleeping in the Barcalounger, snoring, the TV still on with a snowy white screen.

Luke paused. He had omitted the entire sexual episode, and had only referred to Lydia by her first name. In his spoken version, she was a nice divorcee gone wrong. The memory of it aroused him as if Julie were the one to remove her clothes, to blow him. He wondered if Julie was the kind of girl you could do those things to, or if all women were like Lydia, and, if so, was that a good thing or a cause of great worry?

"So that's when you came to New York?"

"Yeah, pretty much. I didn't know anyone here, so I just asked around where there was a YMCA and they sent me to the place I'm stayin'. No ladies allowed, I'm afraid. Not that I was assuming anything," he added hastily.

"You're going to stay?" Julie turned toward the window, and he had the feeling she knew that this angle made her long, graceful neck even more attractive. She focused on the street outside, as if his answer didn't matter a bit; but he could see one of her fingernails picking nervously at a cuticle on the other hand.

"Till I become a star or they draft me, whichever comes first." He gave a short laugh. "Guess I've seen 'bout all the military I ever want to, thank you very much, so I'll probably find some way out."

"This guy I know," she said, "he plays guitar, too. Casey Mahoney? He went down to the draft board wearing makeup and a garter belt. Another guy I know took a lot of speed and got sent to the hospital but he got a 4F."

"Man's gotta do what a man's gotta do," Luke said, trying to mask the sickly fear the subject caused him.

"Are you...I mean...could they draft you?"

"I don't know. I'm temporarily deferred."

The letter had found its way to him before he left Georgia. As soon as he saw it, he knew. It was amazing how such a heart-stopping, life-altering catastrophe could be so innocent looking. **United States Selective Service...please report to the Draft Board...classification physical...**

"What's your problem, Geetar?" Big Dog asked that night. Luke had hardly spoken a word to anyone, and was doing some serious drinking out in the parking lot between sets.

"Draft, man. Heard from Uncle Sam."

The old musician nodded, understanding. "When they wanna see you?"

"Monday morning."

Big Dog reached into his inside jacket pocket, pressed something into Luke's hand. "Take 'em the night before. Don't worry none how you feel, like you head wanna fly off."

"I took them," Luke said to Julie, "all of 'em. I get to this physical, and I think I'm a goner, they told me 'bring a toothbrush and prepare to stay.' I'm pissin' my pants, standin' there with a hundred other fools, and then the doctor checks me over, listens to my heart. And whattaya know? God's lookin' out for me after all: I got a rapid heartbeat. From all the speed, which I don't mention. And high blood pressure. They give me a 1-Y, which gives 'em the option to call me again, any time, see if I'm in better shape. If it had been a 4F, I'd be home free. Now I gotta make sure I don't take care of myself."

She frowned. "Artists shouldn't have to go in the Army."

"'Artists,' huh? Well, I'll tell 'em you said so when it comes my turn. That ought to impress 'em."

"I'll write you a note. 'Please excuse Luke from the military.' Signed, Julie."

Something that felt like an electric current was tripping through his body. This was nothing like Lydia Lickit—it was more than sex, and it confused him.

He placed his open palm on the window pane. "Cold."

Julie did the same; their handprints lingered on the foggy glass.

A car stopped at the corner and moved on again. "Ford Fair lane, '61." he said. "'58 T-Bird. Volkswagen. Brand-new Olds 88."

"What?"

"Game." He stubbed out his cigarette, smiled. "When I was a kid, we were in Bakersfield, California for awhile, right next to the Mojave Desert, and there was nothin' to do. I mean nothin'. I used to sit out by the highway and watch the cars go by. I could tell the sound of a Pontiac engine from a Buick from a Chevrolet, just by the hum at a mile off. And squint one eye closed and identify a Ford from the tip of its grille." "If they were moving by, how would you know if you'd made a mistake?"

"Just *know*, that's all."

"Big, fat, blue car with fins," she challenged, indicating the street. "'59 DeSoto."

"Little, weird squared-off car like a boxy Volkswagen."

"Huh?"

"There," she pointed down the block.

"Hey, dig it, an old Citroen, must be '51 or '52. Don't see many of them around. Used to see 'em all over France."

His hand was inches away on the table. If either of them moved just a fraction, they'd be touching.

"Cars used to be mostly all black, didn't they?" she whispered.

"I'd forgotten that." "Yeah." His pants were so tight, it was all he could do not to reach down and adjust himself.

"And they used to have a lot better hood ornaments."

"Sure did." He was trembling from holding back. "I think I've gotta kiss you, Julie Bradley." He half stood, leaned over the table, touched her lips with his, placed his hand at the nape of her neck, very gently, as if she might vanish with too sudden a movement. They broke apart, stunned.

As if the momentous thing had not occurred, she said, "Rochelle and I had a game like that. I mean, like your car game."

"Rochelle?"

"My best friend. She was at the show tonight. She came backstage."

"Dark hair? Lotta makeup?"

"I guess so."

"Uh-huh, with that other girl, the uh, not-so-pretty one."

"Arlene Slotnick. I can't stand Arlene. Although…" She began to giggle.

"What?"

"Oh, something silly I just thought of."

"What?"

"A party at Arlene's when Rochelle and I were fourteen. We never hung out much with Arlene, but one day she invited us to her house. Her parents had a lot of money, I mean, for our neighbor hood, anyway. Her father was—is— a doctor, so we figured, what the hell, how bad could it be? I was real impressed because everyone there was...kind of, you know, rocky."

He looked perplexed. "What's 'rocky'?"

"You know, hoody. Tight sweaters and skirts. Black leather jackets. Virgin pins."

"You mean white trash."

"Well, no, not exactly. They're mostly Jewish. Who ever heard of *Jewish* white trash?"

"You know, I actually never met a...a Jewish person till I moved up here."

"I'm one. Well, half anyway. Please don't ask which half."

He'd been about to say just that. "And what are virgin pins?"

"Oh brother." She shook her head. "These circular pins...oh, never mind."

"Okay, okay."

She continued, "So I didn't know anyone at this party except Rochelle and Arlene, and everyone was paired off and making out but I didn't have anyone. So I stayed in the corner and put records on the hi-fi. And I played all the wrong sides of the records."

"What are the 'wrong' sides?" He lit up another Marlboro and waved at the waitress for more coffee.

"Oh, you know how you can stack all the 45s on the hi-fi and they flop down one at a time? Well, I put the whole stack on upside down. So instead of getting 'At the Hop,' it played 'Sometimes When I'm All Alone'..." She sang a few bars.

He shook his head, uncomprehending.

"Danny and the Juniors? It's the B side of 'At the Hop'."

"I was listening to B.B. King and Blind Lemon Jefferson."

"Okay, I know it's ridiculous, but we were fourteen! I was *so* depressed. Not only because of the records, but because Rochelle had this real cute, real rocky boyfriend who gave her the front thing off a Volkswagen. You know, the hood ornament? They were about this big." She made an open circle with her thumb and forefinger. "And they were incredible collector's items in junior high. I really think the Volkswagen people stopped putting them on cars because everybody stole them. You'd drill a tiny hole at the top and wear it as a medallion, but it was no fun to steal it yourself. You had to get a boy to steal it for you."

"I'll steal one for you. Then I can get an arrest record and avoid the draft permanently."

The waitress came over again. "Closing up. Even *this* place mops the floor sometimes." She took their cups and left.

He put two dollars on the table.

Outside the cafe, the street was still. Their breath formed clouds in the cold air.

They were kissing again, for a long time. He pulled away first. A part of him wanted to run away, fast and far. Most of him just wanted to fuck her, right then and there. Who was she to confuse him so? They walked along Bleecker, Luke carrying both of their guitars. He sang, "Green, green rocky road, promenade in green, tell me who ya'll love, tell me who ya'll love..." She knew the song and added a harmony line.

"We sound kind of -"

"Yeah."

"- good."

She broke into the Fred Neil song "Bleecker and Mac-Dougal."

He added a harmony.

"Maybe we *should* be a duo," she said, half kidding. "Then at least I wouldn't have to play the guitar by myself."

"You play okay."

"Compared to what?"

He took her hand and just held it. "So what do you think, is this a fate-like thing?"

"How should I know? I'm an atheist."

He'd never met one of *those*, either. Although, when he thought about it, he wasn't sure he actually believed in God. Not the church one, anyhow.

Luke kissed Julie on the corner of Seventh Avenue and Christopher Street, with the empty taxis rattling by and a few stubborn stars blinking over the city. She pulled away and ran down a narrow street, and stopped at a brownstone with a filigreed gate, a tiny front garden, decorated with sculptures of small animals. There were two stone lions on each side of the stoop, miniatures of the lions that flanked the public library.

"Is this where you live? Far out!" he said, amazed.

"I *wish*."

"We'll just have to get famous and buy it."

It seemed absolutely assured at that moment, everything wonderful would come to pass. When they were famous, he would buy a brand-new Aston Martin DB5, just like James Bond.

They reached a shabbier block. "Here. My little cellar." She indicated the steps that led to the basement. "So, goodnight, I guess."

"Yeah, goodnight." He didn't know what else to do, so he handed over her guitar, and started to walk away. "I'll see you soon," he called out.

"Sure," she muttered. She watched until he turned the corner, his boots echoing on the pavement, the sound growing distant. A cat came out from behind a garbage can and sidled up, purring against her legs. "Here, cat. Poor cat." She bent down and touched the animal.

She didn't bother to turn the light on in the apartment but sank onto the sofa in an abrupt despair, that she would never see him again.

Several minutes later, she heard boot heels running on pavement. They stopped at her door. There was a soft knock. Luke stood in the doorway, breathing hard, clutching something in his fist. "Here," he said, pressing it into her hand.

A small, flat medallion off the front of a Volkswagen.

"Now you have one, too," he said.

8

Elliot rose early each morning, stuffed himself into the packed subway train—feeling superior to those drones who had boring, stupid jobs while he was manager of Luke & Julie, the Future Famous—and schlepped around Manhattan with their home-recorded reel-to-reel tapes and fliers of where they would be performing (a night at the Gaslight; at the Village Gate where Odetta was the headliner; a guest set at Gerdes Folk City, after Phil Ochs had taken the audience and gone home). He beseeched the all-powerful A&R reps to hear his clients, please just *listen*, just one song.

He'll get back to you, secretaries said. *Leave your name and number. Who?* they asked rudely. *Sorry. Sorry. Sorry. Goodbye.*

He borrowed money from his mother and rented a tiny office in the Brill Building on 49th and Broadway. People sometimes called it Tin Pan Alley, but that had actually been on West 28th Street and was long gone. This was where a lot of the music business happened now and he was at its center, despite the fact that his office was smaller than the bathroom down the hall. The top half of the door was a cloudy glass with a partly scratched imprint—BUT E FLY PROD—from the last tenant, but as soon as he had the money, he'd have that changed to **Elliot Levine Productions**. A photo of Julie and Luke was the only wall decoration, other than a calendar from a local dry cleaners. They posed with their instruments in front of the Bitter End.

The mail was mostly junk, except for his new subscription to *Happy's Hotsheet*, a music-industry roundup of the latest released records with recommendations and pans by its editor, Marvin "Happy" Becker. After he'd read it through, he turned on the tape recorder, threaded a tape, and began to listen to the first in a small stack of hopefuls, on the chance that he'd find yet another nugget of gold.

9

"Mr. Gorsuch's office," she said for the umpteenth time that morning.

"Rochelle?"

"Hi, Ma." She reached for a cigarette.

Her mother heard the exhale. "You're still smoking? You said you were quitting two months ago!"

"I *am* quitting. But I'm doing it at my own *pace*, okay?"

"At your 'pace,' you'll be quitting after you're breathing out of one of those tubes, like Uncle Morty who dropped dead at forty-five."

"Then I won't have to worry about it, will I? Ma, is *this* what you called about? I'm busy. My boss has been *hocking* me all day."

"I can't call up my daughter? Ever since you moved to the city, we could be on Mars as far as you're concerned, and your brother's graduating junior high—"

Rochelle's intercom buzzed, giving her an excuse to put her mother on hold. She copied down her boss' list of orders in shorthand, then returned to her mother.

"—so can you come out for Ira's party?"

"What? No, can't. Got a date. Just a sec." She pushed hold again, her tension level rising another notch. "*Yes*, Mr. Gorsuch?"

"Let's get Johnny Coffey on the phone—I think he's at his place in the Hamptons—then get Brandon Dilburger and, uh, Arnie, no he's in Europe, call Arnie's office and ask his secretary where we can reach him or have him call us, then get…" The button that held her mother's call was blinking like an angry eye. "…Joel Crampton, Les Schmukler and the dry cleaners and my wife." He clicked off.

"Ma, I've gotta go–"

"A date with who?"

"No one. This guy, Elliot, but it's more like business. He's going to introduce me to some people who could get me a job. A *real* job in the record business."

"The record business? What kind of business is that? A bunch of crooks and dope fiends. That Alan Freed dropped dead from the payola and god knows what. So are you coming this weekend?"

"I'll try. Really," she lied.

Rochelle took a bite of her lemony veal Francese and tried not to look at Elliot. He ate strangely, separating his food and cutting it up like a parent would for a child. At least it wasn't as bad as another date she'd had. He'd taken her to a really nice French restaurant. While they were chatting, sharing a basket of crusty bread, the guy had leaned over the table and, with no apparent awareness that he was in public, licked up the crumbs from the tablecloth.

Elliot said, "It should be a big party, lots of important—"

Their table was next to the rippling fountain. Water cascaded from the open mouth of a sea nymph. The violinist was heading their way, and between that and the rushing water, she could barely hear him.

"What?!"

"Ray Fish heads BigWheel Records! He's having the party. I'm trying to get them to sign Luke & Julie!"

The violinist sawed a syrupy "Love is a Many Splendored Thing." All Rochelle could think of was "love is a long and slender thing," a *faux*-lyric she and Julie had made up when they were thirteen.

The fountain splashed. What made people throw coins into fountains? Did they really expect their wishes to come true? Maybe tossing pennies into some ancient site in Paris or Rome held some magic, but here in the middle of a restaurant? Why not just lob change into the toilet bowl?

The violinist concluded with a screechy flourish. Elliot handed him a dollar and the man backed away, nearly colliding with a waiter bearing a full tray.

"That was—"

"Awful."

"How did you get invited to this party?" she asked. It came out a little ruder than she'd intended: How did *you* get invited?

"Friend of a friend," he replied, too quickly. "Uh, yeah, this guy I know told me about it. I mean, it isn't like there's some official list or they're going to strip search us at the door."

Oh, great. We're crashers. "Well, if somebody asks me how I got there, what am I supposed to say?"

"Say you're with Stan Bernstein."

"Who's Stan Bernstein?"

Elliot shrugged, grinned. "I dunno. But it's worked before."

"This should be some evening."

"Well, I've got Luke and Julie coming and with a little help from the music gods, they'll play. It's a sneak audition."

"Like I said." She finished off her second glass of wine.

He went over the check like it was his tax return.

The cab let them off in front of an ultra-modern highrise on Fifth Avenue, a white slab soaring into the black sky, set back from the street by a circular driveway where three enormous limousines waited. A doorman opened their cab door and escorted them to the elevator. The lobby looked as if it had been transported directly from one of the 1964 World's Fair "Future Living" pavilions, all chrome and Formica and curved angles, as if people in the future would no longer want to sit on a comfortable chair.

"We're here for Mr. Fish's party," Elliot told the doorman with an air of importance.

"And your name, sir?" He held a list.

Oh, shit, here we go, thought Rochelle.

Elliot coughed. "Stan Bernstein."

The man scanned the list. "I only see a Steve Bernstein."

"Must be a misprint," Elliot said smoothly.

"Twenty-eighth floor."

An expressionless elevator operator escorted them up, sparing them the effort of having to push the button themselves. The elevator opened on a small foyer. Sound assaulted their ears as soon as they crossed the threshold, as if they'd broken through an invisible barrier.

Silver lamé, pink chiffon, polka dots, eye-boggling stripes and paisleys, gold mesh stockings and fake see-through lace over flesh-colored body stockings, flashes of jewelry, sleek heads of lacquered women's hair, puffed up and teased into towering coiffures, cleavage and legs, legs encased in op-art hose, bangly earrings and heavy medallions. The men with black pants flaring out slightly above the ankle, loose plaid vests and plain narrow ties; the women in pantsuits or tiny backless cocktail shifts, shorter than she'd seen except in magazines—nearly two inches above the knee—and fishnet stockings. Half the women there wore short white boots just like hers. Sound vibrated through her bones.

The apartment was surrounded in glass, the city beyond and below, the ceiling lofting two stories up. A bartender in a white smock briskly poured and mixed. While Elliot was fetching Rochelle a daiquiri, she foraged a cigarette out of her purse and lit it, jostling her way out of the throng by the bar, nearer to the window. Below was all of Central Park, all of the world. From unseen speakers came the relentless thump of "Woolly Bully." Elliot weaved through the crowd, two drinks held aloft.

Rochelle took hers, and drank nearly half in one swallow. Too weak and too sweet.

"I'm going to the little girls'," she told him, and slipped off—drink, cigarette, freedom. All these people. Money. She could all but smell it. In fact, she *could* smell it: an unmistakable waft of expensive perfumes. The apartment was more a house in a larger building, with several levels, corridors leading off to bedrooms, sitting rooms, a library with walls of old books, rows and rows in identical, gold-trimmed bindings; a half dozen people were passing a joint. Another door turned out to be a closet. Finally, a bathroom.

The toilet, she discovered after a moment of bewildered exploration, was disguised as a rattan chair, like something out of *The Maltese Falcon*. Where the hell was the toilet paper? Hiding behind a little brass door. Swans for spigots. Gilded mirrors. Marble bath. She'd placed her drink on the counter and now she picked it up and watched herself take a sip, impressed by her sophisticated surroundings, only faintly tainted by her jealousy that there were people who lived this way *every single day*, while she was only a tourist.

Somewhere in the multitude out there was the host, record mogul Ray Fish. Probably some old fart with a paunch. She teased the hair that rose in a nest at the crown of her head, and combed down the blunt-cut bangs that hid her eyebrows. Straightened at a pricey salon with a snooty staff that made her feel as if they were doing her a favor by letting her butt touch their chairs, it now fell smoothly to her shoulders, turning up at the ends. Re-lined her eyes with black Mary Quant. Added another layer of silver-white lipstick. Her mouth, which she had once hated, had become her best feature, full-lipped and sexy. If only she were thinner.

Emerging, she bumped into a couple making out in the hall. The music was "Satisfaction" and bodies were writhing in dance frenzy. Her pelvis pumped instinctively to the beat. Instead of returning to the living room where she'd left Elliot, she ascended a curved staircase which led to another floor and a large, masculine room containing a pool table, complete with a full rack of, what were they? Sticks? No. Cues, they were called. A game was going on, the men seriously focused, and a couple of women watched from the sidelines, ornamental and bored. There was a sound she knew well, a muted thop...thop-thop. Darts.

The memory of her brother's old dartboard came back. She'd sneak into his room and mess with it when he was out, just to tick him off. Now, she recalled the poised balance of the tapered, feathered dart in her hand; her eyes narrowing on that small center, the perfect distance of the target, the toss. She smiled, and entered the room.

Three men were gathered around the dartboard. The one throwing wore a leather vest over a red silk shirt open at the neck, black slacks, leather sandals, no socks. His hairline had receded slightly but was long in back, brown streaked with silver and trailing over his shirt collar. He moved in an easy, muscular way, like someone who might leap onto a horse bareback with a leather whip. Tinted frameless glasses shadowed his eyes. She had no idea how old he was. Old, though, maybe forty. But attractive. His hand held the dart delicately, poised. She noticed the way his fingertips adjusted the grip, and how he focused on the target. He let fly. Bullseye. He laughed and turned an expensively capped smile on Rochelle. His two opponents groaned. One of them had a goatee and no mustache, the other was short-haired and clean-cut, in a white jacket and sporting a yachting cap.

"Come on, Ray, you get to practice all the time," the bearded one said to the long-haired man in the red shirt.

"You oughta have a handicap."

"I've got a handicap. You met my ex?" said Ray.

He was the host, Ray Fish, and he was not at all as she had pictured him.

"Wanna toss a few?" offered the yachtsman, addressing Rochelle.

"Why not?" She sensed Ray looking at her body in the tight hip huggers.

"Try not to hit people," the goateed man remarked.

She hurled the dart. Bullseye. The men gave her a round of applause.

"The girl can throw," Ray commented.

"Beginner's luck," muttered the goateed man.

She aimed again, threw. Score. Her mother would say: "Men like to be the best. Sometimes, you have to let them win." She often did just that, played helpless, but for some reason right now, she wanted to show them she was good at *something*.

There was no way she could be the most beautiful woman at the party, or the richest, or the smartest. Maybe she could at least be the best fucking darts player.

Another bullseye, it knocked the first one off the board.

"Who are you, Maid Marian?" Ray joked.

"Rochelle Klein."

"Nice to meet you, Rochelle. I'm Ray."

The yachtsman spoke up. "Department store Klein's?"

"Yeah," she lied automatically.

"My father's firm did some work for Abe Klein," Ray Fish said. He tossed three more darts, matching Rochelle's score. "Your uncle, right?" There was a teasing note in his voice.

"Yes, old Uncle Abe."

"Old Uncle Abe. So, to whom do I owe the pleasure of your company tonight?"

"Stan, I mean, Elliot Levine. That is, he's a friend of Stan Bernstein. I mean, Steve Bernstein."

Ray stared at her.

"Elliot Levine. He's a talent manager. He handles Luke & Julie. The singing duo."

"Ah, the 'singing duo.'" He shrugged. "So many wanna-bees, so little time."

"They're really good."

"I'm sure they are." His attention strayed. "If you'll excuse me?" He strode away.

She headed downstairs toward the louder music, the tail end of the Four Tops' "I Can't Help Myself." Her body saw Luke first and then the thought registered with her brain, so that she felt the jolt before she understood it. He ran his hands through his hair in a nervous gesture that she found particularly appealing.

Quickly, she excused her way through the throng, using her years of practice in the subway to push and slither, motivated by a primal instinct.

"Luke."

Barely a flicker of recognition.

"I'm Rochelle Klein. Julie's friend."

"Sure! Sorry, sugar, I'm not too good on names. Rochelle. I'll remember now." He smiled and dazzled her once again.

She looked up at him through her eyelashes and licked her lips.

"Can I get you a drink?" she asked.

"Great idea. Julie here yet?"

"Haven't seen her. But Elliot's around someplace."

His hand brushed her arm, making her shiver. "What'll I do with this monster?" He tapped the guitar case.

"Follow me." She led him down the hall and opened the door to a large walk-in closet she'd discovered while searching for the bathroom. A row of fur coats hung at one end. The light went on automatically but when the door closed behind them, it went off and they were alone in the muffled dark.

"Hello," he said. "We have to stop meeting like this."

"Yes." She could hear his breath. He smelled faintly of cigarettes and a tangy aftershave. Then, a light went on. His hand had found the switch. They were face to face.

"We don't want to get lost," he said.

"No."

"Might never find the way out."

"Right."

"Starve and die in here. They'd find our skeletons months later."

"We could eat all the pelts," she said, stroking one of the fur coats.

"You've been friends with Julie a long time, right?" he asked. "Sometimes I can't figure her out. You must understand her a little, being her friend and all."

Why was *every*one always asking her about *Julie*? Instead of answering, she stretched her arms up and touched the closet's low ceiling, then ran her hands over the furs. "They ought to put them in storage, that's what you're supposed to do with furs in the summer. I could just take all my clothes off and roll around on them."

"Uh, yeah. Well, I'm pretty thirsty. How 'bout we get those drinks?" He opened the door, and they were hurled back into the startling volume and energy of the party.

Elliot was certain he'd seen Rochelle go upstairs. He followed, a drink balanced in each hand. He nearly collided with Warren Jaffee, the portly manager of a few lackluster acts.

"Levine! How ya doing?" Jaffee was as friendly and about as welcome as a big, slobbering dog on a white suit.

"Great! Just great! You?" He knew Jaffee would tell him whether he asked or not.

"Great! I signed Liz Gainsborough, you know." He lowered his voice to a stage whisper: "I'm getting her out of that crappy Vanguard deal and into some real bucks—can't say where yet, you know how it is." His voice returned to its normal mega-decibels. "Great to see you! Gotta run!"

Elliot watched him barrel back into the crowd, astounded that someone as boorish as Jaffee had landed such a classy act. Where was it written that the people you most disliked/resented/looked down upon were inevitably successful?

Well, no more of that kind of thinking. That was the *old* Elliot, the pre-Luke & Julie Elliot. And, where the hell had Rochelle got to? He tried room after room until he came to the library, possibly the only part of the duplex where guests were not swarming. Built-in bookshelves lined the walls, holding pristine editions of *The Compleat*

Works of Shakespeare. The Canterbury Tales. Plato. A door creaked behind him.

"Like books?" Ray Fish was standing in the doorway.

"Sure, love books, especially old ones," Elliot replied.

"I've got a rare book dealer who finds them for me. I don't have the time."

"I'm Elliot Levine." He whipped a business card from his jacket pocket and handed it to Ray. "I've got a lot of music acts I think you might want to hear—some real talent! And a bunch of songs could be hits. You know that song 'Little Silver Raindrops'?"

"Novelty number?"

"Right. That was mine. The Umbrella Singers stole it, thought it was public domain, and now I gotta sue 'em for my share." He laughed nervously. "Show biz, right?" He cleared his throat. "Here's the thing I wanted to talk to you about. I've got this act I think could really go places. Luke & Julie."

"Somebody else just mentioned them."

"*Really?* Well, they've got something special!"

"And what is that exactly?"

"Well, she's gorgeous and he's a helluva guitar player."

"Talk to my assistant, Spider Allessi, he's around someplace. Tall guy, real pale, like an albino. Can't miss him. He'll set something up." Ray was gone.

Elliot went off to find Rochelle and share the news with her. Then he'd go after his next quarry: Spider Allessi.

Rochelle stood by the window, pretending she was having fun. She spotted a scruffy trio in black jeans, loose vests, long hair and straggly mustaches. One had an untamed beard and a string T-shirt that said FUGS. "Hang on

Sloopy" was blasting from the many speakers. Luke had yet to return from his quest for drinks.

"Rochelle!" Elliot handed her one of the two drinks he held. The ice was melted. "I just talked to Ray Fish!"

Luke came over, interrupting. "I don't think this party is in the right kind of mood to do much listenin'." He also handed a drink to Rochelle.

"We'll wait till it calms down," Elliot assured him.

"And then play for a bunch of passed-out drunks?"

"We'll catch them right before that stage."

"If Julie doesn't show, it won't matter either way, will it?"

Luke crushed his cigarette, half-smoked, into a crystal ashtray.

"You don't think anything's happened to her, do you?" Elliot asked.

"Of course not," Rochelle assured him. "She's just being Julie."

Luke scanned the room.

A few feet away, a man told a loud joke, "…and the adorable little girl is dressed in a frilly dress and she's walking her dog on a ribbon leash, and the old lady says, 'What a pretty dress you're wearing,' and the little girl says, 'Thank you, ma'am,' and the old lady says, 'And what a cute little dog, what's the dog's name?', and she says 'Porky,' and the old lady says, 'What a cute name, why do you call him Porky?' and the cute little girl says, 'Because he fucks pigs.'"

"Help!" sang the Beatles on the hi-fi.

She swallowed one drink down, then the other. Elliot had his hand around her waist and he was rocking slightly to the music. Maybe if she got drunk enough, she'd want to sleep with him. Maybe if Luke got drunk enough, he'd want to sleep with her. Maybe pigs would fly.

"Excuse me," she muttered. Her feet took her up the stairs again, to the billiard room. The three darts players were gone and two couples had taken their place, one of the women giggling as she missed the board entirely. The pool players were the same serious men, wrapped in the cocoon of their game. She wandered out again and took the opposite direction down the hall, and came to a wide, closed, knobless door.

She nudged it, expecting it to open, but the door didn't give. There didn't seem to be a lock on it. Her curiosity aroused, she gave it another shove, and a third, even harder.

It opened.

The spectacular master bedroom was surrounded by glass so that it seemed to float above the city, subtly illuminated by track lighting hidden in the ceiling design and from the glow of the city outside, far below. Imagine waking up to this every morning. Going to sleep in a cloud at night.

A huge white painting dominated one wall. At first, in the dim light, it appeared to be an empty canvas. She took a few steps closer and began to make out almost subliminal images: a *trompe l'oeil* of nude bodies and wild animals. Against the far wall, there was an enormous four-poster bed, covered in a silvery satin throw. The only other furniture was a carved wooden chair with a high back that was set precisely in the center of the room, facing the windows. The chair had leather straps at the back and at the base of its four thick legs. It reminded her of a photo she'd seen as a child, of Ethel Rosenberg, fried in the electric chair on the cover of the *Daily News*. There was something as terrifying and fascinating about the odd wooden chair in Ray Fish's bedroom.

Better leave. Instead, she edged closer to the chair. She reached out a hand, daring herself to touch it. What if it were wired? Twenty thousand volts. Dead!

She closed her eyes and, with one fingertip, touched the smooth wood -

"Boo."

She screamed.

Ray stood in the shadowed doorway. "I'm sorry, I didn't mean to scare you."

"Jesus Horatio Christ!" Not only did he *mean* to scare her, he'd damned well enjoyed it.

"Is He here, too?" Ray remarked.

"You have a hell of a nerve, coming up on me like that!"

"*I* have a hell of a nerve? Last time I noticed, this was *my* place."

"And I'm a guest, and you ought to be more welcoming."

"You're something, aren't you, Miss Klein's Department Store. But I guess this isn't nearly as nice as Old Uncle Abe's estate."

"No, not *nearly* as nice. But, of course, we had to let it go. Couldn't get good help anymore. You know how it is." She began to laugh and it spun out of control, turning into a tearful crash of hormones and futile envy. "Okay, I made it up, alright? I'm *nobody*."

"Oh no, not tears!" He made the sign of the cross with his index fingers. "Here." He thrust a box of tissues in her direction. "Don't cry, okay, I can't...okay...and, and let me tell you something. Around this business, nobody is *nobody*. Because *anybody* can be *somebody*. And I have no idea what I just said."

They laughed.

"Come here." He took her hand and sat her on the bed, putting his arm around her shoulder. "Klein's Department Store, huh? You're quite the cute little bullshitter. You know, you almost had me going."

"Please, forget that. I can't believe the things I come up with sometimes." She dried her eyes with the tissue. "I'm fine now. And I didn't go through your, uh, personal things or anything like that, I swear. You should get back to your guests."

"Guests?" He gave a disdainful shrug. "Fuck 'em. They all just want something. From me, from each other, free booze, free favors. I'd rather talk to you."

"Oh, brother."

"What?"

"You're gonna hate me, too."

"Why is that?" He got up and pushed the door shut. The sounds of the party were distant.

She was keenly aware that they were very alone. With the Chair of Death.

"I was sort of hoping you could maybe help me get a job."

She rose from the bed, walked to the window.

"Okay, let me have it. You're a singer?"

"*No.*"

"Thank God."

"Secretary. But I should do something in the music business, but I have no idea. Is that stupid or what?" She turned to face him. The chair was between them. She took a step toward it. His eyebrow rose slightly. She knew he was aware of her curiosity. Like the darts, this was a game of one-upmanship she wasn't prepared to lose.

"No. I got into music ass backwards myself," he said. "I was working in the ad business, churning out copy: 'Brush your teeth with Ipana'. 'Smoke Kools' and all that crap."

"Was that yours?" Another step toward the chair. Casual.

"No. But I did come up with 'The bird in hand should be Marshall brand.' For a poultry company in Nebraska. My big account."

Rochelle's thigh brushed against the chair. She sat on one arm, her legs slightly apart.

"But we're not here to listen to my life story, are we?" Ray asked.

"We're not?" she murmured.

"I don't think so." He leaned over and pushed some hidden button. Music started from the walls, a quiet, haunting jazz.

"Miles Davis. 'Sketches of Spain'," Ray said. "Want a drink?"

"I've had three watery daiquiris. You should get a better bartender."

"Really. Well, then." He pushed another button, a wall slid open across the room, revealing a private bar, refrigerator, ice machine. He padded over and took out a bottle of tequila, a lemon, a small dish of salt, placed everything on a tray and brought it over to her. She noticed the supple tendons on the tops of his bare, tanned feet.

"Like this," he said, showing her how to suck the lemon, swig the tequila, lick the salt off her hand. While she was practicing, he inserted a small square of hashish in a wooden pipe and lit it, drawing the smoke in with deep savoring breaths.

"Now this is how you get high," he said.

Elliot snaked his way through the crowd, keeping Spider Allessi in view. Spotting him wasn't difficult, since he stood at least six foot three and had a long, horsy face framed by pale shags of whitish-blond hair. Spider stopped in the kitchen to fill a glass with ice from the refrigerator icemaker. He placed a cube in his mouth and sucked on it. Although Spider had the ungainliness of an adolescent, Elliot guessed him to be in his late twenties or early thirties. His eyes were almost colorless, with the pink-rimmed look of a white rat. The gaze never settled on anything for very long. He exuded a powerful aroma of English Leather cologne.

Elliot introduced himself, aware of an unease that even a man as powerful as Ray had not engendered in him. Perhaps it was Spider's waxen, staring gaze, off just an unsettling centimeter.

"I was wondering when it would be a good time for my act to perform."

Spider shrugged, popped another ice cube.

"I want Ray to hear them."

"So then wait." He crunched audibly. The sound made Elliot's teeth ache.

A young flunky burst in, yelling at one of the caterers. "Are you crazy? Are you nuts? You don't have single malt? I told you when I made the arrangements that Mr. Fish wanted single malt scotch!"

"Excuse *me*," the caterer said, fiddling with his black bowtie. "I'm in charge of hors d'oeuvres! You'll have to address your grievances to the bartender!" He turned on his heel and stalked out of the kitchen.

"Can you believe that?" the young assistant said to Spider and Elliot.

"Don't sweat it, Lennie," Spider said coolly.

Lennie turned to Elliot. "'Don't sweat it', he says." He dashed out.

Elliot wished he could make a bottle of single malt scotch suddenly appear and present it to Ray on a silver platter. "So, nice party, huh?" he commented to Spider.

"Lotta broads. Can't be all bad."

"You said it. Wait'll you see this act I got, the chick's a looker." Elliot heard himself talking like some guy who ought to have a fat, wet cigar in his teeth. "They do some original songs. Pop. Folk. The folk sound is really starting to move into the mainstream."

As if to prove his point, the Byrds "Hey, Mister Tambourine Man" began playing.

Heartened, Elliot pushed on. "What BigWheel needs is a subsidiary that's gonna bring out the new artists, the young talent. You got your standard pop department, of course, some of the best singers around, but there's a lot of new stuff happening."

"Yeah?" Spider looked mildly curious, so Elliot pushed on.

"BigWheel should be part of it. Ray could start a new sub-label, call it, oh, hell, I don't know, HotWheels or something, sign up a slew of hot young talent—cheap, cause they're all starving anyway."

"Uh-huh."

"I got a great idea. Give me the word, I'll bring you all the groups on tape, I tape 'em live right in the clubs, you could just listen a minute here, thirty seconds there, you could play 'em for Ray, he could pick what he wants, do some demos."

"No protest singers wailing about the niggers and the unions."

"Don't worry. I'll need a small budget. Expenses, you know."

"I'll run it by Ray."

"How about I call you Monday?"

"Make it Wednesday, I'm goin' to Vegas."

"Great," said Elliot. They shook. Spider's long-fingered hand was like hard steel. When Elliot took his away, he thought a few small bones might be broken.

He left the kitchen, exhaling the tension. What he saw brought a surge of elation into his already adrenalined blood.

Julie was standing by the wall near the bar, in shimmering sheer black hip-hugger slacks and a low-cut translucent blouse with a flesh-colored lining that made her appear nude underneath. Her hair, parted in the center, fell past her waist; she wore very little makeup. What would it take for a woman like that to notice—let alone desire—a man like him?

"Are we really gonna *sing* here?" she growled at him. "It's a fucking zoo."

"When things settle down. I think I made a demo deal with Big Wheel."

"You're kidding."

He held up the first two fingers of his right hand. "Just demos, for now, but, hey!"

"God, Elliot!" Her mood transformed. She kissed him on the cheek. "That's so incredible!"

He beamed and went off to find Luke.

Julie stayed in the corner, watching the party. Hey, wasn't that? Yes, it had to be. Paul Newman. The more she stared at the faces, the more she noticed that they were familiar. News photos coming to life. Norman Mailer. People from movie screens. Album covers. Neil Sedaka. Television programs. The fashion designer Rudi Gernreich with a model, whose breasts were totally exposed. People she was sure she *ought* to recognize. Agents. Record executives. They all knew how to drink a lot of liquor. She wasn't good at drinking and getting drunk. That must mean she was insufficiently hip. Mailer was nose to nose with some actor, and although she could hear them, she could make no sense of the conversation. Her heart throbbed somewhere in her throat. What made her think she could do this? She just had to get the hell out of here.

"Julie? Where are you going?" Luke blocked her way.

"No," she pushed past him toward the door. Luke dashed after her, trying not to knock down party guests.

In the hall, he grabbed her. "What the hell are you doing?"

"I don't know," she said. "It's just all so terrible."

"*What is?* Nothing's terrible. In fact, it's just the opposite, everything is going *great!*"

How could she explain the sensation of falling off a cliff when there was no cliff? Of the commotion in her head when she knew there was no real noise? Of the voices that told her she was worthless, when logically there could be no voices? Was this what *crazy* was?

"Julie, come back," he said, "from wherever it is you go, because it's not a good place."

The apartment door opened and people came out. The noise inside rose and fell.

"Come on." He took her arm and pulled her back inside.

Elliot joined them. "It's time."

"Where's Ray Fish?" Luke wanted to know.

"Don't worry, he can't be far," Elliot assured them. "Just start quietly, they'll come to you. I made sure they're going to turn off the music." At that moment, it stopped in the middle of the Animals' singing "We Gotta Get Out of This Place." A few people looked around.

Luke and Julie set themselves up near the window, the panoramic view a backdrop. Julie gazed out at the window, wondering what it might be like to fall that far, and if you would die on impact, or of fear during the brief flight. Luke strummed a few chords. The sound of the guitar was like a magnet, people began to draw closer, to settle themselves on the floor, the sofa, leaning against the walls. He played out a twelve bar blues, humming quietly. Her voice joined in a higher counterpoint. Luke gave an inward sigh of relief. A few guests swayed in rhythm.

Gradually, others gathered, responding to the live sound. Luke began a steady driving rhythm, and they sang, in perfect harmony, the Fred Neil tune "Tear Down the Walls." Julie's fear was replaced, as it was each time, by the joy of singing with Luke.

Rochelle took another toke. She tasted the mellow, bittersweet tang of the hash flowing into her mouth and throat and down to her lungs, holding her breath as long as she could. "Wow." The stuff insinuated itself into her brain cells. She saw Ray's hand reaching over to her and she was able to examine the movement in minute detail. When it touched her, sensation rippled outward from a small place within her, to an ever-increasing pleasure, from a mere stroking of her bare shoulder. His hand descended down the length of her arm and he placed his finger and then his lips at the crook of her elbow, which was suddenly, extraordinarily, alive.

"You. Are. One. Incredibly. Sexy. Woman," he murmured.

There, again, as if drifting in and out on a warm breeze, was that intoxicating music, somehow familiar, but she was too stoned to be sure. She was falling back on the bed, or she had fallen, it was all happening in segments and at once, his hands slipping her pants off, her blouse, her bra, the rush of air against her skin, she was readier, wetter than she'd ever been, knowing that all the groping in the dark she'd done was kid stuff, even the men—or grown boys who fancied themselves men—and the tricks they were so proud of, as if they wanted a round of applause for simply having thought of this or that.

He pinned her arms back over her head; the immobility made her wild. Yes, she said, unsure whether the words actually came out or remained an echo inside her mind. The spiral of sensation rose unbearably, but still he didn't enter her.

"Please," she said.

He stood up. Was he stopping, was he going to leave? She couldn't bear it.

"Do you like to take risks, Rochelle?" he asked.

She nodded, not knowing if that was the truth.

He lifted her up, easily, considering that he was not a big man, and set her on her feet. Her legs trembled beneath her and she thought she would fall. The music and bright laughter of the party seeped in like a distant radio station and she had no more connection to it than to an invisible frequency. She heard a sound like Luke and Julie singing, but she wasn't quite sure.

He placed her in the chair and tilted it back, again she felt the falling sensation, but the chair had some kind of adjustment that kept it upright, and her legs were spread wide apart. From her position, she was looking directly at the window—the glass so clear it almost might not be there—and she was too close, she could catapult out into space; the tips of skyscrapers glimmered and, above them, a few intrepid stars shone through the city's glow. He came around behind her and placed a blindfold, blocking out even the stars, but she could still see them in her mind. Then she felt him between her legs, and the sensation was so powerful she feared it might kill her and she didn't care, not one bit. Then hands were on her breasts and she wondered with a start if there were someone else in the room, because there were too many hands and mouths all over her. But she wasn't quite sure because she had begun to lose her thoughts to the intensity, it was all exploding from within, her body strained upward and she cried out, over and over.

Where was Ray? Elliot fretted, glancing at the doorway every so often. Luke and Julie went into the final verse of their fourth song. They get could away with maybe another song, but was always best to "leave 'em wanting more." At that moment, Elliot saw Ray Fish, looking a bit disheveled, as if he'd grabbed a quick nap. The guests applauded as the song ended. Elliot studied Ray's reactions: He looked pleased. Elliot allowed himself to relax a degree. The two singers began another song. Ray turned to say something to Spider.

Elliot gave Luke a nod: Wrap it up before they became background music. They finished with Tom Paxton's "Can't Help But Wonder Where I'm Bound," a melancholy drifter's song that allowed the two voices to blend on the chorus. Luke added a few fancy instrumental riffs at the end, and the applause was mixed with cries of "more, more!" When the applause finally died out, Elliot sidled over to Ray.

"Nice sound," Ray commented. "Call the office, we'll set something up."

"I'll do that. Also, I talked to…uh…Spider," Elliot continued, "He has this great idea for me to scout out some more talent in the clubs. Just need your go ahead for, you know, taping expenses, just bare minimum stuff."

"Fine, whatever," Ray said. He walked away.

Despite the abrupt dismissal, Elliot was euphoric.

Rochelle materialized next to him. He blurted out his news, and noticed she was looking at Ray. "Did you meet him? Ray Fish? I'm sorry I didn't get to introduce you, there's been so much going on!"

"We met."

"Did you hear Luke & Julie?"

"I certainly did," she enunciated carefully. The combination of alcohol and drugs made it difficult not to slur. "And they were fab'lous. Of course, they're always fab'lous, an' so are you."

"Maybe I should take you home?"

She tweaked his chin. "Where's my coat?"

"You didn't wear one, remember?"

"Oh, right. Then where's my bag? I know I had a bag."

"Did you leave it somewhere?"

"Uh-oh!"

"What?"

"I forgot…oh, I remember, it's upstairs, I think."

"I'll get it, you'll probably get lost."

"No, that's okay."

"I'll find it. You stay here. Don't go anywhere."

"It's white."

"What?"

"My *pocketbook*," she slurred.

He went up the stairs to the billiard room and searched around, uncomfortable pushing on closed doors. The fragments of a conversation leaked out from behind one.

"You fucking asshole."

"I'm sorry, Spider, I—"

"Get the fuck out of my sight before I cut your little dick off and feed it to you." There was a sharp slap and footsteps running toward the door. "I said get the fuck out, you asslicking little bastard!"

Elliot remained still, holding his breath so as not to be detected. Lennie the caterer rushed through the door, his hand pressed against his face. A moment later, Spider emerged, smoothing back his hair with his hand, and passed a few feet from Elliot without noticing him.

Elliot breathed out. What kind of a man was this Spider? Did Ray know what sort of person he had working for him? Sure, running a big company was tough, and everybody lost it at one time or another. He emerged from his hiding place, first checking to see if Spider was anywhere around. The sweet-sour trace of his aftershave still lingered in the air.

"I couldn't find your bag," he told Rochelle.

"Gotta find it, s'got my keys and everything." She was having trouble keeping herself upright.

Ray approached, gingerly proffering a small white purse in the apologetic way men hold women's things.

"Are you looking for this?" Ray asked. "I found it by the pool table."

Their eyes met, and he winked, just the slightest gesture.

"Thank you all very very much!" Rochelle proclaimed.

"I think I better get her home," Elliot said to Ray.

"Good idea."

"See you next week!" she called out as Ray turned to another departing guest.

"Next week?" Elliot asked. The elevator was waiting and they descended with two other couples.

"I mean," she began, then lowered her voice to a stage whisper, "that you, Mr. Elliot Levine, are not the only one who's going to appear in the offices of BigWheel Records next week. I, Rochelle Klein, have been offered a poss...posish...a job. Firs' thing Monday morning, I am going to tell Mr. Gorsuch to take his dep-o-si-tions, roll them up small, and stick 'em. Pardon my French."

10

Julie pulled on a man's white shirt—one that her ex-boyfriend Casey had left behind—over loose, torn denim shorts. Luke would be by in a few minutes for a rehearsal, and she ought to do something to straighten up the apartment. Sipping stale, reheated coffee from a stained cup, she re-draped an Indian blanket loosely over the couch; like *that* made a difference. Scattered shoes stuck out from underneath the one chair, she kicked them further out of sight.

For days, she had been sleeping in a drugged state—only she hadn't taken any drugs. Her skin hurt, as if she'd been torn from a protective shell. Talking to other people made her impatient, agitated. She might go to sleep with her mind relatively quiet, only to wake up with an ocean of noise in her head: a rushing sound like holding a giant seashell to her ear.

But today was a happy day. BigWheel Records was really interested. Elliot said they could be going into the studio to record demos in just a few weeks. Her reaction to the news had been a wild elation; insomnia and the conviction that she would *never need to sleep again* because she had some inner unquenchable stamina that carried her through the streets of the city.

Luke's familiar knock at the door: two shorts, a space, another knock.

He was holding a white deli bag, damp at the bottom from spilled coffee.

"Hi." As if they were meeting for the first time, as if the wrong word or inflection might wreck their happiness. There was a demon in her that often wanted to torment him, to make him hurt, as if this were the only proof of his feelings.

He embraced her. She kissed the patch of tanned skin on his neck, inhaled his freshly showered scent; they kissed more deeply but a part of her was watching, waiting for Julie to feel passion.

They hadn't slept together right away. She held back for nearly two months of delicious, protracted foreplay, hours of sultry pre-dawn groping in her living room, on the streets and doorways of the unsleeping city, until she was convinced that this time it would be different than it had been with Casey: painful, self-conscious, an act that turned her dead inside.

This time would be different.

It wasn't.

Casey had never figured it out. Maybe he just didn't give a shit, or he thought he was so good he must be satisfying her. She was too self-conscious and ashamed of her lack of sexual sensation to admit it. If he'd really cared, he'd figure it out. Men were so easy to deceive. Now, she almost resented Luke's ability to take pleasure from her body, while she didn't.

She pulled away from him, grabbing the bag: two take-out coffees and her favorite cheese Danish.

"Nice shirt," he said.

"What's *that* supposed to mean?"

"What's *what* supposed to mean?"

"I haven't seen Casey, if that's what you're getting at."

"I wasn't getting at anything."

Luke watched her walk toward the small kitchen, bend over to open the half-sized refrigerator. Her thin shorts rode up, exposing a crescent of one buttock.

"Julie." He put his arms around her from behind.

"We *are* supposed to rehearse, right?"

"Do we have to?"

She slipped from his grasp. "*Yes.*"

"Well, then." He tried to refocus his attention. "Here's the E string you wanted."

Being with Julie was tightrope-walking over a shark-filled moat. There was the wry, funny, manic Julie; the sad, despairing Julie; the nasty angry Julie; the quiet, affectionate, seductive Julie. Having little experience with women, he assumed they were all as volatile.

"What do you think of this song of Elliot's? 'Happy Little Snowflakes'?" he asked.

"He thinks it could be a hit, like 'Little Silver Raindrops'." She twisted a tuning peg, removed the broken string.

"Want me to do that?" He was much faster and efficient at changing guitar strings.

"*No.* I can do it."

He raised his hands in a gesture of surrender. "All yours." Rolled his eyes when she wasn't looking.

"You really like 'Snowflakes'?" she asked.

"Well, actually, I think it's kind of…bad."

"Yeah. That's the word: bad." She thought for a moment.

"We don't *have* to do it, right?"

"I don't know," he said. "He says it's what BigWheel wants, something light and pop. They don't think we can just do a demo of the folk stuff. Shit, I don't know, let's just learn it and maybe we can make it better."

They began to sing:

"Snowflakes, snowflakes, happy little snowflakes
Each one a message from my ba-by
This one is diamonds, this one is pearls
But I'd trade them all for love, I don't mean may-be."

Luke stopped playing. "That has got to be the dumbest song I've ever heard." He pulled the guitar strap from around his shoulder and put the instrument aside.

She stared at him with a mischievous expression. Then she sang:

"Snowjob, snowjob, happy little snowjob"
I'd rather give Elliot a blowjob."

Luke nearly fell over. For a woman with quite a few hang-ups, she had an amazingly crude sense of humor. They howled with laughter, repeating the lines over and over, finally rolled into each other, kissing deeply. He tried to hold back, fearing that any second she'd call a halt, and what if he couldn't stop, what if he...but she let it go on...and on. His hands were under her shirt—*Casey's* shirt—so he tore it off, ripped the goddamn thing, and her breasts were bare, he slipped his fingers under the waistband of her shorts, deftly undoing the button, the zipper, his hand brushed hair, sensations flew up and down his body, centering in his groin, he was painfully swollen. He undid his own pants, oh please, don't let her stop me, then they were naked, his bare skin pressed against her bare skin, he could hardly stand it, but he wanted to last, she was letting him, he nudged her legs apart and went inside, she was like tight warm butter, she gave a soft moan. He wanted to slow down, to make it last but he just couldn't, he was overtaken by a terrible urgency, "God, I love you," he breathed, it was all too much, too much, he would die for her, he would do anything, let me, let me, he wanted to go through her and out the other side, love me, he wanted to go into her heart, he gripped her hair with one hand, slid the other hand under her, raised her toward him, her eyes were closed, she was breathing in rhythm, he was pleasing her, he was a superman, he was –

Luke almost blacked out, lying there unable to move.

After a moment, smothered beneath his weight, she nudged him and he rolled off. Without choosing it, without wanting or understanding why, she had retreated to a place deep inside her mind, where there was little physical sensation.

"Did you? I couldn't wait any longer," he asked.

"I...I don't know, I think I did," she evaded.

"Wait, let me..." He moved down her legs.

"What are you doing?!"

"I want to do you this way." He kissed her lower belly.

"No, uh-uh." She rolled up to a sitting position.

"Why? Women love that."

"'Women' huh? How many have you done *that* to?"

"Thousands. And they swear by it."

She grabbed her shirt, got up. "I gotta shower."

"Please. I want to. You taste so incredibly good."

"*No.*" She closed the door to the bathroom.

He called out, "You're not exactly earthy, you know."

"You want earthy, fuck mud."

"Very ladylike." He reached for his cigarettes, wishing he had some grass.

He picked up the guitar again, stuck the burning cigarette in the taut strings between the tuning pegs, and began playing a song he'd written. For her. When the song was over, Julie was standing by the bathroom door, listening. The shower still rained down in the background.

"I like that. Who wrote it?"

"I did."

"*That's* what we should be recording."

"Come on," he scoffed. "It's just a little ditty."

"It's good!" She went back into the shower, her voice a muffled echo. "Let's work on it!"

"We're still gonna have to do 'Happy Little Blowjobs'," he grumbled.

11

L uke sat at the counter of a small diner on East 53rd that
served breakfast all day, and ordered his regular plate
of eggs and home fries (god, he missed grits!). When the
waitress brought his food, he smiled at her. The first time
he'd done that, her face closed down, like he was trying to
start something. Her, a middle-aged married woman with a
prominent ring on her finger, and here's this hick with the
too-long hair. But now that he was a regular, she smiled
back, handed him the *Daily News* and brought extra coffee
before he had to ask. New Yorkers were peculiar, with
their hard surface and soft inside. He was getting used to
keeping a poker face on the streets and subways, in the
elevator and halls at the YMCA; people looked at you
funny when you said good mornin', like first they needed
to know your name, rank and serial number.

The day stretched ahead, unstructured. The rest of
the world was racing by like they all had Indy cars while
he was peddling a bicycle. Sure, Elliot called regularly
with news, but nothing ever seemed to happen. They
were about to be signed by BigWheel; then that got put
off; or Capitol was interested; but meetings got postponed; they had a commitment for a two week gig at
Folk City; until it inexplicably shrunk to two days. As
July blurred into sweating August, he saw that the year

might end and another begin without real change, and he'd still be poor.

Worse, his time could be running out.

He took the envelope out of his pocket. Another notice from Uncle Sam, checking up on his physical status. Had it changed any since his pre-induction physical? Why, no Mr. Draft Board, I still have that *high blood pressure* you rejected me for, in fact, my goddamn heart is about to explode. He had sent the form back and tried to put it out of his mind, but there would be another, and another.

The restaurant was filling with lunch customers, the indentured office slaves temporarily released into the tropics from the monolith refrigerated buildings. The check floated down in front of him; there was no alternative but to leave.

Julie.

The thought of her awakened his body—not that it took much—the pressure building up inside. He hurried back to his gray-walled room, leaped the four flights of stairs, fumbled with his keys, dragged out the magazines that he kept hidden under the bed—hidden from whom? no one else came in there—and satisfied himself in a minute. Spent and chagrined that he was driven to do this, sometimes several times a day; he cleaned up in the small sink and lay on the bed.

She rarely wanted him that way. He wanted her all the time.

"You don't give a *shit* about me!" he had yelled at her.

"So get out," she had replied, strangely calm. "You're going to leave eventually."

He'd expected: I love you. Instead, he got: Get out. Who could keep up? Who could predict?

"You make it awful difficult to stick around."

She pulled the door open. "GET OUT!"

He had slammed his fist against the wall. Then looked at it in astonished horror. His *musician's* hand.

She rushed over to see if he was all right. The fight, or whatever it was, evaporated. They made love, awkwardly, quickly, he was certain she didn't come, and he was afraid to ask.

"What about BigWheel?" Luke confronted Elliot after a guest set at the Bitter End. "I thought we were going to sign, you told me two months ago they wanted us."

"Everything's under control."

"Don't bullshit me—"

"I'm out there working for you guys every day, you have no idea—"

"Excuse me while I cry—"

Julie broke in. "Shut up, Luke."

"Take it easy, both of you," Elliot interrupted. "I've got a meeting with Ray Fish tomorrow. We've been going back and forth on a contract, and I think we're close. I'll look it over and if everything's kosher, we'll sign. There shouldn't be any problems, but I didn't want to get you guys all excited in case, just on the slim chance it fell through."

"You mean it's really happening?" Julie asked.

"Looks that way." Elliot put an arm around her, hugged her shoulders.

"I'll believe it when I see it," said Luke. He picked up his guitar case. "See ya'll later."

"Where are you going?" Julie stopped him. "We're supposed to go over to Cafe Wha? for a late set!"

"Screw it. Nobody goes there anymore."

"Tonight they are," she said. "Elliot's taping some acts for BigWheel."

"I want the brass to see you guys knock 'em dead," Elliot added.

"I'll meet you," Luke promised, walking away, guitar slung over his shoulder. Julie's anger burned into his back. *Serve them right if I go over to Vietnam and get my fuckin' head blown off.*

He stumbled into the Night Owl. There were a couple of guys on stage he knew slightly, a guitarist and that cookin' harmonica player, John Sebastian. They nodded at him to sit in, and after the set, invited him into the can, where they passed a joint. Cheerfully stoned, he sent a girl out for beers and the playing resumed. Not a girl, really, but one of those waif-like Village chicks who could be seventeen or thirty, with stringy long hair and baggy jeans, loose breasts and looser attitude. The girl leaned against the stage, looking up at him, and when the jamming was over, she followed him out. He knew he was supposed to be some place or other, but damned if he could remember where.

They walked east on 3rd until they reached the outer perimeters of the Village and hit that no-man's land between East and West. He still occasionally got lost in the city if he turned down an unfamiliar street. She led him into a shabby vestibule and up several long, cold stone flights of stairs to a bruised door, with several locks and an iron bar that went across the whole door, and they were in a studio loft. Mattress with tangled sheets. High, bare windows looking uptown and a damp breeze, a blare of sirens from below.

He put down the guitar case, miserable with desire. She came back at him with a fierce passion, slithered down his legs and opened his zipper. Letting her, not having to do anything. Not. One. Thing. Didn't care, he didn't feel fuckall responsible. Didn't try to make it last to impress her. Didn't give a shit if she came or didn't or faked it.

When it was over, he told her he had to leave, he had a gig, and she didn't say anything, make a fuss or object.

"What's your name, honey?" he asked.

"Glinda. Like the Good Witch."

"You sure are, sugar, you're one hell of a good witch."

The Cafe Wha? was crowded, acts lined up in the stairway to the basement room where the show was going on, all the way out to the street. Elliot had set up his tape equipment in the far corner of the stage, hooked up the mikes to the club's sound system. He introduced the acts, reading from a list in his hand. The room was packed full of friends of the performers. Chairs reserved for VIPs had been set up at two large tables in the front. They were the only empty tables.

Luke found Julie standing in the back.

"Hi, babe, sorry I'm late, did I miss anything?" He wiped a bead of sweat from his forehead.

"Go to hell."

"Wait a minute!" He followed her into the kitchen, where two harried waitresses were loading trays with whipped cream topped sundaes and coffees.

"I got here in time, didn't I?" His right hand began to shake, like he suddenly had palsy. He rubbed his face with it and felt the stubble of unshaved beard. He smelled of Glinda.

"I thought you weren't coming. I thought you'd left town or something."

"Left town?" he started to say, but she stomped out of the kitchen.

Fuck you, Julie. Maybe he'd just call up Glinda. But he didn't even have her last name, or number, and he was certain he'd never find that place again and she was sort of a skank when he thought about it. In the men's room, he splashed his face with water from the rusty tap. When he came out, they were being announced.

"Luke & Julie!"

Onstage, Julie began to sing the folk song "Shenandoah" a cappella.

By the second verse, he'd gotten the guitar out and sneaked in, finding the key with a few soft chords. They went full out on the last verse.

> *"Oh, Shenandoah, I'm bound to leave you*
> *Away, you rolling river*
> *Oh, Shenandoah, I'll not deceive you*
> *Away, I'm bound away, 'cross the wide Missouri..."*

Before the applause died down, Luke began his new song, which elicited some stomps and whistles of enthusiasm. They closed with "Mississippi Train", but when he turned to Julie to share a bow, she wasn't there.

She was already on her way up the stairs. He'd never known anyone who could leave a room faster.

The street was teeming with tourists, musicians, people strolling in groups, hand-in-hand pairs, the sidewalk cafes spilling over on this warm fall night. He pushed his way through, calling out. He caught up with her in front of the Cafe Bizarre.

"For Chrissake! Hold up!"

She turned on him, eyes narrowed.

"Goddamn it! What did I *do*??" It wasn't like she could possibly know, although she had an uncanny way of reading his thoughts. He attempted a lighter, teasing approach. "Anyone ever tell you you're a difficult woman?"

She allowed the hint of a smile. "Yes."

"*Yes?*"

"Every guy I've ever known. *Hundreds* of them."

"Well, then fuck me. Hey, you know that joke? Guy takes a girl home after a date and says, 'How about a goodnight fuck?' And she says—"

"'Goodnight, Fuck.'"

He tried to kiss her but she swiveled away and he brushed her neck with his lips, buried his face in her hair. If she knew about Glinda and the others, she'd really hate him. "I love you, girl. Why don't you ever believe me?"

They walked toward her apartment.

She said, "We should live together. Or break up forever."

"All or nothing?"

"Yes."

"Well, we can't live at the Y and this place is pretty small."

"Okay, forget it."

"No, I was agreeing, I'm just saying, maybe we should look for another place first. Or wait till we can afford something better."

"Why is everything always about money? About *not* having money?"

"We'll figure things out."

"I love your new song. You should write more of them."

She kissed him with a slow, deep sensuality. "Goodnight."

He watched her walk away. Funny, she was always afraid he'd leave her, and yet she was always the one leaving.

He showed up late at a party in some roachy one-room on Thompson Street, with plenty of beer and fat jugs of sour

Chablis and the grass fumes so intense you could get a contact high out on the street. The windows were flung wide open to let in any cool air but the atmosphere was thick and static.

Luke was trading riffs with a guitarist when they were joined by a tall, lanky guy, blond hair flopping over his forehead and nearly covering his eyes, like an Afghan hound. He had large, long-fingered hands that moved with easy dexterity on the neck of his Martin guitar.

Casey Mahoney, Julie's ex-boyfriend.

Luke had wanted to loathe him, but he couldn't. Casey was just too good—hell, he didn't even try to hog the spotlight. Felix Pappalardi came in, with his guitarron, and John Sebastian, and Dave Van Ronk, Gram Parsons and Steve Stills. They jammed into the night, some of the best music he'd made in New York. Casey said he was heading back to L.A., and if Luke was ever out there, give him a call. He was getting a new band together, and had a pending deal with Atlantic.

A band, with Casey Mahoney. Luke fast-forwarded to what they might sound like if they really rehearsed, and Atlantic was a major record company, not that BigWheel was small potatoes. What was he thinking? Leaving Julie would be like cutting out a vital organ.

He abandoned what remained of the party, stepping over bodies strewn on the floor and on cushions and beanbag chairs. Never did find out whose place it was. Still too wired to sleep. Dawn gradually lightened the sky. A few janitors were getting to their buildings along Lexington. He walked uptown, block after deserted block. At Fifty-ninth, he turned east, passing the glittering hotels, watching as a taxi stopped in front of the Plaza and a woman slithered out, in a silver evening dress that caught the early sunlight. Hurt his eyes. She bent over to tip the driver and he saw the sheer line of her underwear beneath the dress' thin fabric. Aroused by the image, he jogged the rest of the way into the park, to get it out of his system. He settled on a bench, his hand compulsively reaching for the envelope in his pocket again, like probing a painful tooth.

The draft letters came about every six months, each time in an envelope of a different color: green, blue, orange. What did *that* mean? Which color meant he was *formally and royally fucked*? How many times could he send back a 'no change of health status' when the war escalated over there every day? And when would they want to see him in person again? Maybe the next time, he'd pass, and be winging his way to Vietnam before he could say goodbye to his girl and his career. Get his hands blown off. Come back in a bag.

He could go to Canada.

Too fucking cold.

Hop the next flight to L.A., say goodbye to the torments Julie inflicted on him, join Casey's band and wonder, every time he looked at Casey's hands, what they had made her feel, and if she had loved him more. Did Casey know that Julie was his "old lady" now? Would he give a shit?

Or he could stay here, while the unlucky bastards who got drafted were in some jungle hellhole.

Ducks glided across the pond, the water shining like new metal. A man at the far end was feeding the ducks, calling them by name. "Here, Duke, here, Daisy, here Coriolanus!"

There was a pressure behind his eyes, almost like tears, but the tears would never come, not since he was a boy. When it got to be too much, he'd hit something or drink until the ache went numb, but he never wept.

A song constructed itself, phrase by phrase. He grabbed a pencil from his jacket pocket, tore the plastic wrapper off his cigarette pack and wrote the lyric fragments on the box.

He walked west out of the park and down Broadway, giddy from lack of sleep. Theater marquees announced *Fiddler on the Roof. Funny Girl.* He had never seen a Broadway show. Or gone to Carnegie Hall. Or the new Lincoln Center. Luke looked up, his eyes pierced by the morning sun, at the shiny bronze entrance to the Brill Building, where Elliot had his office. The nutty guy who said things to passersby was already outside the building, perched on his upturned crate, hissing "Garbage!" and "Sex maniacs!" at strangers. That was what he did all day. Like it was his job.

Luke shook his head: New York.

12

Ray's kitchen included every possible luxury, an abundance of fine wood drawers and cabinets, marble counters, a center cutting block, a dishwasher. Rochelle was already beginning to forget that she had once lived with only *one* bathroom, let alone four—well, three and a half—and that she'd had to scrimp at the grocery store, while now all she did was make a phone call to the deli on Madison, even if their prices were triple the supermarket's, and they charged for delivery. In Ray's world, none of this mattered.

"Can I get you something?" she called from the kitchen.

Julie said, "You still eat Mallomars?"

"Does the Pope shit in the woods?" With a formal flourish, Rochelle arranged their favorite cookies artfully on a plate, and placed an open bottle of wine and two glasses (the correct ones for white wine, as Ray had showed her) on a silver tray. The sun was setting over the park, the city lights beginning to sparkle.

Rochelle filled the wine glasses with the Chateau Something-or-other. She noticed Julie's short stubby nails, and the torn, bitten cuticles; while hers were long, perfectly manicured. In contrast to Julie's tight, faded jeans and old T-shirt, Rochelle was dressed in tailored black slacks and a high neck, green silk blouse. Ray liked her to always be perfectly groomed. Since moving in with him, her crush on Luke had cooled. She had certainly gotten the better deal, hadn't she? Julie was stuck in that awful Village "pad," and seemed to fight with Luke every other day.

Julie stared at the demo of a new BigWheel band that had just hit the top-forty.

"That'll be you guys soon."

"Think so?" Julie sounded unconvinced.

"'Course!" Ray had fulfilled one important promise—getting her a job at BigWheel. Her new boss, Joe Gallin, was the Assistant Vice President of Marketing and Distribution. He got the records into the stores, the poster ads on the walls of the record chains, like Goody's and King Karol, and helped devise promotional campaigns. Although her secretarial duties weren't much different than they'd been at Gorsuch, Flaum and Claster, now Rochelle also kept track of store orders, with a deceptively simple filing system she'd devised. Mr. Gallin was a tolerable boss, married and evidently monogamous, so there were no girlfriends calling up, pretending it was business, and at least he didn't have her running his personal errands.

The best feature of her job was its proximity to the Artist and Repertoire department, where music played all day long. The head of A&R was an ex-Bronxite named Manny who favored shiny suits and flowered, wide silk ties. When he liked a song, he had a habit of sticking his left hand in his pants pocket and jingling the change in rhythm. That sound elicited a Pavlovian response in her. She'd oh-so-casually wander down the hall to Manny's office, as if it just happened to be her coffee break. That very afternoon, a bunch of demos had come in and Manny actually asked her opinion about a new Negro group he wanted to sign. After a brief hesitation, she said, "I don't feel it."

"Me, neither. Thanks, Rochelle."

She had smiled all the way back to her desk, and, for the rest of the day had difficulty concentrating on her work.

While Julie took her third Mallomar, Rochelle reached into a low shelf beneath the records and tugged out a battered square, striped box, with a lid that clasped shut. It contained several dozen 45s in file dividers. "Look what I found when I was moving some stuff out of my parents'."

She had been gradually relocating her possessions from Arlene's to Ray's. Soon, she'd have to reveal her actual living arrangements to her parents, but for as long as she could hold out—pretending she was still Arlene's roommate—the subterfuge was easier than the inevitable explosion in the Klein household.

"I don't believe you still have that." Julie pulled out a record at random and read aloud the title of the 1958 hit. "Guess the flip side!" she challenged.

Rochelle immediately responded, correctly. They continued the game for several minutes, then switched roles. Neither of them made many mistakes.

"Where are your records? Back with your Mom?" Rochelle asked.

"Guess so. She's moving. To *France*, if you can believe it,"

Julie replied. "She kicked Ben out. *Finally*."

"Wow. Why?" Rochelle couldn't imagine having a stepfather like Benjamin Lefcourt. He'd seemed odd the first time she'd met him at Julie's house. With hindsight, he was even stranger.

"Got tired of supporting him, I guess. She doesn't even speak French but she's learning it from a book." Julie picked up one of the 45s, read the label and dropped it on the turntable. Ritchie Valens crooned, "Oooh, Donna..."

Rochelle jumped up and wrapped her arms around herself, dancing in place; Julie did the same. They drifted separately in the living room, the last light of the sun casting an amber glow over the two young women and their imaginary partners.

Thirteen-year-old Julie fitted a stack of 45s onto the hi-fi; the first hit the turntable with a plop and a hiss of needle on vinyl, and the strains of her favorite song, "Tragedy," began to play. She closed her eyes and swayed in the center of the living room, singing,

"...oh, oh...tragedy..."

"Look at me!" Rochelle called out. She was facing the corner, embracing herself, moving her hands up and down on her back so it looked as if two people were making out.

"Hello," came a man's voice.

The girls froze in place.

He stood in the doorway, head perched forward. He had thinning light-brown hair mixed with gray and was so tall he practically had to stoop in the low-ceilinged apartment. But for all his height, he probably didn't weigh more than a hundred and thirty pounds. A pair of thick glasses distorted his pink-rimmed, pale blue eyes. Taken together, his stance and height and prominent nose gave the impression of a large, bespectacled bird.

"This is my mother's..." Julie said. "Benjamin Lefcourt."

"So, Rochelle," he boomed, "you're the young lady who keeps our Julie on the phone all night long!" He pronounced her name "Roe-shell," with the accent on the first syllable. "Are you in the same grade as our Julie, young lady?"

"Yes. Eighth grade."

"We're gonna play records before dinner," Julie told him. Benjamin Lefcourt followed them over to the hi-fi. "I wouldn't mind some Vivaldi. How about The Four Seasons?"

"We're gonna play my 45s. I told *Mom. Okay?*"

He smiled, showing large, uneven teeth, and pushed the glasses up on his nose. "I guess this just gives me an incentive to get us into our big new house sooner than later. Then we can all have our own music, in our own rooms." He turned to Rochelle, put his large hand on her shoulder. "I don't know if Julie mentioned it, but we're going to be moving up in the world. Not that Paigey hasn't done a fine job on her own, but I've got some pretty important plans in the works."

He passed by Julie and pinched her waist playfully as he left the room.

As soon as he was gone, Rochelle whispered, "They got *married?*"

Julie had been away at summer camp when letters from her mother began mentioning a man named Benjamin. She thought it was a hugely stupid name, and was dismayed to discover him in her kitchen on the day she returned home. Within a few weeks, he had all but moved in. Her mother said that he was "between jobs" and "waiting for an important deal to come through," at which time they would all be very wealthy. Julie would have her own horse.

She was amazed that any more stuff could be crammed into the small living room, but they'd managed a bunch of Benjamin's things. On the desk, pushed farther into the corner, was a stack of typing paper, a box of carbons and an open book in which he'd pasted some stamps. These had pictures of owls and flowers and foreign people's faces. When she thought of Benjamin poring over that book, his glasses sliding down his nose, just to paste stamps in a folder, it made her feel kind of sad inside.

A few months later, Benjamin and her mother had come home from the City all giggly. Her mother was wearing her nice taffeta dress and high heels, which she usually hated because they hurt her feet. They had been to City Hall. How sickeningly unromantic, Julie thought.

While Benjamin popped a bottle of champagne and nuzzled Paige on the back of her neck, Julie retreated to her room and turned on her portable radio. She had a game: She'd make a wish, and think of a hit song, and then turn the dial to the three rock stations—WINS, WABC and WADO—and if she found that song playing, she'd get her wish. Julie wished that Benjamin would disappear, and she tried to conjure up Ritchie Valens, who had just died in a plane crash with Buddy Holly and the Big Bopper. She sang "Ooh Donna," but it was nowhere to be found on the radio.

"Yeah, they got married, *okay?*" Julie snapped at Rochelle.

Rochelle raised an eyebrow—she'd been practicing in the mirror—and kept her mouth shut.

The record ended and the next flapped down: Rochelle's favorite song, the Five Satins' "In the Still of the Night." Both girls sang along with the back ground vocals, which were widely interpreted as "shut up and shove it up, shut up and shove it up." Julie picked up her cat's front paws, and it staggered about reluctantly on its hind legs, as she led it forward and back. "Do you want to dance with her?" she offered Rochelle.

"I don't think she likes it very much."

The song ended and the cat gratefully fled the room.

"I wrote words to this next song," Julie announced, putting on the instrumental, "Sleepwalk." She closed her eyes and sang. The melancholy lyrics were inspired by a boy in school. She had never gotten up the nerve to speak to him.

"You can really sing," Rochelle said.

"Come *on*, you've heard me sing before."

"Not like that. You should make a record or something."

Julie's mother looked in. An aroma of stuffed cabbage wafted from the kitchen. For dessert, there was an ice box cake, which was made from a horizontal row of flat chocolate cookies, stuck together with fresh whipped cream slathered over the top and sides. "If the concert's over, we can eat. Can you believe Julie wants to go into Show Business! I guess she gets that from my *mother*." She said the words "mother" and "show business" as if they tasted bad. "She was in Show Business, and it didn't get her anywhere. Just having a pretty voice doesn't mean anything." Mrs. Lefcourt laughed a high trill. "You know, I was the only one in my family who didn't have a natural singing voice. Of course, every time I opened my mouth to sing, somebody told me to shut up!"

Rochelle offered, "I can't sing either, Mrs. Bradl—uh, Mrs. Lefcourt."

Benjamin leaned against the doorframe, a highball glass in his hand. The ice rattled, like old bones. "Would anyone else care for a pre-prandial libation?"

The two girls stared at each other.

"A soda pop perhaps?"

"Soda *pop?*" they both echoed.

"Pardon me, young ladies, I'm from Chi*cah*go, where the vernacular differs." He disappeared back into the kitchen.

"What did he say?" Rochelle whispered.

Julie shrugged. "I never know what he's talking about."

"Girls, give me a hand setting the table, please." Julie's mother opened the silverware drawer. The silver place settings were remnants of Paige's ancestors who 'registered' when they married, who kept tea sets and monogrammed linens. Their touch of opulence had always looked out of place in this shabby, cramped apartment. Much of the china had broken over the years, but the silver survived. Paige was supposed to have married 'up' and live in an ivy-covered house in Westchester or Connecticut but she'd tripped on love early on, or perhaps it was just rebellion, bringing home what her parents' would most loathe: a Jewish, multi-married, older journalist—and a Communist, a Red!—who became Julie's father and then moved on, leaving behind a cache of interesting books and not one penny of child support.

At the pale-green Formica kitchen table, Benjamin held out Rochelle's chair, and then Julie's. The seats were green sparkly vinyl, the legs silver aluminum. Paige always sat in the one with the ripped seat, which had been perfunctorily repaired with silver duct tape. Benjamin's hand brushed the side of Julie's breast and lingered there so fleetingly she wasn't certain it happened at all, and she was embarrassed for him. Their plates rested on orange plastic placemats, with an overlaid design of yellow balloons, so deliberately cheerful that it had the opposite effect.

Julie gripped the edge of the table. She should never have invited Rochelle for dinner. This place was just too embarrassing. Rochelle, on the other hand, lived in a beautiful high-rise with actual furniture in the lobby, chained to the floor. The apartment had wall-to-wall carpeting and plastic to keep the sofa and armchairs from getting dirty. Rochelle even had her own, small room, with a high-rise bed that could be opened up into two singles, and a Princess phone. Julie tried to sleep over there whenever she could.

Her mother explained to Rochelle that Benjamin was a "wheeler-dealer" who arranged complicated contracts between businesses. Soon, his latest project would hit "pay dirt", she said, and his "ship will come in." Not only that, but he was writing a biography of Thomas De Quincey.

"Who?" Rochelle asked, taking a tentative bite of the stuffed cabbage. Julie's mother cooked strange things.

"Only one of the greatest minds of the early nineteenth century!" Benjamin boomed, helped along by a third highball. "Why, he was way ahead of his time. He scandalized London with his autobiography, 'Confessions of an English Opium Eater.'"

"An *opium* eater?" Rochelle asked. She began to laugh, and it was contagious, at least to Julie, whose near-hysterical giggle joined hers. Rochelle's laughter turned into a choking cough.

"Are you all right, young lady?" Benjamin asked.

"Fine, I'm fine," she coughed behind her napkin.

"Take a drink of water," Paige urged.

"Sorry, Mrs....Bradl...uh, Mrs...."

"Lefcourt, Rochelle. Lefcourt."

"Why don't we open up the wine, ma petite?" Benjamin suggested.

Paige brought out a bottle of red wine and Benjamin made a great show of removing the cork. He poured a small amount of liquid into his glass, swirled it around and tasted it, making a gargling sound.

"Why don't you send it out to a lab?" Julie remarked.

"That'll be enough out of you," her mother warned.

Benjamin Lefcourt ignored them. "Well, I guess this will have to do."

"I should hope so, considering what it cost," said Paige.

Julie knew that until Benjamin's ship came in her mother was paying for everything. His ship seemed to be taking the long route.

"Think of it as a celebration of our future, my dear." He poured wine into Paige's glass. "Young ladies?"

"Don't be ridiculous, Ben, they're too young."

"Never too young to try the finer things in life."

"We have wine on Passover," Rochelle offered.

"Oh, that, awful sweet grape juice," Benjamin cried, touching his chest as if stricken. "My first wife was of the Jewish persuasion and I sat through many a Seder and many a bottle of sticky Manischewitz. Any Port in a storm," he punned.

Benjamin rose and stumbled into the bathroom, which was just off the kitchen. Julie tensed. A moment later, there came the inevitable watery cascade into the hollow bowl, loud as Niagara Falls, followed by a harsh flush. She could not bring herself to look at Rochelle.

Something slid by her leg and she started. "Here's Mussy!" she said, reaching down for her cat. "Good girl, have you been outside? Do you miss your babies?"

"Is that a new cat?" Rochelle asked.

"Julie takes home every stray she sees," Paige said, "and they all seem to be expecting."

"I didn't even get to name them," Julie said. "She dumped the kittens at the Bide-A-Wee."

"They find homes for them," said Paige.

"They gas them. Little kittens suffocating while poisonous gasses suck away all the oxygen—"

"That's quite enough! You're just too sensitive, you have to develop a tough hide in this world."

"If you'd had her spayed—"

"Do you think I can afford to provide expensive surgery for every animal you decide to drag home?"

Ben came out of the bathroom and poured more wine in his glass. "Paigey?" he asked his wife. She nodded and he topped hers off.

"You know I hate nicknames, Benjamin."

"Paigey," he said under his breath.

For a long minute there was only the sound of eating, silverware scraping plates. Julie was unable to breathe fully, her world tilting like an amusement park ride. Was it possible that the room was getting smaller? That the ceiling and walls could come down upon her at any moment? *She imagined herself on an enormous stage, with the spotlight searing her skin, as if she had strayed too close to the sun...*

"So now I'm officially Julie's stepfather," Benjamin was telling Rochelle.

...and when she began to sing, thousands of people would leap to their feet cheering, and the pain/light was turned to a perfect crystal she controlled with sound...

"Julie?" Rochelle was watching her, with a curious expression.

Her mother spoke for her. "Don't pay any attention, Rochelle, she's doing her silent routine."

Plates were collected. Julie remained still as a statue.

"Well," said Julie's mother, "anyone for dessert? Or, as my mother always said, 'Desert the table.'"

"I could go for some." Benjamin wiped his lips with his napkin and folded it into a smaller and smaller square. "How about the young ladies?"

Julie was distantly aware of chairs being scraped back. Dessert served. She remained inert, a part of her knowing she was there, but unable—or unwilling—to move or speak. After a time, it became late at night, and when Julie roused herself back into the world, Rochelle was gone and her mother and Benjamin had pulled out the convertible sofa and were watching television from their makeshift bed.

Ray's key scraped in the door. He was home earlier than Rochelle expected. She met him in the vestibule, concerned he might be annoyed that she was entertaining. Her boundaries were still being established; she had only just begun to feel comfortable giving instructions to the maid. The only experience she'd had with service people was the occasional cleaning woman—the *schvartze*—that her mother used to hire before special occasions. "Sweetie, Julie's here."

"We're going out. Did you forget?" Ray said.

Rochelle kissed him as he handed her his coat to hang up.

"How ya doing?" he said to Julie.

"'Okay." Julie stretched back, ran her hands through her hair and let it trail slowly down. "How're *you?*"

"Maybe Julie'd like to join us tonight." He glanced at Rochelle. "You better get dressed, we're supposed to meet for drinks at the Carlyle first."

Rochelle looked at her outfit: She'd thought she looked nice, but obviously, not for the first time, she had chosen wrong. "Who are we meeting?"

"You don't know them." He began to pick up and re-file the records they'd played. He stopped in front of Julie. "So, you want to come tonight? Rochelle could lend you a dress or something, god knows she's been buying out the stores."

"I'd love to, but Luke and I have a gig tonight. It's a real important one, too, at the Village Gate. I mean, just a guest set, but a lot of big people are coming to hear us."

"Guess I better sign you two up before it's too late."

Julie offered her sensual, enigmatic half-smile.

Rochelle spoke up. "That's what I've been telling you, you know I discovered her way back in junior high!"

"Yes, honey," Ray said. "Hey, I nearly forgot your present. He dug into his jacket pocket and brought out a small blue Tiffany box.

"Oh, Ray!" She opened it to find a small, gleaming silver heart pendant on a delicate chain. "It's beautiful!" She went upstairs to find the perfect outfit to offset her newest treasure.

Ray winked at Julie. "I'm a pretty nice guy, right? *Right?*" He put his arm around her. She wanted to pull away but was afraid of offending him.

The phone rang and he snatched it up. Julie went up to the bedroom, where Rochelle had tossed a half-dozen beautiful outfits on the bed and the floor, and was sitting, dejectedly, on a peculiar chair in the center of the room, smoking a joint.

She passed it to Julie.

"No, the smoke hurts my voice."

"What the hell am I gonna wear?" Rochelle was saying, "I look like shit, I've got my goddamn period, I've got cramps."

"I better go," Julie said.

"Say hi to your Mom for me."

13

Either her memory was distorted or her mother's apartment had shrunk since she'd last visited. She squinted in the dim lighting. Her mother rarely used more than forty watt bulbs, considering more to be "wasteful." Julie took off her jacket and tossed it over the back of a kitchen chair. Her ears were pink and aching from the cold.

"Why don't you wear a hat?" her mother asked. "Don't you know that over fifty percent of the body's heat is lost through the top of the head?"

Paige stirred spaghetti sauce in the heavy iron skillet. She made it with sautéed onions and chopped meat and tomato paste, and it had always been Julie's favorite meal. Her mother's light hair, held back by two blue barrettes, needed trimming. There was more gray than Julie remembered.

Paige's great aunt had died and left her a small inheritance. She was moving in two weeks and had asked Julie to take what she wanted.

"Why France?"

"Why not? Paris is beautiful."

Julie pulled out a chair and sat limply at the table.

"Why don't you look through your things before dinner?" Paige suggested.

"Okay," she replied, not moving.

"Otherwise," Paige continued, "it will all have to go to Goodwill or into the garbage."

"What about Ben?"

"What about him?"

"*His* stuff is still around."

"Not for long. What do you expect me to do, make a big bonfire?"

"That's what I'd do." After a moment, she asked, "Is he coming back?"

"Of *course* he's not coming back, for heaven's sake. Do you think I'd have him back after everything?"

I don't know why you had him in the first place, she didn't say.

Paige found out that Ben was seeing another woman, practically living with her when he said he was out on business meetings. Julie couldn't imagine that there were more stupid women in the world who would have anything to do with Benjamin Lefcourt.

"I'm not hungry."

"Well, why didn't you say that before I put it on the plate?"

"I thought I was." She pushed away from the table and went into her old room.

It was unchanged. Amazing, that her mother had kept the sole bedroom intact, rather than using it as her own. Paige would say: Oh, the living room couch will do, I'm used to it. When her mother died, Julie thought, the gravestone should say, "I'll make do." There was a closed, musty scent in the air and the windowsill was coated with a layer of soot. The little dusty dish of bobby pins rested on the dresser, next to a small conch shell she'd found at Jones Beach years ago. The wood-framed mirror over the matching maple dresser, both of which had been her mother's in *her* childhood, was streaked with age, its silvery backing wearing away. Yellowed Scotch tape spots on the wall remained where Julie had hung the posters and publicity photos of her adolescent idols: Fabian, Ricky Nelson, Bobby Rydell, Jimmy Clanton, Frankie Avalon.

She sat on the narrow bed, hearing its familiar squeak. This could not have been her life. It was like reading about herself in the third person.

When Julie emerged from her old, stale room, her mother was scraping the uneaten spaghetti off the plates, humming a tuneless tune.

"So, how are things in the glamorous world of Show Business?" Paige asked. "How is Luke?"

"We're going to have a big recording deal." One hand tore at the cuticles of the other. The bittersweet taste of her own blood was strangely soothing.

"Maybe this will be your big break." Paige's expression suggested that she didn't much believe it. "Like that Joan Baez and that Judy Collins. You know who I like? Katey Lacey. She sings such nice songs, you should do one of her songs, you should talk to your record company about that and see what they say."

"I'll do that."

"Well, at least the divorce is almost final." Her mother bent down to open the cabinet under the sink, took out a bottle of scotch, pouring a generous portion into a short glass.

"Want some?"

"I hate that stuff."

"Well, good for you."

"How did you find out?"

"What?"

"About Ben's other woman."

"Women, actually. Oh, one of them called here. One thing led to another, and all the little lies started coming out. Did you have any idea he was Jewish?"

"He *looks* sort of Jewish."

"No, he doesn't, he's much too fair."

"So am I, and I'm half Jewish."

"You can't be 'half Jewish.' Jewish is a religion and we don't have any. Besides, you favor my side of the family."

"What are you *talking* about? All I've ever heard is how I look like my father. My Jewish father! Whose real name wasn't even Bradley!"

"And his name isn't Lefcourt, it's Lefkowitz."

Julie burst out laughing.

"I don't think it's at all funny," Paige said, although the beginning of a smile sneaked through.

"I do. Imagine, lying about being Jewish in *New York*, for god's sake. In *Rego Park*. It's like pretending not to be female in a convent. What an asshole."

"I suppose he is…an asshole," Paige laughed.

Julie grinned at her mother's obvious enjoyment at using the word. "What was my father's real name, anyway?"

Paige shrugged. "Something Russian, it got changed at Ellis Island. I think it ended in 'ovski.'"

"They all end in 'ovski'."

The kettle began to whistle. Paige rose to turn it off.

"I'm having instant coffee, do you want some?"

"Strong."

"And maybe a few cookies?" Her mother reached into their cookie jar and took out a handful of homemade chocolate chip cookies. She arranged them in a circle on a plate.

Julie thought about her mother making the cookies for herself, or in the hope that Julie would visit. Perhaps they could be like real mothers and daughters were, however that was. She'd seen them: in restaurants, and department stores, shopping together, giggling and hugging, touching each other in small, unconscious gestures. She couldn't remember the last time her mother had touched her.

"You can come and visit. Maybe you could learn some French songs."

"I guess I should have taken French instead of Spanish in high school."

"You're good at languages."

It occurred to her that she could now tell people, "My mother lives in France," which sounded classy.

"How will you meet people there?" she asked.

"How does one meet people anywhere? I don't know, I'll just meet them."

"But if you don't speak French."

Paige started clearing the dishes. "I guess if you can learn a French song, I can learn the basics, too. I still remember some from school. I'm not an idiot, you know."

The brief warmth evaporated, like a door had blown open and a storm, always close by, blew in again. The protective wall was thin as a membrane.

"I'll get the rest of my stuff."

At thirteen, she had swallowed five aspirins and waited for the overdose to hit, but felt only a faint grinding in her stomach that went on for hours. She'd sat on her bed, waiting to die, and when nothing happened, she was disappointed.

When Benjamin had come to live with them, after the initial shock and the claustrophobia had given way to resignation, she began to wonder what it might be like to have a father. Hers had left when she was too young to remember, and had only visited occasionally before he died, when she was nine. The first time Benjamin massaged her neck and shoulders, she thought: This is what fathers do. She told herself that again and again.

She pulled out the dusty *Fairy Tales of Hans Christian Anderson*; turned to the beautiful Edmund Dulac illustration of the Snow Queen, sitting on her ice throne, her hair streaming out over her bare shoulders. The tale told of an evil mirror that shatters and sends slivers flying all around the world, getting into people's eyes and turning their hearts to ice. She took that book, and several others, and carefully closed the door behind her, as if something monstrous might escape.

"That's it?"

Julie tossed the books in a grocery bag. "I don't have much space."

"I guess I won't see you before I leave."

There was a second in which they might have hugged each other.

"Have a nice trip."

Her mother was humming under her breath as Julie left.

14

Ray Fish rocked back precariously in his tan leather office chair, inches from the open window behind him. Elliot experienced a shudder from his legs to his belly, less from the thought of Ray plummeting forty-three floors to a splattery death than the concern he might plummet before signing the contract that lay between them on the desk.

The Luke & Julie contract: four years, four LPs. A single to be released from each. A generous promotion budget. At least two of Elliot's songs to be included on each album and given priority for single release, beginning with "Happy Little Snowflakes." Months of lawyerly wrangling had gotten them to this point. Of course, Elliot had been forced to make some concessions, but he was mostly pleased with the final draft.

"Congratulations," said Ray. "You've got a hot young act here."

"Thank you."

"Love that Luke's guitar playing. And the girl's great, too. Yeah, I think they got a real shot. More coffee? Bagel?"

"No. No, thanks." The first bagel was sitting in his stomach like a sunken tire.

Ray toyed with his fountain pen, a silver antique that fed from an inkwell. "Here we are," he said, "two guys who want the same thing. I thought we should just sit down together, no lawyers, no bullshit, and talk man to man. I hate middlemen, don't you? When I started in this business, everything was simple. You signed a one-page agreement, picked out two songs, you went into the studio and the next day you had a record."

I know how you made it in this business, Elliot thought: by signing unknown Negro groups for pennies, adding your own name as composer, and raking in the publishing royalties, which you didn't bother to share with the artists. Poor naive *schvartzes*. So grateful to get a record they gave away all but their firstborn.

"Nowadays," Ray continued, "seems like everybody wants a piece of the action, I got managers and agents up my ass, no offense, and a bunch of putzes calling themselves 'independent producers', whatever that is. My theory's always been that if you get too many cooks in the kitchen, you wind up with shit for supper."

"Right," Elliot was unsure where this was leading. He could hear the traffic, even this high up.

Ray clasped his hands behind his head. "But at least we're all straightened out here. What I wanted to talk to you about—"

The phone rang, and Ray picked it up. "Uh-huh, yes, sure," he said, squinting at a spot over Elliot's head. "Gimme a break, Becker, we're back-ordered fifty thousand and they're gonna hit the stores next week, full radio play, just need a little push in the *Hotsheet* to put it over the top, sure, no problem." He grinned. "Like always, Hap."

Elliot looked down at the ordinary Bic that would change his life. It occurred to him that Ray must be talking to Happy Becker, publisher of *Happy's Hotsheet*. Ray concluded his phone call.

The strains of "Here Comes Santa Claus" drifted in.

"Seems like they start Christmas earlier every year," Ray remarked. "But I love Christmas, don't you?"

"Frankly, I could do without all that *goyishe* good will."

"You're a funny guy, Levine." He buzzed his secretary. "Tell Spider to come in."

A moment later, the towering, oafish Spider Allessi came through the door. "How's it goin'." His pale eyes were hidden behind dark reflector lenses. He was like some mutant creature in a B movie.

"Great to see you again, uh...Spider."

Ray took over. "This is what's on my mind. You familiar with Magic Records?"

"Sure," Elliot replied.

"Well, they're in trouble, so I've made an arrangement with Bob Sanderson, he's the owner, we'll bail 'em out, do some cost-cutting, of course, but they'll be under our umbrella. I thought you might want to head it up."

Elliot sat forward. "Really? What about Sanderson?"

A flicker of a glance passed between Ray and Spider. "He's moving to Florida, sick of the rat race, gonna work in radio."

Elliot was excited: head up his *own* label! Even if it were just a subdivision of BigWheel, he could build it into something bigger. "I could be interested in that," he replied.

"There's nothing more rewarding than creating your own label and watching the money roll in. Of course, there won't be a lot right at the start, like any business it takes time, but with your eye for talent, I know you'll find 'em. So, what do you think?"

"I think it's great! What did you have in mind for the image? I mean, we can't possibly try to duplicate the kind of names BigWheel has."

"I'll leave that up to you, whatever you think'll sell. Hell, it don't cost anything to sign up acts."

Spider said, in a low monotone, "Throw it at the wall and see what sticks."

"What's the time frame?"

"Yesterday. When I move on something, I move fast. Magic Records is a done deal; their inventory's being shipped to our warehouse in Jersey as we speak." Ray rose, stretched his arms up, bent to the right and to the left, doing calisthenics. He sat and moved his neck around, loosening the muscles. "Jesus I could go for a massage." He buzzed his secretary. "Book me an hour with Torvil, will ya?"

Spider cracked his big knuckles.

"So, we'll get some contracts drawn up, of course, but how 'bout we shake on this for now?" Ray said.

"Sounds good to me."

He picked up the Luke & Julie contract, as if they'd been talking about it all along. "So I see it says here you want producing points. There's just a small problem with that, but nothing we can't iron out." He leaned forward, his voice low and exuding regret. "You see, we just don't use outside producers.

That's the way the company's set up. The Da Costas'll produce."

"The *Da Costas?* They do middle of the road pop. What do they know about a...a folk-rock sound like Luke & Julie?"

Ray's eyes narrowed slightly. "Harry and Marty Da Costa know their way around a studio. Helluva track record."

Spider snickered, "'Folk-rock'? Next it'll be 'opera-jazz', or 'calypso-polka'."

Ray ignored him. "Of course, the Da Costas'll have final say on what songs get recorded."

Elliot forced his face muscles into what could pass for a smile. "But my songs are still in. Like we agreed?"

"That's up to them. I was thinking, with you busy running Magic—or whatever you'll want to call it, Levine Records if you like—you probably won't have all that much time left over to hang around the studio, right?"

"I figured Luke & Julie would be on *my* label."

"Oh, shit, oh, shit!" Ray said, gushing apologies. "Did I fuck up? I *hate* when I fuck up." He opened his top drawer and took something out, tossed it across the desk to a startled Elliot, who barely managed to catch it.

An Almond Joy candy bar.

Elliot felt like a seal who'd been thrown a fish.

"I'm addicted to these things," Ray was saying. "No, no, no, Luke & Julie'll stay with BigWheel, didn't I mention that?"

He hit his forehead with mock self-reproach.

"Well, wait a minute. What you're saying is, you don't want me as producer, you don't want me as a songwriter, just what *is* my function in this deal?"

"Elliot, Elliot, you don't want to be a manager forever do you? Groveling around trying to peddle some ungrateful unwashed string pluckers who'll just dump you once they hit the big time? You want some power, don't you?" The secretary came in with a pot of coffee. She refilled Ray's china cup, and Elliot's, too. He picked it up, balancing the delicate saucer gingerly.

"You got root beer?" Spider asked.

Power. Yes, power. "Sure, I've got as much ambition as the next guy, a lot more in fact, but right now I have an agreement with Luke and with Julie, it gives me veto over any recording contract, it gives me final decision over repertoire and publishing and promotion—"

Ray waved his left hand in the air, as if he were shooing a pesky fly. "You'll have to work that out with your artists. I'm just telling you what we want. What we always *get*."

"So, this is a deal-breaker?"

Ray closed his eyes and leaned back again, the unnerving tilt of chair to window ledge. "Jeez, you really got me on the wires here. I offer you a whole record company, and you still want the moon. Lemme think. You really want to produce that much?"

"I think it'd be best for the talent."

"Well, then, no biggie. We'll just work it out with the Da Costas."

Elliot drained the coffee cup to hide his obvious relief.

"Of course," Ray went on, "There's the publishing. BigWheel holds the copyrights. Past and future."

The cup shook in his hand. He put it down carefully on the antique desk.

"BigWheel gets the copyrights to your stuff and anything Bellavita may write. Hey, that's standard, I don't know why we forgot to put it in the first place. Oh, I know what it was—we had a temp that week, she fucked up, but the clause is back." Ray shuffled through the contract, which had begun at six pages and now was more than twenty. "Here—page fourteen A, paragraph 11G, insert, party of the first part—here you go, you can read it."

"Ray, this is kind of last minute. I'll show this to my lawyer, but I hate to spend another month—"

"Sure, take your time."

"—keeping those kids on hold. And this looks like you get my backlist as well, songs I've found for other artists, I mean, this isn't a contract, it's a...well, it's nothing but a holdup."

"Elliot, don't worry so much, you're gonna give your self an ulcer, you gotta look at the whole picture. You know what the great thing about it is? We live in a free country, and if you don't like one deal, you can always take your business somewhere else. Right?"

Ray stood up. The meeting was over. "Think about it, talk to your lawyer, get back to me."

A headache was pounding at the crown of Elliot's head. What was he doing in this league? A dumb schmuck from Flatbush who liked music too much. Ray's dizzying paisley Nehru shirt made his eyes ache.

The blind artist-beggar Moondog was standing outside the building, tall and immobile as a statue, clad in Viking clothes; a familiar vision, a self-creation of the New York streets. Elliot had seen him around the Village, where he recited his poetry and occasionally played his own music on a drum or other homemade instrument. Where did he live?

Elliot walked the few blocks back to his office in a daze. Ray hadn't said anything about money, salary, guarantees of any sort. Maybe he was just blowing hot air. Maybe this was an easy way of getting Elliot out of the picture. Ray didn't need him on the contract, taking producer points. But if he gave up too easily, Ray would lose any respect he had for him.

Elliot reached his building, where its own, personal street regular, a shabby, bearded man, sat outside the doors on a wooden crate, hissing "Garbage! Garbage!" and making rude sounds at pedestrians. If a couple passed by, he'd growl "Sex maniacs!" Even his building's *derelict* had less panache than Ray's.

The windowless cubicle oppressed him further. The walls needed painting; sheet music and papers were stacked up in the corners because he'd run out of file space. Meager ventilation came from a transom that opened into the hallway. You sweated in the summer, froze or suffocated in the winter. Just like where he grew up in Flatbush. Sure, the Brill Building had a certain cachet, you could still hear pianos tinkling in the hallways, but the old guard was moving out: lawyers, promoters, press agents, even dentists, for god's sake, were replacing them.

He called his answering service and wrote down the messages. The next call was to Morty, his lawyer, to tell him about the meeting. Morty said it sounded fishy—that was a joke—but at this point Elliot ought to take it or walk away, enough already.

The papers were in front of him, the contract awaiting nothing more than his signature. An old folk song lyric kept repeating in his head.

In the pines, in the pines, where the sun never shines
And we shivered on the cold, cold ground…

Folk songs were fucking depressing.

He dialed Ray Fish's number.

"I'll see if he's available," the secretary said smoothly.

Ray came on the line, "What's up, Levine?"

"I've been looking this over. Tell you the truth, I don't think it's the deal we're after. Not the way it stands now. I'd be happy to have my lawyer get back to you with a few changes. I'm sure we can work it out in a way that's best for all of us."

There was a silence, but he could hear Ray's breath. "See you around, Levine." The connection was severed with a tiny click.

Elliot held the receiver against his ear for a few more seconds, then placed it quietly back on the receiver.

In the pines, in the pines…

Thinking of things he should have said. But they weren't without options. Vanguard was still sniffing around. Sure, they weren't as rich and powerful a label as BigWheel, and there were a couple of small labels that had shown interest.

Dusk cast shadows over the city, the buildings smothering any remaining light. He got his coat and hat and turned out the light, locked the door.

Elliot browsed through Colony Music, imagining the day when *his* artists would be there; when *his* songs would be in the rows of sheet music at the back of the store. His stomach clenched when he saw the cover for the published sheet music of "Little Silver Raindrops". Written and Arranged by Mark Draper and the Umbrella Singers. The bastards were supposed to reprint the music, with *his* name as 'co-writer' (the best he could get from the lawsuit). Making sure no one was looking, he slipped the copies of the song out of the rack, and hid them from sight behind "Love Me Do".

Outside, he headed for the Times Square subway station, stop ping at a news stand to buy the *Post*. A chill gripped the back of his neck, as if he were being watched. He turned: just an ordinary crowd of people, pushing this way and that, rushing to get home. On the subway platform, he was jostled on all sides by commuters. For once, the closeness, the forced intimacy of the too many people gave him a sense of security. He stood well back from the edge of the platform, the years of his mother's warnings an ingrained habit: don't stand near the edge, you could fall, some maniac could push you. If you ever fall in, watch out for the third rail, you touch that, you're electrocuted.

Elliot noticed a tall man with his head half hidden behind a *Herald Tribune*. He was wearing a New York Yankees baseball cap but Elliot could see tufts of white blond hair sticking out from underneath. Spider Allessi? Elliot stepped forward, to say hello, but the man disappeared into the crowd.

At that moment, the lights began to dim. Then they flashed back on. There was a murmur as the tired commuters looked up.

A woman next to Elliot rolled her eyes, "Christinheaven, now what?"

The lights flickered. Once. Twice. And went out.

15

The crowded elevator moved with an eerie slothfulness, gave a funny little bump, and stalled. Rochelle's stomach did a queasy dip.

The small, enclosed space was plunged into darkness.

"Uh-oh," said someone.

"Don't say 'uh-oh', I don't want to hear 'uh-oh'," said another.

Rochelle clung to the back wall, her hands, beginning to sweat, gripping the metal holding bar.

"At this rate," commented a voice.

"You'd rather go ninety?"

Oh God just get me the fuck out of here.

Someone banged on the door. We're in here get us out of here!! The elevator lurched suddenly. There were screams in the dark. When the doors opened at last, Rochelle shoved her way to the front. She gasped for air as she stepped into the lobby. Then she gasped in shock.

New York City had disappeared. The lobby was lost in shadows. The streetlights on Sixth Avenue had vanished, and only a few flares of car and taxi headlights provided any illumination. Rochelle craned her neck and looked back up at the building, faintly lit from within by scattered emergency lamps. Ray was somewhere up there, in his office.

She turned around, re-entered the lobby and headed for the stairs.

"Miss." A security guard stepped in front of her, pointing an oversized headlamp in her face, as if she were under interrogation.

"I forgot something."

"You work here?" He had a Jamaican accent.

"*Yes.* I just got out of that deathtrap elevator."

"Miss, we're all doing the best we can."

"I have to go back up."

"What floor?"

"Forty-three."

He laughed. "Hope you're in good shape!"

She felt her way to the stairs, and began the climb. At first, there was a little light from the lobby, but as she climbed higher, even this disappeared, and she was in the dark. People passed by, on their way down, laughing and chattering as if it were all a big game. Her legs were strong for the first twenty flights. Did Ray have any candles in the office? Well, there were lots of fun things they could do in the dark. At the twenty-ninth floor, she sat on the steps to rest. Ray might have already left by another staircase. She panted up another eight flights, legs heavy, muscles shaky. Forty one. Forty two. Forty three.

He was at his office window. The silhouettes of the blackened high-rises were barely visible. Two candles burned in ashtrays on his desk. A portable radio was reporting a growing list of emergencies.

"Maybe it's Martians," she said.

"A lot more likely some idiot pulled the wrong switch and the whole city goes down. Makes you wonder."

"I'm going to try to find the ladies room. Have you got a flashlight?"

"'Fraid not. But take one of the candles. What do you want to drink?"

"Anything, as long as it's strong." She held the candle in its dish out before her, stepping carefully. "Well, wish me luck."

"Luck," he responded, distracted.

Even the backup lights had dimmed. She began to wish she'd asked Ray to accompany her. The darkness distorted her sense of distance, and she felt her way slowly along the wall.

The bathroom door creaked as it opened, and of course there was no light inside. The room echoed. She set the candle dish down on the counter, and entered the nearest stall. The burning candle cast writhing shapes of light, like a demented strobe. What if she wasn't alone? There could be a maniac hiding in the next stall. Once she'd seen a cockroach on the floor of this very bathroom. She hated bugs. One could be scuttling around right now and she'd never know it, a really big bug, and its whole family.

She pulled up her pantyhose and quickly washed her hands in the sink, grabbed the candle and began edging back down the hallway to Ray's office.

His door was open, and she could see him crouching on the floor, just behind the desk, the other candle next to him. Curious, she stayed as still as possible. There was the sound of closing, like a lid. He reached up and put the candle back on the desk, and stood. He was holding a small bag. He slipped something else into his upper desk drawer. She heard the tink of metal on metal: a key?

She backed up a few feet, and cleared her throat as she approached.

When she came in, Ray was sitting in his chair, measuring out lines of cocaine on the desk top.

"Ninety nine and one hundred percent pure," he said cheerfully, not looking up. "Take off your clothes."

16

Julie had been in Macy's for hours, spending far more money than she could afford. The spree had begun with a sudden, overwhelming desire for a leather vest but then she could not decide between the brown cowhide or the black suede, so she bought them both, and had to have the black jeans, and the boots, ten pairs of dark patterned hose and the dangly op-art earrings in three colors. The new store credit card and the spending were an extension of the grandly expansive mood that had overtaken her lately, a mood in which every facet of her life—the people in it, her own abilities, the limitless future—were cast in a golden hue. She was incandescent. Had someone reminded her that she did not always feel this way, that there were times— often, and without warning—when she would plunge into despondency, she'd have thought the idea perfectly ridiculous. She had a kind of mood amnesia. Whichever mood she was in was the sole reality that erased the others.

This one was characterized by a driving energy and insomnia. Eating felt unnatural, about as palatable as ingesting paper. Nights, she was wide awake, her back aching from bending over the guitar, writing songs, or talking on the phone to Luke, refusing to let *him* sleep, and calling people all over the country, sometimes strangers whose numbers she dialed at random, drawing them into conversations—

especially easy if they were men—going so far as to make dates. Yes, I'll be in Cincinnati next week on business, lets get together. She never told anyone about these deceptions. It was a way to fill the unsleeping hours. She was deliriously happy, spiraling up and ever upward.

When she exited Macy's revolving doors, and saw the lights beginning to die, the buildings across the street vanishing one by one, she had a surge of pure elation.

A car at the corner of 34th and Broadway screeched to a halt, but not in time to avoid scraping the bumper of a truck turning the corner. Several other drivers slammed on their brakes behind, and there was a pileup, a series of crunches that made her cringe, and freeze in place. The drivers emerged from their cars, shaken but apparently unhurt. They started directing traffic.

There was a phone booth at the corner. While a woman in a hideous red hat monopolized the phone, Julie shifted her packages to one hand, and fished a dime from her purse. She was starting to feel as if her nerves were on the outside of her skin. A line for the phone was forming; everyone had a bizarre theory about the cause of the power outage. No one seemed especially frightened; agitated, yes, curious and annoyed and excited, but not scared. It was in the nature of New Yorkers to take things in stride, and if the city chose to black itself out, well then the only recourse was to figure out the logistics of getting home. The woman finished her call. Julie could barely make out the numbers on the dial.

"Is it dark there, too?" she asked Luke when he answered at her apartment.

"Sure is. All the power's out."

"What is it?"

"I don't know, I was just looking for your portable radio. Is there a flashlight anywhere?"

"The portable's in the desk drawer, I think, but the batteries are probably dead. I don't have a flashlight."

"Everyone should have a flashlight."

"Well, I don't *have* one, okay?"

"Where are you? I'll come get you."

"No, don't come all this way. I'll start walking down Seventh Avenue on the west side of the street. If you walk uptown, we'll meet."

He appeared out of the gloom at Eighteenth Street, jacket open, hair damp; seized her in his arms, and kissed her for a long time, as though they were the lone survivors of a war.

A party atmosphere was beginning to take over the city.

They walked all the way down to the Village. Restaurants glimmered in candlelight, hand-written signs outside offered free food. People mingled in the streets. Music played from open windows, and there was dancing. Julie and Luke dropped off her many packages at the apartment, and went out to join in the festivities.

"Isn't this *fantastic*?" she cried out. A handwritten sign invited the public: FOOD WILL SPOIL, COME IN, BUY A DRINK. The news on the portable radio reported that the blackout was widespread, all along the East coast from as far down as Virginia, and up to New England.

"I could get something to eat," said Luke.

She pulled off her coat and ran ahead, waving it like a flag.

He hurried to catch up with her. "What are you doing, it's cold out!"

"No, it isn't!"

"Yes—look, let's eat somewhere—"

He went into a restaurant on Bleecker Street.

"I don't like this place." She pulled him down the street to another. There were no tables. The next also had a wait.

The one after that was serving only desserts. The one after that…

"We could have gone in that first place," Luke said irritably. "Just *pick* something!"

"You are so fucking boring."

"No, I'm fucking hungry!"

"How can you think about food when all this is going on?"

"I don't know, I just can. It's like sex, something you wouldn't know that much about."

"What?" She stopped walking.

"Nothing, I'm just hungry, and cranky, can we just get–"

"No, I heard you."

"Julie, I didn't mean it, I'm tired and hungry, and this spooks me, let's get off the street!"

They were at the corner of Minetta Lane and Sixth Avenue. Minetta was a small street, really an alley that wound past the rear exit of The Fat Black Pussycat cafe.

The high flying balloon of her mood, a Hindenburg kept aloft by a dangerous and combustive fuel, had been pierced. The descent began slowly, then accelerated until she was hurtling downward into the speed of light.

A great hopelessness washed over her.

Julie, she heard Luke saying. Julie?

"What's wrong? Five minutes ago you said how great you felt. I can't keep up with you!"

She saw herself reach into her purse and pull out a small metal container of aspirin, thinking she might take one, because there was a vague ache in the back of her head. Instead, she bent back the two halves of the little box, separating them. Before he moved to stop her, she dragged the serrated edge along the inside of her left wrist. There was no blood, just a small scrape. No pain. The arm was someone else's.

He grabbed her and wrestled the aspirin box away; it fell to the ground and the pieces scattered, the small white pills rolling to the curb.

"What are you doing, are you crazy?" He pulled her into his arms and they stood there, frozen, in the darkness. "Julie, you have to see someone, talk to a doctor or something, you have to, will you promise me you'll see someone?"

She began to cry.

"Let me see your wrist." He turned it over. "It's just scratched. I don't think the skin is broken. Why did you do that?"

"I don't know. I really don't know."

17

The packed subway was now completely dark. Someone said, "Maybe the city didn't pay the Con Ed bill," and there was nervous laughter. Elliot waited, his heart beating faster. He lifted his hand and could not even see it. The blackness was like a blind pressure against his eyes. There was an eerie silence in the tunnels, as if all the world had gone dead.

"It's the Russians," said a man next to him.

"UFO's," a woman chimed in.

A weary voice remarked, "They couldn't wait till I got to Brooklyn?"

The crowd moved like a live thing, he was propelled along, unable to tell if he was being jostled toward the platform edge or away from it; and the perspiration on his body, from the heat of a thousand people muffled in winter coats, and the station that held its summer humidity into winter, turned to a clammy cold sweat of fear.

Something, someone pushed him.

He braced his feet, afraid to cry out and start a panic, he wasn't even sure the shove was deliberate, but his gut told him that this was the man in the Yankees cap, and that man was Spider.

Someone flicked a lighter nearby, illuminating an array of faces, distorted by shadows.

"Are you crazy, you wanna start a fire?" the lighter wielder was admonished. The light went out. Flashlight beams pierced the platform.

Police!

What is it? What's going on?

The pressure of the hand on Elliot's back disappeared. Cops yelled for attention, a transit officer arrived with a megaphone and announced that there had been a power failure in the city, the trains weren't running, they were to evacuate the subway.

"So how are we supposed to get home?!"

"Are the lights on in Brooklyn?!"

"The power is out all over!"

The cops made their way along the platform, flashlight beams darting over faces, walls, the dank, black tunnels. The crowd was gradually herded back toward the stairs, and Elliot shuffled along with the rest of them. The streets were in a kind of organized pandemonium. Cars inched their way down Broadway, pedestrians volunteering as traffic monitors. Elliot thought he had never seen anything so alien as the darkened skyscrapers, Times Square without its blaze of lights. In the strange beauty, he forgot for a moment about the shove on the platform. The buildings looked as if they had been painted black.

Like a truck ramming him, some force collided and caught him, his arm was suddenly twisted up behind his back. He gasped from the pain and could not speak. A faint scent of English Leather. He tried to dig in his heels, but the man, at least a head taller than Elliot, half dragged him down a side street. No one noticed in the dark. His bladder felt weak, and he feared he couldn't control himself. He was shoved into the alley of a closed theater, a cement wall at his back and he heard the man's hoarse breathing.

"Look, Spider, it's me, Elliot, you know me—"

The man cut him off with a hard punch to the stomach. The air went out of him and his legs buckled. Again the fist connected. He had never known how to fight, and it had been a long time since he'd felt this helpless, in the playgrounds, on the way home from school, when bigger boys picked on him, and he'd never learned to defend himself, thinking that when he grew up, all he'd need was his brains.

His mind exploded in a world of pain, then retreated, and exploded again, as the man connected over and over. He was on the ground, crouched against the wall, trying to protect his face, his insides, but it was no use, he rolled into a ball and wondered if he was going to die, and after a while he didn't care.

Rain? Something wet on his face. His hand came away sticky. Blood. Sirens in the distance. Coming to help him. Please. Terribly dark. Had he gone blind? No, just the blood in his eyes…watch broken, the glass shattered, wallet gone, like a mugging. But he knew this had been no random mugging.

Try to get up. Legs like jello. And the pain, so hard to breathe like knives stabbing in his side. He lurched along, hurt searing his ribs with each step. A flap of skin hung from his lip, his teeth felt loose and he could hardly see through the swelling around his eyes.

"Are you all right, mister?" a woman asked, peering through the shadows.

"…hospital…need a doctor."

"St. Clare's is over on 9th…an emergency room…you'll have to walk…here, lean on me…there's no taxis in this mess…can you…?"

Legs started to give way again; tears mingled with the blood on his face.

"Sure, you can do it," she said, as they hobbled along.

When they got to the emergency waiting room, she apologized for being unable to stay and left him slumped in an orange plastic chair.

He woke up on a cot and couldn't remember what had happened in between, except that there were bandages on his face and his chest was constricted by some sort of binding.

"Is there someone you can call?" a nurse was asking, as she took his blood pressure. She had a round, pale Irish face like a nun.

"We'll make the call for you."

"Rochelle," he mumbled. "My wallet."

"I'll find it," the nurse said. He heard her dial, and speak to someone who answered the phone.

...in the pines, in the pines where the sun never shines and we shivered on the cold, cold ground...

Time passed in breaths of agony.

She was leaning over him.

"Rochelle?" He looked up into her face. Not Rochelle. But familiar.

"Come on, honey," Arlene Slotnick said, "I'm taking you home."

H ow do I know so many details about these people, when I was born just seventeen years ago, and only have my father's notes and a few bits of memorabilia to go on? Well, of course I'm making a lot of it up. The story of Julie, Luke and the rest is "inspired by actual events" to put it cheesily.

I did get some first hand accounts. I tracked Elliot down (yes, he's still alive, unlike some of the others.) We met at a Starbucks on West 57th Street, although he no longer lives in the city. I was carrying my guitar and he laughed that he could be my manager if he was still in the business. He has an amazing memory, and a scrapbook and files and photos from that time. He also has a shitload of bitterness he tries to hide with bad jokes. I guess he hasn't heard of the concept of 'get over it, move on.' I think he loved my grandmother, but she wasn't interested in him that way. No, she went for the bad boys and the guitar players.

I'm not going to make that mistake. I'll do the drummers instead (kidding).

Can you believe how difficult it was to get recorded back then? Even if you had a decent reel-to-reel tape machine, it was probably no more than two tracks. Home made demos sounded like shit. Now, anyone with a computer can make a CD and put it out all over the 'net. I'm working on mine, and

I already sent a track to this Internet radio guy, and he likes it. I just wish my Dad could have heard it; maybe it would have given him something to live for.

I'm not supposed to think that way, at least that's what the 'grief coach' says. I can't blame myself for his illness. You can't save people no matter how much you love them.

COLLECTIBLES

Sheet music: *Happy Little Snowflakes*, copyright 1962 (never recorded)

BigWheel Records contract, signed by Julie Bradley and Luke Bellavita, dated June 5, 1966. [note: It wasn't legal because they were both underage.]

New York Post, November 19, 1965, front page. Headline: BLACKOUT! – from Elliot's scrapbook.

Photo: Luke & Julie album cover—shot in Central Park (never used)—photographer unknown

News Headline (1965): LBJ Stops Bombing and Offers Peace

News Headline (1965): LBJ Sends 50,000 New Troops to Vietnam

Happy's Hotsheet—recording industry Tip Sheet, June 1966—one-liner promo for newly signed BigWheel artists, Luke & Juley [sic]—from the estate of Marvin "Happy" Becker.

Article excerpt: "Payola, in the American music industry, is the illegal corruption practice of payment or other inducement by record companies for the broadcast of recordings on music radio, in which the song is presented as being part of the normal day's broadcast." (Wikipedia)

Part Two

With haunted hearts through the heat and cold,
We never thought we could ever get old.

Bob Dylan, "Bob Dylan's Dream"

18

The BigWheel lawyer pointed with a blunt manicured finger at the various places where Luke and Julie were to sign or initial their names, page after page with highlighted words in bold: THE ARTIST. THE COMPANY d/b/a BIGWHEEL RECORDS.

This was really happening: their own record. An actual advance of seven hundred and fifty dollars, split 50-50, and no manager to take fifteen percent. She had a momentary flash of guilt. Elliot should be here; he got them to Ray in the first place, didn't he? But Ray said this sort of thing happens all the time; and why give up an extra fifteen percent to a loser like Elliot? Ray said he'd get one of the big agencies to handle them.

"I think this calls for a celebration." Ray pressed his intercom as the lawyer left the room. "Theresa, get Marty and Harry in here." He gave a sly wink, and pushed a button under the desk. A bookcase on the opposite wall opened and turned into a bar. "Drink?"

Luke tried not to look impressed. "You got Jim Beam?"

"I've got everything." Ray poured a generous splash into a glass and handed it over. "And for the lady?"

"White Russian?"

He mixed the drink, and then poured himself a single malt scotch. Raising his glass: "To the newest members of the Big-Wheel family."

A sharp wind buffeted the building, whining at the window; the floor vibrated.

"Don't worry, honey," Ray said, "They build these things to sway in the wind; otherwise they'd break off and we'd all go boom."

Ray's secretary escorted two short, bulky men into the office. They had identical, thin mustaches. "Marty and Harry Da Costa," Ray said.

"Look at these kids!" Marty said. An obvious toupee dipped low on his forehead. "They're *babies*, coupla *babies*."

"That's the way it goes now," Harry added. "Every year, younger, soon they'll be recording right outta nursery school." He helped himself to a scotch and soda. "How long you been singing' together?"

"A year, more'less," Luke said.

Marty turned to his brother. "Doris Day was just a kid when she first recorded. Who was it said 'I knew her before she was a virgin'?"

"Oscar. Oscar Levant, that crazy drunk."

"Still plays a helluva piano, when he's sober."

"Jo Stafford, too. Made it real young. And how about Katey Lacey, she was what, seventeen, eighteen when her first record broke?"

Julie and Luke exchanged a glance. Jo Stafford? Katey Lacey? They were stars when dinosaurs walked the earth.

"So when are we going into the studio?" Luke asked.

Ray turned to the Da Costas, he said, "They've got plenty of material, but I want a few of your tunes in there. You heard their demos, you know what kind of sound we're going for. A nice, easy pop, small backup band."

"Actually, I was thinking—" Luke began.

Ray interrupted. "You just worry about playing and singing. We'll worry about selecting the material."

Julie spoke up, "Well, Luke has some songs he's written."

"Uh-huh, 'course you do," Ray said, "but the important thing is to find that first big hit, doesn't matter who wrote it, right? Marty and Harry's track record is golden." He refilled Luke's glass and turned to the Da Costas. "I love these kids, think they're ready to run a record company before they've cut a record!"

Luke downed his drink.

"How you kids fixed for money?" Ray continued. "You okay?" He dug into his pocket. "Here." He handed each of them a bill, "Don't say Ray Fish never gave you anything!" He wrapped up the meeting. "Marty and Harry'll get in touch when their schedule frees up."

Out on the street, Julie and Luke studied the hundred dollar bills Ray had given them.

"I always wondered who was on these things," Luke said.

19

Elliot's rage was almost beautiful, like the pearl of an oyster, honed by the grinding of rough sand that polished and smoothed the intruding object, created out of pain. He nurtured and protected it.

In the days and weeks following the Big Blackout of 1965, Elliot languished in Arlene's apartment on West 10th Street, letting her feed him chicken soup from the Stage Deli; freshly squeezed orange juice, and Cream of Wheat. The loose teeth, the stitches on his lip made eating difficult and he lost twelve pounds. Gradually, the swellings and discolorations faded. The lip scar gave his face an odd but appealing quirk. Looking into the mirror for the first time in weeks, he saw a different person—not that his features were noticeably changed, but there was more of a guarded expression.

He could not prove that the beating was connected to his refusal to sign Ray Fish's contract—and, in fact, he questioned why Fish would take such extreme measures for someone so relatively unimportant. Sheer malice? Nor could he positively identify the man who attacked him, although he was certain it was Spider Allessi. The police, with little to go on, made a half-hearted report and an investigation that generated no clues. Elliot was glad to see the matter die. Arlene wanted the attacker brought to justice; what was wrong with the world was that people didn't do anything, like with that Kitty Genovese in Queens, she said, referring to the woman who was murdered in a middle class neighborhood while dozens of people shut their windows and failed to call the police. Elliot let her think he'd put it behind him but one day, he was certain, fate would catch up with Ray Fish. There had to be ways to give fate a little push.

Luke had called a few days after the Blackout.

"Hey, man, how ya doin'? I heard you got mugged."

"Better." His words were still slurred from the injuries and the stitches.

"Good. Look, Elliot, I know this may be a pretty bad time, but we gotta talk, man."

"I'm listening."

"You know BigWheel wants to sign us, but they don't seem to feel—now it's just their lawyers, you dig, so take it all with a grain of salt—they don't like that we're tied, or whatever, to a, you know, a management deal, they want everything free and clear. No strings."

A numbness crept over him. "You and Julie signed a contract with me."

"Yeah, well, that's the thing. Listen, I really hate this, but who knows if we're gonna get another opportunity like this again? And, well, the lawyer guy said that since we're both under twenty-one, then it could just be null and void anyhow. I just want you to know this isn't our choice, of course, and I hope we can all work together again, I'm *sure* we will, 'cause I got the greatest respect for you, man, but, well, so I just thought I'd tell you."

Elliot pressed the phone receiver to his chest for a moment, wondered if Luke could hear his heart breaking. Then he spoke into it again. "Luke. I won't fight it. Do what you think is best. I wish you luck."

"Thanks, man, you know I—"

But Elliot had hung up.

Sitting in Arlene's living room, watching *The Ed Sullivan Show*, Elliot contemplated the future. Managing a few acts on his own had failed to bring in enough money to pay the rent and he was forced to give up his tiny office in the Brill Building. He liked to write songs, but he didn't have a lot of ideas, and the songs he came up with were, he had to admit it, kind of lightweight. Maybe he had a chance of one hitting big, like "Little Silver Raindrops", but it would always be a gamble.

Each morning, he awakened very early, and remembered where he was, and who he was—or wasn't—and the soul sickness came over him. He wanted to see Ray Fish suffer, in some agonizing, protracted manner.

Until that point in his life, he'd presumed that if you had a few good ideas and worked hard enough, rewards would come. He would look at Arlene, bringing him coffee, studying her college textbooks, glasses resting on her curiously upturned nose, her hair twined around rollers the size of inner tubes, and feel a mixture of contentment and contempt. She thrived on taking care of him, she healed him with her food, her tenderness, her body, her mouth; he was ashamed to tell her that before she went down on him, without his even asking, the only time he had experienced that act was when he'd paid a prostitute, and he was sick with guilt afterward— for having squandered the money as much as having embraced such sordidness.

How could he not love Arlene when she did for him all the time? Yet her devotion was the very thing that kept him from adoring her. How could she love *him*? A schnook, a loser, the guy everybody takes for a ride. He thought of the

Groucho Marx quote: I wouldn't want to join any club that would have me as a member. But as the weeks turned into months, he settled into life with Arlene, and the comforts of her apartment, which were not so very different than his mother's.

Rochelle came by to pick up a few items she'd left behind in her move from Arlene's to Ray's. She wore a silver fox fur coat that she draped across the sofa with a studied nonchalance.

"Are you okay?" she wanted to know. "It must have been so terrible!"

"How's the job?"

"Great! I'm getting to screen tapes and demos and Ray really listens to my opinion. There's still a lot of typing, and boring stuff but it's better than where I was."

Hearing the name—Ray—was like being pierced with a knife. Ray. Ray. Ray. He wanted to check to see if he was bleeding.

After Rochelle left, he smoked one of Arlene's menthol cigarettes, not really enjoying the taste or the feel of the smoke in his lungs, but appreciating the way it seemed to press back the hurt.

Arlene took him to Queens to meet her family. The spacious brick house on a tree-lined street in Forest Hills was a long way from the dreary apartment in Flatbush where he grew up. Her childhood room was still intact, neat and pink, with a long double shelf of books, and stuffed animals on the ruffled bed.

In the white-carpeted split level living room, Dr. Slotnick shook Elliot's hand vigorously. "Arlene tells us you're in the music business?" he inquired. Elliot noticed a row of pictures on the mantle. Arlene as a little girl, a bigger girl, a teen. He assumed it was Arlene. The little girl had a rather large nose, which grew larger as she did. The older teenager looked more like the Arlene he knew.

"Yes, I manage talent. Write songs, too."

"Guess you're waiting for that big hit!" said Mrs. Slotnick.

"Elliot's a genius," stated Arlene.

Her parents regarded the genius in their midst.

"Well, I wouldn't say that," he said.

"If my daughter has faith in you, you should, too," Dr. Slotnick advised.

They dined on roast beef, with tiny potatoes, succotash, challah bread, chocolate cake for dessert. On the subway back to the city, Elliot mentioned to Arlene that he thought he might give law school another try.

Arlene immediately responded, playfully: "So there's this guy who works in the circus, and his entire job consists of shoveling up the elephant shit after the show. So one day, somebody asks him, 'You ever think of getting another job?' and he answers 'What, and give up show biz?'"

Elliot laughed, even though he'd heard it before. "So what are you saying? I should keep hitting my head against a brick wall?"

"You have to do what you love. Even brick walls can be knocked down."

As they walked the two blocks from the subway station to their apartment, she stopped. "Elliot. I have to tell you something."

He knew before the words were out of her mouth.

"—pregnant."

He stumbled slightly on an uneven patch of sidewalk. "Elliot?"

"I heard you." He licked his lips. "Well, then, we'll get married."

Arlene increased her pace, obviously upset by the lack of feeling in his voice. "Well, we don't *have* to," she snapped. "I could always get the name of a doctor from Daddy. It isn't like I could ask *him* to do it!"

He hurried to catch up. "Don't talk crazy. I want to. Get married, that is. It's just that I don't have any money, or even a job."

She waved a hand. "You'll get one. And my parents'll give us money to start out, and I've got my Bat Mitzvah money. I don't care about a big wedding."

"But what about college? Don't you want to graduate?"

"I can always study at home, or finish later."

Perhaps his destiny had been charted out, like a crossword puzzle, and he was simply filling in the blanks.

They eloped at City Hall, and told their families afterward. Both mothers cried. Mrs. Slotnick was particularly disappointed at having been robbed of the opportunity to see her daughter in a beautiful white wedding dress, but they were forgiving people and gave the newlyweds a hefty check.

20

In the back room of The Fat Black Pussycat, androgynous Tiny Tim, gaunt as a scarecrow with long tangled hair and a mannered falsetto, gushed affectionately, "Julie! I'm so delighted to *see* you!" His voice went up oddly in the middle of sentences. "I hope you'll sing your *beautiful* version of 'Summertime'."

"I will, promise," she said, watching as he re-joined his friends, mostly female, and remembering how freaked out she'd been the first time she'd seen Tiny Tim, and amazed that he had girlfriends. But they were always around. Tiny revealed no self-consciousness about his eccentricity. As if he believed he was on a planet where *he* was the norm and everyone else peculiar.

The impressionist comic, Dave Frye, was working on his Nixon imitation with an intense focus. He faced the wall and talked aloud to himself, shifting among the many characters in his repertoire. Dave had appeared on a few TV shows.

Meyer Norman came through the door carrying his beat up guitar case. Luke was right behind him, in conversation with Peter Torkelson, who played banjo and sang. Luke wanted him to play on their record but the Da Costas rejected the idea as 'too folkie.'

"Hey, how's the record coming?" Meyer asked.

"We haven't gone into the studio yet," Luke replied.

"No shit, thought you'd be done by now."

Several months had elapsed since they'd signed their contract. The reason they'd been given was that the Da Costas were finishing up other projects, and wanted to be able to concentrate on Luke & Julie.

Julie unpacked her guitar and began to tune.

"Are you auditioning for this TV thing?" Peter asked Luke.

Julie looked up. "What TV thing?"

"They just want guys, for some TV series about four musicians in a group, like the Beatles, only American."

God, what a stupid idea, Julie thought. She turned to Luke, about to ask if he knew about it.

He read her look. "Ray mentioned something about it but I told him I wasn't interested."

Meyer was saying, "Yeah, man, I went in last week. It was crazy, there were about twenty people sitting there watching, the whole goddamn network."

"I know. I got a callback tomorrow," Peter said.

Meyer's eye twitched. "No shit? Well, good luck, man."

Julie whispered to Luke. "You should audition, I bet it pays a lot."

"What about us?"

"Well..."

"I couldn't do both. And it sounds like bullshit."

The club manager came through the black curtains that separated the music room from the coffee house. "You guys about ready?" he asked Luke and Julie. "We got a nice crowd in there."

After the set, a couple of mangy adolescents followed them out the door to MacDougal Street.

"You think Dylan sold out?" asked a thin kid wearing a tattered denim jacket.

"Yeah, he should never've gone electric," his friend added.

"He sold us out, man," the first kid repeated, his long hair blowing in the autumn wind.

"Dylan can do whatever he goddamn well pleases," Luke snapped.

Julie said, "I think the electric guitar kind of spoils his sound."

The kids left, confused.

Luke laughed. "That's the defining tragedy of their young lives, Dylan going electric."

"Mine was when Richie Valens, the Big Bopper and Buddy Holly died in that plane crash."

They were booked for a week of recording. First, they would have several rehearsals with the Da Costas, to work on the material and the arrangements. Luke was apprehensive when they told him they'd "picked out some potential top-40s."

"What's wrong with that?" Julie argued. "Do you have something against a hit record?"

"Of course not, I just...I don't know, I just had the feeling they didn't understand our sound."

"Why would they have signed us if they wanted us to sound like somebody else?" she asked.

At the first rehearsal, his fears rose. The songs, mainly written by Harry and Marty Da Costa, were light, pop confections—not unlike "Little Silver Raindrops". Gone was the blues-based rhythm of Luke's playing.

"Could you lower the key?" Marty asked, every time they tried a new tune. "Julie, your voice is a little *high*."

"It's gonna be great," Harry enthused, taking a bite of a giant pastrami sandwich. The smell of mustard filled the room.

Luke played one of his compositions, sang the lead with Julie on harmony. The Da Costas listened, politely, then Marty turned to his brother, "Might be good for the B side."

"B side," Harry repeated.

21

"Elliot Levine!"

The face came into focus: Warren Jaffee.

A truck rumbled down Broadway, leaving a trail of black exhaust. Elliot's mood sank, if possible, a notch lower. Had he caught sight of the rival manager first, he would have ducked into Chock Full 'O Nuts for a couple of whole-wheat donuts and a coffee, and avoided the inevitable airing of his troubles.

They exchanged bullshit.

"So how's the lovely and talented Liz Gainsborough?"

"She's amazing," Jaffee said, "But I'm not managing talent anymore. Nah, decided to take the leap to the *real* money. Over at Taylor Pine."

Elliot was familiar with the huge, bi-coastal talent agency.

"...just an Associate for now, but I took Jill with me as my first client, and between her and The Generations—their single's on the charts, you know—I'll be a full agent soon. So, how's it going?"

Elliot couldn't help but reflect on the peculiar stroke of luck that had allowed Warren Jaffee to flourish, while *he* was struggling to stay alive. He raised his voice to be heard over the collective din that was mid-day Manhattan. "A little slow." He lacked the energy to lie.

"Heard you had some problems at BigWheel." Jaffee blew his nose into a sodden handkerchief. "Join the club."

"You, too?"

"Yeah, Fish screwed me out of a deal coupla years back. Took it as a learning experience."

Elliot fingered the bridge of his nose, where a small bone hadn't healed correctly. It didn't hurt anymore, but when he nudged it, which he did often, the cartilage shifted.

Jaffee shook a Marlboro out of his cigarette box and offered one to Elliot, who declined. He shielded the match from the wind. "You ever think of going the agency route, give me a call. 'Course, you gotta start at the bottom."

Elliot's first instinct was to tell Warren Jaffee to cram his cigarette and his job offer, and to start at the bottom, but then he remembered Arlene, four months pregnant, and how she was paying the rent. Well, her father was. He should shove his *own* pride. It was time he stopped feeling sorry for himself, as Arlene had pointed out, more than once.

"I'll give it some thought."

"Here." Jaffee wrote down the name of the head of personnel on the back of a business card. "They'd like someone like you. You got a good eye for talent, you work hard."

Elliot wondered why this person he hardly knew was doing him a favor. As though hearing his doubts, Jaffee said, "Us Fish bait gotta stick together!"

The next morning, Elliot called the number on the card.

22

The air conditioning in Studio A was a wintry breeze. The musicians all seemed to know one another, and joked among themselves. The engineer, who had a concave chest and a stringy beard, hooked up the amplifiers, set out microphones. Luke stayed in a corner, noodling on his guitar. He'd wanted to pick the musicians himself but the Da Costas insisted they knew the best studio men.

"Who *are* these guys?" Julie whispered. "They look…kind of *old*." Maybe they'd started out to be stars and hadn't made it and here they were, playing on somebody else's record. She later learned that the studio musicians earned a ton of money and played with the best people in the business.

The skinny engineer directed them to stand in front of a dangling microphone, encased in foam rubber.

"So you won't pop your consonants," the engineer explained. She was certain there was a condescending tone in his voice. Despite the room's icebox temperature, sweat trickled down under her arms.

The Da Costas were stationed behind the glass in the control room. They said don't worry about mistakes. Anything you messed up while taping could be 'fixed in the mix'. She wasn't sure if they were joking.

When the week was over, they'd recorded twelve songs.

"Five fucking days, that's it?" Luke railed, striding down Broadway, with Julie running to keep up. "Do you know how rich this company is, and all they can give us is five days with the Disgustas and a bunch of hacks?"

"They weren't so bad."

"I could play rings around that other guitar player but would they let me even put down a rhythm track?"

"I guess it's just the way they do things—"

"—next record, I'm gonna have some goddamn *control*."

"I thought we sounded *good*!"

He turned, contrite. "No, it's not us, you were great, it's, I don't know, it's just not right or something."

"You expect everything to be perfect."

The Da Costas didn't want them around for the mix, insisting that it was just drudgework the artists didn't need to bother with.

Ray suggested they get away for a few days, and offered one of his cars. They packed a few things in Luke's duffel bag and picked up the car at the garage under Ray's Fifth Avenue apartment building. Luke's mood was instantly transformed.

It didn't matter that it was an obvious bribe to get them the hell away from the studio.

"Jesus Christ, a '56 XK140!" The car was a deep forest green convertible, the seats tan, soft leather. They peeled out and headed for the East Side Drive, Luke's foot flooring the accelerator, on their way to Cape Cod.

"Can you believe this car?" Luke yelled over the wind. "I've dreamed about driving one of these babies for years. There was a colonel in Germany who had one when we were over there. He got it in England and took it on the ferry across the Channel, through France and into Germany. It was silver, the most beautiful thing you've ever seen. I thought that if I could have one of those, I'd never want anything else." He glanced at her. "Except the most gorgeous girl in the world to go with it."

"I'm not even going to ask which of us takes first place. You know, I can drive, too," she said.

"You'll have to pry this steering wheel out of my cold, dead hands."

The highway ended at Providence, with a complicated detour that left them hopelessly lost. They stopped at a diner for burgers and fries, and plotted the rest of the journey, which would take them up the slow road along Cape Cod. The diner was an old railroad dining car, with a small jukebox mounted on the wall in each booth. They sat overlooking the parking lot, to keep an eye on the car.

"Just think," she mused, flipping through the jukebox selections, "This may be the last time we can go out in public anonymously. Soon, we'll be recognized as those famous singing stars." She dropped in a quarter and selected three songs. "Satisfaction" began to play. It still didn't seem quite real that it would be *their* record on the jukebox. "We'll have to go around in disguise. I think I'll buy a short platinum blonde wig and big dark sunglasses. And one of those Russian head scarves."

"No one will notice you like that."

"Ray says the record will be out in maybe two months. I think your song should be the single, don't you?" Luke had written the music and lyrics, but Ray Fish was somehow on the copyright as a co-writer/arranger. Ray explained that it always worked that way, sharing the credits with the record company's publisher.

"The Disgustas want one of theirs, but I think Ray will go with mine."

Since it was midweek, they were able to find a room in busy, summer-tourist Provincetown, in a small hotel that overlooked the bay. They ate cold shrimp, and lobster dripping with butter, homemade biscuits, with a French white wine. Luke pretended he knew about wines, sniffing the cork with a great flourish.

They drove a few miles to the tip of the peninsula, where fog had settled over the high white dunes. The sand, at dusk, was still warm, its top layer crisp beneath their bare feet.

"Let's have a house overlooking the sea," she said. "If I could always hear the ocean, I think I'd always be happy."

Later that night, the water in the bay lapped impatiently against the dock. She wouldn't let him leave the light on but the moon outlined their bodies as they made love.

23

The legendary Taylor Pine Agency was crowded into the four upper floors—and basement—of an older, sixteen story building just off Sixth Avenue, dwarfed by the new CBS 'Black Rock'. Elliot was acutely aware that it was just two blocks north of BigWheel Records.

The twelfth floor contained the theatrical departments: agents representing actors, directors and writers. The next floor up—fourteen (there was no thirteen)—was the music section, with clients ranging from classical conductors to pop acts to the latest rock stars. Live nightclub bookings were also handled there. Above that was for film agents who flacked for big stars, directors and producers. The top floor was the executive suite, a rarefied, hushed environment—especially compared to the constant phones and chatter of the lower divisions.

On the three main floors, past the reception desk, small offices were lined up along four right-angled corridors, with the secretaries at desks outside the offices. In each office there was an intense and often raspy-voiced man. The outer desks were manned—womanned, really—by young, attractive secretaries.

Like every other ambitious agent in the Taylor Pine 'family', Elliot was first put to work in the basement mailroom, an integral part of the company's training program.

He sorted letters and memos, wheeled a cart through the upstairs hallways delivering to the various offices on the multi-tiered agency, picked up outgoing and incoming and inter-office mail, and acted as an on-call messenger.

When an envelope needed to travel across town, Elliot or one of the other mail 'boys' donned coat, gloves, scarves, and set out into the elements, usually traveling by subway or bus. He enjoyed getting outside in the middle of the day, a brisk relief after the closed windowless room in which paper, endless paper, came and went. He'd stop for a hot dog at the corner Sabrett's, or a slice of pizza if his route took him past a favorite place.

He took advantage of the times he was alone in the mail room, covertly reading through inter-office correspondence and internal memos. He quickly educated himself as to who had the power—and who didn't—and all the little squabbles and rivalries. Which clients were on the verge of departing.

Who was about to be signed. Who'd been dumped. On his rounds, he'd stop and chat with the men in the music-booking department, and in A&R, dropping an opinion now and then, careful to keep it casual. He didn't want them to think he was after their job. Which he was.

Passing an open office door, he overheard a snippet of conversation between Lew Frank, a V.P. who booked pop music acts, and the head of personnel.

"He's an idiot!" Lew was screaming—his usual mode of conversation. "Get me someone with half a brain!"

Elliot paused in the doorway as Lew slammed down the receiver. He noticed that the assistant's desk was empty, and the secretary was typing away, oblivious. He knew Lew's assistant, casually: a slight, passive young man who would probably be better off working in an accounting office.

"Mail."

Lew didn't look up. "Leave it on my desk."

From his many perusals of the 'secret' memos, he was aware that Lew was considered a bit of an over-the-hill hack. His wife was the sister of one of the company's richest board members. His assistants didn't last long. If they were stupid, they took the fall for Lew's screw-ups; if they were clever, they moved on fast.

Framed gold records lined the walls: Lew's clients. One was a record by Katey Lacey, a pop balladeer of the 1950s Elliot long admired. She had recorded for BigWheel Records until her career went into decline. He knew that Lew Frank had personally produced the album.

"Fine singer, Katey Lacey," Elliot offered.

Lew's expression softened. "You said it."

"I always thought her collaborations with Martin Goldenson were her best." The orchestrator had worked with some of the finest singers of that era.

Lew looked up. "What's your name, mailboy?"

"Elliot Levine." He almost added "sir."

"You got taste in music."

Elliot moved on to the next office and cubicle.

A few weeks later, he got a call from personnel. Lew Frank was looking for a new assistant and would Elliot like to apply? It was more a formality. Lew had already determined that Elliot was a *mensch*.

His relatively swift journey from the basement to the fourteenth floor was a source of some kidding—and envy—among his mailroom colleagues.

Tough shit, he thought, as he accepted their false good wishes.

Elliot arrived at work by eight every morning, at least an hour before the secretaries and most of the agents. He'd pass the empty receptionist's desk, carrying his scalding cardboard container of coffee, and occasionally pausing to look at the grainy 1905 photo of the founders, Arthur Taylor and Matthew Pine (born Artur Tymenowicz and Moishe Pinevski), standing in front of their original, modest Tin Pan Alley headquarters.

He was given his own cubicle, slightly larger than the secretary's, just outside Lew Frank's corner office. If Lew had his door fully open, Elliot got a glimpse of the window, which looked out at the tip of Central Park South. Lew generally kept his office door closed, because of complaints from the secretaries who objected to the permeating odor of his ever-present cigar.

Lew talked on the phone all day long, yelling at talent, managers, other agents, publicists, Elliot, and their harried secretary, Barbara Corigliano, a quiet, large-breasted, unnatural redhead who wore tight skirts, spike heels and a stiff pageboy. Lew's voice bellowed out into the corridor, mingling with the barks and blusters, whines and cajoles of a dozen or so other agents on the floor.

Lew had three "celebrity" clients: a long-popular male crooner with a blue-haired following, whose albums and singles still made their way onto the charts; a society bandleader who had hosted his own television variety show for three and a half seasons; and, of course, Katey Lacey, the singer who had become more renowned for her alleged mob connections, affairs and many marriages than for her hits, which had pretty much dried up by the late 1950s. Nevertheless, she prospered on highly paid engagements in Las Vegas and big name nightclubs as well as the occasional TV variety show, recycling her old hits into fragmented medleys that earned bursts of worshipful applause with each familiar opening phrase.

Katey was Elliot's favorite client, always good-humored and bearing gifts when she stopped at the office. Her hair was pulled back severely into her trademark platinum pony-tail, even now that she was too old for it, and her bloodlessly pale skin had a doll-like smoothness. She had a fondness for fine chocolates and generously distributed them among the office staff, along with the blue jokes she couldn't tell in her act.

She leaned down to whisper into Elliot's ear. "Do me a favor, sweetheart, would you personally check over my contract with the Coconut Grove? Last time, Lew messed up my dates so bad, he had me doing a local TV show in Chicago while I was supposed to be onstage in L.A. Thanks, kid." She pecked his cheek, leaving a smudge of crimson lipstick and a trace of her perfume, old-fashioned and flowery.

He blushed, from the combination of Katey's scent and the proximity to a real star. He had grown up listening to her records, seeing her on television.

"Oh, and, could you do me another favor, honey—I don't know what I ever did without you, Elliot—the guy before you was a pinhead, I mean really, he had this little pointy head sitting on this triangular body, he always put me in mind of those road markers, what do you call them? Gnome hats! I need to find a couple of my early LPs on BigWheel, you know I was there before I signed with Columbia, and Lew doesn't have any copies, and he couldn't locate his dick with a compass, so if you can spare a moment."

Lew's voice seeped from behind his office door. "You think we're gonna pick up the tab for the transportation? What am I, a goddamn travel agency?!" Lew's door opened.

"Katey!" he roared. "Gorgeous as ever!" He turned to Elliot. "Listen, this gal needs to go to an opening at the Copa tonight, I want her out and about. You take her, okay?" He went back into his office, slammed the door.

"Well," she said, smiling, "I hope you don't mind."

"No, I...no...sure."

As soon as Katey left, in a flurry of air kisses to the staff, he dialed home and explained to Arlene that he had to work late.

The headliner at the Copa was Bobby Vinton, but the real show was in the audience before the lights went down. Elliot recognized Joey Bishop, whose sitcom had ended the season before with a fizzle, but had helped launch Danny Thomas' daughter, Marlo, in a new show. Joey was sitting with Leslie Neilson, late of *Peyton Place*. A few booths away, Ed McMahon and Paul Anka chatted with two bejeweled women. The agents and managers and record company execs, and their lawyers and stockbrokers, oozed from table to table before the lights went down.

Elliot was, if not completely overwhelmed, then at least whelmed. This was his first official social event as an agency rep, and he could not afford to blow it.

Katey held court gushing over the industry reps that stopped by pay homage (and who would inevitably comment, once out of her earshot, that she looked old.)

"Go on," she encouraged Elliot, "Make the schmooze rounds." She raised her hand to the waiter for another martini, her third since they'd arrived. As he left the table, he was distressed to see that an agent from William Morris quickly took his place, kissed Katey's hand and gave her a business card. She might not be the recording star she once was, but she was a consistent moneymaker, and a "prestige" client.

Christ, that was all he needed, to lose her to another agency.

He shook hands with a couple of producers he'd met before. They perked up when he name-dropped The Taylor

Pine Agency and handed over his new business cards. His next stop was the desk of the maître d'.

"Where can I get some flowers?" he asked. "Fast. For the lady I'm with. Miss Lacey."

"We can arrange it." The man waited until Elliot dug the right amount of money from his pocket, then he picked up his phone and set the floral wheels in motion. Elliot experienced a flush of power. Especially since he knew he'd charge the expense to Taylor Pine. Ray Ray Ray, he thought, with a thrill of imminent triumph. Fuck you, Ray.

He returned to Katey as the lights began to dim, and the Copa Girls came dancing out, the orchestra began the strains of "Blue Velvet", and the star appeared, flanked by two slinky female backup singers. The flowers—along with a complimentary bottle of Moët—arrived between "Roses are Red" and "Mr. Lonely". Katey squeezed Elliot's hand and kissed his cheek.

After the show, she insisted on going backstage. They made the labyrinthine journey through the kitchen; Katey knew the back route well, having played the Copa countless times. Elliot thought of the famous people who appeared here, negotiating the aisles between stainless steel tables and stoves where food was prepared by what looked like illegals, where steam rose from enormous vats and the overhead basement pipes creaked. Katey stopped to introduce him to the diminutive, gargoyle-faced club manager, Jules Podell, whose cursory greeting was squeezed out in a strangled growl. A back elevator took them up several floors to the dressing rooms.

Bobby Vinton wore tan suede slacks and a matching shirt with pearl buttons. His feet, in hand-tooled, pale beige,

Western boots, were propped on the makeup table in his room. He had remarkably blue eyes and seemed pleased to see Katey, who was downing another drink.

The dressing room suite swarmed with well-wishers, hangers-on, fans, musicians, the star's manager and his entourage, the chick backup singers, waiters bringing trays of hors d'oeuvres and drinks.

"Bobby, darling! You were so incredible!" Katey gushed. "This is Elliot, my *agent*!"

He was about to correct her—Lew Frank wouldn't be at all pleased to learn he'd been usurped—but Vinton was shaking Elliot's hand.

"Great to see you, Katey," Vinton said, glancing past her. "I opened for her back before my first record broke," he told Elliot.

"And I just *knew* he'd be a star!"

Bobby rose from his chair and went into the hallway to greet fans, pausing to air kiss Katey's cheek. "Still gorgeous, as always." He was gone. Katey looked after him, as if she didn't know what to do next.

"Why don't we head out?" Elliot suggested tactfully. She was unsteady on her feet.

"Jus' a little longer. Those guys at William Morris want me, you know. They said they could get me a lot more in Vegas than Lew's been getting. And a Broadway show."

Elliot was unsure how to handle this. "Maybe you're right. After all, they have a *lot* of top singers. You'd fit right into the crowd."

"Crowd?"

"Sure, honey. Those guys would love to sign you up, add you to their trophy collection."

"You think so?"

Elliot nudged her in the direction of the elevator.

"Wait! My beautiful flowers!"

He went back and retrieved them, balancing the arrangement in one arm, Katey on the other. Katey's limo pulled up in front of the awning. A light autumn rain was falling, the air almost balmy. Katey hummed "Roses are Red."

"I love married men," she said, sidling up to Elliot, "Especially Jewish married men. They're so…conflicted."

Although Katey's main residence was in L.A., she kept a pied a terre on East 63rd St., just off Lexington Avenue. In the backseat of the limo, Katey leaned her head against Elliot's shoulder, while he sat stiffly in place, unsure what to do with his hands. At her building, the doorman held an umbrella over Katey's head.

The comfortable one-bedroom was furnished in flowered chintz and a thick wall to wall carpet that looked like an immense dead white Angora cat. He declined her offer of a drink.

"Look!" She held up a record album. On the cover was a photograph of a young Katey Lacey, draped on a gold chaise longue, clad in a clingy black velvet gown. Her champagne hair fell over one cheek in a Veronica Lake pageboy. One high-heeled black satin shoe was poised at the end of her toe, the other rested on the floor. *Black Satin Lacey* was the name of the album.

"My only copy," she said. "When it came out, I stupidly gave them away like spare change, and now they're out of print and I don't have any more left."

"How come you left BigWheel?"

"Between you and me, there was somebody at the company, he thought he could run my *life*. He was young and hungry, on his way up, you know…wanted to, control everything. Everything. Kinky son of a bitch." Her eyes were heavy lidded.

"Ray Fish," he said. "We've crossed paths."

"Lucky you," she said dryly. "But I better shut up, he could be your best friend." She put the record on the turntable.

"He's no friend of mine."

"New York was so wonderful then, you probably don't remember. It was the Stork Club and El Morocco, and everyone dressed beautifully. One of my beaus bought me a sailboat."

"But Ray Fish?" he prompted.

"...was like gum stuck to the bottom of my shoe. When I tried to scrape him off, all of a sudden, my recording dates are postponed, no one's available, songs're going to other singers...so I called in some favors. Sort of."

"Sort of?"

"Nothing's for free, Elliot. Don't ever forget that. I got out of my contract but I never saw a penny on those albums. Or the singles. Somehow, the royalties never came my way." She laughed bitterly. "'Course, Ray's got himself in so many pockets, who knows how much he actually makes from little ole BigWheel. Well, one day, somebody's going to bring him down. When the time is right. Oh boy, what I could tell you... but now I really should shut up or I could get in trouble, and we don't want that, do we?"

Elliot refilled her glass and she drank it down gratefully.

"Whatever is said here, stays here," he assured her.

"My records *sold*, believe me. You couldn't turn on WNEW in 1955 without hearing 'My Letter to You'. Until that bastard tried to ruin everything. He didn't, but only because I had some *very important friends*, if you catch my drift."

Elliot nodded. He'd opened a floodgate and the nasty details were just pouring out. How lucky was this?

"He was into a lotta debt from hitting the blackjack tables too often—or was it roulette?—so he had to give up a piece of BigWheel—to Gary Luna! I loved that. Served him right. Remember Payola? They sold Alan Freed down the river? It's still going on, they just got more careful. Gary Luna likes to be around 'artistes', thinks he knows about music. He likes to fuck to my records." She burst out laughing. "I guess I'm shocking this nice Jewish boy."

"Hardly," he said, trying not to blush. *Gary Luna?* The mobster?

She stood in the center of the room, as if there were a spotlight, and began to sing in a voice rich and smooth, even through the alcohol.

> *"These are the words I couldn't say:*
> *When I'm in your arms, I'm swept away*
> *So I'm taking all the lovely things you do*
> *And putting them in my letter to you"*

He was mesmerized. She was a boyhood fantasy come to life.

> *"But words can't take the place of your smile*
> *The poets couldn't match your style...*
> *I'm taking a chance on dreams come true*
> *And keeping them in my letter, darling...*
> *Keeping them in...my letter to you..."*

Her eyes were closed and she swayed to a lush, imaginary accompaniment.

"I never thought I'd be 'old-fashioned' or 'out of style'," she said. "*I* was a rebel, you know, my mother couldn't keep me in the house at night. I had to do everything new that came along, see every new movie, try every new dance. And now there's all this music I don't understand and I'm not even *old*! Okay, I'm forty-two."

More like fifty-two, he thought, not unkindly.

"I guess that's old to you. I don't *feel* old. Most of the time, I feel like seventeen, right? Oh, shit, *you're* just a kid, what do you know?"

He cleared his throat, put a hand over hers, awkwardly. "But you have everything. Talent. Fame. Success. Beauty." He could kiss her, what would be the harm in that?

She gave a brittle laugh. "It's over, don't you think I know that? Money! Who cares? What happened? Doesn't anyone like a pretty melody anymore?" Tears ran down her face. "Why won't any of those fuckers get me a contract now? Gary Luna's richer than God and he knows *every*one."

"You should lie down for a while." He guided her into the bedroom. She let her high heels fall on the rug. Elliot pulled up the white throw that was folded at the end of the bed, and draped it over her.

"You're a nice guy, Elliot honey, I'm just gonna take a little rest and then we'll have some…"

She was out cold.

Elliot placed his hat on his head and went out the door, closing it carefully behind him.

24

The sky outside Ray's office window was a brilliant blue and the sun illuminated a bar of dust motes in the air.

Luke lit a cigarette. "Why haven't we seen an album cover? They took those pictures of us months ago. What's going on?"

"Take it easy, Luke," Ray assured. "Coffee?"

"Fine."

"I'll get right to the point." Ray sipped from his tiny espresso cup. "You know I'm not one to bullshit around. There are a few changes we want to make. Not that the record isn't good, but we're talking marketability. You know we love you both, you're both really fine talents with big futures but we have a few problems with the album as a whole."

The cup in Julie's hands became unusually heavy.

Ray continued, "I take the blame for not seeing this in the original demos, but I thought we could overcome some of the problems when we got into the studio with a band. I thought we could fix it in the mix." Looking at Julie, he said, "I'll tell you straight: We just don't like your sound all that much, honey."

The room compressed into a small box far away. "What?" she heard herself say.

"Now hold on!" Luke stood up. "Julie's voice is—"

"No, no, no," Ray interrupted, and then, more gently, "I don't mean we don't like her *voice*, we're talking about a commercial *sound*. It's the two of you together, well, there's something missing." He was addressing Luke, as if Julie had vanished. "We listened back to your takes singing alone, Luke, and it was obvious you should be fronting your own band. Julie's sound—how can I put this—waters you down. You got that tough, angry edge to your voice and you play guitar like a demon. What can I say?"

"I don't fucking believe this," Luke said. "What about our record?"

"We signed a contract," Julie said.

"As far as the contract goes, we're not obliged to *release* the product. You can check with your lawyers—"

There had been no lawyers; they had been so anxious to sign.

"But, don't worry, honey, we want to cut a single for you, something really commercial. Send you right to the top of the pop charts. I spoke to the Da Costas and they're looking for just the right song, we're thinking a Leslie Gore kind of number." He smiled, "Hey, guys, look at it this way: You'll be getting two records, two big careers. We *love* you guys, we want big futures for both of you." Ray glanced at his Rolex.

Julie tried to bring the room into focus. "So, our record won't be coming out? Ever?"

Luke knew he should be doing something, saying something, but couldn't think of the words. It wasn't like it was his fault. Why did it feel that way? He stood abruptly and crossed to the door. "Come on, Jul." To Ray, he muttered, "We'll get back to you."

"It's for the best, you'll see. Oh, and Merry Christmas." He handed them each an envelope.

"They can't do it, I just won't go along with it," Luke raged. "Can you believe that sonofabitch? Who the hell does he think he is?" In Central Park, they sat on a cold bench. Their breath puffed out in the air. Children in snowsuit cocoons played near the frozen lake.

The foggy sensation that had stolen over her in the office still lingered, and she was locked up inside it. A chestnut vendor pushed his metal cart and the scent cast her memory back to a cold city street. She was a small child in a snowsuit, and someone was leaning over her. It must have been her father, whose voice she could not recall, but he had graceful hands, and he showed her how to peel the chestnut. She had seen him so seldom that she did not know what to call him: "Daddy" stuck in her throat. "Father" was all wrong. So she never addressed him by any name. Funny that she would think of that now. She never thought about her father.

"That bastard Fish, who the *fuck* does he think he is? Merry fucking Christmas."

…your father died, her mother told her one morning. She was nine, and by then, she had never expected him to come back anyway; there was nothing but a small sinking, like the feeling in your stomach when an elevator stops an inch below floor level.

She opened the envelope Ray had given her. A Christmas card signed with the imprint of BigWheel Records, and a check for two hundred dollars.

"Wow. Now I'm rich."

"If Peter, Paul and Mary came in, would he have them all start solo careers? Asshole." Luke saw himself in Ray Fish's office. He'd say fuck you, and Ray would say, no, Luke, we need you, on any terms, please please stay. Yeah, right. Well, so what, there were other record companies.

"I can always go back to Georgia if that's what it comes down to. Who needs this shit?" He said it so loudly, several children and their parents turned around.

She started walking, quickly, down the path, away from him. He jumped up and ran after her. "Julie? What?"

"Nothing, just go away, alright?"

"Don't let that asshole get to you. Tomorrow, I'm going to march right in there, and tell him where he can stick it."

She stopped. "You are?"

He hesitated, then with more vehemence, "Yes, I am, that's exactly what I'm gonna do!"

She didn't say anything.

"Why? You wouldn't do it for me?"

A few seconds went by. "Probably not," she admitted.

"Maybe I love you more," he insisted.

"Maybe you're perfect. *I'm* sure as hell not perfect."

"This isn't about anybody being perfect, this is about doing what's right—for both of us."

"Oh, please!" She was working herself up again. "In fact, maybe you should just hang yourself on a cross and hammer in the nails!"

"I didn't want it this way!" He grabbed her coat-sleeve. "You think this is what I wanted?"

"Like this is something really bad happening to *you*. Really, it must be so *tough* hearing how brilliant you are, yeah, that must really hurt a lot, you're so full of shit you're gonna give it all up!"

Luke was silent for a while. "Look, Jul, it's not a matter of giving it *up*. It's a matter of playing their game. So I make a record first, what's the big deal, long as we get there, right?"

The medallion Luke had given her pressed against her chest like a weight. "You *are* going to take their offer."

"It just seems like, well, you don't want to make enemies in this business, I mean, we don't have any power, but once we *get* it, then we can call the shots. Right?"

"You son of a bitch!" She struck out wildly, her fist hitting his shoulder, and glancing off his neck. Startled, he backed off, hands up like he was being arrested.

"Look, it's not like I started all this or caused it to happen, you don't have to fucking *blame* me, or look at me like that, like I'm...I don't know what." He swiped an icy bare hand over his face. "You say you love me? You wouldn't ask me to make some kind of impossible choice...it's not my fucking *fault!*"

She ripped the chain from around her neck and hurled it as hard as she could into the icy lake. The medallion sank into the water. Her feet pounded the pathway, her breath puffed in front of her face as she ran.

"Jesus, don't go, Julie, please, you're always leaving me, you can't keep running out!" His feet felt stuck to the cement. "It's not my fault!"

She ran down the subway steps and boarded the first train that pulled in. It didn't matter where she went, as long as she was moving. The train took her uptown, to the Bronx, a borough of disorienting unfamiliarity. The sliding doors nearly caught her purse as she jumped out of the train and crossed to the opposite platform. Riding downtown again, she was breathing high and fast at the thought of having nearly been dragged by the subway train. She got off at Christopher Street.

There was a payphone booth on the corner, an old one that looked like an upright coffin. The corrugated inside walls were scratched, as if someone, buried alive, had tried to escape. She called information for the Taylor Pine number.

"Elliot Levine, please," she said. The person on the other end asked her name and she heard herself giving it. A moment later, he came on the phone.

"Julie?"

The ice was closing fast around her heart, and freezing her vocal chords.

"Julie? Is something the matter?"

He sounded as if he cared, but why would he after all they'd done to him? She had never even called him to say goodbye when they broke the contract. The ground seemed to be dropping away. She couldn't breathe.

"Listen to me," Elliot was saying, "If something's happened, we can talk about it. Tell me where you are and I can be there. Is it something about BigWheel?"

"Ray Fish," she whispered.

"What did that bastard do now? I know, I've been there, don't self-destruct, Julie, that's what they want you to do, just hang on, do you understand? Tell me where you are." He paused and when she didn't reply, he continued, "Whatever's wrong, don't take it out on yourself, okay? I could help you now, I'm in a much better position—"

"Thank you, Elliot." She hung up and immediately dropped in another dime, dialed.

"Ray Fish's office."

"This is Julie Bradley. Could you leave a message for Mr. Fish? Tell him: Go fuck yourself."

There was a pause. "Is that the entire message?"

"That's all."

Laughing, she pounded the inside of the phone booth until her hands were bruised but she couldn't feel a thing.

25

"I thought I'd stay a little late and listen to some new tapes that came in," Rochelle told Ray on the phone. He was four floors above her.

"You don't have to listen to that unsolicited junk, that's not your job."

"I just like to." Her desk was piled high with papers that needed filing, letters to type.

"We're going to the Copa."

"That's later."

"We're meeting Spider and his date for drinks first."

"Spider?" She couldn't forget the night they had been in a Village bar and a drunk got nasty with Ray, and before Rochelle could even blink, the drunk was on the floor, with Spider's foot slamming into his kidneys. Then Spider picked the guy up and slung him out the door. Rochelle heard a sickening crunch as the body hit the sidewalk, but nobody did anything. They got into their limo and headed uptown. The next day she looked in the paper to see if the guy had been found dead, but there was nothing.

"What time?" she sighed.

"Seven."

If she stuck around, she wouldn't have much time to get glamorous, the way Ray liked her to look. "Okay, I guess I can listen to this stuff tomorrow night."

"If there's one thing you can count on in this business, it's that every day brings in another hundred pieces of shit. The car's downstairs, I'll drop you off at home, I got an appointment."

"I have a few more things to do, I'll get a cab. Who're we seeing, by the way? At the Copa."

"Katey Lacey."

"*She's* still around?"

"Some of us old timers refuse to fade away."

She put down the phone, smiling.

Joe Gallin came out of his office. "'Night, Rochelle."

"Night, Mr. Gallin." Her boss always left at five exactly. That was why he'd never be anything, Ray had remarked on more than one occasion. Yet when *she* wanted to put in more hours, he teased her: she didn't have to work at all, he said. She could spend the day in the beauty parlor or shopping.

Except that she liked seeing her name on a paycheck each week, even if the paycheck didn't even come close to Ray's daily spending money. She wanted to be more than Ray Fish's girlfriend. Rochelle Klein Productions had a nice sound to it.

She picked up a stack of tapes and brought them into A&R. They let her use the equipment after hours to screen the "slush pile" of demos. The first tape turned out to be a truly awful band that sounded like it had been recorded in a bathroom. She dropped it in the trash, looped the next one into the recorder. Not much better. And so it went until she realized her office phone was ringing, and she dashed down the hall to pick it up.

Ray was calling from a bar. She could hear the muted sounds in the background, and guessed he'd stopped at the Polo Lounge.

"Honey, could you do me a favor? There's a manila envelope in my office I meant to bring home. Could you stop by and pick it up? It's in the desk, top right drawer."

"Sure."

"You better hustle if we're going to make it to the show tonight. And, hey, your friend freaked out."

"Who?"

"That singer. Julie. Left me quite the message."

"Is she okay?"

"How should I know? But good riddance, I don't need any nutcases."

There was no answer at Julie's apartment. Rochelle gathered up her coat and purse, and caught the elevator to Ray's floor. A cleaning woman was pushing her cart through the hallway.

Ray's desk was perfectly organized: the leather bound blotter, the antique marble inkstand and paperweight. Inside the right drawer she found the envelope just as he'd said. Doubly sealed, taped all around the top. She couldn't resist feeling what was inside. It was soft. So it wasn't a tape or record. Like cloth. No, crisper. Money. Yes, it felt like bills.

The night of the Blackout, Ray crouching beneath the desk, taking something out of a hiding place.

What would it hurt to look?

She went to the office door, checked the hallway. Empty. Closed the door and locked it.

Okay, be logical: he had taken something *out of the floor* that night. But the floor was carpeted. She got down on her knees, feeling more than a little silly, and groped around for bumps or seams. Nothing.

Stumped, she sat back on her heels. Then, she saw it: the thinnest of lines in the wood on the inside of the desk, almost perfectly flush to the grain—but not quite. She slipped a long manicured fingernail in between, and felt a tiny space. Her nail chipped. Shit.

Pushing didn't open it further. Nor did pulling. One more try. She pressed sideways. It slid open.

There was a small, gray safe behind the hidden wooden cabinet, with a key lock. Where there was a lock, there had to be a key, but he wouldn't go to so much trouble to hide a safe, and leave the key lying around. Her instinct told her she'd find the key on his personal key ring, the one he always carried.

She put everything back as it was. With the envelope tucked under her arm, she opened the office door and locked it behind her.

Spider Allessi was leaning over the water fountain just down the hall.

Taking a deep breath, she walked in the opposite direction.

"Rochelle!"

She froze.

"See ya later, right?"

"Yeah."

Back at the apartment, she tried Julie's number again but it just rang. She undressed carelessly, letting the clothes fall in a trail on the way into her dressing room. Ray had had the whole place redecorated for her after she moved in, with mirrored glass, a sumptuous closet the size of a small bedroom, an antique vanity table. He introduced her to Pratesi bed linens from Italy. One set of sheets cost more than a month's rent on her parents' apartment in Queens. She was of two minds about the money: she loved spending it without worry, enjoyed the things it bought. But there was a subliminal nagging voice reminding her that people were starving in other parts of the world. She was learning, without a great deal of effort, to turn that voice off.

Rochelle rummaged through her jewelry box, looking for just the right earrings, a pair of pearl and silver drop clip-ons that would set off the silver lamé mini-dress. The earrings weren't there.

"Damn!" She tried Ray's dresser, remembering that the regular maid had been gone and the temporary girl, who was sweet but spoke only Haitian-accented French, put things away in the strangest places: dishes in the cabinet with the pots and pans; socks in the linen drawer. Sure enough, her earrings were in the top drawer, in the marble dish where Ray put his watch and rings at night. Next to the dish was a thick stack of credit cards, wrapped in a wide rubber band.

Ray always carried his credit cards with him, and besides, he didn't have this many. She picked them up. The one on top was American Express, Arnold P. Grayson. Exp date: 11/67. Still good. Who the hell was Arnold P. Grayson? She slipped off the rubber band and looked at the next one. Diners Club. Mitchell Landau.

"What are you doing?"

She jumped, her heart knocking against her chest. "Jesus, Ray, don't do that."

"What are you doing?" he repeated.

"I...I was looking for my earrings. That stupid maid put them in with your stuff. What are all these cards?"

"Nothing for you to worry about."

"Why do you have them?"

"I'm really not in the mood for a fucking interrogation, Rochelle." He took off his jacket and flung it on the bed, pulled a white silk shirt from his closet. She was struggling with the back of her dress. He came over to help, his fingers icy on her back.

"Ooh, cold." She wriggled, then felt his warm lips in the middle of her back.

"I didn't know I was living with Nancy Drew." He reached around for her breasts.

"Ray, I thought we were in a hurry."

"We are." He kept kissing her back, up to the nape of her neck. "Hold that thought. I want you to wait, I want you to think about it." There was a steely edge to his voice.

With sudden force, he spun her around and slapped her face hard, twice, then shoved her; she lost her balance and fell against the bed, slipped to the floor. A numb shock drained her sense of reality. She could not move. Her face stung, and tears sprung to her eyes.

"Get dressed," he snapped. "And stay the fuck out of my stuff." He left the room.

A moment later, the stereo was suddenly pumped up loud: "Goldfingah!" crowed Shirley Bassey. Rochelle got up, a little dizzy, and made her way into the bathroom. She slammed the door as hard as she could. The plaster trickled down somewhere behind the wall.

Spider pulled out his date's chair. "You know, she used to be a Copa Girl," he bragged.

The Copacabana's tiers of tables were filling up fast.

"I have go to the little girls," the date announced, looking at Rochelle expectantly.

Rochelle got up, the men leaped to their feet, the waiter pulled out her chair. She left her mink draped across the seat, and followed Spider's date to the powder room. What was her name? Dinah? Doreen? She'd forgotten it the instant they were introduced.

"Hey, Dierdre," one of the waiters called out, solving the mystery.

They used side-by-side stalls, emerged at the same time, and took seats at the dressing table. A silent attendant sat like an ebony statue next to a small table that offered toilette supplies.

"So how long have you known Ray?" Dierdre asked, leaning into the mirror with a pointy-tipped eyeliner brush, to redraw tiny Twiggy lines beneath her bottom lashes.

"Nearly two years." Her hand shook as she tried to apply makeup. An inner trembling had begun after Ray hit her, and it hadn't faded. There was a slight redness on her cheek, but she'd managed to cover it up. What she couldn't cover was the mixture of rage and grief and disorientation. While one part of her mind told her it was just a slap, no big deal, another screamed warnings she didn't want to hear.

"He seems nice," Dierdre was saying.

Rochelle teased the hair at the crown of her head. Eye drops had taken away the redness from crying. She forced herself to make conversation. "Have you been dating Spider long?"

"Couple weeks, that's all. He's a…funny guy."

"Funny ha-ha or funny weird?"

"Both, I guess. He thinks Ray Fish is God."

"So does Ray Fish."

Deirdre laughed. "Spider said he could help me get an agent. I'm an actress, you know."

"Uh-huh." Rochelle applied another layer of silver white lipstick. "We better get back, the show'll be starting."

"My mother always used to listen to Katey Lacey's records," Dierdre said. "I can't believe I'm gonna get to meet her."

Rochelle sucked in her cheeks and her abdomen as she made her way through the crowded tables. She held her head high, and was so preoccupied with not breaking down, she didn't see Elliot Levine until they were face to face.

"Rochelle," he said formally, putting out his hand. "Nice to see you again."

There was something different about Elliot. It wasn't just the Brooks Brothers suit and quiet paisley tie, but he conveyed a new confidence. She'd heard he was working at the Taylor Pine Agency. "How are *you*?"

"Getting by. Did you see Arlene?"

Arlene waved like she was hailing a cab.

"Come say hello." He led her to their table, in the center of the front tier, a coveted spot. Better than theirs. That would annoy Ray.

Arlene was wearing a bright coral satin pants suit with a high ruffled-neck blouse and long bell sleeves that draped over her hands, the overall effect like of a flock of limp flamingos. A large diamond ring sparkled on Arlene's left ring finger, nestled next to a gold and diamond encrusted wedding ring. Her nails were spectacularly long, painted pearl white.

"Roch*elle*!" squealed Arlene, hugging her. To the others at their table, she said, "This is my ex-roomie! We were *best friends* in high school! It's so good to see you, Rochelle!" Up close, Rochelle noted with some satisfaction that even heavy makeup, carefully applied, and expensive designer clothes could not transform the ferret-faced Arlene into a beauty. She draped a tapered hand over her husband's arm, possessively. "How *are* you, anyway?"

"I'm great, Arlene. I heard about you and Elliot. Congratulations."

"So when are you and *Ray* getting married?"

"Oh we prefer to keep our freedom."

"That's *so* independent of you. I wish *I* could be that way, but of course now we're *expecting*." Arlene said the last word in a hushed, confidential voice.

"You are? When are you due?"

"Three more long months. If I stood up, you'd see I'm a blimp. It's been *so* crazy lately, what with moving and all." Arlene squeezed Elliot's hand. "We're going to L.A.! Elliot's going to run the agency's west coast music department."

"Not the whole division, Rochelle," Elliot put in. "I'm developing new bands."

"That's wonderful. Well, I better get back to Ray before he sends out a posse."

Elliot kissed Rochelle on the cheek. He smelled pleasantly of an understated aftershave. "Give my regards to Ray," he said, deadpan.

Neither Ray nor Spider was at the table when she returned. She scanned the room, finally spotting them deep in conversation in a corner near the entrance. Ray was making sharp angry motions, one hand slapping the other, while Spider leaned against the wall, nodding, a hint of a smile on his colorless face. After a moment, the two men headed back across the room. Rochelle heard Spider say, sotto voce, "Take it easy, they've got air time sewn up...it's all over the radio."

"So what was all *that* about?" she asked Ray, lightly.

"Can't I get another fucking drink around here?" Ray waved at the waiter. "What was *what* all about?"

He turned on her, and she had a shiver of real fear. "I just missed you, that's all," she said.

"Business, honey."

"So how are you girls doin'?" Spider boomed. "Havin' fun?" He put his arm around Ray's shoulder, "I *love* this guy!"

"I'm kind of tired, sweetie, can't we go home?" she asked Ray after the show. Katey Lacey had been in good voice, even if her act was corny and mostly a compilation of ancient hits. She looked kind of frozen, her skin too smooth and pulled tight.

"Come on, babe, I told you we're going to this new club I got a piece of."

"Yeah, Rochelle, you don't want to miss this," Spider insisted. "It's a real head trip."

"I thought we were going to that disco, "Arthur"," Dierdre whined. "I want to meet Sybil Burton."

"Shut up," said Spider.

Rochelle leaned in to whisper to Ray. "We could go another night."

"It's a special invitation."

"Oh, okay, but I'm asleep on my feet."

"Here," he reached into his pocket, slipped a small vial into her hand. "I'll wait for you."

Dierdre happily followed her into the bathroom, and they shared the coke in a stall.

The limousine glided smoothly through a damp New York, glistening from rain that had fallen while they were indoors, downtown past the Village, into a neighborhood of abandoned storefronts, dark streets. Inside the limo, Spider poured champagne; Ray passed around a joint. The events of earlier that evening, Ray's dark expression, the hand flying toward her—all that began to take on an unreality. She *had* been snooping after all. So why was she still so angry? Everyone else was happy and there was something irresistible about riding in a limo with Ray to some glamorous, maybe dangerous adventure.

"Are you sure this is the place?" Dierdre asked, a little fearful.

They had pulled up in front of a plain, unlit doorway where the number 585 was barely visible in faded paint on the door. The chauffeur opened the door and helped the women out.

"Maybe we've time-traveled back to Prohibition," Rochelle remarked.

"Look, there's a camera up there!" Dierdre pointed. As their eyes adjusted to the dimness, Spider found the doorbell and pushed it. A disembodied voice came over a speaker.

"Elysium."

"Ray Fish and party."

A long rasping buzz. Spider pushed the door and it opened onto a staircase.

"Up one flight," instructed the voice. The intercom shut off with a hiss and a click.

"Jeez," Dierdre said as they climbed.

Upstairs, they found themselves in a perfectly ordinary foyer, like the entryway to a modest restaurant. A reservation desk to the left, a coatroom down the hall and to the right. Spider and Ray gave their names and they were shown to the coatroom. On one side were a few wraps, mostly fur stoles; on the opposite rack, a hanging row of white cloaks. The attendant handed them each a cloak. It was long, of an opaque gossamer material and had a hood. The men and the women received the same kind of gown, only in slightly different sizes.

"What, are we supposed to put this on?" Rochelle wanted to know.

"Only if you want to," said a woman's voice, "Clothing underneath it is optional, once you get into the Elysian Room."

They turned to see a beautiful young woman with long straight black hair that brushed her lower back. She had exquisite Eurasian features and wore one of the white gowns and nothing else. Her nude body was clearly silhouetted beneath; her feet were bare. "I'm Tanna, your escort," she told them. The men were wide-eyed. "You may want to check your valuables. And your shoes," she added, smiling.

Spider took off his jacket, revealing a shoulder holster and small gun under his armpit. He unstrapped it and handed it to the escort. "Be hard to smuggle this in, huh?" he said. Ray chuckled, and dumped out the contents of his pocket, a wad of bills and some change, a handful of credit cards.

Tanna handed the men the coat-check receipts and directed all four into a dressing area, with separate cubicles for the men and the women.

"You ain't gettin' me into no ladies nightgown," Rochelle heard Spider say.

"Ah, come on, if I can do it," Ray insisted.

Rochelle slid the caftan-thing over her head, and peeled her dress off underneath. After an instant's hesitation, she removed her underwear, too. Dierdre was less modest, taking off all her clothes and then donning the gown. Rochelle tried not to be obvious about looking at the other woman's body, but couldn't help but notice that Dierdre had the kind of taut, straight, goyishe thighs she'd always wanted. When they were dressed—or undressed—they stared at each other in the diaphanous white costumes.

Dierdre rubbed the material against her inner arm. "Wow, this is so soft."

"Why do I feel I'm at the gynecologist?"

Tanna led them through a series of doorways and a thick white curtain, and into the main area.

"Welcome to Elysium," she said in a mellow voice, opening the curtains.

Rochelle drew in her breath. The room was long, like a wide hallway, and it was decorated in shades of white and off-white, so softly lit that it seemed to glow, like radium, the walls high and draped in various light textured material. There was a succession of identical, carpeted platforms that formed a series of diamonds from the front of the room to the far end. These were each about three feet off the floor, which had been painted, or treated, to appear sparkly, like snow reflecting light. Mist rose from the floor and diffused the air. Music was playing. As they were ushered to their designated space, she saw that each platform was fitted with four sets of headphones. Small bowls of white objects had been carefully placed on the platform. Other groups of people, also wearing the white robes, were sitting or reclining on the carpeted platforms, their headphones in place. The ceiling was draped with a huge white parachute, and there were white balloons, and silk pillows, as well as pieces of satin, marshmallows, Slinkies and various other sensory objects scattered about.

"Geez," said Dierdre.

"Maybe we died," Spider remarked.

"You think this is where they'd send *us*?" Ray remarked.

The men laughed, and it was contagious. Suddenly, none of them could stop laughing.

They were still giggling as the hostess showed them the controls for the stereo headphones, various channels they could tune in individually. She asked if they wanted refreshments.

"A bottle of Dom Perignon," Ray replied.

"I'm sorry, we don't offer liquor, only soft drinks."

"Are you nuts?" He turned to Spider. "I invested in this place?"

The hostess continued, "However, we don't concern ourselves with whatever our guests choose to bring into the club. Or indulge in beforehand. This is a private club."

"I see." Ray reached into his pocket and drew out an aluminum foil packet that held four joints. "Did somebody make this legal when I wasn't looking?"

They lit up and passed the joints around. Rochelle was already far away from anything resembling her home planet, and the celestial surroundings increased the sense of disorientation. She reached into a bowl and took a marshmallow, examining the delicate crust that held in its spongy center, contemplated it for a very long time before biting into it and analyzing in detail the full, sticky sweetness. They were alerted to a group participation game, everyone in the room joining as they hoisted a parachute over their heads, letting it shimmer down, slowly, covering them in silk, hoisting it up again, she could even see little pauses in time between motions, each move separated in split seconds by strobe lights that flickered throughout the room. The white gowns lit up like neon. Ray kissed her, his tongue probing deep, and she was falling, or was she? No, she was sitting back on the platform, earphones wrapped around her head, listening to "19th Nervous Breakdown." Try this, Ray was saying, try that. It began to spin. Time to get dressed. The limo raced through the night.

She was in a bed, their bed, moving in a haze of arousal, a man was there, but he wasn't Ray, because she knew the feel of Ray's hair and this was wirier, he was between her legs, another man was behind her, and there was a woman, too, she heard the whispering voices, the crying out sounds, Ray's among them, and her own. Just relax, Ray's voice said. She was blindfolded. The sensation built and built until she thrashed and screamed, hearing herself from a distance, like a siren receding down a dark street, and then she passed out.

26

The album cover featured a photo of Luke, a little un-shaven, his eyes closed in mid-performance, serious and sexy. He was pleased with the record; the Disgustas had hovered around in the studio but didn't interfere too much. When the release date came, BigWheel threw a party at the Bitter End, and then sent him out on a concert tour, with a backup band. He hadn't had time or budget to get the top musicians, but he lucked out with the bass player. Brewster Henderson was a lanky yellow-haired, twenty-three-year-old from Iowa who accentuated his cowboy good looks with pointy boots and leather fringe vests. BigWheel hooked them up with a decent drummer and a guitarist who dou-bled on keyboard.

The tour was barely publicized, even though it starred The Kinks. The venues were half full and the British band didn't much care for touring in America's heartland, where the audiences weren't familiar with their one hit, "A Well Respected Man."

When the tour ended, BigWheel arranged for Luke to open for The Lovin' Spoonful, who had just scored again with their third big single, "Summer in the City". The crowds were still piling in when Luke's band played, they didn't give a shit about Luke, sometimes they stomped im-patiently for the Big Name. He got so pissed off one night, he kicked over one of the amps—and damned if that didn't get their attention. All of a sudden, the audience went crazy, he took off into a guitar solo like he was possessed and they loved him. But he still had to start anew in every town, win them over by plain hard work.

He called Julie from Allentown, Pennsylvania and Roanoke, Virginia and Yellow Springs, Ohio. There was no answer, but he'd call back, sometimes minutes later and let it ring fifteen, twenty, fifty times. The ringing of the phone was like a drug he felt compelled to take, even if it made him feel worse afterward. When he called from Chicago, a recording said that the number was disconnected. He threw the phone against the motel room wall, denting the cheap plaster.

A moment later, he was dialing Ray Fish's office. The secretary put him right through. Luke was never comfortable talking to Ray. He wanted to simultaneously kill him and beg him to put more effort behind the record.

"Hey, Luke, good to hear from you, I've only got a minute, though. You're in Atlanta, right?"

"Chicago. Atlanta's next. I haven't heard the single."

"Relax, you will, these things take time."

Luke paused. "How's Julie's record coming?"

"I thought you knew, she wanted out of her contract. What can I tell you? We did our best. I'll try to catch the band in Atlanta, I've gotta fly down there for a meeting. The band's already getting some buzz, you just keep on with what you're doing and it'll happen."

In Atlanta, his parents came to the concert with four of his sisters. Luke had to coax them backstage afterward, they were so intimidated. His mother had gained a lot of weight and the sleeves of her yellow sweater were too tight around her upper arms. His father's hair was slicked back with pomade. He could see the comb lines. All of them were pale and shapeless as dough. He'd never realized how cracker they sounded. The oldest of his sisters was married, at eighteen, and had a baby already. She kept worrying about the babysitter. Her husband was in the Army and had just shipped out to Vietnam.

His mother looked at the roadies setting up, young men without shirts, with long, stringy hair and thick brass belt buckles hanging low on soiled jeans, and she shrank back against the wall, stumbled over a nest of cables on the floor.

His father snapped impatiently, "Watch it, Lily May!" as if he weren't ill at ease himself. "Goddamn, will you look at all the hippies," Vinnie commented. He turned to Luke, "You could use a cleanup, too. You look like a goddamn faggot."

"Thanks, Dad."

"You'll come home for Sunday dinner, won't you?" his mother interceded. "We want to meet your Julie, isn't she with you?"

"No. And anyway, we're leaving tomorrow. Packin' up after the show."

His mama looked so disappointed his heart ached.

"I'll be back in a couple three months, we're moving around a lot now, but as soon as I get a break, I'll come home for a nice, long visit."

"We love you, son. You're much better'n that other group."

His father shook his hand, hard, and didn't look him in the eye. His mother clung to him until he had to pry her off and he turned away fast, so as not to see the tears.

"Bye, son," they called out. "Bye, Lucas."

Girls were always around, hanging back stage during concerts, finding the band in the motel. It was like the deluge after a long, long drought. Sometimes he woke up entangled with a lady he didn't remember taking to bed.

Short-skirted, long-haired young girls, with firm, angular, pudgy, soft, lean, voluptuous bodies, they wanted him sweating right off the stage, they wanted souvenirs, his socks, his underwear, used guitar strings. They wanted to be his 'old lady', to just be there, silent and supple, part of his entourage.

He went for days without eating real food, flying along on coffee, Coke and coke, then they'd all gorge, at some Denny's or Howard Johnson's, he stopped keeping track of what city or town, they were all alike, stuffing down huge orders of steaks and eggs, pancakes, burgers, malteds, tuna melts. Like a python, he'd wallow, stuffed and nauseous, in the motel room that smelled of recycled air and plastic, cigarette butts and sweat, listening to the hum of cars on whatever highway, wondering why he was alone when he could have picked from a dozen eager young women. Or why he felt so alone when there was one beside him.

"They oughta have groupie room service," Brewster, the bass player, complained when they were talking horniness one afternoon in the motel's coffee shop. "Get a little lonesome in the middle of the night, dial 'L' for lay."

"Is that all you ever think about?" Luke wanted to know. It was all *he* ever thought about.

"Yeah."

"Where's that waitress?" Luke stood up in the booth, waving the dull-gold plastic coffee pot in her direction.

"She's busy."

Luke tapped his spoon nervously against the table. His head hurt. "What are the symptoms of a brain tumor?" he asked Brewster, whose father was a surgeon back in Cedar Rapids.

"How the hell should I know?"

"My head feels like it's gonna explode."

"I think that's a hangover."

"Dig this, I woke up in the middle of the night and my arm was paralyzed. Maybe it's a stroke."

"Maybe you were sleeping on it. Jesus, Luke, lay back."

A radio droned in the kitchen behind the counter, a fuzzy sound that got on Luke's nerves. Why couldn't someone tune the thing? Then, he noticed a familiar guitar riff. His own. Brewster looked at him at the same time. "Hey, that's you, isn't it?"

"Jesus, that's me," he said, "That's the record! That's it! Holy shit, I'm on the radio!" He jumped up from the booth and gave a yell. "Hey," he called into the kitchen, "Turn that thing up!"

The waitress rushed over, wanting to know if anything was wrong.

"No," he said, "Everything is right!. But I have one question, sugar. Where the heck are we?"

"Logansport, Indiana."

"Logansport, Indiana, I love you!!" The waitress shook her head as she walked away. "Listen, listen everybody! This is a holy moment!"

The patrons stared at him. The music crackled out of the old radio.

He had to call someone, tell someone. Julie. No. She was gone. He'd call his folks.

"Where's the phone?" he asked the waitress. She pointed to the back.

He dropped in a bunch of change, and the phone rang and rang. No one was home.

Luke and Brewster played for the rest of the afternoon in Luke's room with the radio on low in the background, just in case, but they didn't hear the record again. When they stopped playing, it was dark, the sounds in the motel were magnified: a baby crying; voices in the hall. A television, blaring the six o'clock news: "Three astronauts, Virgil Grissom,

Edward White and Roger Chaffee, died in a simulated launching at Cape Kennedy this after noon, the first deaths of the Apollo space program. NASA experts report…"

"Oh, shit, oh, shit, those poor sonsofbitches," said Luke. But he didn't want to feel bad now. He turned the dial from station to station, looking for his record, not finding it. Maybe it was a one-time thing. He paced around the room, lit up a joint, but couldn't erase the image of the three astronauts going up in flames.

He'd noticed the girl at another concert, a different city, her black hair in long braids, and she stared at him all night but never said a word. The bands were having a party backstage after the concert and she stood by the food table watching him and after a while, he went off with some speedhead little blonde.

He kept the portable radio on all the time, in the bus, in the motel rooms. The record finally came on while they were driving between Columbus and Dayton, Ohio. "Luke Bellavita's new single," the DJ said, and Luke felt as if he'd grown three more inches on his dick.

Me, that's me, he said over and over to himself.

"We'll be headlining soon, man," said Brewster.

The girl with the braids turned up in his room in St. Louis and for a moment he thought he was having a déjà vu experience.

"Haven't I seen you someplace before?" he asked her.

She was half-reclined on the chair by the window, wearing tight jeans and a white, off-the-shoulder peasant blouse. Her nipples stood out beneath the fabric.

"Yeah, maybe," she said.

"How the hell did you get in here?"

She shrugged. "I said I was your sister."

There was a slight resemblance. They both had black hair and a similar, squared-off chin; a blunt, straight nose. Her eyes were dark, though, kohl-ringed.

"Well, 'Sis', I'm a little beat, if you don't mind. I prefer to invite people to my room when I want company."

"It was too crowded down there."

"Exactly."

"Okay, I'll go. It wasn't like I was going to sleep with you or anything. I'm not one of those cheap groupies."

"No, of course not."

"I'm *not*." She got up, unfolding long legs and slipping into the leather sandals beside the chair. "See ya."

"What's your name?"

"Elissa."

"Elissa what?"

"I don't like last names. They don't mean anything."

"Unless you want to write a check or get a phone or buy a car."

She gave a disdainful sniff.

"You were at the concert in Atlanta, right?"

She nodded.

"You don't sound like no Georgia girl."

"I've been all over. I've been in Europe."

"Well," he mocked. There was a bare sexiness about her, almost as if she exuded an invisible high frequency his body was picking up.

She reached the door.

"Don't go," he said.

"I just wanted to meet you. No big deal."

"That's all?"

She licked her lips, but it wasn't a bold, sexual gesture. He sensed uncertainty behind the bravado but she crossed the room slowly. Her thigh muscles moved beneath the thin denim. When she was just within reach, he put his hand out and touched her arm. "You don't have to stay. You don't have to go." Their breathing was the only sound in the room. He was sitting on the bed, his legs apart, and she stepped between them, her breasts close to his face. He lifted the blouse and brought his lips to one of her dark nipples. It went rigid beneath his tongue. She leaned her head back. Then she stood up and undid her jeans. The fabric made a soft sighing sound as it slid to the floor. She wore nothing underneath.

He pulled her onto his lap, held her hips while he slipped into her. She was tight and wet and met him with equal fervor. He did it harder and she cried out, an animal sound. He felt an incredible excitement, a building pressure in his groin and in the back of his legs. There was anger in him, that Julie never let him have her, not really, cold bitch, fuck her. As he fucked this Elissa, he was alternately liberated and desperate. Thinking of Julie, and then he stopped thinking altogether; he was a machine of pure sensation.

When it was over, and they had dozed for a while, he was aware of a lifting of his spirits, and only then did he realize how low he had really been, and for how long.

27

Rochelle awoke alone in bed, the sheets askew, blankets on the floor. An empty champagne bottle teetered on the edge of the night table. The room smelled of someone else's perfume. A full ashtray next to the bed. A cigarette with lipstick. Not hers. Not even her brand. She sat up and discovered that there was a bowling ball inside her head. Along with the headache was a cold, clammy feeling. The nausea came on quickly, and she ran for the bathroom, kneeling over the toilet for a long time, until she was empty, her stomach muscles aching.

There had been too many nights like this over the past few months. The glamour—if there had ever been any—was fading fast. She could barely stumble into the office most mornings, and only revived with coffee and a few capsules of speed. She had to tell Ray: no more scenes, no more of this craziness.

After calling her boss to let him know she was taking a sick day, she tried Ray's extension.

"Mr. Fish's office."

"Hi, Lenore, it's Rochelle. Can I speak to him?"

"He hasn't come in yet. I was about to call you. Do *you* know where he is? He's got someone waiting in his office, and a lot of calls."

"I don't know, he left early. I'm home with a bug. Could you ask him to call me when he comes in?"

"Sure thing. Get some rest," said Lenore, clicking off.

A bath refreshed her but she was still nauseated. This was more than a hangover. Her breasts had been sore for days. Was it possible? Yes, of course, they were careless as often as not. She'd forget to take the pill, forget to use the diaphragm; she kept putting off getting an IUD. It was possible, and it might not even be Ray's.

There were seven other women in the waiting room. Even with an appointment weeks in advance, this hotshit Park Avenue OB-GYN kept his patients sitting around for hours. None of the patients, who included well-known actresses and models, ever seemed to think it was out of the ordinary, and they sat passively reading old issues of *Avenue* and *Good Housekeeping* and *Mother's Day*. Since the doctor, via his receptionist, had reluctantly agreed to fit her in, like they were doing her a big favor, she was last on the list.

Many of the others were visibly pregnant. Rochelle put her hands over her belly, so they would assume she was pregnant, too, but she was not wearing anything that resembled a wedding ring—just a single pearl in a platinum band that Ray had given her on Valentine's Day. She surreptitiously turned the ring around, so that only the plain band showed.

It must have happened just after her last period. Which would make her nearly six weeks pregnant—if she was. Because it could always be something else, like cancer or god knows what. There had been all those nights she could barely remember, because Ray kept upping the ante, needing more and more bizarre scenes to keep him satisfied, and she didn't want to be boring, and now maybe a baby would have two heads or four arms. She made a pact with God: if I am pregnant, let it be not a monster and I will be good from now on.

Cosmopolitan offered helpful instructions on "How to Keep Your Man Satisfied". She turned the pages. "Fifteen recipes for your summer barbecue!" "The Long and Short of

Wash-and-Go Hair!" From there, she moved on to *Mother's World*, which had a terrifying article on birth defects, and then *Life*, with vivid photos of maimed and dead soldiers in Vietnam.

"Mrs. Fish?"

The examination room had a small alcove with a mirror and a bench for her things. She removed her skirt and panties and put on the open-backed gown, closed the alcove door behind her and lay down on the paper-covered exam table. There was another long wait for the doctor, during which she drifted off, the murmuring sounds out side the room soothing her into half-sleep.

"Hello, Rochelle, how are we today?" the doctor said, banging through the door.

"We think we may be pregnant."

"Well, let's just take a look. I haven't examined you since—" He looked at her folder— "last April, so I'll check things out and then we'll do a blood test. When was your last period?"

The best thing about this guy was the way he kept the in-struments warmed, although he was rather brusque in his hands-on technique. After he was through, the nurse took her blood—Rochelle looked away when the needle went in—and instructed her to get dressed and see the doctor in his office.

He was on the phone, but glanced up and signaled her to sit. She leafed through a *Reader's Digest*. Eventually, he turned his attention to her.

"Rochelle, I won't know for certain until we get the test back, but from my visual exam, and from what you tell me—and there's nothing to indicate any problems—I'd say you're most likely pregnant."

She nodded, biting her lower lip.

"That *is* good news, isn't it? Your husband—" he glanced at his records—"Mr. Fish will be pleased?"

"Sure."

"Well, then," he snapped her file closed and began to explain how the follow-ups worked. Words like Lamaze filtered through, and she envisioned herself and Ray at the classes, with her panting and him at her side. Right. Like that was going to happen.

"Are you all right?" the doctor asked. "Do you want to lie down?"

"No, I'm fine, just a little dizzy. I didn't get much sleep."

"Well, you'll need to take good care of yourself—" He was off on another healthy motherhood speech, and then she was out in the lobby, telling them to bill her husband, because she'd forgotten her checkbook, and then she was on the muggy street.

She called Ray from a payphone, but he was still out of the office. With a burst of energy, she walked down Madison to a fancy maternity boutique and bought three pricey, dressy outfits, using one of Ray's credit cards. Then she cabbed over to Bergdorf and purchased an array of infant clothes, in yellow and white.

She would surprise him by displaying the baby clothes on the bed when he came home. The idea of it was beginning to excite her. By the end of the day, she had mentally moved into a house in Westchester and decorated the baby's room.

She dialed his office again.

"Lenore, could you put Ray on?"

"Rochelle? I've been trying to call you but there was no answer."

"Doctor's appointment. What's wrong?"

"Well, nothing, exactly, except that Ray hasn't come in all day, or even called."

"Did you try Spider?"

"He left a message that he was driving down to Philly to visit his brother."

"This is weird."

"I know. I had to cancel all Ray's appointments." Lenore sounded indignant.

"I'll call around, but let me know if you hear from him."

She put down the receiver and stared at the baby clothes on the bed. The apartment was eerily quiet. The grandfather clock downstairs chimed, five times. To fill the silence, she picked up the remote and turned on the TV, but nothing interested her. A car ad triggered a thought. Maybe he had driven somewhere on the spur of the moment. She called the garage. No, the Jag was in its spot, and they hadn't had any orders from Ray to get it ready for him. He hadn't ordered a limo, either.

A sudden business trip? He wouldn't have forgotten to tell his secretary. Or her. Well, maybe her, but not Lenore. She checked Ray's top dresser drawer for the stash of credit cards with other people's names. They were gone. He kept a small address book in his desk, and she leafed through it. A few of the names were familiar, people from the record company, but there were many she didn't recognize. He always kept cash beneath his neatly rolled socks. The money was in a manila envelope. Beneath that was another, legal sized white envelope. She slid a fingernail under the seal, opening it without tearing the paper, and unfolded the contents.

Scanning it quickly, she saw that it was a contract, as yet unsigned by Ray, merging BigWheel ("its Holdings, Artists and Investments") into a much larger media company. Ray stood to make a substantial fortune. An addendum listed the "contents of Shield Warehouse & Storage #43, Hackensack, N.J." This could explain his absence: he was away closing the deal. She took a handful of hundred dollar bills and transferred them to her own wallet, putting the rest—slightly over six thousand—back in place, along with the contract.

The grandfather clock awakened her. Six chimes. Morning or night? She had fallen asleep with the TV still droning. Dawn light seeped in. Groggy, disoriented in the quiet apartment, she pulled herself out of bed and started to make coffee, then remembered that it was bad for the baby, and boiled water for herbal tea instead.

At nine, she called Ray's office.

"We have to notify the police," Lenore said.

"*No!* He's just on a trip, he forgot to tell us. If he comes back and finds the police crawling all over, he'll have a conniption."

"Yeah, there's that."

"What are you telling people?" Rochelle asked.

"Like you said, he's on a business trip. But I can't keep this up indefinitely."

"You won't have to. He'll be back."

"Of course he'll be back." Lenore sounded just as uncertain as Rochelle did.

"Look, could you transfer me to Joe, I gotta let him know I'm not coming in again."

She dressed and went out, just as if it were a normal day.

She window-shopped on Madison, stopped for a croissant at the bakery, at the health food store, the deli, the dry cleaners. If she acted like everything was fine, it would be.

The door wasn't locked the way she'd left it.

"Ray?" she called. The newspaper, delivered earlier, was lying on the sill. Rochelle put down the bag of groceries, and picked up the newspaper, gingerly, as if something might crawl out. Using it like a spear, she pushed the door open.

This could not be their apartment. This place was wrecked. She stepped back out to make sure she had gotten off the elevator on the correct floor.

When I go inside again, it will have been my imagination.
Some kind of hormonal hallucination.

The bookshelves had been cleared, as if by a giant hand, and the books were tumbled on the floor. Lamps lay like felled trees on the carpeting that had been ripped up along the walls. Stepping over the rubble, she made her way upstairs to the master bedroom, and found the same destruction. She wondered if whoever had done this had found whatever it was they were looking for.

28

The bus rolled through the night. Julie checked her reflection in the dark window to see if she was still there. A long-haired guy had gotten on with her at Port Authority and asked about the guitar, the whole 'what/where do you play?' conversation.

"Going to San Francisco?" he asked.

"What's the point? Everybody else is going there. With flowers in their fucking hair." She stretched out her legs in their worn-thin jeans. "You?"

"Pittsburgh. My grandmother died."

Julie murmured a condolence sound.

"The cool thing is," he continued, "my sister had a baby last month. Real cute little boy. My first nephew. They named him after me."

If there was one subject that bored her blue, it was babies.

The bus lurched to a stop in Trenton. The guy had dozed off on her shoulder. She slipped out from under him and went to the bathroom in the back of the bus. It reeked of disinfectant. There were wads of damp tissues on the floor.

She held her breath. In her seat again, she tried to read a tattered paperback of *Valley of the Dolls* but it kept reminding her that her own life was far more tragic and extraordinary than the tormented heroines of any novel and her thoughts began to take the form of the third person, a trick that enabled her to pretend she was someone else.

She fell asleep and dreamed that her mother was trying to wake her up to go to school. Her stepfather was in the bathroom; she could hear the flush of water through the apartment's old pipes. He came out, his face pink and scrubbed, wearing the plaid flannel robe her mother had bought him for Christmas. The radio news was all about the presidential campaign. Kennedy would be in their neighborhood on Wednesday. Julie wanted to see him, even if she had to cut school. Then, with dream logic, she was standing in the crowd outside Alexander's department store. Kennedy was on a makeshift platform across the parking lot, his sandy hair wind-tossed, and she could barely see him but the voice resonated out of speakers, and everyone cheered. You're alive, she said, astonished, and she began to cry.

Her seatmate was gone, but he had left a piece of paper with a phone number on it. She put it in her pocket, as if she really would one day call him and they'd get together and find they had things in common, other than one night on a Greyhound.

Somewhere between Houston and Denver, the tour bus lurched to a stop at a gas station. Luke got out to stretch his legs. Elissa was sound asleep, curled up next to the window, her unbraided hair covering most of her face and chest like a dark sheet. He bought a cup of coffee from the sleepy attendant.

Outside, there were millions of stars in the clear and cold night. Despite the friends in the bus, and the beautiful woman, he reeled from the emptiness inside himself.

"Goddamn it," he said aloud, in a hoarse voice. Even when everything was going well, she came and haunted him. Julie. The stars blinked indifferently.

You damn fool, get back on the bus.

He cupped his hands around the warm paper cup, and closed his eyes for a moment in time, fleeting as a prayer.

Elliot touched the cold glass of the airplane window with his fingertips. What were the odds of the window breaking and sucking him out into space?

He'd read the flight magazine, eaten the meal and couldn't concentrate on his work. They were probably over the West by now. At least if it were day he'd be able to see the Rocky Mountains, the Grand Canyon, or one of those other places he didn't quite believe existed.

Weary of sitting, he climbed over the sleeping Arlene, and made his way down the aisle to the bathroom. The 707 gave a sudden lurch, which caused his heart to double up its beats and convince him he would never get to Los Angeles, but would wind up strewn across some national monument.

He already had the business cards: The Taylor Pine Agency. Elliot Levine, Vice President, Artists and Repertoire, Hollywood, California. That sounded damn pretty good. It made the flying almost bearable. He couldn't die now. Not with all he'd been through. This would be a ridiculous time to die.

The plane shimmied and dropped and so did his stomach. There was no way he'd go to the toilet while it was moving, so he staggered back to his seat.

Please, God, let me get to Los Angeles, he intoned. *Alive.*
The plane leveled.
Thank you.

29

The doorman called on the intercom. "A Mr. Jenkins in the lobby to see you, Miss Klein."

She pushed the "talk" button. "I'll come down."

Mr. Jenkins was sitting on one of the overstuffed lobby sofas, tapping a sneakered foot. He was thin and feral, and holding a white envelope. "Miss Rochelle Klein?"

She nodded, and he handed her the envelope, turned and left before she could get a word out. Inside the envelope was a folded piece of paper, a shape she had seen many times before in the law offices where she'd worked.

> State of Nevada, Reno County, subpoenas Miss Rochelle Lisa Klein...to appear before the Grand Jury of the State of Nevada in the case of Nevada v. Ray Fish a/k/a Raymond Fishman a/k/a Donald Raymond a/k/a Donnie Fitch a/k/a Richard Feitzman...at the Reno County courthouse 9:00 AM Tuesday, October 2, 1967.

Mr. Gorsuch, her former boss, listened to her story without expression. The attorney fondled a small, silver-framed picture of his wife and three children, the same one he'd kept on the desk when she'd worked for him, only now the children were bigger, the wife fatter. At the end of her recitation, he leaned back in his leather chair and said, "Well, Rochelle, looks like you've got yourself in a bit of a mess."

"But what do I do?" She indicated the subpoena.

"Your boyfriend? You say he's missing how long?"

"Three weeks. Almost."

"Doesn't he have an attorney or someone who handles his business? Someone at the record company?"

She had the sense of her feet not connecting to the ground, that she'd lost some primitive tie to reality. "Lester Mills, he's the company lawyer."

"Talk to him," he went on, "He'll be in a better position to handle this than I am. You know I'd love to help, but this is out of my field of expertise."

Lester Mills' office was two floors below Ray's.

"You'll have to appear," he said, flicking a finger at the subpoena she'd handed him. "But I doubt if you'll have what they want."

"I don't know anything about Ray's private business. I didn't even know he had, you know, business in Nevada."

"Good. Then that's what you'll tell them. You ought to have a lawyer out there, though. "Here," he wrote a name on a slip of paper. "Ralph Micali's a good man, he'll help you out.

I'll call him first and tell him to expect you."

"But what about Ray?"

Lester Mills' face went solemn. "We've been in touch with the police, of course. You have, too, right?"

"Well, yes, I mean, after the break-in, I called, and they said they were filing a report or something, but they didn't seem very confident they could find who did it. I don't know whether to stay there or not, at the apartment—I mean whoever broke in might come back, right? And they might think I know something, oh, God, this sounds like a bad movie...I...I haven't been thinking very clearly, I guess."

"I can understand that," he said. "Maybe you can move in with family or friends, for the time being."

She could only imagine her parents' reaction to this.

Lester Mills stood up, ready to end the meeting. She was getting very tired of being dismissed by men.

"But there's another problem," she said, "There are bills, the rent. I don't have enough to last very long, my salary isn't much. I thought maybe the company must have some kind of, I don't know, *fund*, or something."

"I've certainly never heard of a provision for anything like this," he said. "Hey, I'd give you something out of my own pocket, but," he chuckled, "I'm mortgaged up to my ass, you should excuse the expression."

"I just meant maybe Ray left some kind of instructions."

"I don't know what to say, Miss Klein, if you're looking for a will—"

"A will?"

"No will can be probated without proof of death—"

"*Death?* I just meant, could I borrow from some of his, you know, accounts or something? Until he gets back. I know it would be all right with Ray."

"The problem is, I'm not authorized to dip into Ray's accounts. He signed everything himself—you can talk to Moe Wagreich, his accountant, if you don't believe me—but there's no power of attorney. And as far as his will goes, he hasn't changed the one he made several years ago, and that leaves everything to his family."

"But his parents are dead."

Mills smiled sourly. "His wife. And his son."

"You mean his ex-wife."

"He was divorced from his first two wives, but the third marriage is still legal."

She started to speak, but nothing came out.

"I'm afraid you aren't in a very strong position, Miss Klein. You want my advice?"

She almost said no, but held back.

"Go to Reno, play dumb, and get on with your life."

"Look, I just need to know. Who's doing Ray's job if Ray isn't here?"

"I guess that would be Mr. Allessi."

She knocked on Spider's door.

"How ya doin', Rochelle," he said as she entered.

"How do you think I'm doing?" It took a massive effort not to break down. "You happen to have any idea where Ray might be?"

"Ray's an adventurous guy, you oughta know that. I don't mean to be disrespectful, but he could've gone off with a broad." He grinned. "Everything else okay?"

"Well, let's see," she said, "Ray's disappeared, the apartment was torn apart, I've been subpoenaed. Just an ordinary day."

Spider lowered his voice. "Subpoena?"

"Something in Reno."

Spider waved his hand. "Don't worry about it, that's all bullshit. They been trying to throw payola charges at us for years, and couldn't make it stick, so they're goin' another way."

His hand was in his pocket, jingling change. He regarded her for a moment, then said, offhandedly, "'Sides, you don't know nothin', do you? About Ray's business?"

"No."

"There you go, then."

Her body was covered in a cold sweat. A scene from some movie or TV show flashed into her head, in which the characters ripped off masks from their faces, only to reveal other masks underneath.

Spider escorted her to the door. "Take care of yourself, honey."

Her desk was just as she'd left it, except for a company envelope resting on top of her covered typewriter. She tore it open and found a memo.

> From: Personnel
> To: R. Klein
>
> Because of recent economic setbacks, we
> find it necessary to scale back on our
> Marketing Department. Enclosed please
> find two weeks severance pay.

She took her furs out of storage and arranged a quick sale. Then she sorted through the jewelry, keeping the delicate diamond and emerald ring Ray had given her on her twenty-first birthday. The money was enough to keep the apartment temporarily. But how long could she stay? The hearing was coming up, and there was the baby.

Nobody paid much attention when she walked through the corridors of BigWheel a month after her abrupt dismissal. Another secretary sat in her place. It was late in the day. She slipped into the stairwell and walked up from the fortieth floor to the forty-fourth. Sat on a step and waited. She remembered the night of the Blackout, and how she and Ray had made love in his office, happy and stoned.

The noises outside the stairwell began to fade. Once, she heard what sounded like footsteps approaching; a door opened and shut several floors below, and all was silence again. She opened the door a crack. The hallways were dimmed. The carts of the cleaning crew creaked, room by room. Still, she waited.

Hours later, stiff and sore from sitting on the hard stairs, she peeked into the hall. Desolate.

Some of the office doors were open, others closed. Panic spread through her. *No: be calm.*

The name on Ray's office door no longer said Ray Fish.

John S. Allessi, President

Slipping in quickly and closing the door behind her, she stumbled against a low table: The furniture had been moved around. Spider, apparently, didn't like having his back to the window. Even the sofa and coffee table were rearranged. But it was the same desk. She went directly to the space underneath, tugged gently at the spot. Nothing. She tried again, and yet a third time. Spider could have discovered the desk's hiding place, taken its contents and sealed it over. Just as she was about to give up, she felt it move. The panel slid back; the secret safe was still there.

From her pocket, she took out a set of keys Ray had kept at home. One was the size of the safe's lock. The key turned easily. She thrust her hand inside, feeling around; a plastic bag, tied with a rubber band; even in the dim light, the white powder was visible; and a paper sack; she felt the crisp edges of paper money. Just let there be a lot of it, she prayed. There was also a small jewelry box. She tossed everything into her large purse and closed the safe. Her hands were trembling.

Even out on the street, she was still shaking.

Reno, Nevada was a lunar, brown-dry desert.

Ralph V. Micali, Esq., a dapper little man in a pale beige suit, picked her up at the Ramada Inn the morning after she arrived. Tufts of white hair showed above his open collar. A thin, gold chain glinted on a leathery neck.

"I sure miss New York," Micali chattered. "I'm from back there, you know? Once a New Yorker, always a New Yorker, right? Say, how about those Mets? You a fan?"

"No, not really, but Ray likes—liked—likes baseball."

Micali helped her into his waiting white limousine. "Ray," he said, with a somber shake of his head. "Sleep okay? Accommodations decent?"

"Norman Bates didn't make an appearance."

"So later, how's about I take you on a tour of the casinos? But first, we've got to get you through this hearing. Not that it's gonna be much of a muchness." He droned on about the Fifth Amendment and how to say nothing politely, and complimented her on her demure suit, and suggested she go into the ladies room and un-tease her hair a little bit, and maybe rub off the lipstick.

The car pulled into a parking lot in front of a low, unadorned building. Inside, it looked more like a day school than a courthouse. The air conditioning was cold enough to keep meat from spoiling. Micali waved at a group of men in the hall. Nausea swept up from her stomach to her throat.

In the bathroom, the wave subsided, and she used a wad of tissue to wipe away the tears that were running down her cheeks. After freshening up, she found Ralph pacing and looking at his watch. He led her into a fluorescent-lit room dominated by a long conference table. A scratched, opaque plastic pitcher of water and a Styrofoam cup were in front of her. The blinds were closed but shards of light came through, and it made her eyes ache.

The head of the Investigating Committee was a large man in a loose gray suit, wearing a too-tight necktie with a design of small frogs.

"Are you acquainted with the man known as–" He reeled off a half-dozen or so of Ray's aliases.

"I know Ray Fish. I don't know any of those others."

"Did you ever know Mr. Fish to have any contact with–" He mentioned a vaguely familiar name.

She hesitated, glanced at Micali. He gave a small shake. "I don't think so," she heard herself say.

"Tell us, Miss Klein, what was the nature of your relationship with Ray Fish?"

"We were engaged."

"I see. And were you planning on marrying him before or after his divorce from his legal wife?"

Rochelle again glanced at Micali, who was doodling on a legal pad. He looked up and cleared his throat. "I object to this line of questioning. Miss Klein's personal virtue or lack thereof is of no consequence here."

"This isn't a *trial*, Mr. Micali, you can't *object*."

He raised and spread his hands, conceding.

The Investigator continued. "Did you know that Mr. Fish has a long criminal record dating back to his first arrest as a juvenile in the state of Pennsylvania, in 1938, when he served a term for..." He consulted his notes. "Check kiting?"

"No. I never heard about that," she replied, picturing checks tied to the tail of a kite, flying away.

"Do you know anything about a warehouse in Newark, New Jersey, where Mr. Fish is alleged to have stashed several million dollars in bootlegged recordings?"

She blinked, amazed. "You're kidding, right? *No*."

"Are you aware of Mr. Fish's investments in casinos in this city of Reno, Nevada?"

"No."

"Have you met this man?" They pushed something down to her. It was a face-front mug shot of Spider Allessi.

"Sure. That's Ray's...associate."

"And just what does he do at BigWheel Records?"

"That's something I've always wondered."

Micali flashed her a warning look.

"Miss Klein, do you realize the seriousness of these proceedings?" the Investigator demanded.

"I think so."

"You *think* so. Well, let me enlighten you. Your fiancé, Mr. Ray Fish, or whatever he's calling himself this week, has made millions off black-market records and cheated artists out of more millions in royalties. He's managed not to pay taxes by laundering money through casinos that don't exist and he's committed bigamy. And that's just the stuff we have on paper. Is this a man you want to protect?"

"I'm not protecting anything. I just don't know."

The Investigator sat back, expelling a long breath, his hands gripping the edge of the table, as if he were about to tip it over onto her. "Do you know Mr. Fish's whereabouts at this time?"

She shook her head.

"Could you answer the question please?"

"What was it again?"

"Do you know where Ray Fish is?"

"No. I don't. Do you?"

Several of the panel members chuckled. The Investigator glared at them and at her.

"I wish I did, Miss Klein. Now, won't you tell us why you didn't report Mr. Fish missing right away? Why did you wait until your apartment was broken into, and even then, you waited to call the police? You're living with this man, and he just up and vanishes and you don't do a thing about it?"

"I didn't know it was my turn to watch him."

"Miss Klein, do you mean to make a mockery of this hearing?"

"I'm sorry, no."

One of the men leaned toward the Investigator and whispered something.

"One more question," the Investigator said, "Have you ever met or heard of Gary Luna?"

A hazy memory tickled the back of her mind. Ray on the phone, upset. The name Gary. Another time, Spider raising his glass to "Luna," which she thought was some foreign toast, like "l'chaim" or "skol."

"No, I never knew anyone by that name."

"Witness dismissed. Reserve the right to recall."

Ray would've gotten a kick out of this ridiculous Western saloon. He'd be suggesting a threesome with one of the cowgirl waitresses. She was exhausted from all the information they had thrown at her, the questions, and the condescension in their eyes and voices. I'm not a whore, she wanted to tell them, I'm just a nice Jewish girl from Queens.

Ralph Micali raised his glass. "You were great, honey. They've got nothing. You're home free."

She wanted to go home and crawl under the covers. She didn't want to be a mother; she wanted her own mother to bring her some Bosco, and she wanted to play her old 45s and giggle with Julie on the phone.

The bar was filling up, a lunchtime crowd. Two men discussed details of the lumber business. Her hands trembled as she lifted the martini glass, knowing she should not be drinking—it was supposed to be bad for the baby—and thinking, what baby? Whose baby? What kind of mother could she possibly be, the way things were? A tiny collection of cells and blood that was already taking over her body.

Micali moved closer to her. "All I'm saying, sweetheart, is that you gotta do what's best for you." He excused himself to go to the 'little boys.'

Pregnant and alone. How would she work? She knew then that what she wanted most was to get out of it, to stop this process she had not asked for.

Would it hurt? Ruin her insides so she could never have children? Some filthy back room, do they give you anesthesia? Arlene's father would know, maybe he did the operations himself. She remembered the quiet, leafy street where Arlene's house was, and Dr. Slotnick's office. But Arlene was married to Elliot and they'd moved to Los Angeles.

"Are you okay?" Micali was back, staring at her, with that baffled annoyance of men who are undone by weeping women. He offered her his handkerchief, a gallant gesture that brought on more tears.

She took a deep breath. "I need a doctor. A particular kind of doctor. For women." At his blank look, she added, "I'm knocked up, for godsake."

He took out his pen and wrote a name and phone number on the cocktail napkin. "Don't take this the wrong way, but there're a lot of "professional girls" out here, if you catch my drift, and this is where they go. Assuming you have the money. He's not cheap, but he's a real doctor, not some quack."

"I have the money. Enough till I find a job." She stared at the number he'd written. "Thanks."

He put his hand over hers. "Ever think of moving out here?"

"It's a hundred and fifteen degrees. *Lizards* live here, for Christ sake." She paused, breathless. "I need to be on a *coast*. I was thinking Los Angeles."

"I know a guy in L.A. who could use an assistant. He's kind of a nutcase but he really knows the music business. Publishes a tip sheet. You know, a newsletter of record releases and recommends. Happy Becker."

"Happy's Hotsheet?"

"Right, that's the one. Told me he's drowning in paperwork. You type and stuff?"

"Yeah, I type. And stuff."

"I handled his last divorce." He took back the cocktail napkin with the name of the doctor, and wrote Happy Becker's number on the other side. "You know, you're a beautiful woman." He touched her chin with his forefinger, looked into her eyes provocatively.

"Excuse me," she said, standing, "I'm feeling kind of nauseous. I'll be right back."

When she returned, the lawyer had paid the check. He was quiet on the drive back to her motel.

"Well," she said. "Thank you for all your help." It occurred to her that he might want to be paid, but decided not to raise the issue if he didn't. He could just bill Ray's 'estate'.

Rochelle went into the motel room, with its canned smell of recycled air and rubbery new carpet. She dialed the number on the cocktail napkin. The doctor answered after six rings.

30

Elliot parked in his reserved spot behind the Taylor Pine offices, a low, tree-shrouded building on Sunset off Cahuenga. The big blue Buick was his third car in the year since he had been in Los Angeles. He was not a naturally gifted driver. His mind tended to wander when he was waiting at a red light and he'd roll slowly into the intersection before it turned green. Or, making a turn onto the freeway, he'd forget to check for oncoming traffic. His first car, a 1962 turquoise and white Plymouth Fury, had ended up with its front end squashed in. The Corvair met a similar fate. The tow truck driver who came to pick it up muttered something about a mercy killing. Miraculously, Elliot emerged unscathed from both accidents. What he really needed was to become rich enough for a driver, he told Arlene. If you live that long, she remarked. She drove their new '68 Dodge Coronet station wagon, which her father had paid for as a moving-to-L.A. gift, and was essential for schlepping the twins and their toddler gear.

They were renting a small house in Westwood. It had a backyard with the requisite swimming pool, although Elliot could barely swim and Arlene didn't like to get her hair wet. Arlene pored obsessively over the *Los Angeles Times* real estate section every weekend, pointing out that with just a little higher payment each month for a mortgage, they could buy their own house, with a Jacuzzi, a two-car garage, and a bigger pool. When they talked about loans and mortgages, Elliot grabbed his Vicks inhaler.

The perpetual white-light sunshine was like too much sugar. He was not a person who could get a tan; he turned pink at the slightest glimmer of the sun. Arlene, on the other hand, bloomed outside. Her newly blonde hair, bestowed by an amazingly expensive Beverly Hills colorist, contrasted sharply with her darkened skin. She wore short white linen dresses, thick black eyeliner and white lipstick.

Elliot was glad to be indoors most of the time, hunkered in his office with his favorite companion, the telephone. Taylor Pine had expanded its recording artists division, shedding some older clients through attrition and replacing them with younger pop artists. He spent late nights at the music clubs, stopping in at the Troubadour and the Whisky, then heading a few blocks east to the Sea Witch, to see the upcoming acts, and scouting out new talent at the underground Bido Lido's on Cahuenga.

One night, guitar player Casey Mahoney stopped in at The Trip to jam with the band that was performing, the Everpresent Fullness. Elliot knew that Casey was in negotiations with Atlantic Records.

"Hi, Casey, I'm Elliot Levine. Taylor Pine Agency." He didn't mention that they'd met a few years before, in the Village.

"Hey," said Casey, looking over his shoulder at a pair of pretty young women coming his way. Elliot put his card in Casey's hand.

Three days later, Elliot called the Beachwood Canyon house that Casey shared with two other musicians. In the background, an electric guitar wah-wah'ed in cacophony with the clunk-clunk of a bass tuning up. Casey finally got on the phone. He wasn't enthusiastic about coming to Elliot's office.

"I hate all that corporate shit, man," he said.

Elliot rolled his eyes. Okay, he'd drive up there. The directions were circuitous, up this hill, turn left, turn right, one of those roads where you had to pull over if another car came from the opposite direction. The house was stuck into the side of the hill that looked at the Hollywood sign. Music vibrated the walls. As good as it sounded, Elliot was grateful he wasn't a neighbor.

The guys improvised for a long time. Elliot found a seat amid the clutter on an old sofa, and sat back to listen, closing his eyes. It was fabulous, energized music.

"Beer?" Casey asked, when they stopped to take a break. He opened the refrigerator. Inside were mostly cans and bottles.

"Soda, if you've got it."

Casey tossed him a Coke.

One of the musicians took out a plastic bag of grass, glanced at Elliot, then at Casey.

"Don't worry, he's cool," Casey assured the others. He laughed. "Meet my agent."

A few minutes later, they were playing again. More guys dropped by, a few with their girlfriends. An eye level haze of cigarette and pot smoke stung Elliot's eyes. He was giddy just from the contact high. One of the young women, with long, hay-straight blonde hair, picked up a guitar and began to sing. The song was witty and rhythmic and very original. Elliot asked if she had any others; yes, lots. And no, she wasn't signed to anyone. She performed two more compositions.

He knew how the first gold miners felt, the ones who got there before the lodes were tapped out. There was as much creativity here as there used to be in the Village, and this time, he was in a position to do something about it.

Long past midnight, he reluctantly got into his car, just as another musician drove up on a big Harley, guitar case slung over his back. Elliot didn't recognize him at first. The curly black hair nearly touched the shoulders of a worn brown leather bomber jacket; slim black jeans were tucked into pointy-toed boots.

Elliot watched Luke Bellavita enter the house. Seeing Luke was like coming upon an old lover, or a child who'd run away from home: painful and gladdening all at once. He waited in the car until the music began again, this time with Luke's unmistakable sound mingled with Casey's: a perfect blend of voices and instruments, a new force of nature. The shimmer prickled the back of his neck and ran down his spine. This was meant to be: a new group featuring Casey and Luke together.

He didn't even mind the dark, steep and winding drive down the hill.

Silver Knight was officially born in Elliot's office at Taylor Pine on a sunny February afternoon in 1968.

The irony of representing Luke again did not escape him. Apprehensive about their upcoming meeting, he kept popping up from his desk and going to the window, watching the parking lot. Luke arrived on his chopper. A girl climbed off the back of the bike. For just a moment, he thought: Julie. Then she took off her helmet and shook out a yard or so of silky dark hair.

Elliot could not conceal a self-satisfied smile as Luke took in the elegant office and the wall-sized window that looked out over Hollywood and the hills.

"Have a seat."

The girl draped her lithe body on the sofa. Luke didn't introduce her. He and Elliot warily regarded one other across the desk. The rest of the band straggled in. Casey Mahoney wore mirrored wraparound sunglasses resting on his freckled nose. The drummer, Billy Colt, was short, like his name, with thickly muscled arms. The bass player, Brewster Henderson from Luke's old band, was dressed like a cowboy . He stared at Elliot with pale, squinted eyes and was amused by nearly everything Elliot said.

When the meeting was over, Elliot asked Luke to stay behind for a few minutes. Luke straddled a chair in front of the desk, lit a cigarette. "I always thought you got the short end when all that shit went down with BigWheel."

"Wasn't much you could do, right?"

"No," Luke said quickly. Then, "I don't know, maybe I should've gone to bat for you."

"Maybe you should've." Elliot felt the old hurt rising, a heat that flushed his face. "Sorry your record didn't go anywhere. It was good."

"They didn't put much behind it. Just threw it into the marketplace, no promotion, nothing. It got some play in the Midwest. Right to the top in Topeka."

"BigWheel was never exactly famous for spending. Sometimes they just signed people so no one else would get them."

He paused. "Have you heard from Julie?"

The musician's leg began to jiggle nervously. "That's old news, man."

"I just wondered what she was up to, I've got some clout now, maybe I could get her a deal."

"I don't spend too much time thinking about it."

Elliot leaned back in his chair, tilting precariously.

Luke took a long drag on his cigarette, then stubbed it out, half-smoked, in the ashtray. "It's spooky about Ray, ain't it? I mean, disappearing like that."

"Yeah. A real loss to humanity."

Luke laughed. "So here we are again. L.A's a funny town, isn't it?"

"You'll do well."

They shook hands and Luke left. A moment later, Elliot heard the motorcycle start up.

31

"Sit." Happy Becker cleared a stack of tapes and papers from the cluttered armchair next to his desk. "It's a mess," he said, as if Rochelle might not have noticed. He settled his considerable bulk on the couch. He blinked three or four times in rapid succession and passed a hand over his scalp, disrupting the few long strands of hair that had been combed up from the nape of his neck and over his forehead.

Happy Becker was the ugliest man she had ever seen.

Every empty space in the office, which was actually the den of his bungalow in the canal district of L.A.'s Venice, was filled with stacks of LPs and 45s and tapes and newspapers and *Happy's Hotsheets*.

"How did you get here anyway?" he asked. "I didn't hear a car."

"I took the bus."

"Bus? Nobody knows where busses go in L.A."

"Well, I found out where one of them goes." Actually, she'd found three of them because that's how many it took to get from Hollywood to Venice when you didn't know where you were going.

"Clever chick." There were food stains on the front of his madras shirt. "You worked in this business before, Ralphie told me."

"I was in A&R at BigWheel Records." Okay, so she was only down the hall from A&R.

"Shame about Ray Fish." Happy lowered his voice. "They say someone gave him a cement life preserver."

She closed her eyes for several seconds, waiting for the dread to pass. Obviously, Happy didn't know about her relationship with Ray. "I couldn't say."

"Hell, who knows, that's just one rumor." He squinted and blinked. She unintentionally squinted and blinked. Would he think she was making fun of him? She forced her eyes wide open.

"I'm a one-man band here, as you can see," he said, gesturing at the office. "Had a girl but she left to get married. You're not engaged or anything?"

"No."

"Want some coffee. A soda?"

"Cold water would be great."

"Sure. Gimme a minute." He lumbered out of the room.

She slumped in the chair, and pressed her hands over her eyes. Since Reno, she had been tired, just tired.

The "procedure" itself had been easy. A thousand dollars bought a legit doctor's office after hours. Even a nurse standing by. There was another woman in the waiting room, tall, in her thirties with a lot of makeup. She was a cocktail waitress in one of the casinos. Don't worry, honey, she assured Rochelle, you get cramps for awhile, and then you're free again.

After another night in the motel, Rochelle flew back to New York to pack up her clothes, and bought a one-way ticket to Los Angeles.

She perused the tapes on Becker's desk, instinctively straightened up a stack of *Happy's Hotsheets*, and emptied an ashtray into the brimming wastebasket. What a slob. The close quarters made her long for a scented bath.

Happy brought in a stained mug of coffee in one hand, a cloudy glass of water in the other, a package of Chips Ahoy! under his armpit. "Dig in," he said.

She lifted the glass of water as if something might jump out of it. Put it down.

"Ralph Micali says you're a real pistol," Happy said, stuffing two cookies into his mouth.

"I type ninety words a minute, take steno faster than you can talk, and I'm very organized."

"Well, as you can see, I could use some help. You know about the tip sheet, how it works?"

"Sure. You keep track of all the record releases, and try to predict what's going to be a hit or a miss."

"That's basically it. Record companies send me their demo pressings, I take a listen, write a review, every Monday morning it's on the desks of every major radio programmer, record company, independent producer. My predictions. It's a little like reading a crystal ball, or like betting on horses, only I'm the inside guy who knows which horses got a pulled tendon or a sore hoof and which ones're fast outta the gate. Don't ask me how I know, it's a gift from God, but I got a sixth sense about what's gonna climb the charts."

"Or maybe," she said, "they play what you recommend and the extra airplay makes the record a hit."

He appraised her for a moment. "You'd think it'd be that way. But sometimes they don't take my advice and they push the hell out of some piece a crap, and nothing happens. And, hell, occasionally I'm wrong and a song I like goes nowhere." He gestured at the stacks of tapes. "I get stuff from all over the country, the world, hoping for a plug. Professional stuff, homemade stuff, the whole *megillah*. I listen to what I can. You could screen the submissions yourself, if you wanna put in the extra hours."

"I'd like that."

"I'll need you to type the *Hotsheet*, answer the phone, keep the fuckin' talent and agents and personal managers off my back, make coffee in the morning, that's basically it. Think you can handle it?" He noticed his desk. "Hey—you moved things around."

"Sorry, I—"

"No, it's great, first time I've seen it in months." He raised himself off the couch and began opening file drawers. "Record company files are here. Columbia, Elektra, Atlantic—"

"Aren't they alphabetized?"

"That's a good idea—I never got around to it. See, this business started real small a coupla years ago and now, it's like an explosion. The stuff just keeps coming. Once in a while, if I can be frank, it comes with a little bit of an incentive."

"Incentive?"

"Com'ere, look at this." She moved over, gingerly, holding her breath against the mildewy smell of his body. She recalled Ralph Micali telling her he'd handled Happy's divorces. The divorces she could understand, but who'd marry him in the first place?

Happy took a package from his desk's middle drawer and handed it to her. It was a 45 wrapped in tissue paper. When she slipped the record out of its paper jacket, a hundred dollar bill fell out.

"What the—?"

"Some a these jerks think that 'cause they send me presents, I'm going to like their garbage more. But, uh-uh, it don't work that way."

"I like a man with integrity."

He grinned. "Now this," he said, pulling over the trash-can, "This is the most important file of all." He dropped the 45 into the can, while pocketing the hundred.

"You're not going to listen to it?"

"I listened. It's shit. I can give you a hundred and twenty five a week."

"I can't work for less than two hundred."

He blinked and squinted rapidly. "One fifty."

"One seventy-five. And I need to be paid in cash. And if any more 'incentives' come along, we split them."

He took a filthy handkerchief from his pants pocket and wiped his neck. "Jesus H. Christ you're a *hondler*. Alright already. When can you start?"

"Now?"

"Okay, kid, you got a deal. But I forgot your name."

"Rochelle Klein. "

"Can I call you Shelly? How about a little kiss to seal the deal?"

"It's Rochelle, not 'Shelly'." She took a letter opener from his desk. "Try to kiss me and you'll be singing falsetto."

He clutched his chest melodramatically. "You're breakin' my heart!"

The airy one-bedroom apartment in Santa Monica cheered her, with its garden outside and birds chirping, and the smell of the ocean four blocks away.

For three weeks, she terrorized an out of work actor moonlighting as a driving instructor until she was just com-petent enough to pass a driving test and get her license.

Under the pseudonym 'Lisa Fishman', she rented a bank safe deposit box and stashed in it the things she'd taken from Ray's desk safe: the tidy little bag of pure cocaine; $17,000 in cash; and a diamond ring which she later sold to a downtown jeweler. The coke was more of a problem. She couldn't exactly post an ad. Eventually, a thinly veiled conversation with a neighbor led to an exchange of drugs for cash, and she added the money to her savings account. She splurged on a blue '67 Chrysler convertible.

Happy cleared a space for her in the corner of his living room, put in another phone line, and a tape recorder. She listened to music all day long, most of it, as Happy predicted, terrible. The unsolicited tapes were often tinny amateur home recordings, sometimes with people talking in the background, or a dog barking, a car squealing by. She felt as if she had her ear to a hidden artery of America, its boisterous garage bands and solitary folkies. Music played continuously while she was on the phone and typing and filing. Happy's workplace was transformed from a junk heap into an efficient office.

One morning, the mail included a package from Big-Wheel Records. How smoothly the company had gone on without Ray. Among the albums they'd sent was one that had been around for a while: Luke Bellavita.

She turned it over, read the liner notes about his roots in Georgia, and coming to Greenwich Village "his arrival coinciding with the crest of the creative coalescence of musical inspiration!" (Who *wrote* this crap?). In the short bio, there was no mention of Julie. A wave of homesickness came over her. She picked up the phone, dialed her parents.

"Mom?"

"Rochelle! Wait a second, let me get Dad on the phone."

"I'm at work, I can't talk long. Have you heard from Julie?"

"No. Why?"

"I just wondered."

"Is everything okay?

"Everything is great!" She heard her father picking up the extension, and pictured the apartment in Queens. The roped off living room, still pristine as the day they moved in. Her little bedroom-turned-guest room.

"How's everything? Are you okay?" her father said.

"I heard there was an earthquake," her mother accused.

"Just a small one."

"'A small earthquake', she says."

"When are you coming home?" Dad asked.

"Why don't you come here for a visit? It's warm." Outside, a rare chilly rain poured into the non-porous ground, causing flooding and traffic snarls all over the city.

"You think your father can just take off from his job any time he wants?" Her mother's voice rose in pitch. "You think *I* can?"

"Selma, calm down," her Dad said.

Happy called from the other room, "Rochelle! We got any fresh coffee?"

"Dad, Ma, I gotta go, send my love to Ira. I love you" She hung up quickly.

Happy stared at her when she brought him his coffee.

"Are you all right?"

"Why does everyone keep asking me that?"

"Sorry."

"I just talked to my parents, that's all."

He nodded. "Nothing like families. Before my mother died, she said to me, 'You didn't turn out like your Dad and I hoped, but I guess God has his ways'."

Rochelle held back a laugh. "That's so awful!"

"And she meant it as praise."

To calm herself on bad nights, she would mentally recite an inventory of her blessings: she had an apartment, a car, a job, a (big) savings account. She never doubted she had done the smart thing about the baby, but she was certain it would have been a boy.

32

Katey Lacey breezed into his office proffering a gold tin of Belgian chocolates.

"Elliot, sweetheart!" She was in town to play the Coconut Grove, following a long engagement at the Sands in Las Vegas. "How's my favorite flack?"

He filled her in on her upcoming TV appearances (*The Merv Griffin Show* and a local daytime morning show) and attempted to reassure her that the new record label was promoting her single, despite a lack of radio play. He made a mental note to put in a call to Happy Becker, maybe he could wrangle a plug in the *Hotsheet*. Katey kissed him on the cheek and left.

His secretary was preparing to leave for the evening, a daily process that involved applying lipstick while staring into a tiny dusty compact mirror, and changing from the shoes she kept under the desk, into another, very similar pair of shoes. Soon she was gone and he had the place to himself.

Elliot had booked Silver Knight at a free concert in Griffith Park, which got them press attention, then a series of paid gigs at the Whisky. Nearby, at the triangular corner of Crescent and Sunset, Pandora's Box had recently closed after a riot broke out between cops and hippies over an imposed curfew. Stephen Stills wrote a song about it and the record was already a hit for Buffalo Springfield. Silver Knight played several weekends at the Troubadour, and a series of appearances at Pacific Ocean Park—"POP"—the amusement pier at the juncture of Venice and Santa Monica. Next door was the old Aragon Ballroom, which was in the process of being turned into the Cheetah.

He planned to head over to the Troubadour later to catch a new client's set. A pang of guilt reminded him that he should stop off at home and see Arlene and the kids—but after a day of talking on the phone, he wanted a quiet escape for himself. He poured his tenth or twelfth cup of stale coffee. From his lower desk drawer, he took out the steno pad on which he kept statistics from all the National League baseball teams. Opening the morning's sports pages, he was pleased to note that the Mets had actually won two games in a row. By the time he finished perusing the baseball articles, it was completely dark outside.

I want...he would think, unable to complete the sentence, because the list grew, and just when he thought he had attained something, it grew smaller in his mind, and the next thing dangled ahead, a diamond carrot. He ought to be satisfied. *Happy's Hotsheet* was plugging Silver Knight's record like crazy. KRLA's DJ Bob Hull booked them into the Hullabaloo for a massive ten-act concert, and the "Real Don Steele" had become another local DJ fan.

The phone rang, a bossy, startling sound.

"Elliot Levine, please." The man's voice was carefully polite, and familiar.

Spider Allessi.

A cold clamminess crept over him; his old dead Nana would have said that a ghost had walked over his grave.

"I'm in town. Let's get together and talk business."

"Sure, Spider. When did you have in mind?"

Hadn't they settled up back in New York? It had been a satisfactory trade. Elliot got the goods on Ray, which allowed Spider to take over BigWheel. What in fuck could Spider want from him now?

"I'll call you, Levine. We can do some business." He hung up.

Elliot had never noticed how tomblike the building was after hours. He felt strangely vulnerable in front of the open window. As he drew the shades, he imagined he saw a man on the street corner, looking up.

In the parking lot, he was aware that the streetlights had not come on yet. Inside his car, with the doors locked, he felt a little bit better. His chest was tight: the lousy air that hung over the city. He turned west onto Sunset. On the radio, the long version of "Light My Fire" was playing. L.A.'s FM radio scene was a lot more innovative than New York's, which was still stuck in the three-minute song format. Here, they played cuts from albums that could run as long as fifteen minutes. He turned up the volume, tapped his fingertips on the steering wheel.

Katey Lacey had given him the idea, planted it in the back of his mind on the night he escorted her to the Copa and then home, where, drunk and chatty, she spilled out everything she knew about Ray Fish. He had just put the pieces together: the separate sets of books, the storage warehouse in New Jersey, Ray's paper trail. It was not all that difficult. Then he turned the whole mess over to an IRS guy his father knew, who in turn passed it up the chain of command. They opened an investigation. This made the goons Ray was in league with very unhappy, Elliot suspected.

There was only one element missing. Not being there to see Ray's face, not getting the opportunity to shove down his despicable throat the knowledge that it was schlemiel Elliot who set his downfall in motion.

'BIG WHEEL' VANISHES
MOB HIT SUSPECTED IN RECORD KING'S
DISAPPEARANCE.
Ray Fish, 41, the co-founder and president of
BigWheel Records, missing since...vanished
without a trace...the door man at his building
last saw...government was investigating the
record industry's...

For a while, Ray's whereabouts were a hot topic in the
media. He was spotted in the Bahamas, while simultaneously seen in Paris and in the Israeli army fighting in the
Six Day War. He was said to have dyed his hair platinum,
shaved his head bald, worn a black wig, and a Hasidic
beard. He was dressed as a woman, and smoking ganja in
Jamaica and skiing in the Alps. Every lead was a dead end.

Elliot scoured the papers daily, obsessed with each detail of Ray's drop from sight. He was waiting for that
crucial phrase: Found Dead. But it never appeared. Ray
had simply vanished without a trace. An ongoing Federal
investigation delved into "irregularities in the recording
industry", but after awhile the papers' coverage of that,
too, dwindled, swallowed up in the more immediate news
of Vietnam.

The Troubadour was crowded, a line had formed outside, but the door sentry swiftly escorted Elliot past the
crowd. He went to his regular seat, rear left. The waitress
appeared immediately, and a Tab was placed in front of
him a moment later. The show had already started, a lackluster rock trio, followed by the band he'd come to see.
Their personal manager had been calling him every day,

saying you gotta catch a set, they're hot, but what Elliot heard didn't exactly excite him. Just a garden-variety band.

He paid the check—they never billed him a cover—and left exactly fifteen percent for a tip, counting it out to the penny. He had parked on a side street just off Sunset Boulevard, to avoid the valet parking charge. The street was dark, tree-shrouded, and he didn't see Spider until he had his key in the car door.

"Elliot. Imagine the coincidence us running into each other in such a big city."

"Life's funny that way," Elliot replied, his voice a little too high.

Spider thumped his back playfully. "Buy you a drink?"

"Actually, I was just on my way home, busy day tomorrow."

"You got time for a nightcap."

"Uh, sure."

"I have a friend wants to meet you. Come on, you drive, I'll navigate, that's what my wife always says, only she can't read a map for shit and we always get lost, but I figure you know your way around this town by now."

Elliot's hand trembled as he opened the car door. For a split second, he considered driving off, fast, driving all night, north to San Francisco, Oregon, Alaska. He reached over and unlocked the passenger side door. Spider got in, bending his ungainly body.

"So, uh, where are we going?"

"Canyonview Terrace, left on Franklin to Canyon, then up to the top."

"Thing is, I gotta call the wife, you know how it is, she'll worry—"

"Plenty a time when we get there," he said cheerfully. *Get where?*

Another one of those terrifyingly steep, twisting roads, made worse by Spider's presence. Up, up, around, precipices on both sides. What were they, goats or something? People were supposed to live on the ground or in sensible high-rises in places like New York.

After a dozen or so loops on a road that needed a Jeep, not a sedan, they reached the top, a plateau on which one immensely large estate had been built for utmost privacy and seclusion. The mansion looked more like a movie set than a home, but perhaps it was more inviting in the daytime. At night, it was insufficiently lit, as if striving for camouflage surrounded by a great black emptiness, the city lights as distant as from an airplane.

The dry hot Santa Anas kicked up, the winds tumbling down from the desert and sucking up any remaining moisture that made its way inland from the coast. He yearned momentarily for a cold winter day, snow on the ground, his breath a cloud in front of his face. He licked his lips, parched from apprehension and the lack of humidity. Spider told Elliot to leave the car in the circular front drive. A ghostly valet came out of the shadows and took it away.

They entered through a soaring cathedral door. Elliot followed Spider down a wide corridor, museum paintings on the walls, and into a room crowded with antiques of some ancient vintage Elliot could not identify, having little interest in interior decoration. But it was the kind he hated, a lot of heavy dark wood with curlicues and cherubs.

"Whose place is this?"

"Luna."

Of course. Gary Luna, the money, the power behind corporations, film companies, records, stars. His reclusiveness was as legendary as his financial empire.

Gary Luna was sunk deep in a brown corduroy Lazy-Boy at the far end of the room, the chair's back to the door. Elliot could see his hand holding a television remote in one hand, a stein of dark liquid in the other. Slowly, he turned in the swivel chair, until Elliot could see him clearly.

He was tiny, almost dwarflike, with feet that did not quite reach the floor. His voice was startlingly high, but assured. An eerie cross between an adolescent boy and an old man.

Luna said, "I've heard a lot about you."

Large rings dominated the delicate forefingers of both hands. One was a snake with emerald eyes, the other a heart encrusted with rubies and diamonds.

"What would you like to drink?" Gary Luna asked. His eyes were dark, the lids fleshy and drooping at the corners, like a turtle's.

Elliot perched tentatively on the edge of a hard, gold-leafed chair. He guessed it was one of those French king periods he could never tell apart. "Just, uh, water would be fine."

Luna snapped his fingers and a flunky—there were at least six of them, all young men—hurried out of the room.

"Like the place?" Luna asked. He didn't wait for Elliot to answer but launched into its history. He bought the hilltop property from an old silent film director, but it was seriously run down, paint peeling, the pool dark algae green and thick with leaves. The director had lost his career in a seamy scandal, and spent his last years living in the pool house, having abandoned the rambling, dust-coated rooms of his castle to several dozen cats and the echoes of the horns and shrieks and music of modern Hollywood that sometimes, mostly at night, were wind-borne up into the canyons.

Elliot glanced around. The wind swept through open doors that led to a vast courtyard. Music drifted in over the wind: Jo Stafford singing "You Belong to Me."

Someone called his name.

"Well, no need to look like I'm a ghost, Elliot, you know perfectly well Mr. Luna and I go way back." Katey Lacey was barefooted, in a white linen caftan, her platinum hair in two long braids.

"Of course." He remembered her drunken ramble about Luna, a name that had meant little to him at the time.

She kissed him on the cheek. "Welcome to our little club."

Turning to Luna, she said sweetly, "Do you have to play that cunt's records?"

"I *like* that song."

"Well, you can hear it on my second album. I do it much better, thank you very much. She covered my version."

Luna snapped his fingers; seconds later, the Jo Stafford record stopped mid-song.

Katey grabbed Elliot's hand and pulled him toward Luna. "Gary, honey, you be nice to this guy, he's my savior at that fucking agency!"

A recorded Katey Lacey began to sing "You Belong to Me."

"I see you've met my son," she added to Elliot.

Elliot glanced around the room. "I'm not sure—"

"Didn't I ever tell you my first ex's name was Allessi?" she said, laughing. "I don't usually admit it 'cause who'd believe I have a thirty year old kid, right! You have to keep up a certain image in this business." She breezed out of the room, her laughter still ringing.

He realized that Gary Luna was talking to him.

"What?"

"It's good that we meet face to face finally."

"Yes, good to meet you, too. I wonder if I could use the phone? To, uh, call my wife, so she won't worry." He was still trying to digest the concept of Katey Lacey as Spider's mother. The flunky brought in a tray with a glass of water for Elliot, beer for Luna and Spider. A phone was finally presented to him. As it rang, he realized that Arlene would have turned off the extension in the bedroom. He didn't know what he was going to say to her anyway.

"I guess she's sleeping," he said.

"Long as she's alone, right?" Spider cracked.

"Yeah."

"Just kidding. No offense."

"None taken." He took a deep breath.

At some unseen signal from Luna, the young men left the room, vanishing like a school of fish. Spider leaned against a wall, under a vast hanging tapestry depicting a gruesome hunting scene, dogs surrounding a torn apart animal.

"Spider tells me you're an okay guy."

"I like to think so."

"We appreciate how you helped us with the Fish problem.

And of course Katey thinks you're a prince. So I guess I owe you."

"No, really, you don't owe me anything."

"I've been giving it some thought," Luna continued. "Katey's mentioned you want to start up your own company. I'd like to invest in something like that. Seems like we could do some business, everybody's happy, everybody's rich. Right?"

"Well."

"Maybe even Katey'll be happy, you take her on as a client, get her away from those douchebags at Taylor Pine—present company excepted. I think the lady's career's still got some mileage, get her a new record deal. A TV variety show. And you got that rock band, Silver Knight? You get Happy Becker to work promotion, you got a hell of a startup company."

"I'm not sure if I have the experience."

"What're you talking about?" Gary Luna's little eyes were steely. "You'd be a fool to turn it down. Right, Spider?"

"Elliot's no fool."

"I'll have my lawyer draw up an agreement. You get your lawyer to look at it. I'm a businessman, everything's on the up and up."

"Sure. Of course. We gotta have paper."

The recorded Katey Lacey sang, "...you belong to me..."

Luna held out his hand. The hard rings left imprints in Elliot's palm.

*W*hen I was ten, I fell in love with three dead men: George Gershwin, Orson Welles and Charlie Chaplin. I didn't know they were dead at the time. My Dad was always renting old black-and-white movies.

My Mom loves classical music, so I knew every note of "Rhapsody in Blue" before I could speak. I don't recall thinking at the time that a person had actually written that music; it seemed to come from the universe, just for me. It wasn't till later that I learned there were such things as composers and I saw a photo of Gershwin, and decided I had to marry him. My mother broke the news that he had died in 1938. Welles was my second heartbreak. I fell in love with the guy in Citizen Kane, *the one who dances with the line of chorus girls when he's celebrating the debut of his newspaper. He has this tremendous charisma. Not only did I learn that he was dead, but that even if he were still around, he'd be tremendously fat and bear no resemblance at all to the young movie star. Except for that resonant, seductive speaking voice. I'm still in love with that voice.*

Then there was Charlie Chaplin. I pretty much knew he was dead, but held out hope. My father took me to see Modern Times *in some old movie theater on the Upper West Side that was about to be turned into a multiplex. The*

*sound track alone is enough to make you cry ("Smile"!),
and Chaplin manages to be funny and sad simultaneously.
When he and Paulette Goddard (who was his wife at the
time—and how lucky can you get, being a movie star and
married to Chaplin!) walk down the road at the end, with
the theme music playing, your heart breaks for them but you
know they will somehow survive.*

*Now I think I'm in love with the young Luke Bellavita,
although there's the slim chance he's my grandfather,
which would be pretty creepy. He was a little too ambitious
to be a nice guy, but I think that people who go after success with that kind of passion usually leave pieces of their
niceness strewn along the road.*

*I wonder if any of them could possibly live up to my ex-
pectations, or if it's better to keep them frozen and forever
young in their music and on the screen.*

*My CD is almost finished. Mom is a good photographer
and she designed the cover. We're doing an homage to my
grandmother, so we went down to the Village and I posed
in the same spot on Jones Street off Bleecker where Dylan
(and a girlfriend) stood for his* Freewheelin' Bob Dylan *album (1962). My mother Photoshopped in the old
background with the VW bus.*

COLLECTIBLES

LP—*Katey Lacey Live at the Coconut Grove* (1967)—
$25.00

Letter announcing the FUGS Cross-Country Vietnam
Protest Caravan (1967)

Handwritten announcement: Turn in Your Draft
Card!! (1967)

Cleveland Plain Dealer (archives) May, 1969
entertainment listings—Holiday Inn Lounge: The
Donny Drake Band [sic].

Poster: An Aquarian Exposition in White Lake, N.Y.
Three Days of Peace & Music, August 15-17 (1969)

Photo: Spahn Movie Ranch, Chatsworth, California
(August 1969)

Part Three

And if I see the day
I'd only have to stay,
So I'll bid farewell in the night and be gone.

Bob Dylan, "Restless Farewell"

33

The blare of a car horn dopplered into the distance.

"Fucking asshole." Donnie's hands gripped the wheel.

Julie woke up, groggy, in the backseat. Donnie's wife, LaTrelle, was asleep in the passenger seat, head leaning back, her mouth open in a snore.

"Where are we?" Julie's voice came out a creaky whisper.

"Past Cleveland. We'll be hitting Toledo in another hour, then figure three more to Bay City, allowing for a pit stop, breakfast, gas..." He kept on talking, giving every single fucking detail of their itinerary. No wonder Donnie was awake and chattering. He kept a ready supply of No-Doze on hand, and often boosted it with a Black Beauty chaser. Her eyes drooped down again. Amazing how she could sleep through just about anything now. Day, night, in the car, in strange motel beds.

The big white Chrysler needed filling about every two hours. The thing probably got less than ten miles per gallon, especially pulling the U-Haul with all their band equipment: Donnie's big Baldwin organ, Al's drums, Mack's guitars, the amps and P.A. system, mikes and wires. They were a self-contained, travel-anywhere "show band", The Donnie Drake Four.

Donnie went on about the gigs he had lined up, stretching through the rest of the year and the next, until 1970, not that she was planning to stay that long. Stuck like the Drakes in lounge limbo? Outside, there was little to look at in the dawn's early light but the distant taillights of Al's car up ahead, where he rode with his wife, Cindy, and their squally baby, and the guitar player, Mack Stepiczki. Julie and Mack usually flipped a coin in secret, the loser having to travel with Al and Cindy and the brat, but it was no treat sharing close quarters with Donnie and LaTrelle, either.

It had to be below freezing out there; gray sky, hard, ice packed ground. She closed her eyes again.

"Bay City, Michigan, everybody out!" Donnie announced.

They stumbled out of the cars in front of a small motel/lodge, on the edge of the Lake Huron waterway. Snow swirled over the slick gray water. A giant freighter with Russian writing on the side moved silently through the narrow passage, sailors hanging over the rail, staring at the shore. The ship was less than a hundred feet away. One of the crewmen waved. Julie waved back and wondered if she was meant to love that sailor, and had missed her chance. The ship disappeared into a snowy shroud.

"Julie, you mind lending a hand?" LaTrelle said, all sweet magnolia and vinegar. She looked a hell of a lot older than the thirty-eight years she claimed. Donnie also insisted he was under forty, and onstage he could get almost away with it, with his boyish grin and bleached out hair. Up close was another story.

Al and Cindy struggled with suitcases and baby paraphernalia. Mack reluctantly held the baby and sang to himself, preoccupied with guitar riffs and masturbation.

At nineteen, he was the youngest in the band, an affable sloth who usually wore a comfortably frayed red T-shirt no matter the weather, and antediluvian jeans. Onstage, he was forced to put on the band "uniform": a dark green suit with wide satin lapels and matching stripe-down-the-trouser legs. As the chick singer, Julie wore glittery long dresses that showed off as much of her as the law allowed.

"Food?" she asked Mack.

"I got stuff from the candy machine in Pittsburgh. I'm gonna hit the sack for a while."

Donnie and LaTrelle were happy to go out in search of a meal. LaTrelle blamed her extra twenty plus pounds on road food and eating late at night.

"I have a slow metabolism," she informed Julie, not for the first time, as they settled into a sticky booth at Denny's, a few miles from the motel. "Do you have any idea what my blood pressure was yesterday?" LaTrelle helped herself to the rolls, buttering them generously.

"Mine was a hundred eighty over ninety five," Donnie told them proudly.

The waitress shuffled over with coffee. Donnie and La-Trelle ordered big platters of burgers and fries. Julie had a craving for pancakes slathered with syrup. They barely spoke during the meal, although LaTrelle eyed Julie's plate with a certain hostility.

"I could use a piece of pie after that long drive," La-Trelle said. "But I really shouldn't..."

"Coconut crème, apple and chocolate chiffon is all we got t'day," the waitress recited.

"Apple," said Donnie.

"No, sweetie, not apple."

"Thought you weren't having any?"

"Well, they all look so good."

The waitress gazed out the window, tapping her pad with a chipped, pearly-nailed fingertip.

"Now, sugar, if you want pie, why don't you order your own?"

"I don't want a whole piece."

"Chocolate chiffon okay?" Donnie asked. LaTrelle nodded.

Donnie grinned helplessly at the waitress. "One big piece of that and two forks."

The Blue Pheasant Restaurant and Lounge was just off Highway 21, conspicuous by the huge neon bird—resembling a turkey more than a pheasant—blinking a flashy welcome. Al was setting up his drums when they got back from the diner. Mack sat cross-legged on the stage, playing the same riff over and over on his Stratocaster.

"If you got nothing to do," Donnie said to Mack, "why don't you give me a hand with this fucking thing?" Mack rose slowly, yawning. Together, they pushed the organ into place and ran the electrical cords into the speaker system.

A man approached purposefully. Even before he introduced himself, Julie knew he was the club owner.

"Hi, I'm Jack Kennedy! No relation to you know who!"

No shit, Julie thought.

"Everybody calls me Jackie K!"

"Hey, nice to meet you, Jackie," said Donnie, offering his hand.

"Jackie K! You know, the Blue Pheasant is like my baby. I've made this place what it is today and I always get the top acts on the circuit. My customers know when they come to see a show at the Blue Pheasant, they're getting as good entertainment as they could in Las Vegas or Los Angeles or New York City! So I'm really lookin' forward to hearing you folks! Anything you need, ask for Jackie K! See you to-night!" He left the room.

"Thanks, Jackie K!" Mack and Julie burst out laughing. Donnie flashed them a 'grow the fuck up' look. Mack pushed back his scraggly hair and squealed a few notes on the guitar.

Mack could make her laugh, and sometimes that got her through the long nights. But he was such a jerk. They were both twenty-one but she felt years older. She was sure he was a virgin the first time she got him into bed, although he'd never admit it. He didn't appear to be aware of whether or not she had orgasms, which she didn't. She slept with Mack so that she'd have someone to torment, someone to hold her when she needed it, and to reject when she wanted to be left alone, which was much of the time.

"Let's take it from the top of the show," said Donnie. He counted off and they began the intro for the 'Hair' medley, with Donnie rasping out lead vocal. Al pitter-patted behind on the drums. Julie closed her eyes and sang backup, then a solo on a snippet of "Good Morning Starshine". Mack launched into a frenzied guitar solo. She glared at him. He'd never be as good as Luke, not if he practiced till he died. They breezed through the rest of the set, concluding with a raucous "I'll Be There", with choreography.

"Sounds good," Donnie declared after they'd finished. "Just a quick meeting, okay?"

Mack groaned and slumped into a chair at the table where LaTrelle was drinking coffee and reading the menu. Al glanced at his watch.

"This is the beginning of a better circuit for us," Donnie proclaimed when they were all seated. "Once the word gets out how good we are, we'll get the bigger rooms, then it's Vegas and New York and the real money." Donnie took a sip of coffee and looked at Julie. "Jackie K likes you. I can tell. Nothin' like a sexy chick to steal the show." He didn't sound happy about it. It really galled Donnie that Julie and Mack occasionally got it on.

She remembered the ad that had brought her into the band: **Top Show Band Seeks Female Lead Singer.** A sign on the bulletin board of a Cincinnati hotel lounge where she stopped in to use the rest room. Called the phone number collect and they took her sight unheard. Mack later told her that the previous singer, their fourth, had quit after some kind of ugly scene with LaTrelle, who accused the singer of fucking Donnie. Of course, LaTrelle would never use the f-word.

"So get some rest," Donnie told them, "Sound check at eight, show at nine."

In her room, Julie turned on the TV and flipped the dial through the three stations: game show, soap opera, religious program. She turned it off and collapsed onto the bed.

Jackie K approached the entertainer's table. "That was pretty good for the first set, people, but if you don't mind a little suggestion, I think you need to do more 'up' stuff and less of that show music. People here don't care much for show tunes. They want to hear what they hear on the radio or the jukebox, see what I mean?"

"Sure, Jackie K, sure," Donnie responded quickly, "More Top Forty."

When the club owner walked away, Donnie leaned in conspiratorially. "He liked us. Or else he wouldn't bother giving us any constructive criticism."

After the second set, Jackie K came over again and suggested they were maybe playing too much rock and roll and the people in Michigan liked a softer sound, so that they could eat their dinners and drink their drinks and have a conversation without getting their ears blasted off.

They opened the third set with their 'love' medley: "The Look of Love", "I'll Never Fall in Love Again", and "Love Walked In", then segued into a Beatles medley, and finished with a tribute to big band oldies, featuring Al's Gene Krupa solo. It was the only time Al seemed fully alive, his eyes closed in drummer heaven, thinned hair flying over his forehead as he pounded the tom-tom.

Jackie K bought a round of drinks, reminding them that this courtesy was just the one time on their first night, and thereafter they'd have to pay for their own drinks and food; some of the bands drank and ate up all his profits. "I had to institute a policy."

There wasn't enough audience for a fourth set. Jackie K let them lock up the instruments in his office.

Julie and Mack rode in the backseat of Al's car, which smelled of old diapers. Al groused about how Donnie didn't know how to run the band, and the music the was crap, because what everybody really wanted to hear was more big band stuff, like his Gene Krupa solo. The car didn't warm up and Julie shivered under her coat, the sequined gown like ice against her skin.

The room was the mess she'd left earlier, makeup spilled in the bathroom, instant coffee, cold and congealed, in a cardboard cup on the dresser. The silence pressed on her eardrums. She tried the TV: test pattern, static, nothing. The knob came off in her hand; she hurled it across the room and watched it bounce and roll under the bed.

Outside, a freighter moaned deeply as it slid along the Lake Huron waterway.

She picked up the phone to call Mack's room, changed her mind and set it down. Why was she in a motel in the middle of the end of the world when she was supposed to be someone?

Mack called her room an hour later and hinted around until she told him to come over. His body was slim and boyish and as he slid into her, she thought of Luke. By the time Mack was finished, she was weeping silently, and wouldn't explain to him just what he had done wrong.

The next day, Julie and Mack borrowed Al's car and drove into town, and went shopping separately. In the bookstore, she leafed through a book of crappy poetry by a guy who used to read his poems in the basket houses and put everyone to sleep.

After a few minutes, Mack was at her shoulder.

"What'd you get?" she asked.

"That new band. Silver Knight. The guitar player is a gas." The picture on the album cover showed four musicians in front of a white Mustang convertible. Luke wore a cowboy hat, his hair touching his shoulders, and a netted silver vest, like knight's mail. Casey had on a top hat and western clothes. The others also sported mixed period clothes. "Oh," she breathed. "He did it."

"You *know* them?"

"Know them?" she said loudly, "I fucked them."

The astonished look on his face made her laugh.

"Well, not all of them. These two." She flicked a forefinger at Luke's and Casey's faces. "And I made a record—well, demos—with him." She touched Luke's image again.

The album had been recorded in Los Angeles. That's where he was now.

"You made a record with Luke Bellavita?"

"Maybe Luke Bellavita made a record with *me*." A queasy lightheadedness swept over her. Too much coffee, crazy hours, not enough sleep. "Where are we, any-way?"

"Bay City, Michigan."

"Got any Valium?"

"No, but I got speed. I think LaTrelle has Librium or some shit. You fucked Luke Bellavita and Casey Mahoney, too?"

"Oh, shut up." She stalked toward the mall exit.

Mack trotted after her. "What's the matter, what did I say? You're the one who brought it up."

"Did you ever feel like you just had to get out of a place, because the air was sucking the breath right out of you? Or the floor was suddenly crooked?"

"When I'm drunk the room kinda spins. Or if I take too much speed I feel like I can't breathe fast enough to keep up with my heartbeat and it could all explode."

"I mean when you're *not* stoned. If you can remember back that far." She sprinted to Al's car, leaned against it, and stared up at the cold winter sky.

"Julie? You okay?"

She shook her head, her throat constricted, thinking about herself in the third person pathetic again. They were in the car. Just moving forward helped. "Drive faster."

"I don't want to get a ticket, Al will have a shitfit."

"You are such a little slug!!"

His foot pushed the accelerator. She glanced over and saw seventy-five, eighty, eighty-five. Good. If it were faster, maybe they would fly off the earth.

34

Elliot had to step around the construction littering the suite of offices, in its last stages of renovation. An artist was carefully stenciling the door:

The Levine Company
Elliot J. Levine, President

The twelfth floor corner office had unobstructed views of the Hollywood Hills on one side, and on the other, beyond the Capitol Records building, the smog-shrouded skyline of downtown L.A. His desk was a smoothly oiled cherry wood.

When he first had to decide the look and design of the offices, he hadn't had any idea where to begin. Fortunately, Luna mentioned an interior designer, and Elliot had put it into his hands. As they proceeded from blueprint to reality, he grew more confident in his preferences: a view, a sense of space and light; a full stereo system with tape decks and two record players on one wall; a fully-stocked bar that could be tucked away. Ray, wouldn't you enjoy this, he gloated.

"Happy Becker on one," his secretary called out.

"Hap, how's it going? Did you give some more thought to my offer?"

"Elliot, I don't know..."

"Let's have coffee."

"You paying? Sure."

They met at Izzy's, a New York style deli in Santa Monica. Elliot was late, and found Happy sitting in a booth across from a blown-up photo of the Manhattan skyline. Pictures of Times Square in bygone days decorated the walls.

"I got hungry waiting," Happy said, indicating his half-finished chocolate shake.

Happy's eyes were tiny squints above puffy, pasty cheeks. Those eyes were now focused on a female customer in a white leather mini dress. "Man, she looks like she plays the skin flute in the Fuck Philharmonic."

Elliot closed his eyes for a beat. Happy's crudeness always embarrassed him. The clothes, too. While Elliot sported a dark grey tailored jacket, Happy wore plaid Bermuda shorts and a pink T-shirt that strained over his paunch.

He ordered a black coffee and a prune Danish from the waitress. "Hear the game last night?"

"Hear it? I was there! Right behind home plate courtesy of a client I shall be so tactful not to name."

"Seaver was incredible. If they keep it up to the All Star Game, they could catch Chicago."

They both nodded sagely, contemplating this wondrous possibility.

"So what's up?" Happy asked. "Let's get the pitch over with so we can go back to talking about what's important, like broads and batting averages."

Elliot drained his coffee and waved for a refill. "Look, Hap, the new company is coming together, the offices are nearly finished. It's going to be big. All the representation, production and publishing under one roof. That means we own the product and don't have to give away all those points to Atlantic or CBS or Shitkicker or whatever Records.

We do our own marketing, have a studio for rehearsing and putting down demos, eventually we'll expand to a full master-quality studio. Everything in-house." Elliot focused on Happy like a laser. "There's room for someone like you. I mean, what're you doing sitting at home writing promos? You could be part of this."

"Levine, I'm flattered, but this isn't 'Judy and Mickey, lets get a barn and put on a show'. It takes bucks, big bucks. And clients."

"I got bucks. And clients. Silver Knight, for one."

Happy laughed. "I can't believe you stole 'em from under Taylor Pine's nose." He finished his shake with a loud rasping slurp.

"Yeah, how about that?" Elliot said with a grin. "There's more unhappy talent at Taylor Pine than stars in the heavens, let alone what's floating around out there undiscovered and unrepresented."

Taylor Pine wasn't about to sue him for stealing their clients—the performers had left on their own. Of course, it helped that Elliot had taken them to Chasens and the Derby for lavish lunches, gone into debt renting a yacht for a cruise to Catalina. He sent vintage champagne and persuaded them that what they needed wasn't a big stuffy old agency, but an energetic upstart, devoted to *them*.

In the weeks before he left Taylor Pine, before anyone knew he was even planning it, he worked later than usual.

When everyone was gone, except the cleaning crew, he went into each office and pored through the Rolodexes, copying all the important names. His hands trembled; he looked over his shoulder at every slight creak and sound. He pulled out files, and made photocopies of the clients' contracts. A few days' later, he'd call the clients, arrange lunch or drinks—and make them a better offer. With Gary Luna's money to back him up.

Elliot continued, "I've got couple of junior agents with A&R experience who are coming in with me and they'll bring some more acts. Then there's you, who can sell snow to Eskimos. Head of Marketing and Promotion. A salary, plus a part of the action. A secretary, some gorgeous young blonde." He raised his eyebrows up and down like Groucho Marx.

"I've got a secretary."

"Fine. Bring her along."

Happy studied him. "So who's paying for all of this? You win the Irish Sweepstakes or something'?"

"I got a silent partner."

"I don't know...shit, it sounds good, but...you know, running my own show, being my own boss. Levine, I'm flattered, but I gotta say no. However..." He drew out the word teasingly. "You may have me on retainer at a special bargain rate. A start-up courtesy. Send me a blonde or two, I'll give you a year at half-price. You know I can smell a hit blindfolded."

"Think about it. You could be missing a big chance."

"It won't be the first. Hey, you know, the girl who works for me is from New York. Maybe you know her."

"Right. It's such a small town." He'd been certain Happy would want the job. Gary Luna would be less than pleased by the turndown, especially if Hap panned any of their clients.

"I don't think he's going to come aboard," Elliot informed Luna on the phone an hour later.

"He's making a mistake."

"That's what I told him." His palms were always sweaty when he talked to Luna, no matter how well he prepared himself.

"Everything else all right?"

"No problems."

"That's what I like to hear." There was a slight echo, either from the connection or some cavernous room in his estate. "Spider and some of the fellas are heading over to the Grove tonight to hear Dionne Warwick," Gary said. "She's got an opening act you oughta take a look at. Comics."

Elliot licked his dry lips. "Sure. I'll be there."

The Coconut Grove was a lavish nightclub that jutted out from the Ambassador Hotel's main building on Wilshire Boulevard. A tier of wide curved steps led up to the entrance. He joined Spider and Luna's gofers and sycophants—Elliot privately thought of them as Lunatics—as they were ushered past the common folk crowding the lobby. The club was a series of banked levels and decorated tables, leading down to a broad raised stage that curved out into the room. Tropical designs were the motif, with flowers and palms in every corner, sparkling silverware and crystal, colorful pink cloth napkins folded like origami. It was the faint lingering essence of Old Hollywood.

They had barely enough time to order drinks when the lights dimmed and the orchestra played a short intro. Two guys came barreling onstage, and told jokes in the Martin and Lewis tradition. Most of the audience laughed heartily, but Elliot stifled a yawn. Was he going to have to sign these bozos? Whose relatives were they?

After the opening act, there was a break while the waiters scurried around taking more orders. He was relieved when Spider pronounced the comics 'real losers'. The room was packed, and he recognized a table of agents from William Morris; rival managers; a couple of execs from Dionne Warwick's label, Scepter Records; and the celebrity quotient, notably Herb Alpert, and Sonny and Cher, who were booked into the Grove next.

He excused himself to make a phone call. The booths were busy and as he waited, foot tapping impatiently, he noticed an attractive woman. A fraction of a second passed before the recognition reached his brain. She was a little thinner, and her hair was longer.

"Rochelle?"

"Elliot?!"

"What are you doing here?"

"I'm seeing the show, what do you think?"

"I mean in L.A."

"I live here."

"Me, too."

"I know. I work for Happy Becker. Your name comes up a lot."

"Oh," he said, and "Oh," again. Happy had mentioned his secretary was from New York. "Well, why didn't you get in touch?"

Ray's ghost rose up between them, a weighty silence.

"It's great to see you," he said.

"How's Arlene?"

"We have twins. Boys."

"That's nice."

The music resumed in the main room.

"Well," she said, "Maybe I'll see you later."

Elliot had just returned to his seat when the orchestra launched into "Do You Know the Way to San Jose?" The audience applauded wildly as the star entered. He rolled his glass of cola between his two palms, cooling them. There was an unfamiliar ache in his chest and a tingling in his groin. Hadn't felt this way since he could barely remember. Arlene flashed into his mind, but she occupied an entirely different compartment. How odd it was that once he had married, and could have sex with his wife fairly often—she was a willing partner—his ardor for her had cooled. This made him sad, so he tried not to examine it, preferring to fantasize about young women he caught glimpses of while driving, or at the clubs where they clung to the musicians. They responded to his prestige, his growing power, and didn't appear to view him as a short, balding man, but as someone to fawn over. Not that he took advantage. At least not yet.

Rochelle glanced at her watch: ten-thirty already. Her escort was a fifty-year-old accountant who did Becker's books, and had a crush on her. She went out with him because he took her to nice places and spent money and didn't push her for anything more than a goodnight kiss. He kissed with his lips tightly closed.

The show wasn't half over and it was a long drive back. Too bad she couldn't just book a room at the Ambassador. If Ray were here, he'd flash some money and they'd have a suite. A limo. She no longer waited moment to moment, breathless, for him to reappear—it had been almost two years—but she still saw reminders of him in strangers: one man's smile, another's eyes, the slouch of a shoulder. Each time, her heart would lurch, shock and relief mingled with fear and disgust with herself for the sexual craving she'd once had for such a liar and thief, and probably worse.

At the next table, a woman with long corn silk blonde hair, and wearing a peek-a-boo white net mini-dress, was also with an older man, a producer or agent with narrow, gray-haired hands. The man fondled the woman's knee under the table, while she appeared to ignore it and watched Dionne Warwick sing "Walk on By". A few minutes later, the producer's hairy hand had crept up between her thighs, and she still acted oblivious. It wasn't too difficult to fill in the rest of their evening: the scotch at his place, somewhere with a view, the blow job, the bland, numb taste of his prick, the woman washing up in the spa tub and staring out at the star-flecked night, feeling hollow and a little unclean, but proud of what she thought of as her own sophistication.

That was the old me—with Ray.

Out of the corner of her eye, Rochelle noticed Elliot making his way to the back of the club.

"Be right back," she whispered to her date. She hurried up the aisle, to the strains of "What the World Needs Now".

Elliot was at the phone booth again. "There ought to be something like a portable phone," he said.

"The cords would be too long."

Inside the booth, his expression changed to dutiful seriousness when the other person—Rochelle guessed it was Arlene—answered.

She watched the parade of hotel guests in the lobby browsing the rows of boutiques

"Everything all right at home?" she asked when Elliot came out.

"Just fine."

They strolled a short distance down the hallway. "Where was RFK shot?" she asked.

"The kitchen off one of the ballrooms, I think."

"Creepy. Let's find it."

They continued down to the end of a long hallway and up the wide staircase. She pushed at a door.

"Maybe we shouldn't," he said.

She ignored his trepidation. "You know what this hotel reminds me of? An ocean liner. Like Wilshire Boulevard is floating somewhere in the Caribbean. That's why there're all those palm trees."

"Imported. They're not native to California," he said.

They were in a large ballroom closed for remodeling. Thick velvet drapes were piled on the shiny wooden floor.

"Neither am I," she said, "Native to California. Or you. I'm not sure I'll ever really belong here."

"It's a city of castaways."

"Who are you: Gilligan or the Skipper?"

"What Jew would set foot on the *Minnow?*"

"Who says none of them were Jewish?"

Elliot smiled. "My grandmother always said coming to this country steerage was cruise enough for her."

She was comfortable with him. The smooth, expensive cut of his suit felt nice against her arm.

"We should go," he said.

"Don't you want to see the Kennedy bloodstains?"

"I think they would've washed them away by now."

The lobby was especially intrusive after the dusky silence of the shuttered ballroom.

"I'd love to see your new office," she said. "Who knows, maybe you'll be hiring. I could think about leaving the wonderful wacky world of Happy Becker."

"Are you serious?"

"I did some A&R work for BigWheel—never got much credit for it—but I think I have an ear for talent. Maybe you could give me some contacts?"

"I could use a secre- an assistant. We're growing. In a year, I promise, you'll have your *own* secretary, your *own* clients."

They were at the entrance to the Coconut Grove. A swell of applause burst louder as the ushers opened the doors.

"Are you serious?"

"Come over to the office tomorrow. Lunch on me." He handed her his card.

"I'll be there."

He could barely concentrate on the remainder of the show. A few minutes later, they were all standing outside the nightclub, waiting for the cars to be brought around. He didn't see Rochelle.

The Luna limo pulled up, the chauffeur ran around to open the back door, and Spider and the others got in, disappearing behind the curtained windows; they drove away. A few tourists gawked, trying to see who was in the limo. Presently, Elliot's Buick appeared. He was glad the others were gone. It really was time for something more impressive, like a Lincoln Continental.

Elliot took Rochelle to the Derby on Wilshire. Since it was across from the Ambassador and the Coconut Grove, there was a sense of continuity to the reunion they'd begun the night before. After ordering and catching up on the intervening years, he turned to business.

"I want you to work for me," he said directly, and went on to name a generous salary. "How soon can you start?"

"I've got to give him some notice. I can't just walk out on Happy."

"No, of course not, I wouldn't expect you to. 'He'll be mad enough at me for stealing you."

"He'll get over it," she said. "I'll help him find someone else."

"One other little thing," Elliot said. "And if this makes you uncomfortable, just say so and it won't be mentioned again."

"What, I have to sleep with the boss?"

He actually blushed. "Of course not!"

"I was only kidding."

"Listen, I need to trust you on this."

She raised an eyebrow.

"It would help if you could, uh, bring Happy's mailing list. All his subscribers. The programmers he, uh, deals with. The record company contacts. If you see what I mean."

"Well, yeah." She sat back, a little unnerved. Annoyed that she'd thought he wanted her to work for him because of her own brilliance. "You're quite a piece of work, Elliot. Do I get the job without the pirated list?"

"Of course."

She toyed with her fork, musing that Happy wouldn't lose anything, so what was the big deal? It was just a list of names. His subscribers, garnered from years of building up the business.

She prowled Ray's office in the dark, opening the safe.

Well, if she'd been able to do *that*, this would be a snap. It was too late to get all moral about it.

"If he catches me and has me arrested, you'll have to bail me out."

"I don't want you to do anything you're not comfortable with."

"You can worry when I start stealing all your clients."

Elliot put out his hand. "It's a deal?"

"Deal."

The waiter brought the baked Alaska, flaming and melting, and divided it up on their plates. Fragrant coffee was poured from a silver pot. Elliot ordered cognac, specifying a vintage year. A moment later two large snifters were set before them.

"Hear anything from Julie?"

Rochelle swirled the deep gold liquid in her glass, inhaling its scent.

"I think she fell off the earth."

35

Julie knew this feeling—the incandescence—but in the past it had only been for short periods, the first weeks of being in love, or anticipating a performance. This time, it lasted and she floated above it, immune to sleep—an exceptional person did not need sleep—just a matter of will, *like performing with the Donnie Drake Four which she did on automatic pilot while her mind raced and spun and she hated the Donnie Drake Four, they hated her, too, and as soon as this lap of the tour was over, they'd dump her in some god-forsaken town and hire another singer, yes, she'd caught Donnie, on several occasions, whispering to Al and they had to be talking about her and that bitch LaTrelle filled Donnie's head with all sorts of anti-Julie bile, i know it i know and they don't think i know that i know, and even Mack was getting weird around her—she would be singing on stage, the Holiday Inn Lounge patrons drinking and talking, maybe dancing right in front of her like she was invisible, a jukebox in a dress for Chrissake, and she saw herself put down the microphone and leave. In elevators, she was not sure what kept her from screaming, or touching herself or attacking someone. What stops us? And this would scare her so much her hands would tremble. In her room, whichever awful lonely sanitized-for-your-protection room she found herself in, awake all night long staring into the bathroom mirror with its invisible traces of vanished visitors, holding her razor poised over her right wrist—what stops me? The bottle of pills called their siren song. It was happening on-stage almost every night. What keeps me here? Nothing. No one.*

So it was no surprise to *her*—that third person *her*—when, in the middle of "Can't Take My Eyes Off You", she walked off the stage. Donnie glanced up from the keyboard, startled. Mack didn't notice at first, he was too busy wringing noise out of the guitar.

Standing on that stage one more microsecond was intolerable and the next second she was leaving, not even a conscious thought, her body took action, and *fuck you all very much*. She snatched her coat from a chair in the back, didn't even pause to put it on as she flew by the club manager and out into the chilly Ohio or was it Indiana night. Her thoughts came so fast they were in danger of a pileup, she would have begun to scream and, thinking of it now, the faces of the audience and the staff and the musicians if she had gone nuts all over the stage, well, now it seemed so incredibly funny!

She walked for quite a long time toward the motel but couldn't find it and began to despair. A car pulled up. In the dark interior a shadow moved, muttered "ride?", so she got in, because it could not possibly be dangerous, not when she was so luminous. She felt the glow sparking from her, light bouncing off metal in bright sun.

She told the driver the name of the motel, smiling brilliantly. Maybe he'd even wait while she picked up her stuff.

Outside the window of whatever car or truck or van it happened to be at that leg of the journey west, each truck stop, diner, hill, mountain, gas station, each place on earth was an inspiration. The scenery turned from red and purple canyons into night-shadowed lavender desert, the scents flying in the window so heady and powerful, she brimmed over, and she licked the salt of tears rolling down her cheeks.

Joe/George/Jim/Ginny/Ned/Alice/Huey drove her, she sat in the passenger seat exchanging small talk about their lives as salesman truck driver college dropout ex-pilot wanderer bull-wrangler divorced waitress magician. They asked about her guitar. I'm going to be famous in L.A., and they believed her—who could doubt her?—asked for her autograph: knew you when, tell everyone you were in my car.

The sunset exploded on the horizon, they were getting closer.

Only going as far as Bakersfield. Sorry.

that's okay she could fly there if she chose she could fly

another night descended, the darkness chirping and crying out. Donnie and LaTrelle and Mack faded into the past, the expressions on their faces, what she imagined they'd said later, the names they must have called her—and it came back again how she'd laughed, and cried out on the gloomy road as lights zoomed by, the earth vibrated total silence...she craned her face up to the stars there had never been so many, so close and clustered she could snatch them from their nests and smear their radiance all over her face, she hurled her own light at them and they winked back that they got it

By the time the rattling Volkswagen bug rolled into hurray-for-Hollywood she was tired but elated to see it for the first time. Just let me out, she told the guy who'd talked her ear off for three hours about the Navy.

Dawn was chilly; cold, really, so she tugged another sweater out of her suitcase. Wasn't it supposed to be hot in California? Anxiety grew inside her that she'd done a deed so terribly wrong and couldn't remember what it was, and where was she? The sun finally began to insinuate itself along the boulevard. Die for coffee. Her arms ached from carrying suitcase and bag and guitar for blocks. She had no idea where to go next and needed a bath. *People are staring at her,* Julie thought, again in third person pathetic, *wondering who she is.* The waitress at the counter smiled. Where you from, honey?

"Everywhere."

The waitress laughed. "I know what you mean."

Julie reached into her overstuffed pocketbook for the worn leather purse where her money was: a hundred and twelve dollars and change. Donnie's band had paid pretty well, and a lot of it in cash, but she'd managed to spend whatever came her way. She paid for the coffee and the donut.

"Is there a hotel that's not too expensive, near here?" she asked the cashier, a fat woman counting out quarters.

"Try the Galaxy, turn right at the corner, up three streets."

The two-story pink building with a courtyard rented by the day, week or month. Julie paid twenty-five dollars for a week; that was as far ahead as she could imagine.

The high mood plummeted into a pit of inertia and hopelessness. She slept, and slept some more. Tomorrow, I will begin, she kept promising herself: she would find a place to play her music and someone would have to hear her, and someone else...it was all too complicated...so in the morning, she slept until it was too late to start the day right; another day vanished like the others.

The guitar leaned against a wall, neglected. In her half-sleep, she thought of ways to die, and occasionally, new ideas popped, ephemeral as soap bubbles, of Things She Would Do to Make a Difference in the World: be a nurse; a journalist in Vietnam; a civil rights lawyer; a leading psychiatrist. She would join a commune or she could just sleep forever.

Days passed, she remained in bed except to eat or to forage for food at a takeout place two blocks away. The television droned, the shadowed room baked in the mid-day sun.

The siege of inertia and sorrow ended. She dragged herself down to the pool. Lacking a bathing suit, she wore shorts and a wife-beater she'd borrowed from Mack and forgotten to return. No one else was around at first; she lay there alone, getting burned, freckled and stupefied. When she opened her eyes, two people reclined side by side in lounge chairs. The man was bony, darkly tanned, with black body hair that crept in a line from his chest to his belly and disappeared under shiny silver shorts. The woman was thin, too, with large, soft breasts that sloped out the sides of her bikini bra. She had a long vertical scar on her stomach. Julie stared at them from behind her sunglasses.

"How ya doing?" the man asked.

"'kay," she replied.

"New to town?"

"Yeah."

"Like it?"

"Haven't seen much yet." She wondered if she looked and sounded like a normal human.

"I can dig it."

The woman whispered to him, and he nodded, looking at Julie.

"You want some fun, meet some real folks, check out the Haunted House. My pal's a bartender. Geordie. Tell him Cash said hey."

"I don't have a car. Yet."

"Coupla blocks that way, you could walk," he nodded over his shoulder. "They got live music."

That night, she put on her favorite outfit, a long peach suede vest with fringes that brushed her knees, over jeans, the material washed and faded so thin the imprint of her hipbones showed through. She dropped a string of blue glass beads over her head, leaving her hair loose, dead straight to the small of her back; slipped on a pair of sandals with wedgie heels and straps that wound around her ankles.

The club was crowded, dark and smoky, with giant eerie wall murals, like the inside of an amusement park horror ride. Janis Joplin screamed her pain from a jukebox. Julie hesitated, unsure why she had come. She'd never been to a bar where she wasn't either playing music or with a guy. Alone seemed lost, naked. She snaked her way through the throng, trying to keep a purposeful expression on her face, as if she'd come to meet someone who hadn't yet arrived.

Buying a drink at the bar seemed like a good idea, but she'd never done that herself either. Guys always bought the drinks. Laughter shrilled in the air. A smoke ring drifted past her face. If only she smoked. Her stomach tightened, and she was about to flee toward the door, when she felt someone lightly touch her breast. She drew back and bumped into someone else. The press of bodies was dizzying. A man—a boy, really—was in front of her and she wasn't sure if he was the one who had touched her or even if it had been on purpose.

His face was flushed, and maybe it was from embarrassment or just drink and the heat inside the club. Lank strands of plain brown hair hung over his forehead. His eyes were pale and bloodshot, wide-spaced. He had the fuzz of a mustache and beard, like someone who was trying to look more mature.

"Ruthie?" he asked her.

"No."

"Sorry, babe, took you for another chick. Fuckin' zoo, ain't it?"

"Yeah. Is there a bartender named Geordie?"

"Damned if I know, this ain't my regular hangout, know what I mean?"

She nodded. It was a relief to have someone to talk to.

His smile didn't quite reach his eyes. Not that they were cold, just a little blank. "You sure got some beautiful hair. You could sell it."

She wasn't sure whether or not he was joking, but then he laughed, and it, too, sounded a little disconnected. Stoned, yeah, stoned. The crowd, like a tide, had nudged them closer to the bar, which was long and wooden, three deep with customers. There were two bartenders and she wondered if one of them was Geordie.

"You want something?" the guy asked.

"A beer'd be okay."

"Got any money?"

"Well, I guess so."

"Just kidding, I'll buy it for you. Hey! Barkeep! Send down a brew!" It didn't appear that anyone was paying attention. "Jerkoffs! I hate when people don't do their jobs right."

One of the bartenders turned around. Julie's benefactor mimed a beer and a moment later one came sailing down the bar. The guy handed it to Julie and watched her take a sip, which made her self-conscious. She coughed and spilled a little bit onto the floor.

"Here, I'll get that for you." He leaned close, dabbing her hand with the corner of his tie-dyed T-shirt. The gesture's awkward formality was touching. She relaxed a little. The beer mug in her hand was an anchor.

"Guess you ain't been here too long, huh?"

"Where?"

"Land o' the sun. You're so white."

"I never tan, anyway."

"Me neither. I like those freckles. I could play connect-the-dots." He traced a pattern on her shoulder.

She couldn't pull away because there was nowhere to go, and anyway it felt good to have someone noticing her.

"Why L.A.?" he asked.

"I don't know. I sing folk stuff."

"Yeah?" He seemed impressed. "You play, too?"

"Guitar."

"Me, too, a little. You good?"

"Yeah. I mean, I think so."

"They'd love you at the ranch."

"What ranch?"

"Friend of mine rents this place," he indicated with his head, "Up north of the city, in the mountains. Some real creative folk up there, they love music n'shit."

"Are there horses?"

"Sure. It's a real ranch. Used to be some movie guy's place, they still use it sometimes to shoot movies and TV. They did some *Bonanzas* there."

"Really?"

"Sure. Some of the guys were in it, background n'shit."

The bar was unbearably noisy. If she fell apart right there no one would catch her, they'd just trample her into the sawdust on the floor.

"...practiced roping but I kept falling off, looked like a real jerk, everybody thought it was hysterical, guess I don't have no future as a stuntman."

Maybe he would take her to this ranch, and she would wake up in the morning with the sound of birds outside her window, someone cooking up a huge breakfast, and she would ride a horse.

"You can hear the coyotes howling at night. Champ—he's the guy rents the place—says the devil shines out of their eyes, and when it gets real cold, they just freeze up and the eyes drop out like marbles you can pick 'em off the ground if you're quick, and it'll give you power."

She shivered despite the heat in the bar.

"Champ's part Indian or something', he's got a lotta crazy ideas. But brilliant, you never met nobody like him. He plays the guitar, too, gonna be a rock star."

Her new friend's attention shifted. He waved to someone near the door, and said, hurriedly, "Gotta go. Something's up. Maybe you'll be here tomorrow night?" He was gone.

Her beer mug was empty. Breathing was difficult with too many people sucking up the oxygen. On the street, it was no better. So many strange faces, she didn't even know the way back to her motel, and turned in the wrong direction, walking for blocks before she realized her mistake. The night was cool and fragrant, some kind of night-blooming flower permeating the air. She thought of the field of poppies in *The Wizard of Oz* and how they felled anyone who in haled their tantalizing poison.

A poster was pasted to the scaffolding around a construction site. A line of posters, all identical. In big block letters, white on black: SILVER KNIGHT at WHISKY A GO GO—Fri. & Sat. only. 10PM.

The next night, she got to the Haunted House earlier. It was less crowded.

"Is Geordie here?" she asked the bartender when he brought her beer.

"Geordie? Naw, he's not here anymore."

"Oh. Where's the Whisky A Go Go?"

"The Whisky? It's on the Strip."

"Is it far?"

He shrugged. "Bout five-ten minutes, that's all."

She'd already learned, the hard way, that when people here gave you directions, they meant driving time, not walking. She took the small yellow spiral notebook out of her purse and began to write, practically nonsense at first, anything to make it look as if she had a reason to be there. The words formed their way into a lyric.

"Hey, Freckles."

He was wearing the same clothes and smelled kind of stale. "I got money. Order anything you want." A thick wad of bills appeared from his jeans pocket.

"Brandy Alexander." Rochelle used to order those, and they sounded glamorous.

"What're you writing? Writing about me?"

"No. I mean. No. Just thoughts, and maybe a song."

"You'll sing it for me?"

She sipped her drink, creamy and sweet. "You ever been to the Whisky?"

"Sure, lots of times."

They found a booth in the back. The guy sat next to her, on the same side, and they both watched the candle flickering in the oval glass wrapped in pink plastic mesh. Bits of black wick floated in the liquid wax. He reached into his pocket with his free hand and took something out, dipped it in the candle flame. A joint. He offered it to her.

She leaned over, inhaled with effort and held her breath.

"That's it," he encouraged, and put his arm around her shoulder, tugging her to him awkwardly. "You're like my girl or something' now, huh."

She shrugged.

"Well, I'll have to tell Champ, hands off."

"Who?"

"At the ranch. You wanna go?"

"Now?"

This was Tuesday. She had to fill in the time until Friday, it didn't much matter how or where.

"'Less you're afraid to ride the back of a bike."

"No. But what if they, well, what if there isn't room, you know, at the ranch?"

"There's always room, that's the great thing, it's like this big family."

She gulped down her drink—powerfully, wonderfully sweet. "Tell me about the horses."

"I dunno, there's a reddish one, and a Paint, I think he used to be in the Westerns, and a coupla retired race horses."

A few minutes later she was climbing on the back of his motorcycle, a big black machine with the image of an Indian on the side.

"I don't even know your name."

"Names don't mean nothin'."

"I gotta call you *some*thing." She wrapped her arms around his middle, over the top of the thin shirt. He was sleek and cool under her hands, like a reptile.

"Everybody calls me Cupid." He turned around and winked.

Through wind-teared eyes she saw the Old West rise and outer space loom above the two-lane highway into Chatsworth. The moon was swollen, illuminating towering silhouettes of mountains that resembled globs of rock stuck together like giant mud castles. She gripped her hands around Cupid's waist; strands of hair stung her cheeks. The motorcycle made a sharp turn down a narrow dirt road that twisted several times before opening onto a clearing.

A low-slung ranch house sprawled in three directions; several low smaller buildings were nearby. There was a railing, the kind cowboys tied their mounts to in western movies, in front of the house and the unmistakable sweet earth scent of horses and hay and manure. As Cupid parked his bike, a big dog bounced out of the shadows and crashed happily into his legs.

"Frecks, say hello to my best friend, Blackie." Hearing his name, the dog, some kind of Lab-Shepherd mix, woofed low and wagged his tail frantically. Julie petted the large smooth head. She followed dog and biker into the main house. The porch gave a sharp crack of rotting wood.

"Loose board, watch out," he warned. "Place needs a little work. Guy who owns it is kinda old, can't take care of things, so we're trying to keep it up."

The interior was lit by a multitude of candles. Several people sat on the floor around a scuffed wooden coffee table. Marijuana permeated the air. She wondered if, all over America, there were living rooms like this, on the outskirts of every town, where the outcasts—the lonely, the displaced and disaffected, the strays and losers and geniuses and seekers—sat on floors in candlelight and pretended they were families.

A blur of names followed, nicknames like Spooky and Snake and Starlight. There were lanky, narrow-eyed guys with bad complexions and stoned voices; longhaired, melancholy girls who regarded the newcomer with suspicion. One was dancing in the middle of the room, turning around and around to "Blackbird." Two others girls stretched out on the couch, a man between them stroking their legs. He had his eyes closed. Then he opened them and fixed Julie with a piercing stare.

"You," he said.

He was a small, wiry man with waves of unwashed brown Jesus hair parted in the center, reaching to his shoulders. Clean-shaven but for a small tuft of beard beneath his lower lip.

"You. Have. The. Gift." His voice was high and thin but the intensity behind it conveyed an unmistakable authority.

"I do?"

"You see into things, into people. I know, because I have the Gift, too."

She was peculiarly, wordlessly flattered. Her cheeks flushed.

He made a small gesture and the two young women rolled off the couch, almost as one, and padded barefoot from the room. "You're Cupid's?"

"No, I mean. He brought me."

"Welcome to our family. I try to make this a home, for people who never had a home or whose lives were poisoned. Know what I mean, to come from a poisoned life? The miracle is that you can have a new life, brand new, new name, new person, and it takes very little, know what I mean?"

"I think so." His words seemed to have a deeper meaning she didn't quite grasp. Blackie the Dog nearly knocked her down. She laughed and the man on the couch laughed, too. He stood up, and was surprisingly short.

"What do you think you might want to do here? We all pitch in." He said this with exaggerated formality, and she almost laughed again, but kept it in. He didn't appear to have much of a sense of humor.

"Uh, I could work with the horses. A little."

"What makes you think we need that?" he said sharply.

"I don't know."

"We have ranch hands. They make movies here, you know. This is a famous place. Do you want to be famous? Are you *meant* to be famous?"

"I don't know."

"You don't know. You *have* to know. *I'm* gonna be famous. I'm gonna be signing a record contract."

"She sings, Champ," Cupid put in, "Don't you, Freckles?"

"Uh, yeah, but I didn't bring my guitar."

Champ softened visibly and became gracious again. "A musician. You see?" he said triumphantly.

One of the girls walked through the room, her arms waving in front of her like she was pretending to be a ghost.

"Charlie, I'm invisible," she chanted.

He ignored the interruption. "I knew she was favored!" He left the room.

36

Luke parked his immaculate, silver '69 Shelby Mustang convertible behind the Whisky. Evading the line that snaked around the block, he dashed up the back stairs to the second floor. The musicians' greenroom looked out over the marquee entrance on the corner, the walls of the building painted flat black with a few touches of red. Eager fans were kept at bay by crafty Mario the doorman, who knew how to create a sense of excitement outside even on nights when it wasn't packed. This night it was all Mario could do to maintain some semblance of order, letting in the VIPs when they pulled up in their big cars, checking the names on a long list. A kid with wiry red hair and shaggy cutoff shorts surreptitiously hawked bootleg tickets from a doorway just off Sunset. Two couples, seated against the wall, looked as if they'd been camped out all day. A pair of slinky women in halter tops and minis tried to catch Mario's attention.

Luke turned away from the window. He checked to see that his signature was still on the wall, from the first time he'd played there—everybody signed The Wall, from the barest unknowns to the biggest stars.

"Hey, man," Brewster greeted him. They slapped hands. Billy lit a joint.

"Not here, asshole," Luke chided, "Take it next door." The adjoining office was the unofficial drug zone.

Casey came in, unloaded his guitars, followed them. "Shit makes me sleepy."

"There's some dust mixed in," Billy said.

"Whoa." Casey took a drag, passed it to Luke.

The lights became brighter.

"Why are premature orgasm and a drum solo alike?" Brewster asked, setting up a joke.

Luke rolled his eyes. "Okay, let's have it."

"You know they're comin', but there ain't a damn thing you can do about it!"

"Fuck you all," Billy said good-naturedly. The joint made its rounds again.

They headed back into the greenroom, still laughing. A flock of groupies were lounging around. Luke suddenly felt old at twenty-five. The damn girls were teenagers. They passed a flask around.

Elissa came up the stairs, a drink in her hand. She touched Luke's arm.

"Hey, babe," he said.

Brewster addressed the guys again. "What does a chick singer do first thing in the morning?"

In unison, Casey and Luke replied, "Gets dressed and goes home."

It was Billy's turn. "What are a chick singer's favorite tempos?"

"Okay, what?" Brewster asked.

"Too fast and too slow!"

"Good one!" Casey said, slapping Billy's hands.

One of the techies had a bottle of decent bourbon, and they all had a taste. Three groupies, who obviously knew each other, giggled in the corner. Luke guessed they were deciding who got which musician.

Casey unpacked his guitar and began tuning up. "*You* oughta have some chick singer jokes," he said to Luke.

"Why's that?"

"You used to work with one, didn't you? Back in the Village? You know, the one I had first."

"We told Mick jokes back then."

Brewster broke in. "Did you hear about the Polack who fell down a hole—"

Casey interrupted. "In *my* neighborhood we told a lotta Wop jokes."

Billy spoke up, "Hey, man, nothin' beats a good nigger joke, right?"

Luke stepped closer to Casey.

"I mean, uh…black." Billy left the room.

The two musicians regarded each other. Luke broke the silence.

"Are we gonna tell jokes or play music?"

Casey slapped Luke on the back. "The ladies. You can't live with 'em and you can't kill 'em."

A plump young woman eased over to Casey, wrapped her arms around his waist from behind. He said to Luke. "I was thinking, maybe we should cut 'Take the Road', 'cause it's kind of down, and replace it with 'Reaction'."

Luke stiffened. It was a song he'd written, while Casey had written "Reaction". "The people seem to like it."

"I always feel like we're losing them."

Luke's jaw tightened. "Song stays."

"Who the fuck died and made you king?"

"The set works, if it ain't broke don't fix it."

Casey's expression turned serious. "No," he said, "Not when it's one of *your* tunes, funny how that always works out, you've got five tunes in the set, I've got two, and Brewster, Brewster can't get one of his in on a bet. He's like goddamn Ringo. Now, what do you make of that?" Casey turned to Brewster, who was checking his amp. "Don't you want your stuff done?"

Brewster shrugged, "'Long as I get paid, I don't give much of a shit."

"Great," muttered Casey.

"You wanna vote on it?" Luke demanded. "Fine. Where's Billy?"

"Next door again, probably." said Brewster.

The drummer appeared, red-eyed and mellow, and took in the tense faces. "What's up?"

Casey said, "Maybe it's just time somebody got it straight that we ain't his backup band."

"Maybe it's time," Luke retorted, in a tight voice, "To get it straight that somebody here writes better songs, like the one that's been playin' on the radio."

"Uh, I think we're all a little road crazy," Brewster suggested.

"Gee, I hate to break this to you, pal, but we're not on the road anymore."

"I figured that out."

Luke twisted a tuning peg with too much force and immediately snapped a string. "Motherfuck!"

Casey went on, "I'm the one who got the record deal in the first place."

"You mean you had a meeting."

"I let Levine bring you in."

"You would've sunk like fossilized shit."

"Knock it off, will you?" Brewster hollered.

Billy slumped down on the couch.

"If I hadn't agreed to bring you in," Casey persisted, "you'd still be passing the hat in the Village."

"Hate to remind you, Mahoney, you thick Mick, but Levine got this band together, and if it wasn't for me—"

"That's right, Bella-fuckingwop-vita, and whatever *did* happen to that chick you used to hang with? At least we got that in common, 'course she was a fresh virgin when I had her, and a real, honest-to-god redhead, and she couldn't keep her mouth offa my dick—"

Luke's fist connected with Casey's face so fast neither of them saw it coming. He kept pummeling blindly, a red haze filled his brain and blocked out all other sensation. He didn't even feel the techies and Brewster and Billy prying him off Casey. Holding him back, but he was too strong and leaped forward again to tear Casey's face off and they were on him again, flung him into a chair, where he breathed in deep, heavy gasps, sweat pouring off his body. His hands were shaking and when he looked down he saw the knuckles were bloodied.

Pain filtered in through the haze. Brewster was yelling, "Did you break your hand, you fucking idiot?!"

He flexed his fingers; it hurt, but didn't they say if you can move it, it ain't broken? They were already starting to swell. "Don't think they're broken," he muttered. A few feet away, Casey's latest girlfriend was dabbing the blood on his chin with a tissue.

Luke got up and stumbled to the bathroom in the hall, barely closed the door before he threw up into the sink. He ran the water and splashed it onto his face and neck. In the mirror, he saw a monster, red-faced and sweating. The face of his father.

After a moment, there was a knock on the bathroom door.

"Luke?" It was Elissa.

"Yeah, babe, give me a few."

"You need anything?"

"I'll be okay." Luke emerged at last to find Casey holding a bag of ice against his jaw. Elissa had found another one for Luke's hand.

"He's quitting!" Billy said accusingly. "The band's over!"

"No, it's not," Luke insisted. He sat down across from Casey. "I was out of line."

"Go fuck yourself," came the slurred reply from behind the ice pack.

At that moment, Elliot Levine came through the door, exuding confidence. He stopped short. "What the *hell* is going on here?"

"How would you like to have two bands?" Brewster suggested. "'Silver', and 'Knight'."

"Give me a fucking break." Elliot checked out Luke's hands, Casey's face. "Get onstage already, you've got a show to do! Are you guys out of your minds?" He shook his head.

"And by the way, the second single's on the charts with a bullet. Just thought you might want to know."

The line was moving at last. For awhile it seemed they were only letting in people on some list. She worried there would be no room, and she'd come all this way for nothing. Cupid had dropped her off, on his way to some rendezvous Champ had organized. It became very important to get into the club right that minute. Easing her way through the crowd, she reached the front.

"I'm supposed to meet someone," she told the guy at the door. He looked her up and down, his face breaking into a smile. "Pass on through, angel."

The club was packed to the rafters, and dark. Black and red upholstered chairs surrounded small tables, with booths against the wall and a bar in the corner. To her immediate right, she saw the stage, where an opening band was playing. Two go-go cages flanking the stage were empty, but the small dance floor in front was packed with writhing bodies. If there was air conditioning, it wasn't working that night.

She found a place in the back corner near the bar, where she could see the stage from across the room.

Elliot Levine was crossing the room in her direction.

She turned her face away, and he passed by without seeing her.

The band ended their set, and recorded music came on. Jimi Hendrix singing "Purple Haze". There was a hush; a disembodied voice announced the star band. Silver Knight came down the steps to the raised stage.

This was no ordinary set. Maybe it was the fight with Casey, or the dull ache in his hand that gave the songs an edge of bitter emotion they'd never had before. Luke played like the devil was waiting at the crossroads.

He appeared to be staring right at her, even though she knew that could not be true, because the white hot light was in his eyes.

After the show, Julie saw Elliot Levine making his way around the room, talking to one person after another. She was bursting with her own secret presence, and was about to step forward, when she saw Elliot and a beautiful woman with long black hair head toward the back. Luke came out— she could barely see him through the crowd—and draped his arm around the bare shoulder of the woman.

She wandered along Sunset Boulevard and eventually thumbed a ride north, back to the ranch.

37

Prowling the long, wide hallways of his company, Elliot thrilled to the medley of typewriter click-clacks, conversations, radios and tapes that drifted out of each office; employees on the phone, in meetings, from sales to distribution to A&R; secretaries and assistants taking dictation, the hum and disorder of lives colliding to succeed. Office doors were open; he liked it that way. A test pressing of the new Silver Knight single was playing in the office of the head of marketing. He paused. The song actually gave him chills.

"Got a minute?" Rochelle asked.

"Sure." Her short dress showed a tantalizing glimpse of cleavage and tanned legs.

"Listen to this band." They went into his office. The built-in wall system included two reel-to-reel tape recorders, a television, and giant speakers mounted a few feet off the floor.

"You look incredible, you know that?"

"Why, Mr. Levine." The demo began to play. Rochelle slipped off her shoes and tucked her feet under her on the couch.

He noticed her perfume, faint but musky. Patchouli? Arlene used it sometimes, but it wasn't the same at all. "They play pretty well, but the songs aren't saying anything." He gave an indifferent shrug, palms up.

When the second song ended, she rose and switched off the tape. "You're not paying attention, are you."

"I don't know why," he admitted, "but I can't seem to concentrate today."

"Maybe," she said slowly, "Maybe it's the heat."

"The heat," he echoed. "But it's a dry heat."

They both laughed.

She handed him the tape. "Try again later."

"I'll do that."

"Well," she said, "I guess I'll be getting back to my office. Or the boss will get on my case." It was their joke.

He smiled. "Maybe we could have a drink later."

"A drink?"

"You know, liquid, over ice, in a glass?"

"I know what it is." She paused at the threshold. "Well, okay. But just a little, I've got to drive."

"Don't worry about that, I'll call a car if necessary."

"I don't intend to get tanked, Elliot."

The phone rang.

"How's it goin'?" Spider Allessi, who had recently grown his hair long over his ears, and took to wearing wild paisley colors and thick gold chains on his hairy chest. "We haven't been getting any play on the Surfer Kids single," Spider said. "I talked to the programmer at KSLA and he said the *Hotsheet* panned it. You need to get some inducement over to the station. Straighten out Becker. He's a loose cannon. Gary's real unhappy about it."

"I know, I talked to him, I'm taking care of it."

"Good. See ya, Levine." Spider hung up.

He went to the liquor cabinet, poured some scotch into a glass and downed it quickly, hating the taste.

"We're starting a little early, I see," Rochelle remarked.

He poured another and handed it to her, accidentally spilling some onto the floor. "Sorry," he muttered, flushing.

She took a paper napkin from the desk, a leftover from a Mexican takeout meal, and wiped up the spill.

"What's going on?" she asked.

"Just stuff about Happy, I'm afraid he may be getting him self into….He doesn't quite get how some things work."

"Like what things?"

"It's complicated, Rochelle."

"I raided his mailing list. You know you can trust me, right?"

He fiddled with a pencil, tossing it in the air and catching it. The second time it dropped on the floor. "Okay," he said at last. "Just tell me this: If, say, I needed something from him—Happy, I mean—some push on a record, do I take the hard line, or butter him up?"

She thought about it. "Happy likes to think of himself as totally independent—which, of course, he isn't—but it changes from day to day, depending on whims, moods, what he ate that morning…"

"That's what I was afraid of."

"So who was that on the phone?"

He faced her. "Spider Allessi." Then he told her everything.

Happy insisted they meet in the lobby of the Garden of Allah Hotel, one of the grandly absurd L.A. fantasies going to seed. Happy was chewing on a Baby Ruth, and Elliot noticed his nails were bitten to the quick.

"So," Elliot prompted, "You got this call."

Happy lowered his voice. "Gary Luna himself. It's like getting a call from God. No, make that Satan. Listen, I run a clean show—"

"Ha."

"Okay, okay, so I take a little bonus now and then, to plug this or that, but I make the decisions."

"So what'd he want?"

"First he's got these Beachboys ripoffs he wants me to play, then he's got some Dago lounge singer, works Vegas, totally owned, they've bought him an LP, they want me to *kvell* in the *Hotsheet*. I said 'hire a fucking press agent'."

"You said that?"

"Well, without the 'fucking'. Then Luna says 'why don't you want to work for Elliot Levine?', and I say, 'I like being an independent operator', and he says 'think about it anyway.' So you tell me, what's going on? Why do they care where I work? You wrapped up with that mob?"

"We've crossed paths now and then, you scratch my back, that kinda thing."

"I don't want to scratch any part of them." There was a rim of chocolate around Happy's lips. "And you shouldn't either."

"What, are you kidding? No way. This is all on the up and up." Elliot switched to what he hoped was a more persuasive tone. "Listen, Hap, you could be rolling in dough—"

"How much does a person need, huh? How many toilets can you shit in at one time, right?"

"Then get a big gold one with marble trim. Look, Hap, Come on already, I mean, look at us, a coupla guys from Brooklyn, we gotta stick together, right?"

"All I want you to do is get those goombahs the fuck off my back."

"Like they'd really take orders from me, are you kidding?"

"Just pass it along to your backscratchers: Happy don't have nothin' they want. Happy isn't for sale."

"Or what?" Elliot shot back.

"Or what what?"

More soothing. "I mean, hey look, that's not, that's not so smart, you know? I mean in the grand scheme of things. It's a small town, right?"

Happy blustered. "Who says I don't have my own connections? Who says?"

There was a pause, while each man contemplated the faux-Arabic architecture of the hotel.

Elliot tried once more. "Listen, Hap, we've had a good relationship, you know you can trust me. I don't wanna see you get in over your head. I'm just looking out for you."

"I'm sure you are, Levine."

"So we're agreed? You write up a nice little plug on the Surfer Boys and the Da—the singer?"

"I'll sleep on it."

Elliot placed an envelope on the seat between them. Happy looked down at it, hesitated, and pushed it back toward Elliot. "Not this time, not those guys."

"Come on, now's not the time to acquire scruples."

Happy hesitated, looked at the envelope. "I don't know, maybe you're right. I had scruples once. They itched." He chuckled, and pushed the envelope back to Elliot. "On the other hand, sometimes you just gotta watch who you get into bed with."

Rochelle put the paste-up on his desk. "Look at the invitation before we send it to the printers. We have plenty of time if you want to make any changes."

THE LEVINE COMPANY/MOONSHADOW RECORDS
COCKTAIL RECEPTION
AUGUST 8, 1969
6-9 PM
CELEBRATING SILVER KNIGHT'S NEW LP
ALL KNIGHT

"Fine," Elliot said, distracted. "By the way, are the caterers set? Call and tell them: good-looking waiters and waitresses, God knows there's plenty of out of work actors." Christ, what if this whole thing was a bust? What if nobody came? "And champagne, decent stuff but not a fortune, and a lot of different appetizers, I hate when they keep passing around the same three half-empty trays."

Whose big idea was this party, anyway? Oh, right, it was his.

He drove home over Laurel Canyon, the sun fading on the horizon as he headed west on Mulholland to Sherman Oaks, where they'd bought a sprawling estate—that was the only word for it. Arlene wanted space and a killer view. The radio reported a fire burning somewhere in the hills, whipped by hot dry winds. A plume of whitish smoke snaked into the sky.

Their leggy French au pair, Jean d'Arc, appeared at the top of the stairs, holding a toddler in each arm.

"Allo, Monsieur Levine." It came out a classy sounding 'Le *Vanh*'.

Elliot stared at Jean d'Arc's slim, tawny limbs. He always made sure not to say her name aloud, since he could never pronounce it in the soft French way, instead it came out more like 'John Dark'. A pink halter top barely covered her small, perfect breasts.

Arlene was in the kitchen. He kissed his wife on the cheek.

"How about a quick swim before dinner?" she asked.

The Valley heat was intense, although it was starting to cool down, and it felt wonderful to slip into the water. He hauled himself out of the pool and into the Jacuzzi, and pushed his tired back and neck muscles against a pulsing jet.

A few moments later, after helping Jean d'Arc put the kids in bed, Arlene joined him, naked. He leaned back and looked up at the stars. If Rochelle were in the hot tub instead of Arlene, life would be just about perfect.

Between the hot tub and the wine, he fell asleep early. A strange sensation awoke him some hours later. The bed was moving around. By itself. At first he thought the toddlers were playing, or that Arlene was having some kind of wild dream, but then he realized foggily that the whole house was rolling, side to side, up and down, like they were being borne away on a runaway freight train. He gripped the side of the mattress, his fright building with the nauseating motion.

"What is it? What is it?" Arlene whispered, terrified. She had his arm in a vise.

"Earthquake." They heard the crack and shatter of falling china. All the neighborhood dogs were barking.

"The boys!" Arlene slipped from the bed in the pitch dark and felt her way out of the room while the floor continued to shudder.

His heart had reached record beats per second, even as the tremor passed, and continued to bludgeon his chest painfully for minutes after. The clock said: 3:20 AM.

Rochelle! He was about to call her when Arlene came back, holding a flashlight. "They never even woke up. I can't deal with the mess now." She turned into her pillow. "What kind of place is this?"

They clung to each other. When he finally fell asleep again, it was near dawn, and light was beginning to seep through the blinds.

Elliot? Someone is calling him and he sees a shadowy figure. He isn't sure if he is dreaming, or dreaming that he is dreaming but he is in an elevator, and it is going too fast, shaking from side to side. The other person in the elevator is Ray Fish. Ray looks slightly different than Elliot remembers, like a cloudy cataract has blurred his features. But Elliot knows it's him, and he feels the old mixture of envy and intimidation and rage.

Elliot realizes that Ray can't see him. It's late at night and now they are in an underground garage. Ray walks to his car, as the ground moves like an amusement park ride. Elliot has to touch the walls to steady himself. He sees the men before Ray does. They step out of the gloom like wraiths, and there is a split second in which Ray might make a lightning fast move, get the key in the ignition of his car, but he doesn't think of it fast enough and, anyway, that kind of stuff only happens in movies.

Is this what happened to you, Ray?

Elliot watches as the two big men flank Ray, each holding one of his arms, squeezing the triceps painfully and it's funny, because that's like the movies, too. Hey, guys, take it easy, Ray says. They do, they actually relax a little. Oddly, Elliot feels the pain in his own arms, and the fear is mounting in him. One of the men is chewing gum, it pops and snaps. Smells like Patchouli.

Is this what happened?

They shove Ray into the backseat of a waiting sedan, a Buick, like Elliot's old car. Elliot realizes their mistake, they have taken him instead. His heart bangs painfully in his chest. No, I'm not the one you want, he screams at them, but no sound comes out.

They blindfold him, and drive for a long time, at first stop-and-start in traffic, then fast and smooth as they leave the city and he wants to tell them that he isn't even in New York, he's in Los Angeles, but that doesn't make any sense! There's the unmistakable rough buzzing of tires on a metal grate. A bridge? Perhaps they have gone uptown to the Triborough, or down and over the Brooklyn Bridge. A damp, briny smell reminds him of the docks at Sheepshead Bay.

The car stops.

They push him out; his knees hit pavement.

He knows he is going to die and wants to keep his dignity, but at the last moment, as he hears the click of a gun near his head, he begins to plead, I'm not Ray Fish, you've got the wrong guy. He offers them anything—money, fame—if they will just let him go. One of them punches him in the face and he is sent reeling back to that nightmarish night in the Blackout of '65; blood seeps around the blindfold, mixed with his tears. It's just so damned unfair. The second man chides the first for lacking control. Just do it, already. No, please. One more second, please.

You're making a mistake. Is that what you said, Ray, when the end came? Is that what everyone says?

One of them places a clear plastic bag over the head of this Ray/Elliot person, and there's the shot, the head blows backward, exploding inside the bag. Only a trace of blood escapes, trickling down the window pane.

They cover the body with an oversize trash bag, neatly tie the top with string and stuff it into a large empty barrel. With the cover fitted on and sealed with silver electrical tape, they roll it into the channel.

It makes a deep satisfying splash, slowly sinks into murky, oil-slicked water. Gulls dive down to see what is going on. The men clean up the car and leave it there, just another stolen New York vehicle. A second car pulls up, a black Lincoln. The two men get in the back, their work finished. Someone turns on the radio. They are unaware of the irony that the song playing is a BigWheel record, but they like it and turn up the volume.

The body sinks deeper into the water, past broken pieces of the old dock, and ragged pilings, and garbage.

Elliot woke up sweat-soaked.

Birds were singing outside and the bed was empty. The radio was on in the kitchen, and there was a rich aroma of coffee. The dream was as unreal as the earthquake.

38

They gave her a cot to sleep on, sharing a room with the girl named Snake, but then Snake went off somewhere and another girl came in. She told Julie that Champ was Krishna and Buddha and Jesus in the same reincarnated form. Julie just nodded and turned her face to the wall, staring at spots and stains she preferred not to think about. The place was not what anyone would call clean, and some of the people were downright dirty, but she made sure her own sheets were washed, along with the shabby navy blanket she used at night. No matter how hot it was during the day, and it was often well over a hundred, the desert dryness brought chill at dusk.

The compound was cluttered with old trucks and pieces of torn up cars; out buildings and barns falling to the ruin of neglect. It was a sad place, with wooden planks placed haphazardly over ruts in the road and in the broken windows. Two indifferent ranch hands spent more time drinking beer and comparing the sexual attributes of the women than tending to their chores. The ranch owner, an elderly man whom Julie glimpsed a couple of times, had been relegated to living in a shack on the edge of his own property. One of the girls brought him food and walked him around in the sun like one of the old horses.

Champ liked her singing and wanted her to play every day, usually at sunset, because later everyone was too fucked up to pay much attention. She went through her repertoire of folk and blues, and he wanted more, so she began to write songs in her room. Or she'd take her guitar outside, walk down the path past the barns to a clearing that looked straight up at the mountains, and sit on a large hot flat rock where the occasional lizard skittled by. Songs would come into her head, sometimes so quickly, it was as if they had been sitting there all along, waiting for her to write them down. Later, she'd sing them for Champ and the others, like Scheherazade spinning tales in exchange for her room and board, and maybe her life.

Julie mucked out stalls and cleaned the tack. She liked to ride early, while the burning sun was still hiding behind the trees. Windy, a retired rodeo horse was her favorite, proud in his heavy Western tack, nuzzling her hand for carrots. They took a few turns around the paddock, before setting out up into the hills. It was this that made all the rest bearable, the loneliness and the weird hostility of the 'family'. No one else rode with her, they didn't seem to have the slightest interest, and most of the time, they were sniggering and whispering, and playing the Beatles' "White Album" until she was almost—but not quite—sick of it. One of the women liked to touch Julie's hair. She was a small, mousy girl; her touching came from a place of distant and hopeless envy.

Cupid had a baby with one of the women, but he never seemed to spend any time with them. Champ slept with all of them and treated them like interchangeable parts on a children's toy. It was only a matter of time until he turned that peculiar gaze on her; it was as if he were saving her for a special occasion. If she ever wanted to leave, she'd have to make some money, get a job maybe, but she wasn't sure how to go about it. Champ said he knew some people in the record business and he'd get her an audition but it was the kind of talk that sounded good at night after a few joints but no one ever remembered the next day.

There had been an earthquake a few nights before, and this spooked them a lot; Champ said it was a sign of the Apocalypse, and meant that the Plan was almost ready to put into action. Julie leaned against a door frame, watching the newest freaks; their mean-looking bikes, Harleys and Indians, parked outside. The house rocked with music. Champ was in high spirits, drinking from a bottle of Tequila. Julie noticed one of the bikers. He wore a leather jacket with the sleeves cut off at the shoulder, and faded jeans. The back of his jacket had a large colorful decal of a hawk; its huge, sinister eyes followed you around the room. That was his name, she recalled: Hawk. His hair was thick and wild, almost black. He reminded her of Luke.

The party wound down. Champ played a few songs he'd written, singing in a high, reedy voice. The songs had a raw energy but were chaotic and rambling and paranoid, delivered in one level of frenzied rage. Then he asked Julie to sing— more of a command—her hands were shaking as she began the opening chords to a Fred Neil tune, "The Other Side of This Life." She saw Hawk watching her, too, and it made her want to be wonderful, to bring him melting to his knees. When she finished singing, Champ was pacing around, muttering to himself, smoking a filter less cigarette.

"You see?? You see??" he said, demanding an answer from one of his acolytes, a tall, rangy girl with droopy dirty-blond hair. The girl shrugged and this enraged him. He turned, lightning fast, and struck her in the side of the head. She staggered and fell and he kicked her. The room went deathly, passively quiet; every one had been through this before.

Julie put the guitar down. Her skin prickled, as if it wanted to flee but was stuck to the rest of her body. She was afraid to breathe. The biker went out the front door. The girl who'd been hit left the room crying and one of the other girls followed her. In the noise and distraction of the crying, Julie also slipped out. The biker was leaning against a tree, smoking a cigarette. It was so late even the birds and crickets had given up. Just that last inanimate hush before dawn. One sound came through: the yip-yip-hoo of a coyote. Another echoed, nearer. In the dim, waning moonlight, she saw shadows leaping from rock to rock down toward the barn.

Hawk stood completely still.

Julie turned her face up to the stars and howled like a coyote. Blackie was on his feet, barking madly. The creatures vanished. She howled again. It felt good.

"Ride?" Hawk asked.

She climbed onto the back of his big Harley, and they were off in an explosion of sound and dirt. They raced down Route 27, taking the twists and turns in the road like a slalom. The lights of the San Fernando Valley stretched out before them on both sides, as if they were flying in from a great height. She rested her head against his back, the bike's vibrations became part of her blood. The road took them over and through Topanga Canyon and the Santa Monica Mountains that many decades ago had been blasted through with ax and dynamite and blood, linking desert, mountains and sea. Feeling the change in the air, she saw the wide expanse of ocean, low clouds of varying shades of gray against the dark sky, and a scattering of stars.

Hawk steered the chopper north along the coast highway, then cut left down a small street that said 'Private'. He stopped, dismounted and lifted her off the back of the bike. He put his finger to his lips for silence.

The Malibu beach homes were sealed, soundless. An occasional light could be seen. A dog barked sharply, several houses away. They froze. Hawk leaned the bike against the side of a house. The dog quieted.

He took Julie's hand and led her through a narrow passage between properties. She could just barely make out the structure of a house under construction. The waves pounded percussively on the beach. She leaned down to take off her sandals, and padded to the water's edge. He was close behind her, walking backward, his eyes on the houses along Malibu.

"Rich fucks," he said at last. "But that's okay. They'll get theirs. When it all comes down."

"When what does?"

"It's all gonna come *down*," he repeated. "You'll see." He took her in his arms. "Ever do it on a motorcycle?"

"No."

"Let's get naked."

"It's cold."

"You won't be for long. Leave your shirt on."

He mounted the bike, and directed her to climb onto his lap, facing him. He slid up inside her. The bike motor revved and they were rolling down the beach.

She wished Luke could see her now, him and his black-haired bitch.

They gathered speed. Sand shot out from under the wheels.

Flashes of dark thoughts rapid fired in her brain. The vibrations of the bike set off a series of sensations from deep within her. She screamed, it was almost like pain, they raced along the shore, cold seawater splashing up against her bare legs; she screamed again in exhilaration and a terrifying triumph.

Julie borrowed one of the pickups and drove into Hollywood, getting lost several times despite consulting a street map which she turned around and around trying to find the right direction. She parked at on a side street, around the corner from the building on Sunset, and sat in the truck for a long time. Her hair and neck were damp, more from nerves than the temperature. She plaited it into two long braids.

Gathering her courage, she turned the corner and stood in front of the building, then went in, taking the elevator up to the twelfth floor:

The Levine Company
Elliot J. Levine, President

39

Rochelle was passing through the reception area, clutching an armful of tapes, when a delicately pretty woman with very long reddish braids came through the front door. She looked like Julie.

It was Julie.

She dropped the tapes onto the reception desk, and they spilled onto the floor. Denise, the receptionist, stooped to pick them up.

"Rochelle?" Julie was wide-eyed with astonishment. "But...Elliot?"

"I work for him. With him. I mean I—listen, come into my office, I don't believe it, I mean, we have so much to catch up on. Wait! I know, let's use Elliot's office. It's nicer, and he's out at a meeting. No, wait a minute, I didn't really say hello!" Rochelle hugged her friend, and had the sense of enfolding a deer that might bolt at any moment. "How are you!?"

"I'm fine. Great!"

She led Julie into Elliot's office. "Pretty nice, huh?"

Julie took in the spectacular view. The expensive furnishings. The wall of sound equipment.

"The house that Silver Knight built, I guess you could call it."

Julie visibly flinched.

"Oh, I'm an idiot, you and Luke—"

"Come on, already, that's ancient history."

"You look fabulous!"

"So do you."

Simultaneously, they said: "Have you lost weight?" Then burst into laughter.

Julie plopped onto the sofa but got up immediately, wandered to the desk and picked up a framed photo: Arlene and twin toddlers. "When did she turn blonde?"

"It's the amazing California sun."

"Those babies, well, I don't mean to be cruel, but they're not exactly…" She looked up at Rochelle, and they began to giggle.

"Maybe they got her looks and his brains," Julie said.

"Hello." Elliot was standing in the doorway.

Julie quickly put the photo back on Elliot's desk.

He took Julie into his arms and held her. Where had she been? What had she been doing? She gave only a cryptic shrug and half smile as a reply.

"Well," he said, clearing his throat, "Is there any chance I might have my office back, girls, uh, ladies, uh, women?"

""Let's go to my office." Rochelle led Julie down the hall.

"Oh boy, what a crappy hostess I am! Do you want a drink? Something to eat? We got coffee and soda and stuff, or we could order out."

"Maybe a soda."

Rochelle went to the desk and buzzed Denise. "Could you get us a couple of Tabs?" She turned to Julie. "Diet okay? Not that *you* ever have to watch your weight."

"Sure." Julie flopped down on a chair, twisted a braid in her fingers. "This is so weird. I mean, I came to see Elliot, to bring him a tape." She took it out of her purse. "I saw him one night at the Whisky. He didn't see me or anything."

"Why didn't you say hello?"

Julie shrugged.

"You can give me the tape, I want to hear it, too."

Julie handed over the reel to reel in its small, flat white box.

"Where are you staying?"

"Oh, some friends' ranch. It's a pretty groovy place, there're horses and everything."

"That sounds nice." Rochelle said. "Luke's playing at the Whisky."

"Yeah. I know."

Denise came in with two cans of soda, and two glasses with ice.

"He never got over you," Rochelle said.

"Oh, please!"

"No, really."

Rochelle felt the distance between them. She wondered if they could ever find their way back to their old, effortless friendship.

"I'd better go," Julie said. "I have, you know, stuff to do."

"There's a recording session at Wally Heider's studio, I was on my way there. Why don't you come, it's right down the street?"

"Who's recording?"

"You know."

"Maybe it's not such a good idea."

"Come on. He'll plotz."

"I guess I can't miss that."

40

L uke pressed the left headphone closer to his ear, while shifting the right one slightly off, giving a workable balance of live and canned sound. The four musicians, usually spread out in the studio, with Billy and the drums behind a screen, were clustered around two mikes. They'd laid down the tracks and the first vocals the week before, and were adding harmonies to the last song on the album. Everyone said it was the best work they'd ever done. They held the last note into space; damn it was good. The track ended.

"Do another?" The voice coming through the speaker belonged to one of the top record producers in the business. Luke knew he'd come a long way from the Disgustas. He noticed Elliot in the control room. Rochelle, too. He began to sing the harmony a third tone over the melody line. Someone else was behind Rochelle, a woman, he couldn't quite make her out. It wasn't Elissa. He closed his eyes, needing to concentrate, but curiosity pulled his focus again. He squinted through the glare of the glass into the shadows on the other side; the visiting stranger stepped forward into the light.

A ceiling pin spot illuminated her hair and face.

It was all he could do to keep singing and even before the closing chords had echoed, he tore the phones off, heard

Casey mutter, 'oh brother', nearly tripped over recording equipment and wires and instruments and mike stands, pulled open the thick double padded door like it was made of straw.

"What took you so long?"

41

"I was busy," she said.

They exited the studio into the hot white glare of the parking lot, leaving a roomful of astonished people. It hadn't been discussed, they just wordlessly fled until, outside, they leaned against one shadowed gritty wall, melded together.

"Let's..." he began.

"...go," she finished, and followed him to his car.

"You always wanted one of these," she said of the Mustang. The top was down, the upholstery baking in the sun. Between shifting gears, he would reach over and touch her left hand, and as soon they were on the freeway, he grasped it firmly, as though she might fly away in the wind. It wasn't a question of where they would go, but how far.

She wanted to ask about the woman with the black hair but it was too hard to shout over the wind, and anyway, maybe she didn't care right now.

"Up the coast, okay?" he yelled.

"Your session?"

"We were finishing up. One last overdub for the single."

She leaned back, impossibly happy. The highway broke out of the hills that rose on both sides; the sea opened before them, fog blending into sky. A hazy orange sun and the air thick with a visible mist. He slowed onto a scenic turnout, and stopped the car facing the Pacific. They weren't far from where she had been with Hawk a few nights ago.

"So," she said, deliberately not looking at him, "What's new?"

He leaned back, out of breath. "Why? Why did you leave like that? Back in New York. Whythefuck? And where have you been all this time?" He struck the steering wheel.

She started to get out of the car but he pulled her back.

"No, I'm sorry, forget it, let's start all over, that's the past! No questions asked." He kissed her, "Oh, god, Julie." Pressed his palm against her cheek, touched her lips with his fingertips, she was moist with wanting him, a profound, real desire flooded through her. She grasped his thick hair and drew him to her, their mouths collided, then softened, it was as if she were being pulled into a vortex of pleasure.

"I have to be inside you," he whispered, "I have to make love to you."

The ocean waves, with bobbing, eternally abiding surfers, rose and fell below. Behind them, a highway of cars blurred by.

"You just want to get me to some cheap motel."

"Sounds good to me," he murmured. "It's not far to Santa Barbara, and there are some towns before then."

On the road again, he pressed the accelerator hard. He remembered the way he'd often felt around Julie, that he was on a minefield at all times, and some of the mines were live, some duds, but you never knew.

Well, shit, at least it was never boring.

He glanced over. She caught his eye, with a gaze so full of lust—and love—he nearly swerved off the road.

God help me, I'm still in love with her.

It was providence, finding the little motel with the coffee shop down the street, in a village along the coast. They even served breakfast all day, plates loaded with eggs, home fries, sour dough toast, and fresh butter. The coffee was strong and smooth.

She polished off everything on her plate and some of his, too.

They clasped hands across the table; underneath, their feet wrapped around one another's legs. "You're still playing music, right?"

Her eyes narrowed. "Of course. Why wouldn't I?"

"No reason," he said quickly. "I got a guitar in the trunk."

Then she was smiling. "Yes, let's sing, later, I've got all these new songs I've written."

They walked to the inn, clinging together. A friendly woman with a sun-bleached ponytail turned over the key to room four. She said, "There's stores a couple of miles north of here. And a K-Mart."

Julie went into the bathroom and found a large, immaculate tub. She put in the stopper and began running hot water into it. There was a small container of bubble bath on the counter.

"What are you doing in there?" he called.

"Come see!"

Julie stood in the half-filled tub, naked, the bubbles touching her ankles. Her hair was loose, Botticelli-rippled from the braids. She struck a "Venus on the half shell" pose.

He removed his jeans and underwear, and folded them neatly, the ingrained military influence; then was suddenly shy, hugely erect, almost painfully so. He knelt on the edge of the tub, and drew her close, burying his head against her stomach.

"Come in," she said, slipping down into the water, and taking him in her hands.

42

He buzzed his secretary again. "Did Luke call in yet?" Sorry, he hadn't.

Elliot slammed down the phone. Fucking musicians. It was like herding cats. He dialed Rochelle's extension. "Could you come to my office?"

He was nervous about the release of Silver Knight's new album. The guys were so perfectionistic they were still tinkering with the mix and it was going to be tight, having it ready in time.

"You have any idea where Luke took off to this time?" he asked Rochelle.

"No, but I'll call around some more."

"Long as he's back for the party."

"He will be."

"And what about Happy?" Elliot asked. "You sent an invitation, right?"

"Yes," she said, exasperated because he'd asked her several times before. "But he never goes to parties, he hardly ever goes out."

"How did he ever manage to get married?" Elliot mused.

"I think one was a mail order bride."

"Ha."

"I'm going to stop by his place tomorrow on my way to work," Rochelle said. "He's lending us some tapes for the party. Maybe I can persuade him to come out of his cave."

"You got the sound equipment rented, right?"

She nodded. It had been her idea to set up a raised stage with amps and mikes so that Silver Knight could do a set, and guest musicians could jam if they wanted. "I'd love to hear Luke and Julie sing together again."

"That's all we need: Luke ditching his band."

"He'd never do that."

"He did it that day at the studio. And he sure left that last chick in the dust."

"That's different," Rochelle retorted.

"Is it?"

"He's always loved her. It's one of those fate things."

He considered this for a moment, swiveled his chair toward the window. A tiny airplane trailed silently across the hazy Los Angeles sky.

"Rochelle. I was thinking. You know I like you."

She put up her hand. "Don't, Elliot."

"If I weren't married?"

"I don't know. You're my friend. Let's leave it at that. Business partners."

A flash of sunlight bounced blindingly off the plane. "Right. You're right. I apologize."

"It's fine. See you later."

Julie's tape was on his desk. He looped it into the machine.

Her voice was a bit thin at first, but part of that was the poor quality of the recording equipment, somebody's home set-up. The song was interesting, an original, but his gut told him it would be a difficult sell commercially. The second had the same problems, with compelling lyrics, but no "hook." There were five altogether. No hit, no single, but plenty of talent that fell into no clear category. Maybe one of the folkie labels would sign her. None of the majors wanted chicks, unless they were R&B. This didn't smell like money. Shitty business, but he didn't create it.

If someone chanced to look up at the fifteenth floor at that moment, they might have seen a lone man at a desk, leaning his face in his hands. Maybe even crying.

Of course, since it was Los Angeles, no one was on the street to look up; they were all in their cars.

43

Rochelle parked a half block from Happy's house, the nearest spot she could find in the narrow streets of Venice, shrouded in early morning fog. She crossed a small bridge spanning one of the many canals, in the neighborhood that had been inspired by its namesake in Italy. The trees and brush around Happy's house had grown thicker over the summer, and the lawn needed a trim. His old red MG was in the narrow driveway. The garage was crammed with boxes of tapes and books and god-knew-what that Happy never threw away.

She could hear music inside the bungalow. The front door was slightly ajar. Rochelle pushed it open, stepped carefully over a stack of old newspapers on the floor.

"Hap?" This was much worse than the last time she was here, and she had a flash of guilt that it was her fault; she had left him in the lurch. He kept saying he was going to hire another assistant, but never got around to it, and now she didn't envy the poor person who'd have to straighten out his mess the way she once had.

"'All you need is love!'" sang the radio.

"It's Rochelle!" A prickle of anxiety caused her to stop. She stood still, listening. Just the radio. Happy must've gone out to the store. This was one neighborhood where you didn't have to drive everywhere.

She reached over Happy's desk and switched off the radio. It was then she noticed the phone was off the hook; it must have been for awhile, because it was silent, no operator message or strident beep-beep. She started to pick up the receiver, but pulled back her hand at the last second. The creeping feeling spread down her back.

A crash in the adjoining room. She spun around. Had there been an earthquake? You didn't usually feel them when you were driving, so she might have missed it. Unnerved, her senses jump-started, she gingerly stepped into the back bedroom. A striped cat hopped off the windowsill. It meowed and rubbed against her legs.

Happy was slumped against a wall of bookshelves. Tapes and LPs and 45s had fallen around him, the white boxes and demo jackets splattered with red. There was a purplish-red pulpy hole where his face had been. Rochelle looked long enough to see that he'd been shot in the torso, too, the wound like a crimson bib draped over his chest and neck.

"Oh, Jesus, oh shit oh shit." With a hand pressed over her face, she stumbled out.

The street was bright and silent, the air ocean-scented. A block away, a woman walked her dog, but there was no one else in sight. If she stepped back inside, would it be gone, nothing more than a gruesome vision? The memories came piling back, and she thought she might actually faint: Ray, the wrecked apartment. The hearing in Reno. Spider Allessi turning up—no, *following* them, keeping tabs on her all this time.

Fingerprints. Had she touched anything? Now she was thinking like a TV criminal. Like she was guilty.

The door knob. The radio.

She had to go back in there.

Using the hem of her dress like a handkerchief, she nudged the door open again, rubbed down the handle.

Anything else?

The radio dial.

A siren sounded down the street, passed by.

Moments later she reached her car, but her hands shook so badly she could barely get the key in the door.

It's my fault: If she hadn't come to L.A. Gone to Reno. Slept with Ray. Been born. Was she forever destined to live in the dark world of Ray Fish, with Spider Allessi shadowing her to the ends of the earth, like that guy on "The Fugitive"? Instinctively, she drove to her apartment, and double locked the door behind her. She poured a half a glass of bourbon and drank it down, then picked up the phone and called Elliot.

As Elliot drove at high speed to Santa Monica, he became aware of a huge white cumulus cloud forming overhead, its sides extended out like grotesque arms. There were rarely any clouds in the Southern California sky. He waited for it to explode into some apocalyptic storm.

After letting Elliot in, she quickly locked the door again. "Nobody saw me, I didn't, you know, touch anything," she said. The salty smell of the ocean, and the blood. Maybe she'd always associate the two. "The place was all a mess, the blood, everywhere. I just got the hell out of there. I had to rub out my fingerprints first. Can you believe it? I was trying to think like that? Like what if somebody saw me, but his house is behind all those trees and things."

"Did you call the police?" he asked.

"No. I guess I should."

"Don't."

"Well, someone has to—"

"Someone will, just not you. Not us. It's not like it's gonna bring him back to life, right?"

Rochelle went into the kitchen to make coffee. She couldn't remember how to do it, and began to cry. Elliot put his arms around her. "It'll be all right," he whispered.

The nightly news had the story, the murder of record tipster Happy Becker, which they were calling a robbery gone wrong. Apparently, recording equipment was missing, and no wallet was found on him. The postman had noticed the door open and called the police, which led to the discovery of the body.

"Are we bad people?" Rochelle asked. "Am I a bad person? Is this how it happens?"

"Of course not. We didn't pull the trigger. He should have listened to me. Why didn't he listen to me?"

As Elliot turned into his driveway, a stray cat darted across the street and hid under a car. Its eyes glowed like molten gold in the darkness.

Even in the house, he didn't feel safe opening the windows wide. He checked twice that the front door was double locked.

44

Streamers of gold and silver cutouts shaped like records decorated The Levine Company's suite of offices. Each guest would receive party gifts: the new Silver Knight single, wrapped in foil with ribbon, a press packet and photos. As Elliot's staff tended to last minute details, two bartenders were setting up, one at each end of the wide lobby. The caterers bustled in the small kitchen.

Elliot chewed a couple of aspirin, washed down by a Tums, then stopped at the reception desk, where **THE LEVINE COMPANY** was mounted in elegant brass on the wall, and rubbed an invisible smudge from the plaque with his handkerchief. When he ran out of things to do, he sat down alone in the reception area, black Italian shoes shining against the even shinier pale marble floor.

Rochelle was gorgeous in a short black lace dress. She assured him, "Everyone comes late, you know that."

Happy's ghost walked across the room. Elliot shivered.

The elevator dinged, the doors slid open.

The first guests were a rookie William Morris agent and his nubile, post-adolescent date. The elevator doors opened and closed and all at once, it seemed, the rooms were jammed. Music played from several speakers, booze flowed, cater/waiters glided through the crowds with tempting trays.

"Fabulous set-up!" an Elektra Records VP shouted at Elliot. "I've got a client I want you to take a look at, great songwriter, but he needs representation!"

"Send me a tape!"

"Even better, I've got one with me!"

He bumped into that actor from "Easy Rider", the one who played the lawyer. Moving along, Elliot found himself surrounded by a bevy of record employees from the West Coast office of BigWheel, who wanted him to send his clients their way. He pocketed business cards, accepted demos with vague promises that he'd listen, knowing he'd pass them along to Rochelle or one of the assistants. He slapped backs and lied and charmed and bullshitted.

The musicians and artists were conspicuous in their flamboyant/shabby clothing, long bell bottoms dragging the floor, low-slung hip huggers and miles of fringe. A few of the women had renounced mini-skirts and were going the other way, with Victorian, floor-length skirts of madras and satin and sheer cottons, and cleavage-baring bodices. Beads were abundant, around necks, dangling on earrings, wrapping ankles. There were snug-fitting Edwardian shirts and stacked boots with pointy toes; see-through plastic dresses and billowing caftans.

Arlene Levine arrived with the next group out of the elevator. Her budget-breaking two-piece ensemble from Holly Harp on Rodeo Drive involved several sheer layers of green silk chiffon. Arlene was fond of her jewelry, and this night wore most of it. She found her husband amid a crowd of guests, and kissed him hello; he put his arm around her waist, giving her a distracted squeeze as Rochelle approached.

"Rochelle!" Arlene gushed, "You look *fabulous!*"

"So do *you!*" She looks just like a frog on a lily pad, Rochelle thought.

"We have to have you over, I've said that so many times, but Elliot's always *work*ing." Arlene mock-frowned. "I've become such a hausfrau! Are you seeing anyone?"

"No one to speak of." Rochelle excused herself to circulate among the guests.

"Of course, you go back to work," Arlene said, "I'll just find myself a little drink!"

There was a large back room, which would eventually be a recording studio, but now was a stage set for Silver Knight to perform, along with musicians who might want to join in an impromptu jam session. Stephen Stills, David Crosby and Richie Furay had already pulled out their guitars and were playing, while Joni Mitchell stood by, humming along quietly.

Rochelle was deep in conversation with a record producer and his new artist, James Taylor, whose debut album was about to be released. Elliot approached, and introductions were made all around. Deals, he smelled deals, and happiness welled up in him.

The others moved on and for a moment, Elliot and Rochelle were alone at the sidelines, listening to the live music. He still couldn't relax. "Silver Knight here yet?"

"I saw all the guys but Luke."

"Shit."

"Don't worry, Elliot."

"I'm going to look." He excused his way through the people crowding in to listen.

A body pressed close to Rochelle. Dark reflector glasses covered his eyes and his white-blond hair was much longer than the last time she'd seen him, but he was unmistakable.

"Hey, Spider."

"You're lookin' good, Rochelle. Nice digs Elliot's put together."

A whiff of strong cologne made her a little ill.

"Glad to see you landed on your feet, Rochelle," he said.

"See ya 'round, Spider."

Luke came out of the elevator, his guitar in a thick leather case slung over his left shoulder. His right hand held Julie's. She was in some sheer nearly naked dress.

Jesus, Elliot thought. Forget singing: She should be in the movies. He scanned the room for the few film people there. On Monday, he'd be sure to set up some meetings for Julie.

"Julie," Luke handed her a small packet, "this is for you."

It was flat and wrapped in white tissue paper, tied haphazardly with a piece of string.

"Not very fancy, I know."

She slipped off the wrapping: a metal medallion, with a pretty, inlaid design on one side, the other side plain. A tiny hole had been drilled at the top, and a thin gold chain looped through.

"My Volkswagen medallion?!" She saw it flying through the air that awful day after they'd left Ray's office, when she threw it into the lake in Central Park.

He nodded, bashful. "Well, it's not the same one."

"I can't believe you remembered that." She bit her lip. "Where'd you get it?"

"Let's just say there's another ole Bug somewhere without its emblem. Look, maybe this was stupid, bringing back bad memories, I should have gotten you a gold bracelet or a real necklace—and I will–"

"No, I love this. I love *you*." She turned so he could fasten the clasp around her neck.

Irv Gallion from Gladstone Music sidled up to Elliot to propose a buyout of some of his recently acquired publishing rights. They threw around some figures, and made plans to meet at the Gladstone offices after Elliot returned from the music festival in New York.

"Did he say two million?" Rochelle asked Elliot.

"That's just the starting figure. I'm not making a move till after that music festival back east, I think it'll give Silver Knight some big exposure."

A worried look crossed his face: Luna—and Spider— would never let go of them. He began to understand why people hired hit men. Had anyone hired a hit man to kill a hit man? It was almost funny. He had almost everything he'd dreamed of. He was thirty years old, just under the wire. So when would he feel like a grand success? When would it be enough?

He passed the scruffy, talented singer-songwriter Tim Buckley, and went off to chat with a program director from KRLA. At the same time, he had his antennae out for other conversations that drifted by.

"I was snorkeling off Baja and I saw a mermaid—they were shooting a porn film!" a man was telling his female companion, who reached over to the hors d'oeuvre tray that floated by on a waiter's arm.

Rochelle was trapped in a corner, listening to the wife of a high-powered entertainment attorney.

"You just scream and scream and it gets all the anger out."

"Then what?" Rochelle asked.

"You relive your birth. You should read the Janov book."

Rochelle wondered why anyone would want to relive their birth.

The attorney told Elliot about a client he represented. "Ricky Nelson. The Ozzie and Harriet kid. He's calling himself Rick now and he's after a serious career. You should take a listen. He's going to be playing the Ash Grove."

Hands covered Elliot's eyes from behind, startling him. "Guess who, dahling?"

The perfume was unmistakable. "Katey, my love."

"Quite a gala you've thrown together, Mr. Levine," Katey Lacey exclaimed. "Gary sends his regards but you know he never leaves the manse. I guess my first born is floating around here someplace, yes?"

Elliot saw Spider's head bobbing above the crowd.

"Congrats, Elliot, really," Katey said, kissing the air.

He moved on through the multitude, until a woman he remembered as Evie something or other, the wife of an agent, blocked his path, grabbed his face in both her hands and shouted, "Meditate!" and went on her way, and another beautiful young lady remarked, "I was at Esalen in June and they told me Mick had been there the week before, I just missed him!"

He recalled that she designed album covers and was a lesbian.

He bumped into Rochelle again.

"How are you holding up?"

"I'm all right," she said. "I've had a few of these kirs." She held up a pink-tinted drink. "I saw Ricky Nelson! I had a big crush on him when I was in the seventh grade."

In a crisp English accent, a well-dressed woman said to a familiar-looking starlet, "There's nothing to it, you just suck till he's hard then put the plaster on his cock and leave it on for thirty minutes. I've got Jimi's with me—do you want to see it? It's in the car. I'm bringing it to London to give to him. You know, his needed a lot more plaster than any of the others."

Luke spotted Julie with Casey Mahoney. She twisted a long strand of hair between her fingers, and drew it slowly across her lips. Casey leaned down to her, resting a hand on the wall behind her. Luke's fists tightened. He started across the room, but felt a firm hand on his arm.

"Time to play that set," Rochelle said.

When the band launched into the first of four songs, the place went wild. People danced in halls, the offices, all the way out to the lobby. Casey was really hot-dogging it up on his guitar, Luke thought, as they traded riffs, each one trying to outdo the other. His fingers seemed to have a life of their own, racing up and down the neck, squeezing bends and blues licks and wails out of the Telecaster. Gram Parsons, of the Byrds, joined them for what was turning into an all-star jam session.

Changing to acoustic guitar, Luke began the intro to a new song. He didn't see Julie in the crowd. Where the hell was she?

Julie felt herself growing smaller, diminished by the crowd of Important People, and the furor over Luke and Casey and the band. The doubts flooded in, the belong-inglessness. The invisibility. At the same time, she wanted to be happy for him, she knew she was a selfish bitch, but the falling feeling took her breath. There was noise in her head, voices urging *get out get out you nobody you nothing you piece of shit*, and an irresistible desire to smash everything to pieces.

When the elevator didn't come right away, she headed toward the door marked with a red exit sign.

"Julie!" Rochelle grabbed her by the wrist. "Don't go."

"I can't do this."

Rochelle saw the pain and panic in her friend's eyes. "Come on into my office where it's quiet, we'll talk. But you can't walk out on him again. You can't walk out on *you*."

"There *is* no me, Rochelle. I'm not a real person."

"Don't be ridiculous." Now, she wanted to slap her. Or shake her. How could she keep throwing it all away? "Please. Give yourself a chance. And don't hurt Luke again!"

"Why not? Now he's all yours, That's what you always wanted, isn't it?"

"Maybe once, but not anymore. And he only wants you, anyway. I just want all of us to be happy. You have some kind of depression disease, and maybe a doctor can help. I know someone—"

"Like there's some magic pill? Oh, Rochelle, sometimes things are broken that you just can't fix." She pulled away.

Rochelle heard her friend's footsteps echoing down all fifteen flights.

A million city lights replaced the sunset. Elliot knew the party, now winding down, had been a success.

"I heard Paul was coming," said Corto, a hirsute DJ from a pirate radio station. "They're breaking up, you know."

Katey Lacey interrupted, "Corto, you're crazy. He's always saying that. Why would they break up when they're making billions of dollars staying together? Right, Elliot? The Beatles will be around till the turn of the century."

"I don't want to think about old Beatles," Elliot said.

"Corto," Katey called out. "I'll probably see you tomorrow night at Roman and Sharon's." She turned to Elliot. "They've got the prettiest place up in Benedict Canyon, and

Spider wants to get in with the in crowd. That should be fun," she laughed. "Want to come along, Elliot? Bring your wife. Or whoever."

"I'll try."

"Great!" Katey called out, "See you tomorrow!"

When the last of the guests had disappeared, the catering crew finished the cleanup. Rochelle collapsed in Elliot's office. She kicked off her shoes.

"Went well," she said, with a satisfied sigh. "You're a genius."

"You're right."

45

Champ emptied the contents of two burlap sacks on the scratched wooden table: dozens of knives, switchblades, grooved Gurkhas with gleaming silver blades, several machetes. The family examined them with sensual delight. Cupid hefted a machete, making slashing gestures in the air, until Champ told him to quit it. He and a few of the guys retreated to the barn for some secret pow-wow.

Snake had a box of paint bottles she'd ripped off some crafts store in the Valley. Small bottles of watercolors and an assortment of brushes. Body painting party!

But Champ's gone out, someone protested.

When he gets back we'll all be painted.

Spooky said to Julie, "Would you like to join us, Your Majesty?" She offered a toke. It went down harsh, but struck Julie's brain fast. Golden. Thoughts were sliding around like worms in her head. Hawk came in, bringing a cool gust of night air as the loose screen door slammed behind him. The others took off their clothes. Cut-offs, jeans and tie-dyed T-shirts hit the floor, Julie's among them. She still wore the medallion despite the temptation to tear it off, but it was almost superstition that compelled her to keep it this time.

They sang "Little Piggies," yelling the lyrics. Newspapers were spread on the floor. The girls painted each other and themselves, the paint dripping onto the newspapers, and leaving misty red spatters on the walls and floor. Julie picked up a brush, gazing down at the clean white canvas that was her body. She felt a tickle on her right shoulder, making its way in a wriggly line to her lower back. Another one was at her front, painting rings around her nipples.

"What are you drawing?" she asked.

Ruthie had an odd, fixed stare. Champ's veins, she said.

Cupid dumped a small bottle of yellow paint on his head, and smeared it all down his neck and shoulders. He rolled on the floor, whooping. The door got painted, and the walls, with nonsense works and phrases and snatches of song lyrics. Julie rolled on the floor uncaring if her hair was gooped with paint, keeping her legs tight together or else they'd be in there too with their paints and brushes, but even the touching didn't seem to matter any more; this was someone else's body. The same way it had been when her stepfather came into her room early in the morning. Sitting on the edge of the bed whispering 'Jewel?' a test if she was asleep, *she pretended, keeping her breathing even and slow, and she'd hear his breath deepen, a raspy sound, as he ran his hands over her back innocent at first but then he touched her breast but it must be an accident, right? because this was not how fathers touched their daughters, she'd pretend she was not alive—not dead exactly—but in a small curled mind-space. No one could find her there.*

"Born to Be Wild" shook the house.

"We gotta be armed," Champ railed. "The shit's gonna come down tonight, tomorrow, any second, any hour. The pigs are going to start the war and we're ready. You're little piggies or you're warriors. It's Blacks against Whites when the world comes down. Here, man, take this salvation, you gonna wait till they come or you gonna go our and take 'em by surprise? That's right sit there on your fat white asses while they come with their guns and their tear gas cannons and bombs and blow your guts to the sky."

Julie cradled a machine gun, thinking how people like to joke, when you're carrying a guitar case, 'You got a gun in there?'

Champ sliced a razor-sharp sword through the air. "I need to take something apart just for practice. Any volunteers?"

There was a murmur of nervous laughter.

"Where's that cat?"

Julie's stomach clenched.

"Saw it sleepin' in the kitchen," Spirit said.

"Come on, not the cat," Hawk said.

"You like the kitty?"

"Well yeah."

"How 'bout you take its place, you like it that much?"

"Come on, man."

Julie and the others looked from Hawk to Champ and back again.

"You runnin' things around here now, man?

"'Course not, Charlie, gimme a break, all I'm sayin' is…it catches stuff, rats 'n things, it's good for something."

"You're right, 'cause this place is full of rats and wastes of space, those on this earth taking us down, and that cat is good for another eight lives, but yours has just run out."

Hawk backed against the door. He turned and tried to open it but the latch stuck and his hands were slippery with sweat.

Unseen in the commotion, Julie slunk into the kitchen. The cat was curled up in a circle on a filthy throw rug. "Scat!" she whispered, nudging it with her foot. The cat raised an eye and settled back down. "Scat!" she hissed again. She gave the rug a hard tug. The cat fled.

There was a horrible shriek. Julie froze behind the door, just able to see a sliver of the living room. Hawk was on his back on the floor, blood flowing from a nearly severed arm. His neck was sliced from ear to ear, and in his eyes an expression of shock and sorrow.

Some of the women keened and wept. Some were laughing. Champ roared in savage triumph, his raised sword smeared with blood. He drew one forefinger the length of it. With the blood, he wrote on the front door in large block letters: D E A T H

Clutching the medallion like a talisman, Julie stole out the back door, and into the barn. The horses stirred; a soft whinny, a clump of hooves on the sodden hay. Her mind was a blank of sheer panic. She had to get out of this house of horrors. A door slammed. Footsteps and laughter. The silhouettes of Champ and the others passed in front of the open barn. They climbed into the truck and sped off along the rutted road, tires spewing pebbles all the way down the hill. The engine faded away. Her breathing was harsh and fast in the quiet night. Even the crickets had gone still.

They were all gone. Weren't they? Would they notice she wasn't with them? Would they come back looking for her? Kill her? As often as she'd wanted to kill herself, she knew now that she didn't want to die. And she never wanted to kill anyone. As crazy as she'd always been, she was not this kind of crazy.

A night bird cried. There were things hiding in the dark: black widow spiders, wild animals, rattlesnakes and scorpions and poisonous plants. Yet just over the hill, the benign San Fernando Valley sparkled in suburban oblivion, and beyond that, Los Angeles; towns and roads, diners, gas stations and America.

The old floor creaked as she went back inside. Someone had dragged Hawk's body out the back and dumped him in the compost, leaving a trail of blood. So much blood. She heard a snapping sound, and spun around. Just the house settling.

In the dark, she pulled the duffel from under her cot and stuffed her belongings inside. When the bag was full, she tugged the drawstring tight and grabbed the guitar case in her other hand.

Several vehicles were still parked in the driveway: Cupid's bike, someone's pickup truck, a couple of broken-down cars that belonged to the ranch owner. But she could barely drive a stick shift, let alone a motorcycle, and the keys were inside the house. One old car was a blue and white Chevy, '53 or '54 (Luke would know!) and didn't look too bad inside. She knew it ran, barely. The upholstery was torn, like it had transported a wild animal. The backseat was filled with junk, piles of old newspapers, planks of wood, a broken baby seat.

"Like the car?"

Julie's heart crashed into her chest. It was Bruce, one of the guys who tried to look like Champ, tried to act like Champ, and was hopelessly stupid and violent. He'd been in prison, but so had most of the guys. They considered themselves rebels but they were nothing but fucking criminals.

Bruce stared fish-eyed at her. "Going someplace?" He swung a keychain around his fingers, up, down.

"No." She looked at him straight on. "You?"

"Someone has to hold the fort."

He couldn't see her bag and her guitar in the shadows. Unless he moved a few feet to the right. She leaned against the car, faking indifference. "I thought I left some weed out here."

"I got some inside. And acid, mushrooms, whatever the lady wants."

"Cool. I'll be right in." She made herself smile.

For a few seconds, he didn't move, but then she saw the thought begin to register that there was going to be sex. He went in the house.

She ran, duffel slung over one shoulder, guitar banging against her leg. The road wasn't far and death was chasing her. The dirt path opened into Route 27. The road sloped down. She kept walking. The ground vibrated as a big rig loomed up behind her. She decided to risk it.

46

Elliot and Rochelle and the four musicians took up the first class cabin of the 727.

Luke barely heard the stewardess describe the necessary precautions about what to do if they crashed to earth or sea, nor did he pay attention to the pilot's congenial guide to the sights they'd be flying over en route to New York.

"May I get you a drink, sir?" a female voice repeated, finally making its way through the fog in his head.

"Sure, ma'am. bourbon, and some ice, if you got it,"

Next to him, Brewster ordered a Budweiser.

Luke stubbed out his cigarette in the armrest ashtray, poured the whiskey into the glass, watching how it cascaded over crystal clear ice cubes—like the water washing over the rocks on the beach that first day he and Julie drove up the coast, the cool bathwater shimmering down her body as she stood, and the taste of her.

Shut up.

He downed the drink in one swallow, and poured another.

"Isn't this a groove?" Brewster said. "I can't believe Elliot got us the gig. Do you know who's gonna be there?" He proceeded to name every big name in the business.

"What did you do, kill off some other band to get us into that concert?" Luke asked Elliot.

"Cancellation." Elliot mentioned a famous lead singer who had stumbled on drugs.

"Well hell, fuck him, lucky us, right?"

"Yes, exactly." Elliot took in Luke's morose mood. "I'd think you'd be a little happier about it."

Luke rubbed the calloused fingertips of his left hand on his neck, pulled at the T-shirt like it was choking him. "When do you know, man? When you've 'made it'? When's it supposed to make you happy?"

Elliot gazed out the window at the wingtip's flashing red light. "I guess," he finally answered, "When it doesn't matter so much any more."

"That's it? That's fucking *it?*"

"Far as I know."

"I lose my girl. The draft's still hanging over my head. I mean, what's the fucking point?"

"What am I, a guru? You want me to read your Tarot cards? Your astrology chart?" Elliot asked. "It's like that joke about the guy who wants to know the meaning of life, so he travels around the world, ten, twenty times, trying to find the expert, the Great One who knows the Meaning of Life. He hears about this monk who lives waaaay up in the highest mountains of Tibet, and the only way you can get to him is to climb the mountain. So the guy, the searcher, uses the last of his worldly goods to pay a bunch of Sherpas to take him up there, only they all die on the journey, but our schmuck is soooo determined, he keeps going, and finally, he reaches the summit, and the monk's sanctuary. He goes inside, and there he is: the monk, sitting on a rug, meditating. The guy waits for another ten hours, until the monk comes out of his prayers, and he tells him how long he's searched for the Meaning of Life, because only the monk knows the eternal truth.

"So this monk looks at him for a long, long time, and finally, he speaks. 'Life,' he says slowly, 'Is a circle.'

"The guy thinks about this—it's not what he expected—and he looks at the monk and says, 'It is?' And the monk says, 'It isn't?'"

Elliot sipped his champagne. The stewardess was there, pouring more. He didn't even like champagne. It gave him a headache. Especially in the morning. He hadn't even had time for a decent crap before the car picked him up for the drive to LAX, let alone his regular perusal of the newspapers and trades. He'd barely had three hours sleep.

Luke was unimpressed and not amused. "Great. I should've known you wouldn't get it."

Elliot reddened. "*I* don't get it? Listen, you think you've got some kind of warranty that nothing bad is going to happen to you, or you'll stay the same as when you started out? Pieces of you get taken out, maybe just a little at a time so you don't notice it at first, like a hangnail or a lock of hair, but then, it's an appendix, so who cares? Or tonsils, you don't need them either. But then one day, you realize something came in the night and tore out a chunk of your stomach, or took some of the blood out of your veins, and it's on to your heart, piece by piece by piece. The bullshit goes on, and it's: You want this or that? You gotta make a trade. A liver, a leg, a brain. A life. It's your life, or someone else's, and after awhile you just don't give a shit. I guess that's success. At least it's survival."

The 727 hummed, trembled, dropped, righted itself.

"*B'ruch a'toh adonai,*" Elliot muttered.

A fragment of a tune strayed through Luke's head: a new song wanting to get out. He'd better get back to his seat and write it down before it vanished. It was one way to purge this ache in his chest.

Rochelle passed Elliot *The New York Times*.

"God, I miss the *Post* and the *News*," he said.

"And walking," she added.

"Even the subways." He spread out the front page, and saw large black headlines, about a film star and her friends who had been brutally slaughtered in a house high up in Benedict Canyon over the weekend.

"Oh my god."

Quickly, he scanned the article for the names of the dead, until he came to one that he knew. He nudged Rochelle, and pointed a finger, watched as her eyes grew wider.

"Oh my god."

"Spider was there."

"Spider." She tried to take this in. "Katey? What about Katey?"

He read the names again. "No, thank God. I guess she didn't go at the last minute."

"But all those others. It's horrible."

He could have been there. It could just as easily have been Elliot Levine's name among the list of the dead. Maybe there was such a thing as a guardian angel. Spider murdered! Slaughtered! Elliot pondered the grotesque way in which prayers are sometimes answered.

47

The record company put Luke and Brewster in a small but comfortable Greenwich Village hotel; Casey had his own pad and Billy crashed with a girlfriend. They rehearsed at Electric Lady, Jimi Hendrix's new recording studio on 8th Street.

After the rehearsal, Elliot and the band chowed down on huge burgers and piles of fries at an icily air-conditioned Greek coffee shop on Sixth Avenue. Luke savored a toothache-cold beer.

Brewster was obsessed with the murders in L.A. "I talked to that guy at your party, they chopped him up but good, and that pregnant actress, she was beautiful. Geez, it could have been me, it could have been any of us. They say the guy who masterminded the whole thing was a musician, and he had all these chicks under a spell or something, so they'd go and murder people when he told them to."

"Do you mind if I just eat my lunch?" Luke said.

"Yeah, why don't we change the subject, okay?" Casey put in.

Elliot forced his mind away from the carnage and onto the concert. "The promoters say they've sold some fifty thousand tickets and expect more at the gate. It will get a lot of media coverage."

"Yeah, they're gonna notice us instead of Jimi Hendrix," Casey said.

"They'll notice you, alright."

"If it rains, we'll all get electrocuted," Luke said, only half-joking.

"Wouldn't that be the perfect ending for rock and roll?" Brewster remarked. "All those people who say it's the devil's music could feel so smug."

"Don't worry," Elliot assured them. "It's safe, and besides, what're the odds it'll rain? Listen, guys, I gotta go." He tossed some money on the table. "This ought to cover it. Don't forget, we've got a charter bus day after tomorrow."

"I'm gonna drive up myself," Luke told him. "I hate that bus. You seen the wheels I rented? I could get to there and back before you guys get out of Manhattan!"

Elliot rubbed his right hand over his eyes. "Luke, do this for me, okay? I want all of you in the same place, getting there at the same time, I don't want you lost and driving to Buffalo by mistake, okay?"

"Will you be on the bus, Levine?"

"Rochelle and I are going a day ahead."

"Just take the fucking bus, Bellavita," Casey said.

Brewster jumped in, "Hey, it'll be fun. We'll sing 'A hundred bottles of beer on the wall' and blow up some rubbers and float them out the windows. Didn't you ever go to camp?"

"You sure know how to tempt a guy. Alright. The pissmobile."

"It's only about an hour and a half to Monticello," Elliot said, "And a little more to the concert site."

48

The Kharman Ghia had two bumper stickers on it: Ithaca College and Fuck Profanity. This last driver, she'd thumbed him down in the flat middle of Kansas, was going all the way, he said, all the way to New York. She couldn't believe her luck. Five rides cross country, no crazies. This guy was cheerful, not that she was really listening to his monologue of growing up in Missouri, and how he'd heard about that music thing and knew he just had to be there. He passed her a beer, the bottle tasting faintly of spearmint. She'd slept on and off, and they'd driven straight through, just stopping for food and the bathroom. All she wanted was to get far, far from the ranch in the hills above Los Angeles, and forget she had ever been there.

They passed through Pennsylvania, and she wondered where the Donnie Drake Four was right now, maybe they were still in perpetual lounge purgatory. On through New Jersey to the New York Thruway and the turnoff at Route 17, and that's where the traffic began to slow. Lines and lines of cars, bumper to bumper, filled with young people.

"What the—?"

"You don't think they're all going, do you?" Julie said.

"No it's probably an accident up ahead."

But as they crept along, it became more apparent that nearly all the drivers and their passengers had one common destination.

"Doesn't it seem that everyone in the world is our age?" Julie marveled aloud.

"Everyone who matters," her companion agreed.

And everyone appeared to be on that highway.

Slowly, slowly, the trail of music seekers crept closer to Mecca. The guys in the car next to them passed a fat joint at three miles an hour. The humid day made everybody stoned even without a drug. Radios coordinated, all finding the same station blasting "I Can't Get No Satisfaction." Cars rocked to the rhythm.

Hours later they turned onto Farmers Road. She said, I'll get out and walk; she was stiff from sitting so long and it felt good to stretch out. The music drew her toward a blessed inferno, a snake pit of joyful souls. The ground had already turned to mud from earlier rains. A low rumble of thunder threatened.

49

The bus navigated the curves of Route 17, into the Catskills.

"Ever play the Borscht Belt?" Brewster asked the others.

Billy nodded. "Spent a year one month backing up some lounge act at one of those damn places. Best part was the pool, which was huge, and the horny Jewish chicks."

"I played a weekend for a singer. Had me reading charts, stuff like," Brewster affected a mock-operatic baritone, "'Once in a lifetime!' The audience didn't clap with their hands like regular people, they tap on the table with sticks. It sounded like a fuckin' hailstorm, scared the shit outta me."

The others laughed. Casey said, "I never played before fifty thousand people, what's that gonna be like?"

"Scary," said Brewster.

They reached Monticello, a sleepy Catskills town known for its proximity to the resorts, and for its racetrack. Now it was crawling with longhairs and hippie-mobiles. The bus pulled up in front of a four-story building off Main Street. Elliot and Rochelle were waiting for them in the lobby.

Elliot explained the logistics of getting to the concert. Way more people showed up than the promoters had expected, and the roads were too clogged to drive to the site, so they'd be helicoptered.

"Like an airlift?" Billy asked.

Brewster turned to him. "Yeah, Billy, they're going to drop you and your drums from three thousand feet and hope you land on the stage."

"I meant with parachutes."

"Guys, guys, let's be serious here. The helicopter can land in a field about a quarter mile from the stage, then they'll drive you over."

Rochelle took over, "I'm afraid you won't get a real sound check; during the break, the roadies'll set up, lucky we got the equipment shipped in before everything got crazy, and let's hope nothing blows up. Even if it does, there's plenty more amps to plug into."

"How many people are at this thing? In the audience?" Casey wanted to know.

"I don't exactly how many. No one does. They're crashing the gate, they're climbing over the fences, and now the promoters gave up and are letting them in for free."

The lobby was crammed with people.

"Hey, Luke!"

It was that asshole Meyer Norman from a hundred years ago in the Village. He was in full, hirsute hippie regalia. Meyer acted as if they were long lost best friends, and managed to mention every big name he'd ever met.

"You playin'?" Luke asked when he got a word in.

"Nooooo," Meyer replied, as if that were equivalent to sweeping up. "I'm producing, you know," he named a string of bands Luke hadn't heard of. "Got a great deal with Reprise."

God help us all, Luke thought. "Good for you," he said.

50

S he walked through the main gate into a strange new
world. Lightning cracked across the sky. Three heavy
drops of rain struck her face; her sandals were thick with
mud. She slid them off and carried them looped over her
wrist. Onstage, Creedence Clearwater Revival was
chooglin'. The wind whipped up a frenzy. People huddled
under little tents they'd constructed from ponchos. Thousands more were oblivious to the rain and stood half-naked,
moving to the music. The skies cracked again, eliciting
shouts and excited screams from the mob. The stage was
invisible behind a sheet of rain.

"'Scuse me," she said as she tripped over a pair of
muddy feet. A man and two women were seated on the sopping ground, arms linked, eyes closed.

"Lost?" asked the man. "You can stay here." He lifted
the poncho that scarcely covered the three of them.

"That's okay," she said, "thanks." She stumbled on,
passing a row of stinking Port-O-Sans. A long line of people
waited to use them.

"Born on the bayou!"

The skies really opened up.

"Cut the power!" A chant began, spreading throughout
miles of fields. "Fuck the rain! Fuck the rain!" The band on
stage kept going. Julie slipped between bodies, over bodies,

drawn toward the music. Country Joe and the Fish were on and the crowd was wild and wet.

Julie sat cross-legged under a table at the ravaged concession stand. The water streamed like a curtain. A smoothly muscled young man with long, sun-bleached hair, wearing military shorts and nothing else, intoned "Fine acid, first-class dope, shop at Joe's." He turned to Julie with a smile, "Free sample?" proffering a sugar cube.

"No, thanks," she said.

"No, really. Here." He slipped it into her pocket and moved away.

The announcer, Fillmore East roadie Chip Monck, talked into an echoing microphone. "A two or three-year-old girl is at the Hog Farm first-aid station and pretty unhappy...Kenny Irwin, please go to the information booth for your insulin..."

She moved forward a few feet, heard someone say, "I hear Dylan's coming, he's gonna be airlifted in tonight to close the concert."

The rumor spread quickly. The rain abated and the concert resumed. The Hog Farm had free food. The mud stained map she'd picked up showed they were way on the other side, so she set out again. On a paved road that formed one of the borders of the concert grounds, she breathed in the moist country air, and listened. She was behind the puppet theater and could see the puppeteers' backs, their hands hidden by a curtain, a frenzy of voices and movement. On the other side, children squealed with delight. On the Free Stage, a haphazardly erected platform, a band played a loose mixture of rock and jazz.

Her nerves were buzzing. She sat down on a blanket with several people. Who're you, they asked, friendly. Julie, she said. We're Earthlight. A woman gave her a ripe plum and the juice spurted out when she bit into it. It was deeply sweet and thrilled her senses. They made room for her to lay back and rest, looking up at the pointed treetops that came together like a cathedral ceiling.

She forgot she was hungry and drifted off.

"They want you over at the site," Elliot told Luke. "The rain stopped and you should be on in the next couple of hours." Elliot's driver took them by limo to the heliport just outside town. It was a big Huey loaned from a nearby Air Force base, just like the choppers being used in Vietnam. Luke climbed in, gripped with excitement, dread and guilt as they rose into the air. How strange that he was here in this Huey and not skimming low over the Asian jungle.

Billy lightly tapped his sticks on the tops of his denim-clad thighs, while Casey stared down. Brewster caught Luke's eye, raised his eyebrow and grinned. "Some shit, huh?" he said. Luke managed a crooked smile.

When she awakened, she didn't know why she was among strangers and on the ground. The Paul Butterfield Blues Band had just begun their set. Slipping a hand into her pocket, she found the sugar cube and licked her finger, savoring the sweetness.

At the stage, roadies hauled wires, amps, instruments, mike stands, as each new band had to be set up without too much gap between acts. Behind the scaffolding, performers and their entourages intermingled with middle-aged men sporting headbands around their graying heads, and beads dangling on their necks; the managers, agents, promoters, record execs, and their foxy women.

She wasn't hungry anymore, there must have been a tiny bit of acid on the sugar because the trampled green grass had gotten greener, the mud slick and oozy like shiny melted chocolate, the sky a most interesting shade of puce. It would be easy to just walk backstage as if she belonged.

"Hey, pretty lady?" A hand grasped her arm. It belonged to a big-bearded roadie-type, long stringy brown hair caught behind his head in a ponytail. "Sorry, no visitors past this point."

She leaned her forehead against the wire fence for a moment, watching, and then moved down to a wide, protected area amid trees and tents that formed the performers' dressing rooms. A new band was arriving by helicopter, and then shuttled over, equipment and all, in a farmer's flatbed truck.

From where she stood, it was difficult to be sure who the musicians were. A skinny guy came up next to her, a pair of binoculars hanging from a cord around his neck.

"You see Dylan?" he wanted to know. He peered through the glasses.

"He's not coming."

"Aw shit. But I met Jerry Garcia, he gave me a guitar pick!"

She reached for the binoculars. "Can I borrow those?"

"Sure." He fondled the flat, white plastic pick. "You see anyone? Is Hendrix there?"

"No. I see...I see..."

Luke Bellavita.

"Who? Who do you see?"

She lowered the field glasses, and handed them back.

Well, somebody's farm will never be the same, Luke thought. There could not be so many people in one place at one time. The chopper dropped down, hovering: more detail, more humans, and a stage. So many, and he'd give them everything that he had to give. Maybe if they screamed until their throats were raw, if they worshipped him like a fucking god, it would fill this emptiness, it would get her out of his head.

Rochelle's shoes were sopping despite the planks laid down in the backstage area. If she could only get a little closer; they were keeping everyone but the musicians away from the band shell. She needed to go to the bathroom, but the idea of those portable outhouses...still...this was pretty incredible. Isn't that...? Yeah, it is. Everyone was here. Here she was, too.

Yeah, this was pretty incredible.

Elliot took in the crowd that stretched in every direction, a panorama to the horizon, and the brilliant parade of music stars backstage, some passing so close to him he could smell their performance sweat.

Please, he thought, just don't let it rain again for the next thirty minutes.

Julie came to a large pond. Tiny insects skittered across the top. A beautiful young man floated motionless on his back, his naked body gleaming in the fading light, arms flung wide in a posture of ecstatic surrender. His simple delight only sharpened the despair that pressed down on her. She covered her face with her hands, wondering if she had come to the end of everything.

On stage, the announcer instructed someone to meet his brother by the main gate. The mike squealed. He introduced the next group: Silver Knight.

The music invaded her tired soul. Nothing else really mattered. A long sinuous guitar note reached out like a saving hand. An invisible energy lifted her. She slipped off her clothes, abandoning them on the grass where they fell, and waded into the pond. The water reached her chest, the thin chain around her neck and its emblem bobbed on the surface.

She stretched her arms to the sky, and added her voice to the music that spilled out into the universe.

Postscript

*M*y grandmother Julie was last seen in Toronto in the
late 1970s. She sang at coffeehouses and was living
with a well-known Canadian singer-songwriter who would
prefer to remain anonymous. I found him on Facebook. "It
was a difficult time," he told me in a phone conversation.
"She was bi-polar, you know, and had long periods of deep
depression, and then she'd be up all night and flying around,
spinning out new ideas and songs. She painted, too, beautiful wild colors, weird animals and nightmarish scary shit,
and then the whole down cycle would start over again. She
tried to kill herself with pills, with razors, with the gas oven.
I don't know if she actually wanted to die, or just make the
pain stop. We went to doctors, and they gave her a lot of different drugs. Some helped for a while, but it never lasted. I
didn't know how to handle it.

"It was like a roller coaster and I had to get off or it
would have killed me, too."

He thinks she went back to New York City. She talked
about it a lot, about going home.

COLLECTIBLES

Grammy awards—Silver Knight, 1970, 1972, 1973. Luke Bellavita, My Own Road, 1975

Hollywood Reporter, August 6, 1979: Luke Bellavita, 35, former lead guitarist in the groundbreaking folk-rock band, Silver Knight, who had even greater success as a solo artist, was killed in a car crash in Malibu early Sunday morning. His vehicle, a vintage 1962 Ferrari GTO, plunged into the canyon below. Alcohol may have been a factor. He is survived by his companion, Elissa Myles, their son, Julian, 6, and his mother, Lily May Bellavita, of Columbus, Georgia.

Los Angeles Times, May 8, 2005—The Rock and Roll Hall of Fame added four new members to its growing roster of music luminaries, including the posthumous recognition of late guitar legend Luke Bellavita, as well as his former bandmate, Casey Mahoney, who died in February after a long battle with lung cancer.

Gold Record: *My Own Road*, Luke Bellavita—donated to the Rock and Roll Hall of Fame by Elissa Myles.

Magazine article: *Avenue*, February 26, 2006—Arlene Slotnick Levine is a force to be reckoned with as she prepares her annual fundraiser at the Hotel Pierre for Save the Animals, the charity she founded in 1980, following her high profile divorce from record mogul Elliot Levine.

Photo, *West Palm Beach Herald*, March, 2003—Retired pop music visionary Elliott Levine and his main squeeze, former model Krista Buddwing, at the reopening of Donald Trump's newly restored Mar-a-Lago estate. Google Images.

Small article in *Hollywood Reporter*: 1950s' songstress Katey Lacey opening for Bobby Vinton in Branson, Missouri, April 14-30, 1978.

DVD: *The Oprah Winfrey Show*, October 2006. Rochelle Klein discusses her new book, *Living Well in Spite of Everything*, and shares her investment strategies.

Video clip (YouTube): *The Larry King Show*, October 2006: Guest Rochelle Klein.

Draft card (burned at edges): Brewster Henderson

The New York Times, July 28, 1980: "Meadowlands Body May Be Missing Mogul". Construction on the final phase of the Meadowlands Sports Complex turned up human remains that have been tentatively identified as the body of Ray Fish, one-time CEO of defunct BigWheel Records, who vanished under mysterious circumstances in 1968. At the time he dropped from sight, Mr. Fish had been called to testify before a Senate Committee investigating corruption In the recording industry.

New York Post, July 29, 1980, front-page headline: SLEEPING WITH THE FISHES??

Certificate of Birth: Gender: Male. St. Vincent's Hospital, New York, N.Y. May 1, 1970. Mother: Julie Bradley. Father: Unknown.

Certificate of Adoption: Gender: Male. Help Our Children Foundation, Borough of Brooklyn, New York, March 1971. Anonymous.

LP (one small scratch but in good overall condition)— *Introducing Julie Bradley*, Pine Tree Records, 1974— InternetVinylCollectors.com

Most Promising Female Vocalist, 1974, Juno Awards (Toronto, Ontario): Julie Bradley. Small watercolor painting: Blue Cat, signed JB '78.

CD: Juliette—*Where We Are Now*—14 original songs, available at CDBaby.com

Acknowledgments

To those who inspired, badgered and encouraged me to finish this novel and get it out there, I'd like to offer a greatly appreciative thank you. When the book was just a glimmer, the late Phyllis Levy, friend and mentor, was always there for me. My writer/editor friend, Ken Salikof, provided support and invaluable input. My gratitude also goes to Scott Rudin and Eli Bush for their inspiration; early readers Alan Rachins, Barbara Caplan-Bennett, Jay Siegel and Merlin Snider for their sage suggestions; and the Queens 'gang' who endured the first three chords I ever learned on the world's worst guitar. Lastly and mostly, to my husband, Steve Kaplan, who has persevered all these years in staying married to me through the many ups and downs.

About the Author

Kathrin King Segal is a writer, singer, songwriter and actor who spent the first half of her life in New York City and currently lives in Los Angeles with her husband. She began her singing career in the Greenwich Village folk scene and experienced and/or observed many of the places, people and events recreated in *We Were Stardust*.

Made in the USA
Charleston, SC
25 October 2011